THE FIRST TIME

ALSO BY JOY FIELDING

JOY FIELDING

The FIRST TIME

SEAL BOOKS

This book is a work of fiction. Names, characters, places and incidents are products of the author's imagination or are used fictitiously. Any resemblance to actual events or locales or persons, living or dead, is entirely coincidental.

 A Pocket Star Book published by
POCKET BOOKS, a division of Simon & Schuster, Inc.
1230 Avenue of the Americas, New York, NY 10020

Copyright © 2000 by Joy Fielding

Originally published in hardcover in 2000 by Pocket Books

ISBN: 0-7434-6714-0

First Pocket Books paperback printing September 2001

10 9 8 7 6 5 4 3 2 1

POCKET STAR BOOKS and colophon are registered trademarks of Simon & Schuster, Inc.

For information regarding special discounts for bulk purchases, please contact Simon & Schuster Special Sales at 1-800-456-6798 or business @simonandschuster.com

Cover art by Lisa Litwack

Printed in the U.S.A.

To Larry Mirkin

Acknowledgments

I would like to take this opportunity to thank the following people: Larry Mirkin, for his friendship and warmly critical eye; Dr. Keith Meloff, for giving of his valuable time and sharing his invaluable medical expertise; Beverley Slopen, for her unfailingly generous words and wise counsel; Owen Laster, for his never-ending enthusiasm and unflagging support; Linda Marrow, for her vision, insight, and grace; John Pearce, for never doubting me; and finally, to my husband, Warren, and my daughters, Shannon and Annie, to borrow a phrase from a fan from the Czech Republic—"Thank you—That you exist!"

ONE

She was thinking of ways to kill her husband.

Martha Hart, called Mattie by everyone but her mother, who regularly insisted Martha was a perfectly lovely name—"You don't see Martha Stewart changing her name, do you?"—was swimming back and forth across the long, rectangular pool that occupied most of her spacious backyard. Mattie swam every morning from the beginning of May until mid-October, barring lightning or an early Chicago snowfall, fifty minutes, one hundred lengths of precisely executed breaststroke and front crawl, back and forth across the well-heated forty-foot expanse. Usually she was in the water by seven o'clock, so that she could be finished before Jake left for work and Kim for school, but today she'd overslept, or rather, hadn't slept at all until just minutes before the alarm clock went off. Jake, of course, had experienced no such trouble sleeping and was out of bed and in the shower before she'd had time to open her eyes. "Feeling all right?" he'd asked her, already dressed and out the door in a handsome blur before she was able to formulate a response.

She could use a butcher knife, Mattie thought now, pushing at the water with clenched fists, slicing the imaginary foot-long blade through the air and into her husband's heart with each rise and fall of her arms. She reached the end of the pool, using her feet to propel herself off the concrete, and made her way back to the other side, the motion reminding her that a well-timed push down a flight of stairs might be the easier way to dispatch Jake. Or she could poison him, add a sprinkling of arsenic, like freshly grated Parmesan cheese, to his favorite pasta, like the kind they had for dinner last night, before he supposedly went back to the office to work on today's all-important closing argument for the jury, and she'd found the hotel receipt in his jacket pocket—the jacket he'd asked her to send to the cleaners—that announced his latest infidelity as boldly as a headline in a supermarket tabloid.

She could shoot him, she thought, squeezing the water as it passed through her fingers, as if squeezing the trigger of a gun, her eyes following the imaginary bullet as it splashed across the pool's surface toward its unsuspecting target, as her errant husband rose to address the jury. She watched him button his dark blue jacket just seconds before the bullet ripped through it, his dark red blood slowly oozing into the neat diagonal lines of his blue-and-gold striped tie, the boyish little half-smile that emanated as much from his eyes as his lips freezing, fading, then disappearing altogether as he fell, facedown, to the hard floor of the stately old courtroom.

Ladies and gentlemen of the jury, have you reached your verdict?

"Death to the infidel!" Mattie shouted, kicking at the water as if it were a pesky blanket twisted around her ankles, her feet feeling unexpectedly heavy, as if newly attached to large cement blocks. For a second, Mattie felt as if her legs were foreign objects, as if they belonged to someone else and had been grafted haphazardly onto her torso, serving no other purpose than to weigh her down. She tried to stand, but the bottoms of her feet couldn't find the bottom of the pool, although the water level was only five feet high and she was almost eight inches taller. "Damn it," Mattie muttered, losing the rhythm of her breathing and swallowing a mouthful of chlorine. She gasped loudly, throwing herself toward the side of the pool, her body doubling up and over the edge of the pool to rest against its border of smooth brown stone, as invisible hands continued to pull at her legs, trying to drag her back under. "Serves me right," she muttered between painful coughing spasms. "Serves me right for having such evil thoughts."

She wiped some errant spittle from her mouth, then burst into a fit of hysterical laughter, the laughter mingling with her coughing, one feeding off the other, the unpleasant sounds bouncing off the water, echoing loudly in her ears. Why am I laughing? she wondered, unable to stop.

"What's going on?" The voice came from somewhere above her head. "Mom? Mom, are you okay?"

Mattie brought her hand up across her forehead to shield her eyes from the sun's harsh rays, focused on her like a flashlight, and stared toward the large cedar deck that extended off the kitchen at the back of her red-brick, two-story home. Her daughter Kim was silhouetted against the autumn sky, the sun's glare rendering the teenager's normally outsize features curiously indistinct. It didn't matter. Mattie knew the lines and contours of her only child's face and figure as well as her own, maybe better: the huge blue eyes that were darker than her father's, bigger than her mother's; the long, straight nose she'd inherited from her dad; the bow-shaped mouth she'd gotten from her mom; the budding breasts that had skipped a generation, moving directly from Mattie's mother to her child, and that were, even at the tender age of fifteen, already a force to be reckoned with. Kim was tall, like both her parents, and skinny, as her mother had been at her age, although her posture was much better than Mattie's had been at fifteen, better, in fact, than it was now. Kim didn't have to be reminded to push her shoulders back or hold her head up high, and as she leaned against the sturdy wood slats of the railing, swaying like a young sapling in a gentle breeze, Mattie marveled at her daughter's easy confidence, wondering whether she'd played any part in its development at all.

"Are you all right?" Kim asked again, craning her long, elegant neck toward the pool. Her shoulder-length, naturally blond hair was pulled tightly back against her scalp and twisted into a neat little bun at the top of her head. Her Miss Grundy look, Mattie sometimes teased. "Is someone there with you?"

"I'm fine," Mattie said, although her continued coughing rendered the words unintelligible, and she had to repeat them. "I'm fine," she said again, then laughed out loud.

"What's so funny?" Kim giggled, a slight, trepid sound seeking inclusion into whatever it was her mother found so amusing.

"My foot fell asleep," Mattie told her, gradually lowering both feet to the bottom of the pool, relieved to find herself standing.

"While you were swimming?"

"Yeah. Funny, huh?"

Kim shrugged, a shrug that said, Not *that* funny, not *laugh-out-loud* funny, and leaned further forward, out of the shadow. "Are you sure you're okay?"

"I'm fine. I just swallowed a mouthful of water." Mattie coughed again, as if for emphasis. She noticed that Kim was wearing her leather jacket, and for the first time that morning became aware of the late September chill.

"I'm going to school now," Kim said, then didn't move. "What are you up to today?"

"I have an appointment this afternoon with a client to look at some photographs."

"What about this morning?"

"This morning?"

"Dad's giving his summation to the jury this morning," Kim stated.

Mattie nodded, not sure where this conversation was headed. She looked toward the large maple tree that loomed majestically over her neighbor's backyard, at the deep red that was seeping into the green foliage, as if the leaves were slowly bleeding to death, and waited for her daughter to continue.

"I bet he'd really appreciate it if you were to go to the courthouse to cheer him on. You know, like you do when I'm in a school play. For support and stuff."

And stuff, Mattie thought, but didn't say, choosing to cough instead.

"Anyway, I'm going now."

"Okay, sweetie. Have a good day."

"You too. Give Dad a kiss for me for good luck."

"Have a good day," Mattie repeated, watching Kim disappear inside the house. Alone again, she closed her eyes, allowing her body to sink below the water's smooth surface. Water immediately covered her mouth and filled her ears, silencing the white noise of nature, blocking out the casual sounds of morning. No longer were dogs barking in neighboring yards, birds singing in nearby trees, cars honking their impatience on the street. Everything was quiet, peaceful, and still. There were no more faithless husbands, no more inquiring teenage minds.

How does she do it? Mattie wondered. What kind of radar did the child possess? Mattie hadn't said anything to Kim about her discovery of Jake's most recent betrayal. Nor had she said anything to anyone else, not to any of her friends, not to her mother, not to Jake. She almost laughed. When was the last time she'd confided anything in her mother? And as for Jake, she wasn't ready to confront him yet. She needed time to think things through, to gather her thoughts, as a squirrel stores away nuts for winter, to make sure she was well fortified for whatever course of action she chose to follow in the long, cold months ahead.

Mattie opened her eyes under the water, pushed her chin-length, dark blond hair away from her face. That's right, girl, she told herself. It's time to open your eyes. *The time for hesitating's through,* she heard Jim Morrison wail from somewhere deep inside her head. *Come on, baby, light my fire.* Was that what she was waiting for—for someone to light a fire under her? How many hotel receipts did she have to find before she finally did something about it? It was time to take action. It was time to admit certain indisputable facts about her marriage. *Ladies and gentlemen of the jury, at this time I would like to submit this hotel receipt into evidence.* "Damn you anyway, Jason Hart," Mattie sputtered, gasping for air as her head broke through the surface of the water, her husband's given name feeling strange and awkward in her mouth. She hadn't called him anything but Jake since their first introduction sixteen years ago.

Light my fire. Light my fire. Light my fire.

"Mattie, I'd like you to meet Jake Hart," her friend Lisa had said. "He's that friend of Todd's I was telling you about."

"Jake," Mattie repeated, liking the sound. "Is that short for Jackson?"

"Actually, it's short for Jason, but nobody ever calls me that."

"Nice to meet you, Jake." Mattie glanced around the main room of the Loyola University library, half expecting one of the more studious-minded patrons to jump up and *ssh* them into silence.

"And what about 'Mattie'? Short for Matilda?"

"Martha," she admitted, sheepishly. How could her mother have saddled her with such an old-fashioned, unattractive name, more suited to one of her beloved dogs than her only daughter? "But please call me Mattie."

"I'd like to . . . call you, that is."

Mattie nodded, her eyes focused on the young man's mouth, on the wide upper lip that protruded over the thinner one on the bottom. It was a very sensual mouth, she thought, already projecting ahead to what it would be like to kiss that mouth, to feel those lips brush lightly against her own. "I'm sorry," she heard herself stammer. "What did you say?"

"I said that I understand you're majoring in art history."

Again she nodded, forcing her gaze to his blue eyes, roughly the same shade as her own, except that his lashes were longer, she noted, something that didn't strike her as altogether fair. Was it fair that one man could have such long lashes *and* such a sensual mouth?

"And what exactly is it that art historians do?"

"Beats me," Mattie heard herself say, her voice a touch too loud, so that this time someone did say *"Ssh!"*

"You feel like going somewhere for a cup of coffee?" He took her arm and led her out of the library without waiting for her reply, as if there were never any doubt what her reply would be. As there was no doubt later when he asked her if she wanted to go to the movies that night, and then later, when he invited her back to the apartment he shared with several of his law school classmates, and later still, when he invited her into his bed. And then it was too late. Within two short months of that first introduction, two months after she enthusiastically surrendered to the seductive fullness of his lashes and the unspoken gentleness of his overbite, she discovered she was pregnant, this on the very day he'd decided they were moving too fast, that they needed to slow down, cool down, call the whole thing off, at least temporarily. "I'm pregnant," she offered numbly, unable to say more.

They talked about abortion; they talked about adoption; ultimately they stopped talking and got married. Or got married and stopped talking, Mattie thought now, emerging from the water into the brisk fall air and grabbing at the large magenta towel folded neatly on the white canvas deck chair, sprinkled liberally with fallen leaves. She used one end of the towel to dry the ends of her hair, wrapping the rest of it tightly around her body, like a straitjacket. Jake had never really wanted to get married, Mattie understood now—as she'd understood then, although they'd both pretended, at least in the beginning, that their marriage would have been inevitable. After a short break, he'd have realized how much he loved her and come back to her.

Except that he didn't love her. Not then. Not now.

And truth be told, Mattie wasn't sure that she'd ever really loved him.

That she'd been attracted to him was beyond question. That she'd been mesmerized by his good looks and effortless charm, of that there was never any doubt. But that she'd actually been *in love* with him, that she didn't know. She hadn't had time to find out. Everything had happened too fast. And then, suddenly, there was no time left.

Mattie secured the towel at her breast and ran up the dozen wooden steps toward her kitchen, pulling open the sliding glass door and stepping inside, dripping onto the large, dark blue ceramic tile floor. Normally, this room made her smile. It was all blues and sunny yellows, with stainless steel appliances and a round, stone-topped table, decorated with hand-painted pieces of fruit, and surrounded by four wicker-and-wrought-iron chairs. Mattie had been dreaming of such a kitchen since seeing a picture layout in *Architectural Digest* on the kitchens of Provence. She'd personally supervised the kitchen's renovation the previous year, four years to the day after they'd moved into the three-bedroom house on Walnut Drive. Jake had been against the renovation, just as he'd been against moving to the suburbs, even if Evanston was only a fifteen-minute drive from downtown Chicago. He'd wanted to stay in their apartment on Lakeshore Drive, despite agreeing with all Mattie's arguments that the suburbs were safer, the choice of schools better, the space unquestionably bigger. He claimed his opposition to the move was all about convenience, but Mattie knew it was really about permanence. There was something too settled about a house in the suburbs, especially for a man with one foot out the door. "It'll be better for Kim," Mattie argued, and Jake finally agreed. Anything for Kim. The reason he'd married her in the first place.

The first time he'd been unfaithful was just after their second wedding anniversary. She'd stumbled on the incriminating evidence while going through the pockets of his jeans before putting them in the wash, extricating several amorous little notes, the *i*'s dotted with tiny hearts. She'd ripped them up, flushed them down the toilet, but pieces of the pale lavender stationery had floated back stubbornly to the surface of the bowl, refusing to be dismissed so easily. An omen of what lay ahead, she thought now, though she'd missed the symbolism at the time. Throughout the almost sixteen years of their marriage, there'd been a succession of such notes, of unfamiliar phone numbers on scraps of paper left lying carelessly around, nameless voices lingering on the answering machine, the not-so-quiet whispers of friends, and now this, the latest, a receipt for a room at the Ritz-Carlton, dated several months ago, around the time she was suggesting the possibility of a second child, the receipt left in the pocket of a jacket he'd asked her to take to the cleaners.

Did he have to be so blatant? Was her discovery of his indiscretions necessary to validate his experience? Were his conquests somehow less real without her, even if she had thus far refused to acknowledge them? And was acknowledging his affairs precisely what he was trying to force her to do? Because he knew that if he forced her to acknowledge his infidelities, if he forced her to actually confront him, then that would mean the end of their marriage. Was that what he wanted?

Was that what she wanted?

Maybe she was as tired of this charade of a marriage as her reluctant husband. "Maybe," she said out loud, staring at her reflection in the smoky glass door of the microwave oven. She wasn't unattractive—tall, blond, blue-eyed, the stereotype of the all-American girl—and she was only thirty-six years old, hardly old enough to be put out to pasture. Men still found her desirable. "I could have an affair," she whispered toward her gray, tear-streaked reflection.

Her image looked surprised, aghast, dismayed. *You tried that once. Remember?*

Mattie turned away, stared resolutely at the floor. "That was only that one time, and it was just to get even."

So, get even again.

Mattie shook her head, drops of water from her wet hair forming little puddles at her feet. The affair, if you could properly call a one-night stand an affair, had taken place four years ago, just before they'd moved to Evanston. It had been fast, furious, and eminently forgettable, except that she hadn't been able to forget it, not really, although she'd be hard pressed to recall the details of the man's face, having done her best to avoid actually looking at him, even as he was pounding his way inside her. He was a lawyer, like her husband, although with a different firm and a different area of expertise. An entertainment lawyer, she recalled his volunteering, along with the information that he was married and the father of three. She'd been hired by his firm to buy art for their walls, and he was trying to explain what the firm had in mind before he leaned in closer, told her what *he* had in mind. Instead of being shocked, instead of being angry, as she'd been earlier in the day when she'd overheard her husband on the phone making dinner plans with his latest paramour, she'd arranged to meet him later in the week, so that on the same evening her husband was in bed with another woman, she was in bed with another man, wondering, with joyless irony, if their orgasms were simultaneous.

She never saw the man again, although he'd called several times, ostensibly to discuss the paintings she was selecting for the firm. Ultimately he stopped calling, and the firm hired another dealer whose taste in art was "more in keeping with the sort of thing we had in mind." She never said anything about the affair to Jake, although surely that had been the point—where was the sweetness of revenge if the injured party remained unaware of the injury? But somehow she couldn't bring herself to tell him, not because she didn't want to hurt him, as she'd tried to convince herself at the time, but because she was afraid that if she told him, she would be handing him the excuse he needed to leave her.

And so she'd said nothing, and life continued as it always had. They carried on the pretense of a life together—talking pleasantly over the table at breakfast, going out for dinner with friends, making love several times a week, *more* when he was having an affair, fighting over anything and everything, except what they were really fighting about. *You're fucking other women!* she screamed underneath her rants about wanting to renovate the kitchen. *I don't want to be here!* he shouted beneath his protests that she was spending too much money, that she had to cut back. Sometimes their angry voices would wake up Kim, who'd come running into their bedroom, immediately taking her mother's side, so that it was two against one, another joyless irony Mattie doubted was lost on Jake, who was only there because of his daughter.

Maybe Kim was right, Mattie thought now, glancing at the phone on the wall beside her. Maybe all that was needed was a little show of support, something to let her husband know that she appreciated how hard he worked, how hard he tried—had always tried—to do the right thing. She reached for the phone, hesitated, decided to call her friend Lisa instead. Lisa would know how to advise her. She always knew what to do. And besides, Lisa was a doctor. Didn't doctors have an answer for everything? Mattie pressed in the first few numbers, then impatiently dropped the receiver back into its carriage. How could she disturb her friend in the middle of her undoubtedly busy day? Surely she could solve her own problems. Mattie quickly punched in the proper sequence of numbers, waited as Jake's private line rang once, twice, three times. He knows it's me, Mattie thought, trying to shake away the annoying tingle that had returned to tease the bottom of her right foot. He's deciding whether or not to pick up.

"The joys of call display," she sneered, picturing Jake sitting behind the heavy oak desk that occupied a full third of his less-than-spacious office on the forty-second floor of the John Hancock Building in downtown Chicago. The office, one of 320 similar offices making up the prestigious law firm of Richardson, Buckley and Lang, had floor-to-ceiling windows overlooking Michigan Avenue, and stylish Berber carpeting, but was too small by half to contain Jake's growing practice, a practice that seemed to be skyrocketing daily, especially since the press had lately turned him into something of a local celebrity. It seemed her husband had a knack for choosing seemingly impossible cases, and winning. Still, Mattie doubted that even Jake's considerable skill and formidable charm would be enough to win an acquittal for a young man who'd admitted to killing his mother in an act of undeniable premeditation, and then proudly boasted of the killing to his friends.

Was it possible Jake had already left for court? Mattie glanced at the two digital clocks on the other side of the room. The clock on the microwave oven said it was 8:32; the clock on the regular oven below it read 8:34.

She was about to hang up when the phone was answered between the fourth and fifth ring. "Mattie, what's up?" Jake's voice was strong, hurried, a voice that announced it had little time for small talk.

"Jake, hi," Mattie began, her own voice delicate and tentative. "You were out the door so fast this morning, I didn't get a chance to wish you good luck."

"I'm sorry. I couldn't wait for you to get up. I had to go—"

"No, that's fine. I didn't mean to imply—" Not on the phone ten seconds, and already she'd managed to make him uncomfortable. "I just wanted to wish you good luck. Not that you'll need it. I'm sure you'll be brilliant."

"You can never have too much good luck," Jake said.

Words to write on a fortune cookie, Mattie thought.

"Look, Mattie. I really have to get going. I appreciate your call—"

"I was thinking of coming to court this morning."

"Please don't do that," he said quickly. Far too quickly. "I mean, it's not really necessary."

"I know what you mean," she said, not bothering to disguise her disappointment. Obviously, there was a reason he didn't want her in court. Mattie wondered what the reason looked like, then pushed the unwelcome thought aside. "Anyway, I just called to wish you good luck." How many times had she said that already? Three? Four? Didn't she know when it was time to say good-bye, time to exit gracefully, time to pack up her good wishes and her pride and move on?

"I'll see you later." Jake's voice resonated with that fake, too-cheery tone that was too big for the thought being expressed. "Take care of yourself."

"Jake—" Mattie began. But either he didn't hear her or he pretended not to, and the only response Mattie got was the sound of the receiver being dropped into its carriage. What had she been about to say? That she knew all about his latest affair, that it was time for them to admit that neither was happy in this prolonged farce of a marriage, that it was time to call it a day? *The party's over*, she heard faint voices sing as she hung up the phone.

Mattie moved slowly out of the kitchen into the large center hallway. But her right foot had fallen asleep again, and she had trouble securing her footing. She stumbled, hopping for several seconds on her left foot across the blue-and-gold needlepoint rug while her right heel sought in vain to find the floor. She realized she was falling, and even more frightening, that she could do nothing to stop it, ultimately giving in to the inevitable, and crashing down hard on her rear end. She sat for several seconds in stunned silence, temporarily overwhelmed by the indignity of it all. "Damn you, Jake," she said finally, choking down unwanted tears. "Why couldn't you have just loved me? Would it have been so hard?"

Maybe the security of knowing her husband loved her would have given her the courage to love him in return.

Mattie made no move to get up. Instead, she sat in the middle of the hallway, her wet bathing suit soaking into the fine French needlepoint of the large area rug, and laughed so hard she cried.

Two

"Excuse me," Mattie said, crawling across the stubborn knees of a heavyset woman, dressed in varying shades of blue, toward the vacant seat smack in the middle of the eighth and last row of the visitors' block of courtroom 703. "Sorry. Excuse me," she repeated to an elderly couple seated beside the woman in blue, and then again, "Sorry," to the attractive young blonde she would be sitting beside for the better part of the morning. Was she the reason Jake didn't want her in court this morning?

Mattie unbuttoned her camel-colored coat, shrugging it off her shoulders with as little movement as possible, feeling it bunch at her elbows, pinning her arms uncomfortably to her sides so that she was forced to wiggle around in her seat in a vain effort to dislodge it, disturbing not only the attractive blonde to her right but the equally attractive blonde she now noticed to her left. Was there no end to the number of attractive blondes in Chicago, and did they all have to be in her husband's courtroom this morning? Maybe she was in the wrong room. Maybe instead of *Cook County versus Douglas Bryant,* she'd stumbled into some sort of attractive-young-blondes convention. Were they all sleeping with her husband?

Mattie's eyes shot to the front of the room, locating her husband at the defense table, his head lowered in quiet conversation with his client, a coarse-looking boy of nineteen, who appeared distinctly uncomfortable in the brown suit and paisley tie he'd obviously been advised to wear, the expression on his face curiously blank, as if he, like Mattie, had wandered into the wrong room and wasn't quite sure what he was doing here.

What was *she* doing here? Mattie wondered suddenly. Hadn't her husband specifically told her not to come? Hadn't Lisa advised the same thing when she gave in and called her? She should get up now and leave, just get up and slink away before he saw her. It had been a mistake to come here. What had she been thinking? That he'd be grateful for her support, as Kim had suggested? Was that why she was here? For support? Or had she come hoping to catch a glimpse of his latest mistress?

Mistress, Mattie thought, chewing the word over in her mouth, fighting the sudden urge to gag as she craned her neck across the rows of spectators, sighting two young brunettes giggling at the far end of the first row. Too young, Mattie decided. And too immature.

Definitely not Jake's type, although, truth be told, she wasn't sure what her husband's type actually was. Certainly not me, she thought, eyes flitting briefly across a head of brown curls occupying the aisle seat of the second row before moving on down the rows, stopping at the perfect profile of a raven-haired woman she recognized as one of the junior partners in her husband's firm, a woman who had joined Richardson, Buckley and Lang at approximately the same time as Jake. Shannon something-or-other. Wasn't her specialty estate planning, or something equally nondescript? What was *she* doing here?

As if aware she was under observation, Shannon whatever-her-name-was did a slow turn in Mattie's direction, eyes stopping directly on Mattie, a slow smile tugging at the corners of her mouth. She's trying to figure out where she knows me from, Mattie understood, recognizing the look, smiling confidently back. Mattie Hart, her smile announced, wife of Jake, the man of the hour, the man we're all here to see, the man you possibly saw last night in rather more intimate surroundings.

Shannon whatever-she-called-herself broke into a huge grin of recognition. Oh, that Mattie Hart, the grin said. "How are you?" she mouthed silently.

"Never better," Mattie answered out loud, giving the sleeve bunched around her elbow another tug, hearing the lining rip. "You?"

"Great," came the instant reply.

"I've been meaning to call you," Mattie heard herself announce, almost afraid of what she was going to say next. "I want to change my will." She did? When had she decided that?

The smile vanished from Shannon whatever's lips. "What?" she said.

So maybe her specialty isn't estate planning, Mattie thought, lowering her gaze, signaling the end of the conversation, looking back several seconds later, relieved that Shannon whoever-she-was-and-was-she-sleeping-with-her-husband had returned her attention to the front of the courtroom.

You don't want to be here, Mattie decided. You definitely don't want to be here. Get up now. Get up and go before you make a complete fool of yourself. I want to change my will? Where had that come from?

"Let me help you with that," the blonde to her left volunteered, tugging at Mattie's stubborn coat sleeve before Mattie had time to object, smiling at Mattie the way Mattie smiled at her mother, the expression a little forced, containing more pity than goodwill.

"Thank you." Mattie flashed the woman her most sincere smile, a smile that said, This is the way it's done, but the young woman had already turned away, was staring toward the front of the stately old courtroom, holding her breath expectantly. Mattie straightened the folds of her gray wool skirt, fidgeted with the collar of her white cotton blouse. The blonde to her right, who was wearing a pink angora sweater and navy slacks, shot her a sideways glance that said, Don't you ever sit still? which Mattie pretended not to notice. She should have worn something else, something less schoolmarmish, something less Miss Grundyish, she thought, smiling at the image of Kim that popped into her brain. Something softer, like a pink angora sweater, she thought, glancing enviously at the woman beside her. Although she'd never liked angora. It always made her sneeze. As if on cue, Mattie felt a sneeze building in the upper recesses of her nose, had barely time to fumble in her purse for a tissue, before burying her nose inside it, the force of her sneeze ricocheting through the room. Had Jake heard her? "Bless you," both blondes said in unison, inching away from her side.

"Thank you," Mattie said, stealing a glance in her husband's direction, relieved to find him still deep in conversation with his client. "Sorry." She sneezed again, apologized again.

A woman in the row in front of her swiveled around in her seat, soft brown eyes flecked with gold. "Are you all right?" Her voice was deep and vaguely raspy, older than the round face it emanated from, a face surrounded by a halo of frantic red curls. Nothing quite matched, Mattie thought absently, thanking the woman for her concern.

And then there was a slight stir as the county clerk asked everyone to rise, and the judge, an attractive black woman, whose curly dark hair was flecked with specks of gray, like ashes, assumed her seat at the head of the courtroom. It was only then that Mattie noticed the jury, seven men and five women, plus two men who served as alternates, most of the jurors hovering around middle age, although several looked scarcely out of their teens, and one man was likely closer to seventy. Of the fourteen, six were white, four were black, three were Hispanic, and one was Asian. Their faces reflected varying degrees of interest, earnestness, and fatigue. The trial had been going on for almost three weeks. Both sides had presented their cases. The jury had, no doubt, heard all it wanted to hear. Now what they wanted was to get back to their jobs, their families, the lives they'd put on hold. It was time to make a decision, then move on.

Me too, Mattie thought, leaning forward in her seat as the judge directed the prosecution to proceed. Time for me to make a decision and move on.

Light my fire. Light my fire. Light my fire.

One of the assistant state's attorneys was instantly on his feet, doing up the button of his gray suit jacket, the way lawyers always did on TV, and walking toward the jury. He was a tall man, about forty, with a thin face and a long nose that hooked at its tip, rather like a candle dripping wax. There was a noticeable stir in the visitors' block as everyone inched forward simultaneously, their silence heavy, like a dense fog, waiting for the lawyer's voice to lead them toward the light. "Ladies and gentlemen of the jury," the prosecutor began, making deliberate eye contact with each juror, then smiling. "Good morning." The jury smiled back dutifully, one woman's smile disappearing into an aborted yawn. "I want to thank you for your patience these last few weeks." He paused briefly, swallowed, his large Adam's apple bobbing into view above the pale blue collar of his shirt. "It's my job to recount for you the simple facts of this case."

Mattie coughed, a sudden, violent spasm that brought tears to her eyes.

"Are you sure you're all right?" the blonde to her left asked, offering Mattie another tissue, while the blonde on Mattie's right rolled her eyes in exasperation. It's

you, isn't it? Mattie thought, wiping at her tears with
the tissue. You're the one sleeping with my husband.

"On the night of February twenty-fourth," the
prosecuting attorney continued, "Douglas Bryant
returned home from an evening of drinking with his
friends and was confronted by his mother, Constance
Fisher. There was an argument, and Douglas Bryant
stormed out of the house. He went back to the bar, had
a few more drinks, then returned home at about two
A.M., by which time his mother had gone to bed. He
walked into the kitchen, took a long, sharp knife from
one of the drawers, proceeded to his mother's bedroom, and with deliberate calm plunged the knife into
his mother's stomach. One can only imagine the horror that Constance Fisher felt at realizing what was
happening to her, and she made a valiant effort to ward
off her son's repeated blows. In all, Douglas Bryant
stabbed his mother a total of fourteen times. One
thrust punctured a lung, another went straight for her
heart. As if this weren't enough, Douglas Bryant then
slashed his mother's throat with such force he almost
severed her head from her body. He then returned to
the kitchen, where he used the knife to make himself a
sandwich, took a shower, and went to bed. The next
morning, he went to school and boasted of the killing
to his fellow students, one of whom called the police."

The assistant state's attorney continued to go over
the so-called simple facts of the case, reminding the
jury of the witnesses who'd confirmed that Constance
Fisher was afraid of her son, that the murder weapon
was covered with Douglas Bryant's fingerprints, that
his clothing was covered with his mother's blood, sim-

ple fact after simple fact, each item damning enough in itself, devastating when added together. What could Jake Hart possibly say that would mitigate the horror of what Mattie had just heard?

"It sounds pretty clear-cut," she heard Jake agree, as if he were privy to her thoughts, as if he were speaking directly to her. Her eyes shot toward her husband as Jake rose to his feet, the jacket of his conservative blue suit already buttoned. She was gratified to note that he'd taken her advice and selected a white shirt instead of a blue one, although the deep burgundy tie he was wearing was unfamiliar to her. He smiled, a little Elvis-like curling of his upper lip, and began addressing the jury in the soft, conversational, even intimate fashion that was his trademark. He makes you feel as if you're the only person in the room, Mattie marveled, watching as each member of the jury unknowingly succumbed to his spell, leaning forward, giving him their undivided attention. The women to either side of Mattie fidgeted expectantly in their seats, their shapely rear ends nervously polishing the hard wooden bench beneath them.

Did he have to be so damned attractive? Mattie wondered, knowing Jake had always considered his looks as much a curse as a blessing, how hard he'd worked to play down his naturally handsome features in the fourteen years he'd been practicing law, the last eight with Richardson, Buckley and Lang. Jake knew that many of his colleagues groused that it had all come too easily for him: the good looks, the high marks, the instinct that told him which cases to take on and which to reject. But Mattie knew that Jake worked as hard as anyone at the firm, possibly harder, arriving at the office before eight each morning and rarely leaving before eight at night. Assuming he was actually in his office and not in a room at the Ritz-Carlton, Mattie thought, wincing as if she'd been struck.

"The way Mr. Doren presents it, everything in this case is either black or white," Jake said, rubbing the side of his aquiline nose. "Constance Fisher was a dedicated mother and loyal friend, loved by all who knew her. Her son was a hothead who was failing at school and going out drinking every night. She was a saint; he was a holy terror. She lived in mortal fear; he was her mortal enemy. She dreamed of a better life for her son; he was every mother's worst nightmare." Jake paused and looked toward his client, who shifted uncomfortably in his seat. "It certainly sounds simple enough," Jake continued, eyes returning to the jury, effortlessly catching them in his invisible net. "Except that things are rarely as simple as they sound. And we all know that." Several of the jurors smiled their agreement. "Just as we know that when we mix black and white together, we get gray. And different shades of gray at that."

Mattie watched her husband turn his back on the jury and walk over to where his client sat, confident that the eyes of each juror were on him. She watched him reach out and touch his client's shoulder. "So, let's take a few minutes and examine the varying shades of gray. Can we do that?" he asked, turning back to the jury, as if asking their permission. Mattie noticed one of the women jurors actually nodding her head in reply. "Firstly, let's take a closer look at Constance Fisher, dedicated mother and loyal friend. Well, I don't believe in blaming the victim," Jake Hart said, and Mattie chuckled, knowing he was about to do just that. "I think that Constance Fisher *was* a dedicated mother and loyal friend."

But? Mattie waited.

"But I also know she was a frustrated and bitter woman who verbally abused her son almost every day of his life, and often resorted to physical violence as well." Jake paused, let the weight of his words sink in. "Now, I'm not trying to tell you that Douglas Bryant was an easy kid to mother. He wasn't. He was many of the things that the prosecution claims, and those of us who have children," he said, subtly aligning himself with the jurors, "understand just how frustrated his mother must have been, trying to deal with this kid who wouldn't listen, who blamed her for his father walking out when he was a small boy, who was instrumental in the failure of her second marriage to Gene Fisher, who refused to show her the love and respect she felt she deserved. But stop for a minute," Jake said, doing just that as the courtroom held its breath, waiting for him to continue.

How often had he rehearsed that moment? Mattie wondered, aware she was holding her breath, just like everyone else. How many seconds had he programmed that pause to last?

"Stop and consider the source of all that anger," Jake continued after five full seconds had elapsed, instantly sucking his audience back in. "Little boys aren't born bad. No little boy starts out hating his mother."

Mattie brought her hand to her mouth. So this was why he'd taken this case, she realized. And why he would win.

It was personal.

A lawyer's practice is almost always a reflection of his own personality, he'd once told her. By extension, did that make the courtroom the legal equivalent of the psychiatrist's couch?

Mattie listened carefully as her husband recounted the horrors of the almost daily abuse Douglas Bryant had suffered at the hands of his mother—the washing his mouth out with soap when he was a child, the constant bad-mouthing, calling him stupid and worthless, the frequent beatings that resulted in oft-documented bruises and occasional broken bones—which resulted in Douglas Bryant's lashing out uncontrollably when he could no longer cope with the abuse, a textbook case of "child abuse syndrome," Jake intoned solemnly, referring to the earlier testimony of several expert psychiatrists.

Was that what it was like for you? Mattie asked her husband silently, doubting she would ever receive a satisfactory answer. When they'd first started dating, Jake had made several veiled references to his troubled childhood, something Mattie related to instantly, being the survivor of a difficult childhood herself. But the more they'd dated, the less Jake confided, and whenever she pressed him for details, he'd clam right up, disappear into a funk for days at a time, until she learned not to ask any questions about his family. We have so much in common, she thought now, as she'd thought often during the many strained silences of their years together—the crazy mothers, the absent fathers, the lack of any real familial warmth.

Instead of siblings, Mattie had shared her childhood

with her mother's many dogs, never less than six, sometimes as many as eleven, all doted upon and adored, so much easier to love than a troublesome child who looked just like the father who'd abandoned them. And while Jake hadn't been an only child—he'd had an older brother who died in a boating accident, and a younger brother who had disappeared into a drug-filled haze several years before she came along—Mattie knew her husband's adolescence had been as lonely and pain-filled as her own.

No—worse. Much worse.

Why wouldn't you ever talk to me about it? she wondered now, inadvertently raising her hand as if wanting to ask the question out loud. The motion caught her husband's eye, distracting him from his summation. Maybe I could have helped you, she offered silently, their eyes locking across the room. His handsome face registered surprise, confusion, anger, and fear, all in less than a fraction of a second, all invisible to everyone but her. I know you so well, she thought, feeling a strange tickle at the back of her throat. And yet, I don't know you at all.

Certainly you don't know me.

And then suddenly the tickle at the back of her throat exploded, and she was laughing out loud, laughing so loud that everyone was turning around to look at her, laughing so uncontrollably that the judge was banging with her gavel, just like they do on TV, Mattie thought, laughing louder still, watching a uniformed officer approach. She caught the look of abject horror on her husband's face as she jumped to her feet and propelled herself out of the row, trailing her coat along the floor after her. Reaching the large marble-framed wooden door at the back of the courtroom, Mattie turned back, her eyes briefly connecting with the horrified eyes of the woman with curly red hair from the row in front of hers. I always wanted curls like that, Mattie found herself thinking as the officer quickly ushered her out the door. If he said anything to her, she couldn't hear it over her laughter, which continued unabated down seven flights of stairs and across the main lobby, down the outside steps, and onto the street.

THREE

O rder. Order in the court."

The judge was banging on her desk with her gavel, bouncing up and down in her high-backed leather chair, while the gallery before her buzzed nervously, like bees whose hive has been unexpectedly disturbed. Some of the spectators were whispering behind closed palms, others laughing openly. Several members of the jury talked animatedly among themselves. "What on earth . . . ?" "What do you suppose . . . ?" "What was that all about?"

Jake Hart stood in the center of the old courtroom, with its high ceiling, large side windows, and dark paneling, halfway between his client and the jury, too stunned to move, his shock rooting him firmly to the worn brown carpet beneath his black shoes, his fury spinning an invisible, protective cocoon around him, the noise and confusion of the courtroom swooping, like newly wakened bats, around his head. He felt like a grenade whose string had been pulled. If he took one step, if he so much as breathed, he would explode. It was important that he stay very still. He had to refocus, regroup, reclaim lost ground.

What the hell had happened?

It had been going so well, everything proceeding exactly according to plan. He'd worked for weeks on his summation—not only on the words he spoke, but on the way in which he spoke them, his inflection, the stress he placed on certain syllables, favoring this one over that, the pacing of his sentences, when to pause, when to continue. He'd memorized the words, perfected the cadence. It was going to be the speech of his life, the closing argument that would pull everything together, cap the highest-profile case of his career, a case the firm's senior partners had expressed serious reservations about his taking on, a case they'd argued was hopeless, that didn't stand the proverbial snowball's chance in hell. It was also the case that would almost certainly guarantee him a partnership should he win it, propel him to the top of his profession at the ripe old age of thirty-eight.

And he'd done it. All his hard work had paid off. He'd had the jury in the palm of his hand, hanging on his every phrase. *Child abuse syndrome*—what the hell was that before he'd raised it as a defense? "The parallels with wife abuse syndrome are unmistakable and undeniable," he'd been about to continue. "Indeed, the abused child is more vulnerable than the abused wife because the child has even less control over the situation, even less ability to choose his environment, to pack up his bags and get the hell out." The words had been at the tip of his tongue; he'd taken a breath, was preparing to release them, when someone had landed a sucker punch to his solar plexus and knocked the wind right out of him.

What had happened?

He'd seen something out of the corner of his eye, some vague movement, as if someone were trying to get his attention, and he'd looked over, and there she was, Mattie, his wife, whom he'd specifically asked not to come to court this morning, there she was, and she was laughing, and not just some silly little giggle but this hideous, full-throated guffaw, laughing at something, he didn't know what, perhaps laughing at what he was saying, at the audacity of his argument, maybe just laughing her contempt, at the proceedings, at the process, at *him*, and then Judge Berg was banging her gavel and calling for order, and Mattie was clumsily tripping over the laps of the people beside her, dragging her coat along the floor after her as she was escorted from the room, all the while surrounded by this hysterical, insane cackle he could still hear popping in his ears, like wires that are short-circuiting.

Five more minutes. That was all the time he'd needed. Another five minutes and he would have been finished with his closing argument. It would have been time for the prosecution's rebuttal. Then Mattie could have pulled any stunt her little heart desired. She could have jumped up and down like some deranged jack-in-the-box, taken off all her clothes, if she wanted to, and laughed her fool head off.

What was the matter with her?

Maybe she wasn't feeling well, Jake thought, struggling to be charitable. She'd slept in this morning, which was unusual in itself, and then that strange phone call to his office, that little-girl voice on the telephone, raw with vulnerability, suggesting she might come to court. There was nothing vulnerable about the Mattie Hart Jake knew. She was as strong and as forceful as a gale wind. And as potentially destructive. Had she deliberately set out to sabotage him? Was that her motive for showing up in court this morning after he'd specifically asked her not to?

"This court will come to order," Jake heard the judge proclaim loudly, although no order came.

"What's happening?" the defendant asked, his eyes those of a trapped and frightened child.

I know those eyes, Jake thought, his own childhood reflected back at him. I know that fear.

He pushed the unwanted memory aside, tried to do the same with his wife. But Mattie stood before him like a slender block of stone, delicate to look at but stunningly difficult to dislodge. As she'd always been, from the moment they'd first met.

God, not that crap again, Jake thought, forcing one foot in front of the other, breaking free of his protective cocoon, now more like a coffin, to take his seat beside his client. He lifted the boy's ice-cold hands inside his own.

"Your hands are so cold," Douglas Bryant said.

"Sorry." Jake almost laughed, except that there had been enough laughter in the court for one morning.

"We'll take a half-hour recess," the judge instructed,

as all around Jake, the courtroom began emptying out, the people pulled as if by magnets toward the various exits. Jake felt Douglas Bryant's hands slip through his fingers as he was led away. He watched the jury file out. What can I do to win you back? Jake wondered. What can I say that will obliterate the outrage my wife has perpetrated on this courtroom?

Did anyone realize she was his wife?

"Jake—"

The voice was familiar, soft, achingly feminine. He looked up. Oh God, he thought, feeling suddenly sick to his stomach. Why did she have to be here?

"Are you all right?"

He nodded, said nothing.

Shannon Graham reached out as if to touch him, stopped mere inches from his shoulder, her hand fluttering aimlessly in the air. "Is there anything I can do?" she asked.

He shook his head. He knew she was really asking what the hell had happened, but since he didn't know the answer any better than she did, he said nothing.

"Is something wrong with Mattie?"

He shrugged.

"She said something strange to me this morning," Shannon continued when Jake failed to respond. "Out of the blue, she said she wanted to change her will."

"What?" Jake's head snapped back, as if someone had yanked a fistful of his hair.

It was Shannon's turn to shrug. "Anyway, if there's anything I can do . . ." she offered again, her voice drifting away.

"You can keep this quiet," Jake said, although he

could feel Shannon Graham already rehearsing her speech to the other lawyers in the firm even as she walked away. There was something anticipatory, even eager, in her gait, as if she could barely wait to get where she was going. It didn't matter. Mattie's outburst would be old news before Shannon Graham left the building. The legal profession was the same as any other in that regard. It loved gossip. Exaggerated tales of his wife's behavior were no doubt already sprinting through the hallowed halls of justice on their way across town, leaping from the rundown corner of California Avenue and Twenty-fifth Street where the courthouse was situated to the swank Miracle Mile of Michigan Avenue, home of Richardson, Buckley and Lang. "Did you hear about the stunt Mattie Hart pulled in court today?" "What's the matter with Jake Hart's wife?" "It was the damnedest thing. She just started laughing—right in the middle of his summation."

Sometimes he wished she would just disappear.

Not that he wished Mattie any actual harm. It wasn't that he wanted her dead, or anything like that. He just wanted her gone, out of his life, out of his head. For weeks he'd been thinking of ways to tell her it was over, that he'd fallen in love with someone else, that he was leaving her. He'd rehearsed the words as if preparing his closing argument for the jury, which was exactly what it was, he thought now, the summation of his marriage, with Mattie the jury, the judge, the Lord High Executioner.

"It's nobody's fault," the speech always began, then faltered, because truth be told, it was somebody's fault. It was *his* fault. Although it was her fault as well, a little voice now interjected. Her fault for getting pregnant in the first place, for insisting on having the baby, for pouncing on his reluctant offer of marriage, even though she knew it wasn't what he wanted, that they weren't right for one another, that it was a mistake, that he would always resent her.

"We've given it our best shot," the speech continued. But he hadn't given it his best shot, and they both knew it. Although Mattie wasn't altogether blameless, the little voice insisted, louder now. In the beginning, she'd wrapped herself totally in the cloak of motherhood, nursing Kim at all hours of the day and night, shutting him out. And while it was true that he'd had no interest in changing diapers, and babies made him nervous, that didn't mean he didn't love his daughter, or that he liked being relegated to the role of casual observer in her life. He envied the easy rapport Kim shared with her mother, was envious of their bond. Kim was definitely her mother's daughter. It was too late for her to be Daddy's little girl.

And then last month Mattie had suddenly floated the idea of having another child, slipping it into the middle of a casual conversation, trying to disguise her enthusiasm as indifference, as if it were just another idea, something she hadn't been thinking about night and day. And he'd known then that he couldn't afford to wait much longer, or he would be trapped again. He had to tell Mattie he was leaving.

Except that he hadn't told her. And now there was the distinct possibility that he'd waited too long, that she was already pregnant, that her confused and raging hormones were responsible for her strange behavior in court this morning. "Please, no," he heard himself say out loud. "Anything but that."

"Anything but what?"

He looked up at the sound of her voice, reached out his hand for her to take, felt a rush of excitement as her fingers laced themselves through his. What the hell? Who cared who saw them together? Besides, the courtroom was empty. It was easy to be brave.

"That was your wife, wasn't it?" she asked, her voice full of late nights and too many cigarettes. She lowered herself into the defendant's chair, leaning her head toward his so that her thick red curls brushed against his cheek, like a cat against a bare leg. Just last night he'd gathered those auburn curls inside the palm of his hand and squeezed them, mesmerized by their softness. And she'd looked up at him and smiled that wondrously wide smile that threatened to spill over the borders of her round face, her lips parting to reveal a bottom row of charmingly crooked teeth. What was it about her that he found so incredibly attractive?

Like the expensive silk blouse and faded denim jeans she'd artfully combined, everything about Honey Novak was mix and match. Her hair might be red and curly, but her eyebrows were defiantly black and straight. Her bosom was too big for her otherwise spindly frame, her legs too long for someone barely five foot two, and her nose slightly bent and off-angle, giving her a vaguely scattered look. She wasn't a great beauty by anyone's definition, and at thirty-four, hardly anyone's idea of a younger woman. Objectively speaking, his wife was the more attractive of the two. And yet he'd always been intimidated by Mattie's sunny, all-American good looks. They made him feel like a fraud.

"That was Mattie," he agreed.

Honey said nothing, which was typical of Honey, who rarely spoke when she had nothing to say. They'd met several months ago at the health club in his building. He was on the treadmill, walking a brisk 4.5 miles per hour; she was jogging along beside him, the mileage on her machine registering an impressive 7.2. He made casual conversation; she replied with assorted smiles and grunts. After a few weeks he'd asked her out for coffee, and she said yes, despite the fact she knew he was married. It was just coffee, after all. The following week, coffee spilled into dinner, and the week after that, dinner served as merely an hors d'oeuvre to a passion-filled night at the Ritz-Carlton hotel. One of many, although the locale quickly shifted to her charmingly cluttered one-bedroom apartment in Lincoln Park.

He hadn't meant to fall in love. Love was the last thing on his agenda. Didn't he already have enough complications in his life? A one-night stand was one thing, a casual affair, as meaningless as it was brief; that was all he thought he'd signed on for. The same for her, Honey confided later. She was newly divorced, childless by choice, working as a freelance writer while trying to write a novel, and looking after two ornery cats recently abandoned by a neighboring tenant in her building. The last thing she needed, she'd told him one night, as she perched naked on his stomach in the casual chaos of her bedroom, the cats playing with their exposed toes, was to fall in love with a married man.

"Do you think she knows?" Honey asked finally. "About us?"

Jake shrugged, as he had shrugged earlier. Anything is possible, he thought, a notion that once suggested limitless freedom, but which he now found almost overwhelmingly claustrophobic.

"What are you going to do?" Honey asked.

"I can't go home," he told her, his voice flat, his eyes flashing rage. "I don't think I could look at her."

"She looked scared to death."

"What?" What was Honey talking about?

"I saw the look on her face when she was leaving," Honey explained. "She looked terrified."

"She has good reason to be terrified."

"This goes beyond reason."

"That's for sure." Jake slapped his hands against his thighs, relished the sting. "Anyway, one thing at a time." He patted the burgundy silk tie Honey had given him for good luck the night before.

"You had them," Honey said, nodding toward the empty jury box. "You'll get them back."

Jake nodded, his mind already racing ahead to when court resumed. What would he say? Mattie had disrupted the most important trial of his career by laughing out loud in the middle of his summation, exposing him to ridicule, and his client to a possible mistrial. The jury, indeed everyone in the courtroom, would be waiting to see how he handled it. He couldn't just ignore what had happened. He had to use it. Use it to his advantage.

To do that he had to wrap his anger at Mattie's startling outburst into a neat little packet and tuck it away in a back drawer of his mind, to be opened later. This would be difficult, but not impossible. Jake had learned, almost from infancy, that his very survival depended on his ability to compartmentalize, and now someone else's survival depended on it as well. Douglas Bryant's fate, indeed his life, was in Jake's hands, and Jake would save him because he understood him, because he had been privy to the same rage and frustration that had driven the boy to kill. There but for the grace of God go I, Jake thought, suddenly stiffening in his chair, dropping Honey's hand, as the doors of the courtroom opened and people hurried to reclaim their seats.

"I love you, Jason Hart," Honey told him.

Jake smiled. Honey was the only person in the world he allowed to call him Jason, the name his mother had given him, the name she'd screamed while beating him— *Bad boy Jason! Bad boy Jason!*—until the words blended together, merged as one in his mind. *Badboyjason, badboyjason, badboyjason.* Only on Honey's lips did the words separate, become something other than a curse, something other than an all-inclusive definition. Only with Honey could Jason Hart leave the bad little boy behind and become the man he'd always wanted to be.

"You need a few minutes alone," Honey stated simply, already on her feet. Mattie would have put a question mark at the end of the sentence, forcing him to make the decision, to feel guilty for shutting her out, for sending her away. But Honey always knew when to approach and when to withdraw.

"Don't go far," he told her, almost under his breath.

"Seventh row, center," she told him.

Jake smiled, watching her sly wiggle—sly because she knew he was watching—as she made her way back to the visitors' block. Seconds later the jury filed back into the room, and Douglas Bryant resumed his seat at the defense table.

"Seat's still warm," Douglas Bryant observed.

Jake smiled reassuringly, patting the defendant's hand as the clerk called the court to order and the room instantly stilled. The judge returned to her seat, dark eyes wary, scanning the courtroom for potential trouble spots. "If there are any more outbursts," she warned, "I'll have this room cleared of spectators."

Jake thought the warning unnecessary. Never had he heard a courtroom so still. They're all waiting, he thought. Waiting to see how I handle things, waiting to hear what I have to say.

"Is the defense ready to continue with its closing argument?" Judge Berg asked.

Jake Hart rose to his feet. "Ready, Your Honor."

Ready or not, Jake thought, taking a deep breath, looking toward the jury, taking another deep breath, then looking directly at the seat Mattie had occupied earlier. "You just heard a woman laugh," he began, acknowledging the incident head-on, though not the woman's identity. "We don't know why she laughed. It's not important, although it certainly was unsettling." He chuckled softly, allowing the courtroom to chuckle along with him, to relieve some of the tension still remaining. "But the truth can be equally unsettling," Jake continued, gently grabbing the jury by its collective throat, "and the truth in this case is that Douglas Bryant is on trial for his life." He paused, training his deep blue eyes on each member of the jury, allowing angry tears to fill those eyes, knowing the jury would mistake his fury at Mattie for compassion toward the defendant. "Douglas Bryant is on trial for his life," Jake repeated. "And that is no laughing matter."

The jury sighed, like a lover responding to a well-placed caress. He'd done it, Jake thought, watching several of the women shed compassionate tears of their own. Mattie had inadvertently handed him the biggest win of his career. He'd get the not-guilty verdict, the great publicity, the offer of partnership.

And he owed it all to Mattie. As usual, he owed everything to his wife.

Four

Mattie stood on the outside steps of the Art Institute of Chicago, feeling the cold breeze whip across her face. "Harder," she muttered under her breath, pushing her face forward as if daring the wind to strike her. Go on, knock me down. Send me flying. Humiliate me in front of all these well-heeled patrons of the arts. It's no less than I deserve. Payback time for the way I humiliated my husband in court this morning. "Go on," she whispered, still trying to make sense of what had happened. "Give it your best shot."

"Mattie?"

Mattie spun around at the sound of her name, her mouth opening in an exaggerated smile as Roy Crawford, a man with the weathered face of a boxer and the lithe build of a dancer, approached, gray eyes twinkling beneath a full head of gray hair. He walked with his shoulders, Mattie observed, studying him as he strutted confidently toward her, right shoulder, left shoulder, right shoulder. Definitely cock of the walk, in his casual black trousers and cream-colored turtleneck, no coat, despite the increasing chill. Roy Crawford had made his first million before the age of thirty and had recently celebrated his fiftieth birthday by shedding wife number three and moving in with his youngest daughter's closest friend.

"Roy," she acknowledged, shaking his hand enthusiastically. "I'm so glad you were able to get away early."

"I own the company," he said easily. "I set the rules. That's quite a grip you've got there."

"I'm so sorry." Mattie immediately released her stranglehold on his fingers.

"Nothing to be sorry about."

Nothing to be sorry about, Mattie repeated silently, her mind spinning back to courtroom 703, the memory of what she'd done flashing before her as if caught in a strobe light, revealing images frozen in time and forever seared inside her brain. Nothing to be sorry about. Ah, but that's where you're wrong, Mr. Crawford. There's everything to be sorry about. Starting with her ill-advised trip to court this morning, continuing with the scene she'd created, and not just any scene, the mother of all scenes, the scene from hell. Scenes from a marriage, Mattie thought sadly, knowing her husband would never forgive her, that her marriage was over, her sorry excuse for a marriage, her marriage that never really was, despite nearly sixteen years and the daughter it produced, the only thing in her life that she didn't have to be sorry about.

"I'm really so sorry," Mattie repeated, and promptly burst into tears.

"Mattie?" Roy Crawford's gray eyes shifted warily from side to side, his lips pursing, relaxing, then pursing again as he reached for Mattie, gathered her now-shaking body into his arms. "What's wrong? What's the matter?"

"I'm so sorry," Mattie repeated again, unable to say anything else. What was happening to her? First the laughter in the courthouse, and now tears on the steps of Chicago's famed Art Institute. Maybe it was environmental, some insidious form of lead poisoning. Maybe she was allergic to majestic old buildings. Whatever it was, she didn't want to leave the comfort and security of Roy Crawford's arms. It had been a long time since someone had held her with such overt tenderness. Even when she and Jake made love, and their lovemaking had remained surprisingly passionate throughout the years, it was this tenderness that was lacking. She realized now just how much she'd missed it. How much she'd missed. "I'm so sorry."

Roy Crawford pulled back, though not away, his strong hands still resting on her upper arms, his wide fingers kneading the flesh beneath her coat. "What can I do?"

Poor guy, Mattie thought. He didn't do anything, and yet he looks so guilty, as if he were used to making women cry and ready to assume full responsibility, regardless of his innocence. Mattie wondered for a moment whether this was the way all men felt, if they went through life afraid of the power of a woman's tears. "Give me a minute. I'll be fine." Mattie offered

Roy Crawford what she hoped was her most reassuring smile. But she felt her lips wobbling all over her chin and tasted salty tears burrowing between tightly clenched teeth, and Roy Crawford looked anything but reassured. In fact, he looked terrified.

Who could blame him? He thought he was meeting with his art dealer to view a photography exhibition, and what did he meet up with instead? Every man's worst nightmare—a hysterical woman carrying on in a public place! No wonder Roy Crawford looked as if he wished the earth would open up and swallow him whole.

Still, the look of discomfort on Roy Crawford's face was nothing in comparison to the look of sheer horror that had overtaken her husband's entire being during her earlier outburst in court. What he must have thought! What he must be thinking now! He'd never forgive her, that much was certain. Her marriage was over, and it had ended not with accusations and recriminations but with laughter.

Mattie had fled the courthouse, hooting with laughter as she ran along California Avenue between Twenty-fifth and Twenty-sixth Streets, not the best area in the city, she knew, noticing a drunk zigzagging across the street to avoid her. Even the winos want to get away from me, she'd thought, laughing louder, hearing footsteps and looking behind her, hoping to see Jake, instead seeing two black men with knitted wool caps pulled down around their ears, who looked the other way as they hurried past.

Her car, a white Intrepid in need of a wash, was parked at an expired meter two blocks from the courthouse. Mattie had fumbled in her purse for her keys, found them, dropped them to the sidewalk, retrieved them, dropped them again. Securing them tightly between her fingers, she'd tried repeatedly to open her car door. But the key kept turning over in her fingers, and the door remained stubbornly closed. "I must be having a stroke," she'd announced to the row of decaying small buildings beside her. "That's it. I'm having a stroke."

More likely a nervous breakdown, Mattie decided. How else to explain this outrageous behavior? How else to explain her complete and utter lack of control?

The key suddenly slid into the car door. Mattie had taken a deep breath, then another, shaking her fingers, wriggling her toes inside her black suede pumps. Everything seemed to be working okay. And she'd stopped laughing, she noted gratefully, sliding behind the wheel and checking her reflection in the rearview mirror, using her car phone to call Roy Crawford, to ask if they could change the time of their meeting, possibly view the exhibition early, then discuss possible purchases afterward at lunch, her treat.

Some treat, Mattie thought now, wiping away the last of her tears, struggling for at least a semblance of control. Why hadn't Jake followed her? Surely he had to have realized that something was wrong. Surely he had to know that her outburst hadn't been designed to sabotage him. Although how could he know that when she wasn't sure of it herself?

"Think you're okay now?" Roy Crawford was asking, his eyes pleading for a simple yes.

"I'm fine," Mattie told him, obligingly. "Thank you."

"We could do this another time."

"No, really, I'm fine."

"Do you want to talk about it?" This time Roy Crawford's eyes begged for a simple no.

"I don't think so." Mattie took a deep breath, watched Roy Crawford do the same. He has a very big head, she thought absently. "Shall we go inside?"

Minutes later, they were standing in front of a naked woman, artfully angled around an antiquated washstand so that only her buttocks and the curve of her left breast were exposed to the camera's prying eye.

"Willy Ronis is a member of the famous triumvirate of French photographers," Mattie was explaining in her best professional voice, trying to keep her mind in the present tense, her trained eye on the stunning display of black-and-white photographs that lined the walls of one of the institute's more intimate downstairs rooms.

When we mix black and white together, she heard Jake interrupt, *we get gray. And different shades of gray at that.*

Go away, Jake, Mattie instructed silently. I'll see you in court, she thought, and almost laughed, biting down hard on her bottom lip to ensure her silence. "The other two members of the group, of course, are Henri Cartier-Bresson and Robert Doisneau," Mattie continued when she thought it was safe. "This particular picture, entitled *Nu provencal,* is probably Ronis's most popular and widely exhibited photograph."

So let's take a few minutes and examine the varying shades of gray.

Let's not, Mattie thought. "An interest in the nude

female form is a distinguishing feature of Ronis's work," she said.

"Is there some reason you're shouting?" Roy Crawford interrupted.

"Was I shouting?"

"Just a little. Nothing to get upset about," he added quickly.

Mattie shook her head in an effort to rid herself of her husband's voice once and for all. "Sorry."

"Please don't apologize," Roy said, obviously frightened she was going to start crying again. Then he smiled, a big loopy grin that went perfectly with his big head, and Mattie understood in that instant why women of all ages found him so attractive. Part rogue, part little boy—a deadly combination.

"I've always wanted to go to France," Mattie said, lowering her voice and concentrating on the photographs, trying to assure herself she was capable of normal, adult conversation, despite the fact she was undoubtedly in the middle of a total nervous collapse.

"You've never been?"

"Not yet."

"I would have thought someone of your background and interests would have been to France long ago."

"One day," Mattie said, thinking of the many times she'd tried to sell Jake on the idea of a Paris vacation, and of his persistent refusals. Not enough time, he'd said, when what he really meant was too much time. Too much time to spend alone together. Not enough love. Mattie made a mental note to call her travel agent when she got home. She hadn't gone to Paris for her honeymoon. Maybe she'd go there for her divorce.

"Anyway," she continued, the word stabbing at the air, startling them both, "this photograph is of Ronis's wife in their summer cottage."

"It's very erotic," Roy commented. "Don't you think?"

"I think what makes it so sensual," Mattie agreed, "is the almost tangible depiction of the atmosphere— you can actually feel the warmth of the sun coming in the open window, smell the air, feel the texture of the old stone floor. The nudity is part of the eroticism, but only part of it."

"Makes you want to take off your clothes and jump right in the picture with her."

"An interesting idea," Mattie said, trying not to picture Roy Crawford naked, as she led her client toward another group of photographs—two men sleeping on a park bench, workers on strike relaxing on a Paris street, carpenters at work in the French countryside. "There's an innocence to these early pictures," Mattie said, the disquieting thought suddenly occurring to her that Roy Crawford might be flirting with her, "that's missing from most of his later photographs. While his sympathy with the working class remains a hallmark of his work, there's more tension in the pictures Ronis took after World War II. Like this one," she said, directing Roy Crawford to a later photo entitled *Christmas*, wherein a man, a haunted expression on his solemn face, stood alone amid a crowd of people outside a Paris department store. "There isn't the same connection between people," Mattie explained, "and that distance often becomes the subject of the photograph. Did that make any sense?"

"There's a distance between people," Roy reiterated. "Makes sense to me."

Mattie nodded. Me too, she thought, as they studied these later photographs for several minutes in silence. She felt Roy's arm brush against the side of her own, waited for it to withdraw, was strangely pleased when it didn't. Maybe not so much distance after all, she thought.

"I prefer these."

Mattie felt Roy Crawford pulling away from her side, like a Band-Aid being slowly ripped from a still-fresh wound. He returned to the earlier nudes, gazing intently at the body of a young woman slouched provocatively on a chair, her head and neck just outside the camera's range, one breast exposed, her pronounced triangle of pubic hair the focal point of the picture, her long bare legs stretching toward the camera. A man's clothed leg appeared slyly in the left corner of the frame.

"The composition of this photograph is especially interesting," Mattie began. "And, of course, the juxtaposition of the different textures—the wood, the stone—"

"The bare flesh."

"The bare flesh," Mattie repeated. *Was* he flirting with her?

"The simple things in life," Roy Crawford said.

Things are rarely as simple as they sound, Mattie heard her husband say. *And we all know that.*

"Let's have a look in here." Mattie led Roy Crawford into a second set of rooms.

"What do we have here?"

"Danny Lyon," Mattie told him, resuming her most professional voice. "Probably one of the most influential photographers in America today. As you can see, he's a very different kind of photographer from Willy Ronis, although he does share Ronis's interest in everyday people and current events. These are photographs he took of the burgeoning civil rights movement between 1962 and 1964, after he left our very own University of Chicago to hitchhike south and become the first staff photographer for SNCC, which you may remember stands for—"

"Student Nonviolent Coordinating Committee. Yes, I remember it well. I was fourteen years old at the time. And you weren't even a twinkle in your father's eye."

A twinkle he extinguished when he left, Mattie thought. "Actually, I was born in 1962," she said. He had to be flirting with her.

"Which makes you—"

"About twice as old as your current girlfriend." Mattie quickly motioned toward the first grouping of photographs, Roy Crawford's easy laughter trailing after her. "So, what do you think? Anything catch your eye?"

"Many things," Roy Crawford said, ignoring the photographs, looking directly at Mattie.

"Are you flirting with me?" Mattie asked with a directness that surprised both of them.

"I believe I am." Roy Crawford smiled that big loopy grin.

"I'm a married woman." Mattie tapped at the thin gold band on the appropriate finger of her left hand.

"Your point being?"

Mattie smiled, realized she was enjoying herself rather more than she should. "Roy," she began, a pesky smile threatening to destroy the intended seriousness of her tone, "you've been my client now for how many years—five, six?"

"Longer than my last two marriages combined," he agreed.

"And during those years, I've furnished your various homes and offices with art."

"You've brought culture and good taste to my boorish existence," Roy Crawford conceded gallantly.

"And in all that time, you've never hit on me."

"I guess that's right."

"So, why now?"

Roy Crawford looked confused. His eyebrows, black as opposed to gray, bunched together at the top of his nose, creating one long bushy line.

"What's different?" Mattie pressed.

"You're different."

"I'm different?"

"There's something different about you," Roy repeated.

"You think that just because I fell apart earlier, I might be easy prey?"

"I was hoping."

Mattie found herself laughing out loud. It scared her, forced her to strangle the sound in her throat before she could hear it again. So now I'm afraid of my own laughter, Mattie thought, swallowing hard. "Maybe we've seen enough photographs for one day."

"Time for lunch?"

Mattie twisted her wedding ring until the skin around it grew sore. It would be so easy, she thought, picturing Roy Crawford's big head between her slim thighs. What was she worrying about? Her husband was cheating on her, wasn't he? And her marriage was over, wasn't it?

Wasn't it?

"Would you mind terribly if we postponed our lunch till another day?" she heard herself ask, dropping her hands to her sides.

In response, Roy Crawford immediately lifted his hands into the air, as if one act were predicated on the other. "Your call," he said easily.

"I'll make it up to you," Mattie told him minutes later, waving good-bye on the front steps.

"I'm counting on it," he called after her.

That was really smart, Mattie thought, locating her car in the parking lot around the corner from the gallery, climbing inside. And professional. Very professional. Probably she'd never hear from Roy Crawford again, although even as the thought was crossing her mind, it was being replaced by something else, the sight of her naked body slouching provocatively on a chair, Roy Crawford's shoe protruding slyly into the corner of her imagination. "God, you're a sick person," Mattie said, banishing the troubling image with a determined shake of her head.

Mattie gave her ticket to the parking lot attendant, who waved her away without any refund on her deposit. She pulled out of the lot, turned right at the first corner, left at the one after that, paying no real attention to where she was headed, wondering what to do with the rest of her day. A woman without a plan, she thought, trying to figure out what she'd say to Jake when he came home—if he came home. Maybe she should see a psychiatrist, she decided, someone who could help her deal with her frustrations, with all her pent-up hostility, before it was too late, although it was already too late, she realized. Her marriage was over. "My marriage is over," she said simply.

Nothing is ever as simple as it sounds.

Mattie saw the traffic light several blocks ahead, registered the color red, and transferred her foot from the gas pedal to the brake. But it was as if the brake had suddenly disappeared. Frantically, Mattie began pounding her heel against the floor of the car, but she felt nothing. Her foot was asleep, she was kicking at air, and the car was going much too fast. There was no way she was going to be able to slow down, let alone stop, and there were people in the crosswalk, a man and two little children, for God's sake, and she was going to hit them, she was going to drive her car into two innocent little children, and there was nothing she could do to stop it. She was crazy or she was having some sort of seizure, but either way, a man and two little kids would be dead if she didn't do something about it soon. She had to do something.

In the next instant, Mattie twisted the wheel of the car sharply to the left, catapulting her into the lane of oncoming traffic and directly into the path of an approaching vehicle. The driver of the car, a black Mercedes, swerved to avoid a head-on collision. Mattie heard the squeal of tires, the crash of metal, the shattering of glass. There was a loud pop, like an explosion, as Mattie's airbag burst open, smacking her in the chest like a giant fist, pinning her to her seat, pushing up against her face like an unwelcome suitor, robbing her of breathing space. Black and white colliding, she thought, clinging to consciousness, trying to remember what Jake had said in his summation about few things being black or white, only varying shades of gray. She tasted blood, saw the driver emerge from the other car, screaming and gesticulating wildly. She thought of Kim, beautiful sweet wonderful Kim, and wondered how her daughter would manage without her.

And then, mercifully, everything disappeared into varying shades of gray, and she saw nothing at all.

FIVE

Kim's earliest memory was of her parents fighting.

She sat at the back of the classroom, blue ballpoint pen scribbling a series of connecting hearts across the cover of her English notebook, her head tilted toward the teacher at the green chalkboard at the front of the class, although Kim was barely aware of his presence, hadn't heard a word he'd said all period. She shifted in her seat, looked toward the window that occupied one whole wall of the tenth-grade classroom. Not that there was anything outside to see. What was once a grassy courtyard had been paved over the previous year and filled with portables, three in all, ugly prefabricated gray structures with tiny little windows too high to look out or see in, in rooms that were either too hot or too cold. Kim closed her eyes, leaned back in her seat, wondering which it would be by the time her math class rolled around. What was she doing in this stupid school any-way? Hadn't the whole point of moving to the suburbs been to get her out of overcrowded classrooms and into an environment more conducive to learning?

Wasn't that what all the yelling had been about?

Not that her parents did that much actual yelling. No, their anger was quieter, trickier to get a handle on. It was the kind that lay coiled and sleepy, like snakes in a basket, until someone got careless and removed the protective lid, forgetting that the key word here was *coiled*, not *sleepy*, and that the anger was always there, ready and waiting, eager to strike. How many times had she woken up in the middle of the night, roused to consciousness by the sound of strained whispers hiss-ing through tightly clenched teeth, and run into her parents' bedroom to find her father pacing the floor and her mother in tears? "What's the matter?" she would demand of her father. "Why is Mom crying? What did you do to make Mom cry?"

Kim remembered how frightened she'd been the first time she'd witnessed such a scene. She'd been, how old? Three, maybe four? She was having her afternoon nap, sleeping in her small blue brass bed, nose to nose with a large stuffed Big Bird, a slightly ratty Oscar the Grouch tucked tightly underneath her arm. Maybe she'd been dreaming, maybe not. But suddenly she was awake, and she was frightened, although she wasn't sure why. It was then that she became aware of muffled noises from the other bedroom, Mommy and Daddy whispering, but not the way people usually whispered. These were really loud whispers, as cold and biting as a winter wind, whispers that made her cover Big Bird's ears and hide him under the covers beside Oscar the Grouch when she went to investigate.

Kim slouched down in her seat, her right hand absently patting the tight little bun at the top of her head, checking to make sure there were no stray hairs at the base of her neck, that everything was tightly secured and in its proper place, the way she liked it. Miss Grundy, her mother sometimes teased, a laugh in her voice.

Kim liked it when her mother laughed. It made her feel secure. If her mother was laughing, it meant she was happy, and if she was happy, it meant everything was all right, her parents were going to stay together. She wasn't about to become an unpleasant statistic and hopeless cliché, the child of a broken home, the product of a bitter divorce, like so many of her friends and classmates.

If her mother was laughing, then all was right with the world, Kim reassured herself, trying to block out the eerie sound of her mother's laughter earlier in the day, a grating sound that was anything but happy — frantic as opposed to abandoned, closer to hysteria than genuine mirth, and like the angry whispers of Kim's first childhood memory, too loud. Much, much too loud.

Was that it? Had her parents had another fight? Her father had gone out again last night after dinner, supposedly back to the office to prepare for today's trial. But wasn't one of the reasons they'd moved to the suburbs so that he'd have space for an office at home, one that came complete with computer, printer, and fax machine? Had it really been necessary for him to drive back into the city? Or was there another reason, a reason who was young and pretty and half his age, like the reason Andy Reese's father found to walk out on his family? Or Pam Baker's father, who was rumored to have more than one reason for abandoning his.

Or the reason Kim had seen her father kissing on a street corner, full on the lips in the middle of a sunny afternoon around the time they'd moved to Evanston, a reason who was plump and dark-haired and looked nothing like her mother at all.

Was that the reason she'd come down for breakfast this morning and found her mother standing alone in the middle of the backyard pool laughing like a lunatic?

Kim had never said anything to her mother about seeing her father with another woman. Instead she'd tried to convince herself that the woman was merely a friend, no, less than that, an acquaintance, maybe even a business acquaintance, perhaps a grateful client, although since when did one kiss clients, however grateful they may be, on the lips like that? Full on the mouth, she thought, the way Teddy Cranston had kissed her on Saturday night, his tongue gently teasing the tip of her own.

Kim brought her fingers to her lips, feeling them tingling still, as she relived the softness of Teddy's touch, so unlike the kisses of other boys her age. Of course Teddy was a few years older than the other boys she'd dated. He was seventeen and a senior, heading off to college next fall, either Columbia or NYU, he told her confidently, depending on whether he decided to study medicine or the movies. But Saturday night, he'd seemed more interested in getting his hand inside her sweater than in getting into either medical or film school, and she'd been tempted, really tempted, to let him. All the other girls were doing it. That and more. Lots of girls her age had already gone all the way. She heard them giggling about it in the school washrooms as they hunched over the condom dispensaries. Guys hated condoms, she heard them complain, so most times they didn't bother using them, especially after they'd done it a few times and knew the guy was all right. "You should try it, Kimbo," one of the girls had teased, aiming a packet of condoms at her head.

"Yeah," several of the other girls joined in, pelting her with condoms. "Try it. You'll like it."

Would she? Kim wondered, feeling Teddy's invisible hand at her breast.

Her breasts, Kim thought with wonder, watching the swell of her no-longer-child's bosom rise and fall with each breath. Last year at this time, her breasts were virtually nonexistent, and suddenly, about six months ago, there they were. No notice, no warning, no *I think you'd better prepare yourself*. Overnight she'd gone from an A to a C cup, and the world suddenly snapped to attention. Only with breast size, it seemed, was a C preferred to an A.

Kim recalled the hoots and hollers of the boys the first time she wore her new white Gap T-shirt to school last spring, the envious looks of the girls, the not-so-veiled glances of her teachers. Overnight, everything changed. She was suddenly popular, the object of great conjecture and gossip. Everyone, it seemed, had an opinion as to her new status—she was a slut; she was an ice queen; she was a cock tease—as if her breasts had swallowed her previous self whole, and were now totally responsible for her behavior. Surprisingly, Kim discovered, she was no longer required to have opinions. It was enough she had breasts. Indeed, her teachers seemed surprised she was capable of coherent thought at all.

Even her parents were affected by this sudden and unexpected development. Her mother looked at her with a combination of amazement and concern, while her father avoided looking at her altogether and, when he did, focused so hard on her face that Kim always felt he was about to fall over.

Her phone started ringing night and day. Girls who'd never given her the time of day suddenly wanted to be her friend. Guys who'd never spoken to her in class, nerds and jocks alike, were calling her after school to ask her out: Gerry McDougal, captain of the football team; Marty Peshkin, star debater; Teddy Cranston of the melting chocolate brown eyes.

Once again, Kim's lips tingled with the remembrance of Teddy's gentle touch. Once again she felt his hand brush against her breast, so softly, as if it were an accident, as if he hadn't meant to do it. But of course he'd meant exactly that. Why else was he there?

"Don't," she'd said softly, and he'd pretended not to hear, so she said it again, louder this time, and this time he listened, although he tried again later, and she was forced to say it again. "Don't," she said, thinking of her mother. "Please don't."

"Don't be in too big a rush," her mother had cautioned during one of their earlier talks about sex. "You have so much time. And even with all the precautions in the world, accidents do happen." A slight blush suddenly stained her cheek.

"Like me?" Kim asked, having figured out long ago

that a baby weighing over nine pounds was unlikely to have been three months premature.

"The best accident that ever happened to me," her mother said, not insulting her intelligence by denying the obvious, wrapping Kim in her arms, kissing her forehead.

"Would you and Daddy have gotten married anyway?" Kim pressed.

"Absolutely," her mother said, giving her the answer Kim wanted to hear.

I don't think so, Kim thought now. She wasn't blind to the way her parents looked at one another, quick glances in unguarded moments that shouted their true feelings even louder than the angry whispers that emanated with increasing regularity from behind their closed bedroom door. No way her parents would be together had it not been for her unexpected interference. She had trapped them into marriage, into being together. But the trap was old and no longer strong enough to hold them. It was only a matter of time before one of them worked up the strength and the courage to break free. And then where would little Kimbo be?

One thing was certain: she would never allow her hormones to trap her into a loveless marriage. She would choose wisely and well. Although how much choice did she really have? Hadn't both her grandmothers been abandoned by their husbands? Kim fidgeted uncomfortably in her seat. Were the women in her family fated to choose faithless men who would one day walk out on them? Maybe it was inevitable, possibly even genetic. Perhaps it was some sort of ancient family curse.

Kim shrugged, as if trying to physically rid herself of the unpleasant thought, the sudden movement knocking her notebook to the floor, attracting the teacher's unwanted attention. Mr. Bill Loewi, whose broad nose was too big for the rest of his narrow face and whose overly ruddy complexion betrayed his fondness for booze, turned from the chalkboard on which he was writing and stared toward the back of the class. "Problem?" he asked, as Kim scrambled to pick up her notebook, knocking over her copy of *Romeo and Juliet.*

"No, sir," Kim said quickly, reaching for the book.

Caroline Smith, who sat in the row beside her, and whose big mouth was inversely proportionate to the size of her brain, leaned sideways, reaching for the slender text at the same time as Kim. "Thinking about Teddy?" she asked. She slid the index finger of her right hand into the hole created by the index finger and thumb of her left and waggled it in and out suggestively.

"Get a life," Kim said under her breath.

"Get laid," came the instant retort.

"Something you want to share with the rest of the class?" Mr. Loewi asked.

Caroline Smith giggled. "No, sir."

"No, sir," Kim concurred, returning the book to her desk, and her eyes to the front of the room.

"Why don't we read a few lines from the text," Mr. Loewi suggested. "Page thirty-four. Romeo declaring his love for Juliet. Kim," he said to Kim's breasts, "why don't you be Juliet."

Teddy was waiting for her after class, slouching beside her locker when she went to retrieve her lunch. "I thought we could eat outside," he suggested, unfolding his lanky frame and stretching to his full height, an

inch or two above six feet. He took Kim's hand, leading her down the locker-lined hallway, pretending to
ignore the looks and whispers of the other kids. He
was used to the attention. It came with being athletic,
rich, and "so gorgeous you could die," according to
the caption under his picture in the latest school year-
book. "It's really nice out," he was saying.

"Then leave it out," Caroline Smith volunteered
from somewhere beside them. Annie Turofsky and
Jodi Bates laughed uproariously by Caroline's side.

The Three Muskatits, Kim sneered. They dressed
identically, in tight jeans and tighter scoop-necked
sweaters, wore their long brown hair straight and
parted to one side, and their noses had all been bobbed
by the same plastic surgeon, although Caroline insisted
her nose job was because of a deviated septum.

"You girls are a class act," Teddy said.

"Try us—" Annie Turofsky began.

"You'll like us," Jodi finished.

"Not likely," Teddy said under his breath, picking
up the pace, ushering Kim toward the side door.

"Party on Saturday night," Caroline called after
them. "Sabrina Hollander's house. Her parents are
away for the weekend. Bring your own whatever."

"A party full of stoned fifteen-year-old girls," Teddy
said, his voice dripping sarcasm, as he pushed open the
heavy door to the outside world. "Can't wait."

"I'm a fifteen-year-old girl," Kim reminded him, as
a cold gust of wind slapped her in the face.

"You're not like the others," Teddy said.

"I'm not?"

"You're more mature."

A C cup, Kim thought, but didn't say. She didn't want to scare Teddy away by being too clever, too knowing, too *mature*.

"How about over there?" Teddy pointed toward the students' parking lot.

"What's over there?" Kim asked.

"My car."

"Oh." She dropped her lunchbag to the ground, listened as the can of Coke she'd packed that morning began to fizz, and wondered if it was about to explode. "I thought you wanted to eat outside."

"It's colder than I realized." He scooped up her lunchbag from the pavement without any obvious concern and took hold of her elbow, leading her toward the dark green, late-model Chevrolet at the farthest corner of the lot.

Had he parked it there deliberately? Kim wondered, feeling her heartbeat quicken and her breathing become short, almost painful.

Teddy pointed a remote control unit toward the car, and it squealed like a frightened pig, signaling that the doors were now open. "Let's get in the back," he said casually. "There's more room there."

Kim crawled into the backseat of the car and immediately tore into her lunch bag for her sandwich. "Tuna," she said awkwardly, holding it out for his inspection. "I made it myself." She started unwrapping it, stopped when she felt his breath against her cheek. She turned toward him, their noses colliding gently. "Sorry, I didn't realize you were so close—" she began, but his lips stopped her. She heard a low moan, pulled back sharply when she realized it came from her.

"What's wrong?"

"Nothing," she said, facing directly ahead, as if she were at a drive-in movie, talking a mile a minute, the way she always did when she was nervous, when she wanted to regain control. It wasn't that she didn't *want* to kiss him. It was that she wanted to kiss him so badly, she could barely see straight. "I just think maybe we should eat. I'm in classes all afternoon, and then I promised my grandmother, my mother's mother, Grandma Viv," she explained, knowing that Teddy, whose hand was massaging the back of her neck, couldn't have cared less about her Grandma Viv, "I told her that I'd come by after school. She had to have one of her dogs put to sleep yesterday. It was really sick and everything, and she said it was looking at her with those eyes, you know, those eyes that said it was time, but still, she's really upset about it, so I said I'd drop by. She'll be okay in a few days, once one of her other dogs has its litter. Then she'll have something to take her mind off Duke. That was the dog's name. It was part collie, part cocker spaniel. Really smart. My grandmother says that mutts are much smarter than purebreds. Do you have a dog?"

"A yellow Lab," Teddy said, a sly smile spreading from his lips to his eyes as he lifted the tunafish sandwich from Kim's hand and returned it to its bag. "Purebred."

Kim rolled her eyes, then closed them. "I'm sure it's a really smart dog."

"He's as dumb as dirt." Teddy ran his fingers across the top of Kim's lips. "Your grandmother was right."

"I don't have a dog," Kim said, eyes opening as the tips of Teddy's fingers disappeared inside her mouth, making speaking all but impossible. "My mother hates dogs," she persisted stubbornly, talking around them. "She says she's allergic, but I don't think she is. I just don't think she likes them."

"What about you?" Teddy was asking, his voice husky, as he leaned forward to kiss the side of Kim's mouth. "What do you like?"

"What do I like?"

"Do you like this?" He began kissing the side of her neck.

Oh yes, Kim answered silently, holding her breath, aware of the growing tingle beneath her flesh.

"What about this?" His lips moved toward her eyes, brushing against the lashes of her closed lids. "Or this?" He covered her mouth with his own. She felt his tongue gently prying her lips apart, as one hand caressed the nape of her neck and the other hand began its slow slide across the front of her sweater. Could anything feel more delicious? she wondered, her entire body vibrating. Except that the vibrations weren't internal; they were coming from somewhere outside her body.

"Oh, my God," she said, her hand slapping the pocket of her jeans. "It's my beeper."

"Ignore it," Teddy said, trying to coax her back into his arms.

"I can't. I'm one of those compulsive personalities. I have to know who it is." Kim extricated her beeper, pressed the button to see who was paging her, and watched the unfamiliar number flash across its face, followed by the numbers 911, indicating an emergency. "Something's wrong," she said. "I have to get to a phone."

Six

"Oh, my God, get me out of here. Get me out of here."

"Try to stay calm, Mattie. It's important for you to keep very still."

"Get me out of here. I can't breathe. I can't breathe."

"You're breathing fine, Mattie. Just stay calm. I'm taking you out now."

Mattie felt the narrow table on which she was lying start to move, propelling her, feet first, out of the monstrous MRI machine. She tried to suck in the surrounding air, but it was as if someone were standing on her chest in stiletto heels. The heels dug into her thin blue hospital gown, piercing her flesh, puncturing her lungs, making even shallow breathing painful, almost impossible.

"You can open your eyes now, Mattie."

Mattie opened her eyes, felt them instantly fill with tears. "I'm sorry," she told the female medical technician, who was small, dark, and alarmingly young. "I don't think I can do this."

"It's pretty scary," the technician agreed, gently patting Mattie's bruised forearm. "But the doctor was pretty anxious for the results."

"Has someone called my husband?"

"I believe he's been notified, yes."

"What about Lisa Katzman?" Mattie propped herself up on her elbows, inadvertently dislodging the pillows that had been placed on either side of her head. Pain, like thousands of tiny daggers, shot through her joints. There wasn't a part of her that didn't ache. Damn airbag almost killed me, Mattie thought, manipulating her sore jaw.

"Dr. Katzman will be waiting for you when we're finished in here." The technician, whose name tag identified her as Noreen Aliwallia, managed a small smile as she repositioned the pillows.

"How long will that be?"

"About forty-five minutes."

"Forty-five minutes?!"

"I know it sounds like a long time—"

"It *is* a long time. You know what it feels like inside that thing? It feels like being buried alive." Why am I giving her a hard time? Mattie wondered, longing for the sound of her friend Lisa's reassuring voice, the voice of calm and reason that had soothed her since childhood.

"You were in a car accident," Noreen Aliwallia reminded Mattie patiently. "You lost consciousness.

You suffered a serious concussion. The MRI is to make sure there aren't any hidden hematomas."

Mattie nodded, trying to recall exactly what the initials MRI stood for. Something about magnetic imaging, whatever that meant. A fancy name for X rays. The neurologist had already explained it to her when she'd regained consciousness in the emergency room, but she was only barely paying attention, her mind trying to come to grips with exactly what had happened. Her head was pounding, her mouth tasted of dried blood, and she was having difficulty remembering the precise order of things. Everything hurt, although they told her that, miraculously, no bones were broken. Then suddenly she was being wheeled into the basement of whatever hospital she was in—they'd told her which one it was, but she couldn't remember—and this young woman, this x-ray technician with the mellifluous name, Noreen Aliwallia, who looked like she was fresh out of high school, asked her to lie down on this really narrow table and put her head inside a coffinlike box.

The MRI machine resembled a large steel tunnel. It took up most of the small, windowless room, whose dingy white walls were void of adornment. At the entrance to the tunnel was a rectangular box with a circular hole. Mattie had been given a set of ear plugs—"It gets a little noisy in there," she was told—and pillows were placed on both sides of her head to keep it still. A buzzer was placed in her hand, to use if she felt she was about to sneeze or cough or do anything that might disturb the operation of the machine. If she moved at any time during the procedure, Noreen explained, the X ray would be ruined, and they'd have to start over from the beginning. Close your eyes, Noreen had advised. Think pleasant thoughts.

The panic started almost as soon as Mattie's head was fitted inside the box, and the top of the box was extended past her face to her chest, so that even with her eyes closed, it felt as if she were lying in her grave, as if she were suffocating. Then the table on which she was lying began its slow slide into the long narrow tunnel, and she felt like one of those Russian dolls, a doll within a doll within a doll, and she knew she had to get out of this damn machine that was worse than the accident, worse than the air bag, worse than anything she'd experienced in her entire life. She had to get out or she would die, and so she started screaming for the technician to help her, forgetting about the buzzer, forgetting about everything but her panic, until Noreen told her she could open her eyes, and she started to cry, because she hurt all over, and she was acting like a baby, and she'd never felt so alone in her entire life.

And now Noreen Aliwallia was asking her to push all that fear and loneliness aside and do it again, and Mattie was thinking, no, she'd rather risk internal bleeding in her brain and whatever else might be lurking there than go through that again. She'd always harbored a secret fear of suffocating, of being buried alive. She couldn't do it. She wouldn't do it.

"You'll bring me out if I start to panic?" she heard herself ask. What was the matter with her? Was she crazy?

"Just press the buzzer. I'll bring you right out." Noreen's surprisingly strong arms lowered Mattie's shoulders back to the table. "Just try to relax. You might even fall asleep."

Oh God, oh God, oh God, Mattie thought, eyes tightly closed, left hand gripping the buzzer against the pounding of her heart, as once again her head was placed inside the box, the top of which slid down over her face to her chest, plunging her into total darkness and abject despair. I can't breathe, Mattie thought. I'm suffocating.

"So, how long have you known Dr. Katzman?" Noreen asked, obviously straining to distract Mattie.

"Since forever," Mattie replied through tightly clenched teeth, picturing Dr. Lisa Katzman as a freckle-faced child. "She's been my best friend since we were three years old."

"That's amazing," Noreen said, her words trailing off as she abandoned Mattie's side. "I'm going to start the machine now, Mattie. How are you doing?"

Not great, Mattie thought, as the table beneath her began to move, carrying her into the body of the machine. Stay calm. Stay calm. It'll all be over soon. Forty-five minutes. That's not so long. It's very long. It's almost an hour, for God's sake. I can't do this. I have to get out. I can't breathe. I'm suffocating.

"The first series of X rays are going to start now," Noreen said. "It's going to sound a bit like horses' hooves, and it'll last about five minutes."

"And then what?" Keep breathing, Mattie told herself. Stay calm. Think pleasant thoughts.

"And then there'll be a break of a few minutes, and then some more X rays. Five in all. Are you ready?"

No, I'm not ready, Mattie screamed silently over the sound of horses approaching from the distance. This is interesting, Mattie found herself thinking, her panic temporarily diverted by the loud clip-clop, clip-clop, as behind tightly closed eyes, a team of black-and-white stallions raced toward her. Black and white, she mused. Things are rarely black or white, only varying shades of gray. Where had she heard that?

The accident, she thought, suddenly back in her car, watching helplessly as it swerved into oncoming traffic. Black and white colliding. Varying shades of gray. What had she been thinking?

"You okay, Mattie?"

Mattie grunted, trying to pretend the top of the box wasn't inches from her nose. I have lots of space, she told herself. I'm lying on an empty, white, sandy beach in the Bahamas, and my eyes are closed, and the ocean is lapping at my toes. And a hundred horses are galloping toward me, she thought, about to bury me alive beneath the sand, as the noise of the second set of X rays began. Stay calm. Stay calm. The buzzer is in your hand. You can press it at any time. Think positive thoughts. Think calm. You're on a beach in the Bahamas. No, it's not working. You're not on a beach in the Bahamas. You're on a table in a hospital in the middle of Chicago. They're taking pictures of the inside of your head. What will they say when they discover it's empty?

I can't breathe. I'm suffocating. I have to get out of here.

Think positive thoughts. Think about lying in your bed. No, that's no good. When was the last time you felt safe and secure in bed? Not since I was a little girl, Mattie thought, immediately picturing herself as a sober-faced child, lying under her blue-and-white quilt, her father sitting by her head, his backside propped against the headboard as he read to her from one of her favorite bedtime stories. "That's all for tonight, Mattie," she heard him say, kissing her forehead, the soft prickle of his mustache grazing her tender skin.

"Will you sit with me until I fall asleep?" she'd ask, the same question every night.

And every night he'd answer, "You're a big girl now, you don't need me to sit with you," even as he was settling in at the foot of her bed, even when her mother was calling him, even when she was standing right outside the door, one impatient hand folded over the other, and still he'd sit at the foot of her bed until she fell asleep, no matter how long it took.

"Third set coming up now," Noreen announced.

How much time had elapsed? Mattie wondered, about to ask the question out loud when the sound of fresh horses stopped her. That, and another sound. The sound of banging, as if someone were hammering on the top of the tunnel. How was she supposed to fall asleep if they kept up that loud banging?

The noise reminded her of when she renovated the kitchen, the workmen tearing out the existing cabinets, replacing them with newer designs, Jake refusing to let her exchange their old electric range for the gas oven she preferred, complaining about the mess, about not being able to find anything, about not being able to think with that incessant racket.

Oh, God—Jake. This morning in the courtroom. His summation. Her laughter, so unexpected, so inappropriate. The look on Jake's face. The judge pounding her gavel, the unpleasant sound foreshadowing the banging of the X ray machine. So loud. Did it have to be so loud? And that vibration in her ears, like a swarm of pesky bees, except this was worse because it felt as if the bees were inside her, that they were buzzing around frantically in her skull, desperate to find a way out.

"Is it almost over?" Mattie asked, as the horses retreated and the vibrations shuddered to a halt.

"Three down. Two to go. You're doing great."

Just a few more minutes, Mattie, she heard her father say. *You're doing great.*

When can I see it? her child's voice asked impatiently.

Right . . . now. Her father backed away from his makeshift easel in the middle of the unfinished basement, standing back proudly as she rushed to his side.

Mattie stared long and hard at the portrait her father had been working on for weeks, desperate to keep the disappointment out of her face. The picture didn't look anything like her at all.

What do you think?

I think you should stick to selling insurance, her mother's voice announced from out of nowhere. Mattie hadn't even heard her come downstairs.

I think it's beautiful, Mattie said, immediately coming to her father's defense.

Whatever happened to that picture? Mattie wondered now. Had her father taken it with him when he abruptly quit his job and left town? She almost cried out, stopping herself in time, before she ruined the X rays and they had to start over from the beginning. That's what I'd like to do with my life, she thought.

Start over from the beginning. Do it right this time. Find a father who wouldn't leave. Find a mother who preferred people to pets. Choose a husband who chose her over other women. Discover something about herself that someone else could love.

"Here we go. Number four."

Almost over, Mattie told herself, as the increasingly invasive vibrations from the fourth series of X rays began. She felt as if she were holding her breath under water, as if her lungs were about to burst. She pictured herself hunched over the side of her backyard pool, waiting for her foot to stop tingling. What a strange day, she thought, recalling her spill on the carpet as her sleeping foot failed to find the floor. She'd started the day with thoughts of killing her husband and ended up almost killing herself. Not to mention that little court-room episode in between.

Mattie wondered if Jake would be waiting for her when she was released, or if he'd already packed his bags and left. Like her father, who'd left for greener pastures. For parts unknown. For he's a jolly good fellow. God help me. I have to get out of here, Mattie thought, before I completely lose my mind.

"Last one."

Mattie took a deep breath, although her body remained rigid. Premature rigor mortis, she thought, perfectly suitable for being buried alive. She braced herself for the approach of the galloping herd, already anticipating the banging above and beside her head, dreading the coming vibrations. Was Jake here? she wondered. Had they been able to reach him? How had he reacted to the news of her accident? Did he care at all? Was he relieved, or disappointed, when he found out she was still alive?

The vibrations filled her mouth, invading her teeth, like a dentist's drill. Soon the drill would shatter her teeth and assault her roots, boring a hole through her gums directly into her brain. Talk about hidden hematomas. She couldn't let that happen. She had to get out. She had to get out now. She didn't care if the ordeal was almost over, that the X rays would be ruined. She had to get out of this damn machine. Get out now.

"That's it. We're done," Noreen Aliwallia announced, as Mattie felt her body being spit out of the machine and the lid of the coffin lifted from her head. Mattie sucked at the air with the eagerness and ferocity of a newborn baby at her mother's breast. "You were great," Noreen Aliwallia said.

"So, tell me exactly what happened," Lisa Katzman was saying, her voice deep and strong, in surprising contrast to her tiny, birdlike frame. Short brown hair hugged a narrow oval face dusted with freckles; her nose turned up sharply at its slender tip; her mouth curved down into a natural frown, so that only her eyes revealed when she was smiling. She sat perched at the side of Mattie's hospital bed, wearing a white lab coat over black sweater and pants, the pants tucked inside ankle-length, black leather boots. She had on her best doctor's face, but Mattie could see the worry staining her friend's soft brown eyes.

"I wish I knew." Mattie adjusted the meager pillow at her back, stared at the decorative floral print on the pale green wall behind Lisa's head.

"You told the neurologist your foot fell asleep?"

"Yeah. It was the damnedest thing. I couldn't feel the brake. I kept poking at where I knew it should be, but I couldn't feel anything. It was creepy."

"Has this happened before?"

"It happened earlier in the day. I couldn't feel the floor, and I fell. Is Jake here?"

"He was. He had to get back to work."

"How did he seem?"

"Jake? Fine. Concerned about you, of course."

Of course, Mattie thought.

"So, this afternoon and this morning, those are the only times this sort of thing has happened?"

"Well, no. It's happened before. You know how sometimes your foot falls asleep." Mattie's voice drifted to a stop. Why was Lisa asking her these questions? "What are you getting at?"

"How many times?" Lisa asked, ignoring Mattie's question, lips twitching downward, eyes still smiling, trying to act as if these queries were strictly routine. "Once a week? Every day?"

"Maybe a few times a week."

"How long has this been going on?"

"I don't know. A couple of months, maybe."

"Why didn't you say anything about this before?"

"I didn't think there was anything to worry about. I can't call you over every little thing."

Lisa gave her a look that said, Since when?

"I don't understand the problem," Mattie continued. "Doesn't everybody's foot fall asleep occasionally?"

"Was today the first time you fell?"

Mattie nodded vigorously. She was becoming increasingly uncomfortable with the conversation, had no interest in pursuing it further. Where was Lisa Katzman, her friend? Lisa Katzman, the doctor, was starting to get on her nerves. "Has anybody contacted Kim?"

"Jake called her. He'll bring her by later to see you. He thinks she should stay at your mother's until you come home."

"My mother's? Poor kid. She'll never forgive me."

"You won't be here long enough for her to work up a serious hate. Jake told me that you laughed out loud in the middle of his address to the jury," Lisa said, as if one thought naturally followed the other.

"He told you that? Oh God, was he very upset?"

"I thought you decided not to go to the courthouse." The look on Lisa's face said, Why do you ask my advice if you're not going to take it?

I couldn't help myself, Mattie answered with her eyes, the conversation continuing silently for several seconds, no need for words.

"Why did you laugh?" Lisa asked suddenly.

"I don't know," Mattie answered honestly. "It just kind of popped out."

"Were you thinking of something funny?"

"Not that I remember."

"You just started laughing?"

"Yes," Mattie agreed. "Why? What has that got to do with anything?"

"Has that happened before?"

"Has *what* happened before?"

"Laughing for no reason. Or crying. Any reactions that are out of whack with the situation."

"It's happened a few times," Mattie told her, thinking

of her tears on the steps of the Art Institute, feeling adrift and wobbly, like a balloon that was slowly losing air.

"In the last couple of months?"

"Yes."

"What about your hands? Any tingling sensation there?"

"No." She paused. "Well, sometimes I have trouble with my keys."

"What kind of trouble?"

"They don't always want to fit in the lock."

Lisa looked alarmed, tried to disguise it by coughing into her hand. "Any problems swallowing?"

"No."

"Is there anything you're not telling me?"

"Like what?" Mattie asked. "You know I tell you everything." She paused, brushed some imaginary hairs away from her forehead. She'd told Lisa all about Jake's latest affair. "You think this could be stress related?"

"Could be." Lisa leaned over, took Mattie's hands in her own, tried to push her lips into a smile. "Let's wait till we get the results of the MRI."

"And then what?"

Lisa straightened her shoulders, assumed her most professional demeanor. "Let's take this thing one day at a time, shall we?" But the smile in her eyes was gone, and only the frown remained.

SEVEN

Two days later Jake picked Mattie up at the hospital. She looked lost inside the jeans and sweatshirt she'd asked him to bring from home—so thin, so bruised, so delicate in her movements he worried she might collapse before he got her to the car. He realized that he was uncomfortable seeing her this way, not because he felt her pain—part of him was still so angry with her that he was glad she was in pain—but because such frailty was a form of dependence, and he didn't want Mattie to be dependent. Not on him. Not anymore.

Jake flinched at the selfishness of his thoughts, waiting as the orderly assisted Mattie out of the wheelchair that hospital policy dictated be taken to the lobby. Mattie smiled, a tentative and token gesture that only emphasized her obvious discomfort, and shuffled slowly toward him, pale purple blotches staining her cheeks, large yellow circles rimming her eyes, like old-fashioned monocles. Jake knew that he should be the one helping her, the one whispering words of reassurance in her ear, but all he could manage was a tired smile of his own and a few careless words about her looking pretty good for a woman whose car had collapsed around her like an accordion.

Jake dutifully took Mattie's elbow, adjusting his gait to hers as he slowly led her out the front door of the hospital. Immediately, Mattie raised a trembling hand to her eyes, shielding them from the harsh light of the midday sun. "Wait here," Jake told her at the top of the outside steps. "I'll get the car."

"I can come with you," she offered, her voice weak.

"No. It'll be faster this way. I'll just be half a second. The car's right there." He pointed vaguely toward the parking lot. "I'll be right back."

He walked quickly to the lot, his head lowered against the cool autumn winds, and located his dark green BMW, climbing inside, money already in hand to pay the attendant. By the time he got back, two minutes at most, Mattie had made her way down the stairs and was waiting for him by the side of the road. She was asserting her independence, letting him know she could take care of herself. Good, he thought. That's exactly what we want.

Why was it that he had an abundance of compassion for a killer like Douglas Bryant and, curiously, none at all for his wife? Couldn't he get past his anger at her bizarre behavior and show some genuine concern for her welfare? She was obviously as puzzled by what had happened as he was, although they hadn't actually discussed it. Besides, what was the point in talking about it now? It was over and done with.

As their marriage would be by the end of the day.

He'd already taken most of his clothes over to Honey's, transferred his toiletries to the bathroom downstairs. Kim was still staying with Mattie's mother. By the time she returned home tomorrow, he'd be all but gone. Of course he'd wait a few days before actually leaving, until Mattie was stronger, until he was comfortable she could function on her own. He'd talk to Kim later, explain the reasons he was leaving, try to convince her of the merits of his case. Jake laughed, pulling the car to the curb in front of Mattie, running around to open her door. Kim would be much harder to win over than any jury. She was every inch her mother's daughter. He doubted he stood a chance.

"Watch your head," he advised, guiding Mattie inside the car.

"I'm fine," she told him.

She was fine, Jake repeated with relief. There were no broken bones, no crippling injuries, no bruises that wouldn't be gone by the end of next month. The MRI had showed no internal bleeding, no tumors, no abnormalities of any kind. "There's nothing in my head at all," Mattie had laughed over the telephone, with obvious relief, the sound of her laughter a bitter reminder of the scene she had caused.

"Tired?" he asked her now, pulling into the street and heading toward Lakeshore Drive.

"A little."

"Maybe you'll sleep for a while when we get home."

"Maybe."

They said nothing further until they reached Sheraton Road in Evanston. How had he let himself get roped into living all the way out here? Jake wondered, eyes drifting from the stately mansions on his left to the cold waters of Lake Michigan on his right. Absently, he checked his watch, was surprised to see it was almost two o'clock. He wondered what Honey was doing, whether she was wondering the same thing about him.

"Do you think she knows?" Honey had asked him again the other night. "About me," she added, unnecessarily, when he failed to respond. "Do you think that's why she did it? Out of spite?"

He shook his head. Who knew why women did anything?

"She's very pretty."

"I guess," he said.

"What happens when she gets out of the hospital?" Honey asked, lying beside him in bed.

"What happens now?" Mattie was asking, sitting beside him in the front seat of the car.

"What?" Jake found himself gripping the wheel so tightly his fingers cramped. Mattie was truly a mind reader. She could just reach into his brain whenever she felt like it and pull out whatever stray thoughts were lurking about. He'd have to be more careful. Even his thoughts weren't safe.

"Are you going back to the office after you drop me off?"

"No," he said. "I hadn't planned to."

"That's nice," she told him simply. No, "Oh please, don't stay home on my account." No, "It's really not necessary." No false sentiments. No words she thought he wanted to hear.

She would not make this easy for him.

"Congratulations again," Mattie offered quietly, staring into her lap. She'd called his office from the hospital shortly after the verdict was announced. A mere twenty-seven hours after the jury had retired to deliberate, Douglas Bryant was a free man, and Jake Hart was a star. "I heard the good news," she'd ventured weakly. "I wanted to congratulate you." He'd brushed her good wishes aside, was about to do the same now. "I'm so sorry—" she began.

"Don't," he interrupted.

"—for the scene I caused."

"It's over."

"I don't know what came over me."

"It doesn't matter now."

"Lisa thinks there might be a medical explanation."

"A medical explanation?" Jake felt the bile rise in his throat, coating his voice in derision. How dare Mattie try to find a medical excuse for her appalling behavior? "That's a good one."

"You're still angry," Mattie said, stating the obvious.

"No. I'm not. Forget it."

"I think we should talk about it."

"What's to talk about?" he asked, the large BMW beginning to feel like a small cell. Did she always have to start things in places where he couldn't just get up and walk out? Was that why she often waited until they were in the car to have these discussions? Because then *he couldn't leave*?

"You have to know that I would never deliberately embarrass you like that."

"Do I?" he asked, feeling himself being sucked in, despite his best intentions. "Why did you come to court, Mattie?"

"Why did you ask me not to?" she countered.

"Objection," he said. "Irrelevant and argumentative."

"Sorry," Mattie apologized quickly. "I wasn't trying to upset you."

You don't have to try, Jake thought, but didn't say, deciding that the best course was to say nothing at all until after they were home. He reached over and turned up the volume on the radio, catching Mattie wince out of the corner of his eye. A medical reason for embarrassing him in court, he marveled. He wasn't getting out a moment too soon.

It wasn't until after her nap that she noticed his clothes were gone.

He heard her wandering around above his head, opening and closing closet doors, pulling open dresser drawers. He pictured the puzzled expression tugging at her even features, making creases in her brow, distorting the gentle curve of her lips. "Jake?" he heard her call, her footsteps on the stairs.

He was sitting on the smaller of two burgundy leather sofas in what was originally a den but was now his office, facing an elegant marble-framed fireplace that was flanked on either side by built-in bookshelves, the books neatly arranged in alphabetical order, one side for fiction, the other for biographies and legal texts. Various college diplomas hung on the wood-paneled walls; a floral needlepoint rug, in shades of blue and rose, lay across the hardwood floor. His desk, a special-order, hand-carved oak table, home to the latest in computer technology, sat at the far end of the room, in front of a wall of windows, overlooking the wide, tree-lined street. All in all, a room that was both practical and pleasing to the eye, a room in which to work or relax. Mattie had done a nice job with it. He should have used it more, he thought, fighting off unwanted twinges of guilt.

Not guilty! he wanted to jump up and shout. I am not guilty. Not guilty. Not guilty.

"What's going on, Jake?" Mattie asked from the doorway.

Reluctantly, he turned his head toward her, an involuntary shudder disturbing his otherwise placid demeanor, a demeanor he'd been practicing since Mattie lay down several hours ago for her nap. Did she have to look so damn vulnerable? he wondered, staring past the swelling beneath her eyes. Sleep had darkened her bruises, deepened the scratches on her face and neck. Now was probably the wrong time to do this. Maybe he should wait until she was fully recovered, at least until the bruises disappeared.

Except by then another month would be gone, another month of feeling guilty and alone and trapped and resentful, and by then something else would have come up. Something else to keep him here. And he couldn't risk that. If he stayed, he would suffocate. If he didn't leave, and leave now, he would die. It was as simple as that.

In a way, Mattie's strange outburst in court had been a blessing in disguise. It had given him the courage at long last to do what needed to be done. He shouldn't feel guilty. He was only giving voice to what both of them had been thinking for years.

Jake stood up and motioned Mattie toward the sofas, but she shook her head, no, choosing to stand. Stubborn as ever, Jake thought. And tough. Tougher than he was. She'd be just fine.

"Where are all your things?" she asked.

Jake sank back into his seat, heard the squish of leather as he tried to find a comfortable position. Maybe Mattie didn't need to sit down, but he **sure** did. "I think it's best if I move out," he heard himself say.

The color drained from her face, further accentuating the blotches of conflicting hues that stained her skin, so that she looked like a portrait by one of those German expressionist painters she was so crazy about. "If this is about what happened in court—"

"This isn't about what happened in court."

"I've apologized—"

"This isn't about that."

"What is it about?" she asked, lips barely moving, voice flat.

"It's not about blame. It's nobody's fault," he said, trying to find his place in the script he'd been rehearsing for weeks.

"What is it about?" she repeated.

Jake watched Mattie's body fold into the wall, as if she were using it for support. Was she going to faint? "Don't you think you should sit down?"

"I don't want to sit down," Mattie said, spitting

each word into the space between them. "I can't believe you're doing this now."

"I'm not leaving right away. Not for a few days," he backtracked, as she tossed his words aside with a wave of her hand, a shake of her head.

"I just got home from the hospital, for God's sake. I was in a car accident, in case you've forgotten. It hurts me to breathe."

It hurts me to breathe too, Jake wanted to shout. Instead, he said, "I'm sorry."

"You're sorry?"

"I wish things were different."

"That's obvious," Mattie said, a scoff in her voice, her bruised hand pulling the hair at the top of her head with such vehemence Jake thought she might rip it right out of her scalp. "So, let me see if I've got this straight," she began, not giving him the chance to interject. "You're leaving me, but it has nothing to do with the scene I created in court, that was probably just a catalyst. It's nobody's fault, this isn't about blame. Right? And you're sorry you had to tell me as soon as I got home from the hospital, you know the timing sucks, but there's never going to be a good time for this sort of thing. How am I doing so far? Oh, yes, we haven't been happy in years, we only got married in the first place because of Kim, we've given it our best shot, fifteen years is nothing to sneeze at. We should feel proud, not sad. Right? This is going to work out great for both of us. In fact, you're probably doing me a favor." She paused, arched one eyebrow. "What do you say? Think I'm onto something?"

Jake released a deep whoosh of air from his lungs,

said nothing. He'd been a fool to think he might emerge from this discussion unscathed. Mattie would have her pound of flesh. By the time he walked out the front door, he'd be as battered and bruised as she was.

Mattie walked to the fireplace, leaned against it, her back to him. "Are you moving in with your little friend?"

Jake felt his body turn to ice. "What?"

"I think you heard me."

He looked toward the window, not sure how to respond. What was happening? Even Mattie's outburst had been somewhat expected. But not this. This wasn't part of the script. What should he tell her? How much should he tell her? How much did she really want to know? How much did she already know? "I'm not sure I understand," he said, stalling.

Mattie spun around, eyes on fire, ready for battle. "Oh, please," she said. "Don't insult my intelligence. You think I don't know about your latest girlfriend?"

How could she know? Jake thought, wondering how he could have come to this confrontation so unprepared. Didn't a good attorney always do his homework? Didn't he come to the table with all the pertinent facts at hand, so that there would be no unpleasant surprises? Still, how could Mattie know? Was she just posturing? Should he continue to feign ignorance? Call her bluff? "How did you find out?" he asked, opting for full disclosure.

"The same way I always find out." She shook her head, a gesture rife with disgust. "For such a smart lawyer, you can be awfully stupid."

Jake felt his back stiffen. "I was hoping we wouldn't make this personal," he said.

"Not personal? You're leaving me for another woman, and you don't think it's personal?"

"I was hoping we wouldn't get into name calling. That we could still be friends," he offered weakly.

"You want to be friends?"

"If that's possible."

"When have we ever been friends?" she asked, her voice incredulous.

He looked toward the floor, fixating on the arcs and swirls in the dark wood grain. "Doesn't that tell you anything?"

"No. What should it tell me?"

"Mattie," Jake began, then stopped. What was he going to say? She was right. They'd never been friends. Why on earth would they start now? "How long have you known?"

"About this one? Not long." She shrugged, winced, walked to the window, stared out at the street. "By the way, how was your room at the Ritz-Carlton? It's always been one of my favorite hotels."

"You had me followed?"

Mattie laughed, a harsh, angry sound that scratched at the air like a cat's claws, leaving almost visible scars. "Irrelevant and argumentative," she snapped, using his earlier words as a weapon against him.

"What were you planning to do about it?"

"I hadn't made up my mind."

There was a long pause during which neither spoke. So she knew all about his affair. Jake wondered if Mattie had spotted Honey in court, if that had prompted her outburst. Was she really as vindictive as that? Or had her laughter been as spontaneous as

Mattie claimed, as upsetting to her as it had been to him? He didn't know, Jake realized, wincing with invisible pain of his own. He didn't know his wife of fifteen years very well at all.

"Maybe your subconscious made it up for you," Jake said simply.

"Maybe," she agreed quietly, turning slowly toward him, silhouetted against the fading light of day. Even in this light, Jake could see that the anger had left her eyes. Its sudden departure had softened her stance, released the tight arch of her shoulders. She looked smaller, more achingly vulnerable than at any time he could remember. "So, it's over," was all she said.

Jake wasn't sure what had prompted the abrupt change in Mattie's attitude, whether she realized he was right, or that there was nothing to be gained by arguing, or that she simply didn't have the strength for further protestations. Maybe she was as grateful as he was that everything was finally out in the open, so that they could get on with their lives. She was still young. She was undeniably lovely, even covered in bruises. He turned away, dismayed by the unexpected stirring in his loins. What was wrong with him, for God's sake? Wasn't this precisely what had gotten them into this mess in the first place?

"I think you should go now," Mattie said.

"What?" Jake was confused by this sudden turn of events, his mind twisting and turning like a sailboat caught in an unexpected eddy. Hadn't he already told her he would stay a few days, until she was feeling stronger? Hadn't he shown her that, despite everything, he was still prepared to be responsible, caring, magnanimous? How could she be so dismissive?

"There's no reason for you to stay," Mattie told him matter-of-factly. "I'll be fine."

"Why don't I stay until tomorrow—" he began.

"I'd rather you didn't. Really, there's no need."

Jake sat absolutely still for several moments before pushing himself off the sofa, only to find himself standing motionless in the center of the room, not sure what was expected of him at this point, whether he should stick with his game plan, insist that he stay, whether he should wave and walk out the door, whether he should give Mattie a final kiss good-bye.

"Good-bye, Jake," Mattie told him evenly, once again reaching inside his head, making the decision for him. "You're doing the right thing," she said, catching him by surprise. "Maybe not for the right reason. But it *is* the right thing."

Jake smiled, torn between the conflicting urges to take her in his arms or jump up and down for joy. It was over, he was free, and aside from a few tense moments, it had been relatively painless, even easy. Of course, this was just the beginning. They hadn't started talking about money, about dividing their assets. Who knew what would happen once the lawyers got involved?

Lawyers, he thought, leaving the room and crossing the large central foyer to the front door. Definitely a breed apart.

"I'll call you tomorrow," he said, as Mattie, only steps behind him, jumped ahead of him to open the door, as if he were a guest in her home, and an unwelcome guest at that. Even before he reached his car, Jake heard the front door close behind him.

EIGHT

"What do you mean, you just let him walk out of here? Are you crazy?"

"I'm fine, Lisa. There was no reason for him to stay."

"No reason for him to stay?" Lisa pushed a stray wave of hair away from her forehead. Mattie understood that the gesture was born of frustration more with Mattie than with her hair, which always looked perfect. "How about the fact that you were in a serious car accident, that you suffered a concussion, that you just got home from the hospital today?"

"I can manage."

"You can manage," Lisa repeated numbly, getting up from her seat at the kitchen table to pour herself another cup of coffee. She'd driven to Evanston to check on Mattie as soon as her office hours were through, and she was still wearing her white doctor's robe over her navy sweater and pants. Mattie had made a fresh pot of coffee, unfrozen some banana-cranberry muffins, and calmly announced to her horrified friend that she and Jake had decided to separate. "What if you fall?" Lisa was asking, a not unreasonable question considering that Mattie had already experienced one near-tumble since Jake's departure, although she'd said nothing about it to Lisa.

"I'll get up," Mattie said.

"Don't be glib."

"Don't be worried."

"Don't be stupid."

Mattie felt the unexpected rebuke as sharply as a slap on the wrist. It stung, brought angry tears to her eyes. Lisa Katzman might look like a tiny little sparrow, Mattie thought, but she had the talons of an eagle. "Great bedside manner, doctor. Is that how you talk to all your patients?"

Lisa folded bony arms across her flat chest, pushed one thin lip inside the other, took a long, deep breath. "I'm talking to you as a friend."

"Are you sure?"

Lisa Katzman returned to the table without her coffee. She sat down, took Mattie's hands in her own. "Okay, I admit my concern is more than personal."

"That's what I don't understand," Mattie said, not sure whether she really wanted to get into all this, especially now. "The neurologist said the MRI was clear. There's nothing wrong with me."

"The MRI was clear," Lisa agreed.

"There's nothing wrong with me," Mattie repeated, waiting for the accompanying echo from her friend.

"There's another test I'd like you to take."

"What? Why?"

"Just to tie up some loose ends."

"What loose ends? What kind of test?"

"It's called an electromyogram."

"What's that?"

"An electromyogram tests the electrical activity of muscles," Lisa began, "and, unfortunately, to do that, they have to insert needle electrodes directly into the muscles, which can be a bit unpleasant."

"A bit unpleasant?"

"There's a crackling sound when the needles are inserted into the muscles, sort of like popcorn popping," Lisa explained. "It can be somewhat disconcerting."

"Oh, really? You think?" Mattie asked, not even trying to disguise her sarcasm.

"I think you can handle it," Lisa told her.

"I think I'll pass."

"I think you should think about it."

Mattie rubbed the bridge at the top of her nose, trying to keep the headache that was building behind her eyes at bay. She was liking this conversation even less than the earlier one with Jake. Increasingly, she was wishing she was back on the outside steps of the Art Institute with Roy Crawford and his big lecherous head. "What's going on here, Lisa? What horrible disease do you think I have?"

"I don't know that you have anything," Lisa said,

her voice even, giving nothing away. "I'm just being extra cautious because you're my friend."

"You're just being cautious," Mattie repeated.

"I want to eliminate some possible muscular disorders. Let me try to get something set up for next week, okay?"

Mattie felt a giant wave of fatigue wash across her body. She didn't want to argue. Not with her husband. Not with her best friend. She just wanted to crawl into bed and get this horrible day over with. "How long does this test take?"

"About an hour. Sometimes longer."

"How much longer?" Mattie asked.

"It can take two, occasionally even three hours."

"Two or three hours?! You want me to sit there and let some sadist stick needle electrodes into my muscles for two or three hours?"

"It usually only takes an hour," Lisa said again, trying to sound reassuring, failing miserably.

"This is some sort of sick joke, right?"

"It's no joke, Mattie. I wouldn't ask you to do this if I didn't feel it was important."

"I'll think about it," Mattie said, after a long pause in which she purposefully thought of nothing at all.

"Promise?"

"I'm not a child, Lisa. I said I'd think about it. That's exactly what I'll do."

"I've upset you," Lisa said softly. "I'm sorry. I didn't want to do that."

Mattie nodded, feeling as helpless as she had in the seconds prior to her accident, as if she were still trapped inside the speeding car and unable to find the brakes. There was no way to stop; there was no slowing down. No matter what she did, no matter how hard she tried, she was going to crash and burn.

Light my fire. Light my fire. Light my fire.

"Do you want me to talk to Jake?" Lisa was asking.

"I definitely don't want you to talk to Jake," Mattie said sharply, fresh anger propelling her words. "Why would you talk to Jake?"

"Just to keep him in the loop."

"He opted out of the loop, remember?"

"The bastard," Lisa snarled.

"No," Mattie protested, then, "Well, yes." She laughed, was grateful when Lisa laughed with her. If Lisa was laughing, then things weren't as bad as her manner suggested. There was nothing seriously wrong with her. She wouldn't have to have this horribly invasive test where they stuck needles directly into her muscles and the muscles made crackling noises, like popcorn popping, and even if she did, the test would show nothing, just like the MRI.

"I have an idea," Lisa announced. "What do you say I sleep over here tonight?"

"What? That's a lousy idea."

"Come on. Fred can manage the boys for one night. It'll be like the pajama parties we had when we were teenagers. We can order pizza, watch TV, do each other's hair. It'll be great."

Mattie smiled at her friend's generosity. "I'm fine, Lisa. Really. I don't need you to spend the night. But thanks. I appreciate the offer."

"I just don't like the idea of you being alone on your first night back from the hospital, that's all."

"What if I want to be alone?"

"Do you?"

Mattie gave the question a moment's serious thought. "Yes," she said, finally, her entire body groaning with fatigue. "Yes, I really do."

The house had never felt so large, so empty, so quiet.

After Lisa's departure, Mattie walked from room to room as if in a trance, stroking the pale yellow walls, admiring the decor as if seeing everything for the first time. Over here, we have the dining room, big enough to seat twelve people comfortably for dinner, something every newly single woman desperately needs. And over here, the spacious living room, complete with oversize sofa in soft beige Ultrasuede, perfect for the hardworking man of the house, except, of course, that the man of the house was no longer *in* the house.

Where are you, Jake Hart? Mattie wondered, knowing the answer, knowing he was with *her*, his new love, in her apartment, or maybe even in a romantic room at the Ritz-Carlton, that they were celebrating his newfound freedom by making love and drinking champagne and having a high old time, while Mattie got to wander aimlessly around a big empty house in the suburbs, worrying about some stupid test that was going to make her muscles go pop.

Mattie circled the large center hallway once, then again, this time making the circle smaller, and then again smaller still. Narrowing my horizons, she thought, tripping over her feet, wondering whether she'd get to stay in the house or whether her horizons would shrink to the size of a small, two-bedroom apartment.

Rotating her tingling foot, she hopped toward the stairs, located just to the right of Jake's office, and lowered herself onto the bottom step, massaging her foot until the tingling stopped. "Bad circulation, that's all it is. Runs in the family." Did it? She stared toward the kitchen, wondering what to do next. "I can do anything I want," she announced to the empty house. I can buy myself a new gas oven. I can watch TV till three in the morning. I can talk on the phone all night. I can read the newspaper and leave it lying all over the white broadloom in the master bedroom, now that the master is no longer in residence. "I can even watch TV while reading the newspaper *and* talking on the phone," she continued out loud, laughing. "And nobody can stop me. Nobody can shake his head in disapproval. Nobody can judge me and find me wanting."

Wanting, Mattie repeated silently. What exactly did she want?

What did she want to do with her life, now that Jake was no longer a part of it?

She'd known of his plans the second she opened the bedroom closet and found most of his clothes gone. Still, she dismissed the evidence of her own eyes, as she'd been dismissing such evidence for years, her mind scrambling for other explanations—he'd sent everything to the cleaners; he'd decided to splurge on a whole new wardrobe; he'd moved his things into the guest bedroom to give her more space while she recuperated. The list of improbable excuses had followed her down the stairs and into Jake's office, where he sat waiting for her. "What's going on, Jake?" she'd asked from the doorway. "Where are all your things?"

"I think it's best if I move out," he'd told her. Plain. Simple. Right to the point.

And then the unnecessary embellishments—it was nobody's fault; it wasn't about blame; he was sorry; he hoped they could still be friends.

Mattie reached for the wooden banister and hoisted herself into a standing position, gingerly placing one foot in front of the other as she made her way up the stairs to her bedroom. Maybe she'd redecorate the house again, she thought, reaching the large upstairs hall that mirrored the one directly below. Paint the walls a deep orange, Jake's least favorite color. Replace all the masculine leathers with more feminine floral chintz. Throw out the neat white shutters on the windows and bring in yards and yards of frilly lace, even though she hated chintz and lace. That wasn't the point. The point was that Jake hated them, and the house was now hers to do with as she pleased. No one could tell her what to do or how to do it. Certainly not Jake. No second opinions required. She didn't have to consult or compromise.

At least not yet. Not until Jake came back at her with his list of demands. She'd see where all this lovely talk of friendship went when they started trying to hammer out a settlement. She thought of her friend Terry, of the hell her ex-husband put her through, refusing to leave the house until she agreed to forfeit her right to a share of his pension, nickel-and-diming her to death, forever late in his child support payments. Would it be that way for her once Jake's guilty conscience eased?

Mattie made a decent living as an art dealer, was

used to paying her own way, had even managed to put some money aside. She'd always hoped to use that money so that she and Jake could take a belated honeymoon trip to Paris, but it didn't look like she'd be honeymooning anytime soon. How far would that money take her? she wondered now. How long would it last? Money had never been an issue in her marriage to Jake. Would all that change when he was made a partner? Would he want to keep everything for his new woman, his new life?

Mattie marched into her bedroom and flipped on the TV, listening as the sound of rapid gunfire filled the air, obliterating such unpleasant thoughts. She looked toward her king-size bed, the powder blue duvet still twisted and disheveled from her earlier nap, as if there were still someone lying beneath it. "I can sleep on whatever side of the bed I want," she said, deliberately bouncing down on Jake's side, cognizant of his smell clinging stubbornly to his pillow, tossing the pillow to the floor, then stepping on it as she climbed out of bed. "I can close the damn window." Over fifteen years of freezing to death every night because Jake insisted on sleeping with the window open. She marched to the window and slammed it down with authority.

Mattie located the television's remote control unit on the overstuffed blue corduroy chair at the side of the bed. "All mine," she cackled, pressing her thumb to the appropriate button, watching as channel after channel flipped into view, disappearing before anything had time to register on her brain. She dropped the remote and headed for the bathroom, pulling off her jeans and baggy sweatshirt, confronting herself in the wall of mirrors surrounding the white porcelain sink. The first thing I'm going to do, she decided, is get rid of all these mirrors.

She stripped off her bra and panties, stared with dismay at her bruised and naked body. "Oh, yes, they'll be lined up around the block." She began pouring water for a bath. "I'm going to use up all the hot water," she announced loudly, the sound of her voice bouncing off the almond-colored marble tiles covering the walls, echoing loudly in her ears. I'm going to use up all the hot water and then I'm going to check myself into a loony bin, she thought, the by-now familiar tingling returning to the bottom of her right foot.

Mattie limped toward the toilet, lowered the seat, sat down, massaged her foot. But this time the tingling didn't stop, even after several minutes, and she was forced to crawl across the cold floor to turn off the water pouring into the tub before it overflowed. She caught sight of herself, down on her hands and knees, in a small sliver of mirror not hidden by steam, and turned away, feeling suddenly queasy. "Bad circulation, that's all it is," she said, lowering herself carefully into the hot water, watching her skin flush red. Red and purple and yellow and brown, Mattie thought, counting the colors, her body a canvas. She closed her eyes, rested her head against the back of the tub, the water lapping at the scratches on her chin, the way she remembered her mother's dogs licking at her mother's face.

It was strange in the house without Jake.

Not that she wasn't used to his absence. Jake worked impossible hours, was never really here even when he was sitting right beside her. Occasionally he'd gone away on business, and she'd spent the night alone in their bed. But this was different. This time, he wasn't coming back.

When he'd first announced he was leaving, Mattie felt as if she'd been punched in the stomach by an invisible fist. It had taken all her strength, all her resolve, not to cave forward or cry out. Why? Wasn't it a relief to finally have everything out in the open, not to spend every day waiting for the ax to fall? Yes, she'd be lonely. But the last fifteen years had taught her that there was nothing lonelier than an unhappy marriage.

The phone rang.

Mattie debated whether or not to answer it, finally giving in, grabbing a towel, and limping toward the phone, located on Jake's side of the bed. Maybe it was Lisa, calling again to check on how she was doing. Or Kim. Or Jake, she thought, lifting the phone to her ear. "Hello?"

"Martha?" The word hacked at the air, like a knife-wielding assailant.

Mattie sank down onto the bed, wounded before the conversation had even begun. "Mother," she said, afraid to say more.

"I won't take up much of your time," her mother began. Mattie quickly translated this to mean that her mother didn't want to spend long on the phone. "I'm just calling to see how you're doing."

"I'm doing fine, thank you," Mattie said over the sound of dogs barking in the background. "And you?"

"Well, you know, getting older is no picnic."

You're barely sixty, Mattie thought, but didn't say. What was the point?

"I'm sorry I didn't get to the hospital to see you. You know how I am about hospitals."

"No apologies necessary."

"Jake says you're still pretty banged up."

"When did you talk to Jake?" Mattie asked.

"He came by to take Kim out for dinner."

"He did?"

"About an hour ago."

"Did he say anything else?"

"Like what?"

"How's Kim?" Mattie asked, changing the subject.

"She's a lovely girl," her mother said, with the kind of emotion she usually reserved for her dogs. "She was a big help to me when Lucy was having her litter."

Mattie almost laughed. Of course there'd be a connection, she thought, rotating her right foot, the stubborn tingle refusing to go away. "Listen, Mom, you caught me in the tub. I'm standing here, dripping wet."

"Well, then, you'd better go." Mattie heard the relief in her mother's voice. "I just called to see how you were."

I was fine, Mattie thought. "I'll be fine," was what she said. "Good-bye, Mother. Thanks for calling."

"Good-bye, Martha."

Mattie hung up the phone and transferred all her weight to her errant right foot, sighing with relief at the feel of the carpet beneath her toes. "I'll be fine," she repeated, returning to the bathroom, climbing back into the tub, the water not as hot or soothing as before. "I'll be fine."

NINE

"Are you all right?" Kim cleared her throat in a vain effort to stop her voice from quavering. Why was she asking that? Wasn't the answer obvious? Never before had she seen her mother so obviously not all right. Her skin was almost transparent beneath its palette of fading bruises. Her normally vibrant blue eyes were coated with a dull glaze of fear and pain. The ghost of former tears had left wiggly streaks through the makeup she'd so carefully applied only hours earlier. Her hands were shaking, her steps small and unsure. Kim had never seen her mother looking so helpless. It took all her strength to keep from bursting into tears. "Mom, are you okay?"

Say yes, say yes, say yes.

"Your mother needs to rest for a few minutes," Kim heard someone say. Only then did she notice the burly-looking woman at her mother's elbow. Did she have to look so healthy? Kim wondered angrily, interpreting the woman's shiny olive skin and flashing dark eyes as something of a rebuke, as if, by being in such obvious good health, she was somehow robbing her mother of hers.

"Who are you?" Kim asked.

"Rosie Mendoza," the woman answered, tapping the hospital identity tag hanging around her neck and leading Mattie to a chair, one of approximately a dozen that lined the wall of the fourth-floor hospital corridor. "Dr. Vance's assistant."

"Is my mother okay?"

"I'm fine, sweetie," Mattie whispered, although she didn't sound fine. She sounded weak and scared and in a great deal of pain. "I just need to sit down for a few minutes."

"She needs to go home and crawl into bed," Rosie Mendoza advised.

"But then she'll be fine, right?" Kim lowered herself into the seat next to Mattie's, clutching her mother's hand.

"The doctor should have the test results in a day or two," Rosie Mendoza said. "He'll get in touch with Dr. Katzman as soon as he has anything."

"Thank you," Mattie said, eyes on the short brown boots peeking out from underneath her brown slacks, her body motionless.

"Did it hurt?" Kim asked her mother after Rosie Mendoza's departure.

Say no, say no, say no.

"Yes," Mattie answered. "It hurt like hell."

"Where did they put the needles?"

Don't tell me.

Mattie pointed gingerly to her shoulders and thighs, opened her hands, palms up. Only then did Kim notice the fresh Band-Aid stretched across the inside of her mother's left hand. "How many?"

"Too many."

"Does it still hurt?"

Say no, say no, say no.

"Not too much," Mattie said, although Kim could see she was lying.

Why was she asking her mother these questions when she didn't want to know the answers? Wasn't it enough to know that her mother had spent the last hour and a half undergoing some unpleasant and, her mother had assured her, completely unnecessary test, designed to show the pattern of nerve activity in her body, a test she'd only agreed to in order to get Lisa Katzman off her back? Kim felt a surge of anger charge through her body. Why had her mother's closest friend put her through something so awful if it was so unnecessary?

"Do you want a cup of coffee or something?" Kim asked her mother, refusing to consider the possibility that Lisa might have a different opinion of the merits of the test.

Mattie shook her head no. "I'll just sit here for a few minutes. Then we can go."

"How are we going to get home?" Kim asked suddenly. Her mother had insisted on driving into the city, despite Lisa's admonition that she should let someone else do the driving, that she might feel too weak and unsettled after the test, especially since she was still recovering from her accident. But Mattie had stubbornly refused to burden any of her friends, and she wouldn't let Kim call Grandma Viv, claiming Kim's grandmother was useless in any kind of emergency, at least those involving human beings. As for Jake, Mattie wouldn't even consider asking him, and Kim had agreed with her mother. They didn't need Jake. What did they want with a man who'd made it clear he'd rather be with another woman? Mattie didn't need her soon-to-be ex-husband's help any more than Kim needed her soon-to-be former father.

"I'll always be here for you," he'd tried to tell her that awful night exactly one week ago, when he'd picked her up at her grandmother's small house in the once run-down, now trendy area of the city known as Old Town. "I'm still your father. Nothing's ever going to change that."

"You're changing it," Kim protested.

"I'm moving out of the house," Jake argued. "Not out of your life."

"Out of sight," Kim said coldly, "out of mind."

"You understand that this has nothing to do with you."

"It has everything to do with me," Kim countered, deliberately misinterpreting his words.

"Sometimes things happen."

"Oh, really? Things happen? All by themselves? They just happen?" Kim was aware she was raising her voice. She relished the sound of its outrage, the way it made the man sitting across from her in the small Italian restaurant squirm. "You're trying to tell me this is something beyond your control?"

"I'm trying to tell you that I love you, that I'll always be here for you."

"Except you'll be somewhere else."

"I'll be living somewhere else."

"So you'll be *there* for me," Kim said, proud of her own cleverness. It made her feel powerful, kept her heart from sliding right out of her chest and crashing to the hard tile floor, shattering into thousands of tiny pieces.

"I love you, Kim," her father said again.

"Now I'm just like everybody else," Kim said in return.

And so when Lisa called to tell Mattie she'd been able to book the electromyogram for Thursday of the following week, Kim immediately volunteered to accompany her mother to the hospital, even though it meant missing an afternoon of school. Surprisingly, her mother agreed. "We girls have to stick together," Kim told her, climbing into bed beside her mother later that night, as she'd been doing every night since Jake left, her arm draping protectively across Mattie's hip, as she slowed her breathing to match her mother's, their bodies rising and falling in unison, breathing as one.

"Are you going to be able to drive home?" Kim asked her mother now.

"Give me a few more minutes," Mattie said.

But twenty minutes later, Mattie was still staring at her feet, afraid, or unable, to move. Her complexion remained a ghostly white beneath the mustard yellow and soiled lavender of her bruises. Her hands still trembled. "You better call your father," Mattie said, fresh tears falling the length of her cheeks.

"We can take a cab," Kim protested.

"Call your father," Mattie insisted.

"But—"

"Don't argue. Please. Call him."

Reluctantly, Kim did as she was told. Locating a pay phone beside a busy bank of elevators at the end of the long corridor, she punched in the numbers of her father's private line, hoping he was in court, with clients, otherwise unavailable. "I don't understand why we just can't take a taxi," she muttered under her breath, watching an elderly man in a stained blue hospital gown wander toward her, dragging his IV unit alongside him. Now she understood why her grandmother had such an aversion to hospitals. They were harsh, harmful places, full of wounded bodies and lost souls. Even people who were healthy when they walked in, like her mother, limped out in pain, frail echoes of their former selves. Kim felt vaguely nauseated, wondered whether she'd picked up some deadly virus just sitting outside the doctor's office. How many hands had fingered those same old magazines? How many germs had she been exposed to during the interminable minutes she'd waited for her mother? Kim rubbed her hands against her jeans, as if trying to rid herself of any stray bacteria. She felt dizzy and flushed, as if she might faint.

"Jake Hart," her father suddenly announced, his voice a bucket of ice water tossed at her face.

Kim snapped to attention, her shoulders stiffening, her knees buckling. She pushed a strand of imaginary hair away from her forehead, stared at the newly stilled bank of elevator doors. What was she supposed to say?

Hi, Daddy? Hello, Father? Hi there, Jake? "It's Kim," she said finally, as the old man trailing his IV did an abrupt about-face and began retracing his steps along the corridor. Kim noticed flashes of bare white buttocks between the halves of his pale blue hospital gown. What horrible tests had they put him through? Kim wondered.

"Kim, sweetheart—"

"I'm at Michael Reese County General with Mom," Kim said without further preamble.

"Has something happened?"

Kim buried her chin into the cowl neck of her dusty rose sweater, her lips folding one inside the other, an impatient sigh escaping, hurrying toward her heart. "We need your help," she said.

Forty minutes later, Jake met his wife and daughter inside the front entrance of the downtown hospital. "I'm sorry I took so long getting here," he apologized, as Kim glared her displeasure. "I got corraled in the hall on my way out of the office."

"You're a busy man," Kim sneered.

"Thanks for coming," Mattie told him.

"Is the car in the lot?"

Mattie handed him the keys to the rental car. Her Intrepid, all but totaled in the accident, was a write-off. "It's a white Oldsmobile."

"I'll find it. Are you okay?"

"She's fine," Kim said, snaking her arm through her mother's.

"How are you, sweetheart?" Jake asked his daughter, reaching out as if to stroke her hair.

"Great," Kim replied stiffly, leaning out of his

reach, relishing the hurt look in her father's eyes. "Could you get the car? Mom needs to be in bed."

"I'll be right back."

Minutes later Kim's father pulled the white Oldsmobile up to the curb, jumping out to help Mattie into the front seat, relegating Kim to the back.

Kim made an exaggerated show of trying to get comfortable, bouncing around in the backseat, deliberately careless with the chunky heels of her black leather boots, scraping them against the back of her father's seat repeatedly, as she crossed, then uncrossed, her legs. Who designed these cars anyway? Did they think that all backseat passengers were under ten years of age? Didn't they know that grown-ups needed more leg room? That they might want to sit without their knees circling their chins? She'd spent a lot of time in the backseats of cars lately, Kim realized, thinking back to last Saturday night, hearing Teddy's whispered pleas warm against her ear. *Come on, Kim. You know you want to.*

"You all right back there, sweetheart?" her father asked, scaring Teddy away.

Who the hell do you think you are? Kim demanded silently, angry eyes burrowing deep holes in the back of her father's head. The white knight riding in on his white horse to save the day? Is that how you see yourself? Well, I've got news for you, Jake Hart, famous attorney-at-law and general all-around shit. This isn't a white horse. It's a white Oldsmobile. And we don't need your help. In fact, we don't need you at all. We've been getting along very nicely without you. Actually, we've hardly even noticed you're gone.

"I'm sorry we had to bother you," she heard her mother say, her voice stronger than before, though lacking its usual resonance. Why wasn't she angrier? Why did she have to be so damn polite?

"You should have called me earlier," Jake said. "There was no need for you to drive into the city."

"Mom isn't an invalid," Kim said.

"No, but she was in a major car accident less than ten days ago, and she's still not fully recovered."

"You sound like Lisa."

"It's common sense."

"I'm fine," Mattie said.

"She's fine," Kim echoed. How dare he say anything to criticize her mother! What Mattie did, what *they* did, was no longer any of his concern. He had no right to criticize or pass judgment. He'd forfeited that right the day he walked out. Kim stretched her hand toward the front seat, resting it on her mother's shoulder. She should never have called him. She should have called her grandmother or Lisa or another of her mother's many friends. Anyone but Jake. They didn't need Jake.

The fact was that her father had never been a huge part of her day-to-day life. Ever since Kim could remember, her father was someone who waved to her each morning on his way to work, and who kissed her good night if he was home in time to tuck her in. Her mother was the one who accompanied her to school, took her to the doctor and the dentist, drove her to her lessons in piano and ballet, attended each and every parent-teacher meeting, school play, after-school sporting event, stayed home with her when she was sick. It wasn't that her father didn't care. It was just that he had too many other places to be. Other places he'd *rather* be.

As Kim grew into her teens, she saw even less of him, their busy schedules at constant odds. Since moving to Evanston, she'd hardly seen her father at all. And now Jake Hart was more like a ghost than a man, haunting the halls he no longer inhabited, his presence defined, possibly even enhanced, by his absence.

At first, Kim worried that her mother might fall apart. But her mother, despite her injuries, had been coping with Jake's defection surprisingly well. All Mattie's worries were reserved for Kim. "It looks much worse than it is," she'd quickly assured Kim, who'd almost fainted at the sight of her mother's beautiful face covered in ugly bruises. And then later, "How are you, sweetie? Do you want to talk about it?" She'd even tried sticking up for Jake. "Don't be too hard on him, sweetie. He's your father, and he loves you."

Bullshit, Kim thought. Her father didn't love her. He'd never wanted her.

She didn't want him now.

After that, they rarely mentioned him. Her mother's bruises changed colors as effortlessly as the outside leaves, growing fainter every day. The scratches healed. The stiffness left her joints. She went about the business of everyday life, renting a car, shopping for groceries, even contacting several clients, making appointments for the coming weeks. Aside from the occasional problem with her foot falling asleep, her mother was doing just fine.

They both were.

They didn't need him.

"How are you doing back there, Kim?" her father asked, giving the question a second try. She saw him looking at her through the rearview mirror, his eyes reflecting both concern and hope.

Kim grunted, said nothing. If her mother wanted to be civil and agreeable regarding their separation, that was her business. It didn't mean Kim had to. *Somebody* had to play the jilted wife.

"Looks like I'm going to be offered a partnership in the near future," Jake said. "That's what took me so long getting here. People kept stopping me in the halls to congratulate me."

"That's wonderful," Kim heard Mattie say. "You've worked very hard. You deserve it."

You deserve to rot in hell, Kim thought.

"How are you going to get back to the city?" Mattie asked, as Jake turned the car onto Walnut Drive.

"I've arranged for someone to pick me up in about half an hour."

"Your girlfriend?" Kim's voice was sharp, slashing at the air like a razor. "And don't look at Mom that way," she said, almost before he had the chance. "She didn't say anything."

"We need to talk, Kimmy," her father began.

"Don't call me Kimmy. I hate Kimmy." He'd called her Kimmy when she was a little girl, she remembered, faint memories flooding back, filling her eyes with unexpected tears.

"Please, Kim," he said. "I think it's important."

"Who cares what you think?"

"What's going on?" her mother asked, and for an

instant Kim thought she was speaking to her, that her mother was angry, that she was taking his side against hers.

And then she saw the police car parked outside their house and the two uniformed officers standing outside her front door. What was happening?

"It's probably about the accident," Jake said.

"I've already talked to the police," her mother said as Jake pulled the car into the driveway and stepped out of the car.

"Problems?" he asked.

Kim helped her mother out of the front seat, her eyes on the young man and woman in neat blue uniforms. The man, who identified himself as Officer Peter Slezak, was about five foot eleven, had arms the size of tree trunks, and wore his hair so short, it was difficult to tell what color it was. The woman, whom Officer Slezak introduced as his partner, Officer Judy Taggart, was about five foot seven, and approximately the same width as one of Officer Slezak's thighs. She wore her brown hair pulled back into a ponytail, and there was a large pimple on her chin she'd tried to conceal with makeup. Kim absently felt her chin for any pimples of her own.

"Is this your house?" Officer Slezak asked.

"Yes," Jake answered.

No, Kim almost screamed. It's not your house.

"Is there a problem?" Mattie stepped forward, took charge.

"Are you all right, ma'am?" Officer Taggart stared openly at the bruises on Mattie's face.

"Is this about the accident?" Jake asked.

"It wasn't exactly an accident," Officer Slezak said.

"I'm sorry?" Mattie said, her way of saying, Excuse me, as if apologizing in advance.

"Maybe you should tell us what this is about," Jake said, resuming control.

"We're looking for Kim Hart."

"Kim?" Her mother gasped.

Kim stepped forward, a dull ache building in the pit of her stomach. "I'm Kim Hart."

"We'd like to ask you a few questions."

"About?" Jake interrupted.

"Why don't we go inside?" Mattie suggested, walking up the steps to the front door. Kim noticed that her mother was having trouble with the key and gently lifted it from her hand, easily fitting it into the lock and pushing open the door.

Seconds later they were grouped around the kitchen table, the officers having declined Mattie's offer of coffee.

"What can you tell us about the party at Sabrina Hollander's house last Saturday night?" Officer Slezak began, staring directly at Kim's chest as Officer Taggart produced a notebook and pen from the back pocket of her well-pressed trousers.

"There was a party." Kim shrugged, aware of her heart pumping wildly beneath her breasts, wondering whether that was what Officer Slezak was staring at.

"Were you there?"

"Maybe for an hour."

"What time was that?"

"Around nine."

"So you left the Hollander house at about ten?"

"Not even that," Kim said.

"What was happening at the party?"

"Not much." People were dancing, drinking beer, passing around the occasional joint. Teddy had convinced her to try a few tokes before they adjourned to the backseat of his car. Had somebody reported seeing her do drugs? Was that why the police were here? To arrest her?

"What are you getting at, officers?" Jake Hart asked.

"Sabrina Hollander threw a little party while her parents were out of town. Two hundred kids showed up."

"Two hundred kids," Kim repeated breathlessly, deciding that she must have fallen asleep in the car, and that this whole episode was part of an unpleasant dream.

"Someone decided it would be fun to trash the house," Officer Slezak continued. "They slashed paintings, ripped up the carpets, defecated on the furniture, punched holes in the walls. Altogether there was almost a hundred thousand dollars worth of damage."

"Oh, my God," Mattie said, covering her bruised lips with her bandaged hand.

"I don't know anything about that," Kim said, feeling numb.

"You didn't see anything while you were there, hear anybody talking?"

"No. Nothing."

"But people were drinking, doing drugs," Officer Taggart stated, as if this were a fact not open to dispute.

"People were drinking beer," Kim qualified, her voice weak, her eyes drifting toward the backyard pool, wishing she could disappear without a trace beneath its smooth blue surface.

"And you said you left the party at ten o'clock?"

"She's already answered that," Jake interjected. A better lawyer than a father, Kim thought, reluctant gratitude mixing with her resentment.

"But you did know about the incident," Officer Slezak said.

"I heard some of the kids talking about it at school," Kim conceded, trying to ignore the look of surprise that fell across her mother's face like a shroud.

"What did they say?"

"Just that they heard things got out of hand. The place got wrecked."

"Did they say who was responsible?"

"Apparently some kids crashed the party. Nobody knew them."

"You're sure?"

"She's answered the question." Jake's voice resonated quiet authority. "I should explain that, in addition to being Kim's father, I'm also an attorney."

Not to mention an adulterer, Kim added silently.

"I thought I recognized you," Officer Slezak said, his voice flat, decidedly unimpressed. "You're the guy who let that kid who murdered his mother get off scot-free."

Way to go, Dad, Kim thought. I'll be lucky if they don't hang me.

Minutes later Officer Slezak slapped his giant haunches, signaling the meeting's end. Officer Taggart quickly folded up her notebook and returned it to her back pocket. Kim walked them to the front door, closed it after them, leaned her forehead against its hard oak grain.

"Is there anything you're not telling us?" her father asked, coming up behind her.

"In a few months I'll have my driver's license, and we won't have to call you anymore," Kim said defiantly, pushing past him and disappearing up the stairs. Minutes later she watched from her bedroom window as her father walked down the front path to the street. He looked up, as if he knew she was sitting there, and waved.

She didn't wave back.

TEN

The following Monday, Mattie was on the phone with Roy Crawford when the call-waiting signal sounded. "Can you hold just a minute, Roy? I'm sorry. I won't be a second." Mattie wondered why she hadn't chosen to ignore the signal, as she often did when talking to important clients. She already had voice mail to take messages. What did she need with call-waiting? Except that Kim had been so adamant about keeping it, and these days, most of the calls were for Kim. Maybe it was time for her daughter to get her own line, although it seemed an unnecessary expense in light of Jake's departure. And sooner or later she was going to have to start giving serious thought to her financial situation. "Hello," Mattie said into the phone, amazed at the number of irrelevant thoughts she could crowd into the space of a second.

"Mattie, it's Lisa."

Mattie stared vacantly toward the sliding glass door of her kitchen, noting the sun shining incongruously through heavy gray skies. She didn't want to talk to Lisa. Lisa was only going to tell her more things she didn't want to hear. "Lisa, can I call you back in a few minutes? I'm on the other line."

"This can't wait."

Mattie felt her entire body go numb. "Why don't I like the sound of that?"

"I need to see you in my office."

"I'm not having any more tests."

"No more tests. Look, I've already called Jake. He's picking you up in half an hour."

"What?" Mattie shrieked. "What do you mean, you called Jake? You can't do that."

"I already did."

"You had no right. Look, this is ridiculous. Hold on a minute." Mattie pressed the hold button, returned to her earlier conversation with Roy Crawford, her breath coming in short, ragged gasps. "Roy, can I call you right back?"

"Why don't I just pick you up for lunch at around twelve o'clock?"

"Fine," Mattie said, immediately returning to the other line, barking into Lisa's ear. "What do you mean, you called Jake? I didn't give you permission to discuss my case with him."

"I haven't discussed anything with him."

"Then why is he picking me up in half an hour?"

"Because I told him it was important."

"If it's so important, why don't I just drive over to your office right now?"

"Because I don't think you should be driving."

"I'm perfectly capable of driving," Mattie argued, trying to gain some control over the conversation, over the events unfolding, over her life.

"Mattie," Lisa said, a slight catch in her voice, "Dr. Vance just called me with your test results."

Mattie held her breath. "And?" The word tumbled from her lips before she could stop it.

There was a long pause before Lisa continued. "It's a little complicated. I'd rather discuss everything with you in person."

"Why did you call Jake?"

"He's your husband, Mattie. He should know what's going on."

"We're separated."

"He should be here."

"But he isn't, is he?" Mattie buried her head in the still-bandaged palm of her hand, hearing the unpleasant echo of her muscle going pop.

"Look," Lisa said, regaining control of her voice and adopting the same tone Mattie often took with Kim when trying to convince her daughter to do something she didn't want to do. "Let Jake be your chauffeur. Nothing more. If you don't want him in on the discussion, you can decide that when you get here. But at least this way, somebody will be here to drive you home. Please, Mattie. Do this for me."

"Jake's a busy man," Mattie said, her thoughts translated into words. "He just can't take off first thing on a Monday morning. What did you say to him, Lisa?"

"Just that I thought it was very important for him to be here."

"A matter of life and death?" Mattie heard herself say.

Lisa said nothing.

"Am I dying?" Mattie asked.

"It's complicated," Lisa said after a pause that lasted several seconds too long, and for the first time Mattie heard tears in the measured cadences of Lisa's voice. "Please, Mattie. Let Jake pick you up. We'll talk when you get here."

Mattie nodded, hanging up the phone without another word, trying to keep her growing panic at bay. Complicated, she thought. Why did things always have to be so damn complicated? She checked her watch against the two clocks in the kitchen, discovering it was five minutes faster than the later of the two. "Which means I have even less time than I thought," she said, fighting back tears, grateful that Kim was at school and not here to have to deal with this. Kim already had too much on her plate, Mattie thought, leaving the kitchen, wandering up the stairs in a daze. She reached her room, pulled back the blue duvet, and crawled into the freshly made bed fully clothed.

She was still lying there thirty minutes later, the duvet pulled tightly up around her chin, when she heard the doorbell ring, followed quickly by the sound of a key turning in the lock and someone opening the door.

"Mattie?" Jake called from the front hall. "Mattie, it's Jake. Are you ready? We should get going."

Mattie pushed herself off the pillow, fluffed out the dark blond hair that was flattened against her left cheek, tucked her green silk blouse into her black pants, and took a long, deep breath. She'd have to ask Jake to return his key, she thought. "I'll be right down," she said.

Five minutes later, sitting on the side of the bed and listening as Jake's footsteps bounded up the stairs, she realized she hadn't moved.

"You have something called amyotrophic lateral sclerosis," Lisa was explaining, her voice breaking, as Mattie sat rigid next to Jake in one of Lisa's small examining rooms.

"Sounds serious," Mattie said, refusing to look at her friend, staring at the eye chart behind her head.

"It is," Lisa whispered.

"Why haven't I ever heard of it?" Mattie demanded, as if this made some sort of difference, as if, by knowing something about it, she could have prevented getting it.

"You probably know it by its more common name, Lou Gehrig's disease."

"Oh, God," Mattie gasped. Beside her, she felt Jake slump in his chair.

"Are you all right? Do you want a glass of water?"

Mattie shook her head. What she wanted was to get out of here. What she wanted was to be asleep in her bed. What she wanted was her life back. "What does that mean, exactly? I mean, I know Lou Gehrig was a famous baseball player. I know he died of some horrible disease. And now you're saying, what? That I have this same disease? How do you know?"

"Dr. Vance faxed me the results of the electromyogram first thing this morning. They're quite conclusive." Lisa offered Mattie the pale manila folder containing the results. Jake took the folder from Lisa's shaking hands when Mattie failed to do so. "He asked me if I wanted to be the one to tell you—"

Don't tell me, Mattie thought. "Tell me," she said over the loud ringing in her ears.

"The test showed extensive denervation—"

"Speak English," Mattie snapped.

"There's irreversible damage to the motor neurons in the spinal cord and brain stem."

"Meaning?"

"The nerve cells are dying," Lisa explained softly.

"The nerve cells are dying," Mattie repeated, trying to make sense of the words. "The nerve cells are dying. What does that mean? Does that mean *I'm* dying?"

There was absolute silence. No one moved. No one breathed.

"Yes," Lisa said finally, her voice barely audible. "Oh, God, Mattie. I'm so sorry." Tears filled her eyes, threatening to spill down her cheeks.

"So, wait," Mattie said, jumping to her feet, pacing back and forth in the small space between the examining table and the door. "I don't understand. If I have this amyotrophic whatever-the-hell-it-is, how come it didn't show up on the MRI? The MRI said everything was fine," she reminded them.

"The MRI tests for other things."

"It tests for multiple sclerosis," Mattie argued. "It showed I didn't have that, and it's a sclerosis."

"ALS is different," Lisa explained patiently, pronouncing each letter individually.

"ALS?" Mattie demanded.

"It's short for—"

"I know what it's short for," Mattie snapped. "I'm not an idiot. My brain cells aren't dead yet."

"Mattie—" Jake said, then stopped.

"The disease won't affect your mental faculties," Lisa said.

"No?" Mattie stopped pacing. "So, what exactly will it affect?"

"Maybe you should sit down."

"Maybe I don't want to sit down, Lisa. Maybe I just want you to tell me what's going to happen to me, so I can get out of here and get on with the rest of my life." Mattie almost laughed. The rest of her life, she thought. That was a good one. "How long do I have?"

"We can't know exactly. It's unusual for ALS to strike someone your age—"

"How long, Lisa?" Mattie insisted.

"A year." The threatened tears began tumbling down her cheeks. "Maybe two," she added quickly. "Possibly even three."

"Oh, God." Mattie felt her knees buckle, her body disappearing under her, so that her head felt like a giant lead balloon spiraling through a stormy sky, about to crash into the ground below. Both Lisa and Jake jumped from their seats, caught Mattie before she hit the floor.

"Take deep breaths," Lisa urged, as worried hands secured Mattie in her chair. Mattie heard the sound of water running, felt the pressure of a glass at her lips. "Sip it slowly," Lisa instructed, as Mattie tasted cold water on the tip of her tongue, mingling with the warm salt of her tears. "Are you okay?" Lisa asked after several seconds.

"No," Mattie said softly. "I'm dying. Haven't you heard?"

"I'm so sorry," Lisa cried, holding tightly onto Mattie's hands.

Mattie noticed that Jake was leaning against the door, looking as if someone had kicked the air out of him. What's your problem? Mattie wanted to ask. Upset because you can't work your magic here? Upset because you can't save me from the death sentence a higher court just handed down? "A year," Mattie repeated.

"Maybe two or three," Lisa said hopefully.

"And what happens to me during that year or two or three?"

"It's impossible to predict the exact course of the disease," Lisa said. "It affects different people in different ways, and even on an individual basis, there's no symmetrical evolution."

"Please, Lisa. I don't have a lot of time." Mattie smiled, and Lisa laughed sadly, despite herself.

"Okay," Lisa said. "Okay. You want it straight? Here it is." She paused, swallowed, took one deep breath, then another. "ALS is a debilitating and ultimately fatal condition that leaves its victims mentally acute but increasingly unable to control their own bodies," she recited, as if by rote, accompanied by a steady stream of tears. "As it progresses, you'll lose the ability to walk. You've already begun feeling the tingling in your legs. You've started falling. It will only get worse. Eventually, you won't be able to walk at all. You'll be in a wheelchair." She took another deep breath, as if she were dragging on a cigarette. "You told me you sometimes have trouble fitting keys into locks. That's an early symptom of ALS. Eventually your hands will be rendered useless. Your body will start contorting in on itself, even as your mind stays sharp and focused."

"I'll be a prisoner of my own body," Mattie acknowledged quietly.

Lisa nodded, making no move to wipe away her tears. "Your speech will become slurred, difficult. You'll have trouble swallowing. At some point, you'll probably require a feeding tube."

"How will I die?"

"Mattie, please—"

"Tell me, Lisa. How will I die?"

"You'll start gagging, choking. In the end you'll suffocate."

"Oh, God." Mattie recalled her panic inside the MRI. Forty-five minutes of feeling as if she were being buried alive. And now she was expected to endure up to three years of the same sensation. No, it couldn't be. She felt perfectly fine. She couldn't be dying. There had to be some sort of mistake. "I want a second opinion."

"Of course."

"But no more tests. I was fine till I started having all these tests."

"No more tests," Lisa agreed, swiping the tears from her eyes. "I'll talk to Dr. Vance. Get his recommendations."

"Because this has to be some sort of mistake," Mattie continued. "Just because my foot sometimes falls asleep and I have trouble with my keys—"

"Mattie's outburst in the courtroom—" Jake began, stopped by Mattie's angry glare.

"It's part of what's happening," Lisa told him. "No one really understands why, except that sudden unexplained outbursts, laughing and crying for no apparent reason, are another hallmark of the disease in some cases."

"I really don't want to talk about this anymore," Mattie said, jumping to her feet.

"Dr. Vance wants you to start taking a drug called Riluzole," Lisa said quickly. "It's a neuroprotective drug that prevents the premature death of cells. You take one pill a day, and there are no side effects. It's expensive, but well worth it."

"And what exactly is the point of taking this drug?" Mattie asked, feeling her earlier anger return. Hadn't she already told Lisa that she wanted a second opinion? Why were they discussing medication as if any new opinions were foregone conclusions?

"It offers a few extra months."

"Months being unable to move, months of choking, months of being mentally acute while my body caves in around me? Thank you very much, Lisa, but I don't think so."

"The Riluzole slows the progress of the disease."

"In other words, it postpones the inevitable."

"Science is discovering new ways of treatment all the time," Lisa began.

Mattie cut her off. "Oh, please, Lisa, not the 'wonders of medical science, miracles can happen' speech. It doesn't become you."

"Please, Mattie," Lisa said, scribbling out a prescription and offering it to Mattie, who refused it.

"I said I wanted a second opinion."

Jake took the prescription from Lisa's hand, tucked it in the pocket of his pinstriped gray suit. Next to his receipt for a room at the Ritz-Carlton, Mattie thought bitterly.

"What are you giving that to him for?" Mattie demanded of Lisa.

"I just thought we should have it," Jake offered weakly.

"*We?* Who's this *we?*"

"Mattie—"

"No. You have no rights here. You gave up those rights, remember? I just brought you along as my chauffeur."

"Mattie—"

"No. This is none of your business. *I* am none of your business."

"You're the mother of my child," Jake said simply.

Oh, God, Kim, Mattie thought, grabbing her stomach, doubling over as if she'd been struck. How would she tell Kim? That she wouldn't be around to see her graduate from high school. That she wouldn't be there to see her off to college. That she wouldn't be able to dance at her wedding, or hold her first grandchild in her arms. That she was going to slowly choke to death in front of her daughter's beautiful, terrified eyes.

"The mother of your child," Mattie repeated. Of course. That's all she'd ever been to him. The mother of his child. She was pathetic, she thought, straightening up, pushing her shoulders back and her chin out. "I want to go home now," she said, glancing at her watch, noting it was closing in on eleven-thirty. "I have a date."

"What?!"

The look on Jake's face was almost worth the anguish of the morning, Mattie thought. "Can I have sex?" she asked Lisa suddenly.

"What?!" Jake said again.

"Can I?" Mattie repeated, ignoring her husband, focusing on her friend.

"As long as it's comfortable," Lisa said.

"Good," Mattie said. "Because I want to have sex."

"Mattie—" Jake started, then stopped, his hands dropping lifelessly to his sides.

"Not with you," Mattie told her husband. "Isn't that a relief? Your services are no longer required in that department. You bailed just in time. Now nobody can accuse you of being a no-good, miserable son-of-a-bitch for walking out on your wife when you found out she was dying. Your timing is as impeccable as ever."

"So what do we do now?" he asked helplessly.

"It's very simple," Mattie said. "You live. I die. Now, do you think you could drive me home? I really do have a date."

Jake said nothing. He reached over, opened the door to the small room, sucked in a deep breath of air.

"I'll call you as soon as I make the arrangements," Lisa said.

"No rush," Mattie told her, and walked from the room.

ELEVEN

They didn't speak at all on the drive back from Lisa's office, Mattie too numb, too angry, Jake too numbed by her anger, to say anything. Instead they listened to the radio, louder than Jake usually played it, louder than Mattie normally liked it, but today, just the right volume. The rock music blasted its way into the BMW the way water fills a car sinking into a river, seeping in from every available opening, quickly filling all empty space, drowning everything in its path. The noise of the music blocked their ears and closed their mouths, although Mattie had no idea what the singers were shouting about. That was okay, she thought, focusing her attention on the road ahead. She didn't have to know what they were shouting about. It was enough they were shouting.

Jake drove slowly south along the Edens Expressway from Old Orchard Road, where Lisa's office was situated, his hands strangling the wheel as if he were afraid that, should he loosen his grip, he would lose control altogether. Mattie saw the tense white skin pulling at his knuckles, distorting the raised and ragged boundaries of the scar that covered three of those knuckles, the result of a childhood accident he'd always refused to discuss. Was he tense because of the shocking news Mattie had just received, or because he was driving her to a possible tryst with another man? Did he really care about either?

Mattie had called home from the car to check her messages and learned that Roy was running an hour behind schedule. He'd suggested meeting at a steakhouse called Black Ram, located on Oakton Road in nearby Des Plaines. No problem, Mattie thought, except for Jake, who insisted on driving her.

"You can let me out over there," Mattie said suddenly, pointing toward the Old Orchard Shopping Center, just off the expressway on Golf Road.

Jake immediately flipped off the radio, the resulting silence as deafening as the shrieking it replaced. "Why there?"

"I have over an hour to kill." Mattie almost laughed at her choice of words. "I might as well walk around the mall."

"How will you get to the restaurant?"

Mattie thought that if he'd only worried about her as much before he walked out, they might still be together. "Jake, I'm fine."

"You're not fine," he insisted, confusion lining his face like a series of unfriendly new wrinkles.

"Well, I still have about a year left, so you don't have to worry about me."

"For God's sake, Mattie, that's not the point."

"No. The point is that I'm a big girl. And I'm not your responsibility anymore. I don't think I need your permission to go to the mall."

Jake sighed his frustration, shook his head, turned the car onto Golf Road, signaling at the entrance to the large upscale shopping center. "Why don't we go somewhere for a cup of coffee?" he suggested, obviously deciding to try a different approach.

"I'm having lunch in an hour," she reminded him.

"We need to talk."

"I don't want to talk."

"Mattie," Jake began, pulling into the first available parking spot, between a red Dodge and a silver Toyota, shutting off the engine. "You've just had a terrible shock. We both have."

"I said I don't want to talk about it," Mattie insisted. "As far as I'm concerned, the whole thing is a huge mistake. End of discussion."

"We need to figure out what we're going to do, how we're going to tell Kim, what steps we should be taking—"

"How come when you don't want to talk about something, then we don't talk about it, but when I say the discussion is over, that doesn't matter?" Mattie demanded angrily.

"I just want to help you," Jake said, his voice cracking, threatening to break.

Mattie turned away, not wanting to acknowledge Jake's pain. If she acknowledged it, she'd have to feel it, and she couldn't afford to do that. "Lighten up, Jake," Mattie said, opening the car door. "There's nothing to worry about. It's all a big mistake. I'm perfectly fine."

Jake leaned back against the dark leather headrest, his eyes drifting toward the tinted sunroof above his head. "Can I call you later?"

"What will your girlfriend say about that?" Mattie stepped out of the car, not waiting for a reply.

"Mattie—"

"How'd you get that scar on the back of your knuckles?" she asked, surprising them both, then waited, leaning on the car door, watching the remaining color drain from Jake's worried face, and the blue of his eyes go from murky to opaque. Spotlight on you now, Jake, she thought, knowing how uncomfortable he was discussing his past. Would he plead memory loss, grow sullen and evasive? Or would he make something up, tell her anything to get her off his back?

Jake absently massaged the spot in question. "When I was about four years old, my mother held a hot iron over my hand," he said quietly.

"My God." Mattie's eyes immediately filled with tears. "Why didn't you ever tell me?"

He shrugged. "What was the point?"

"The point was, I was your wife."

"And what could you have done?"

"I don't know. Maybe I could have helped."

"That's all I want now, Mattie," Jake said, managing to shift the focus of the conversation back to her, to get himself out of the spotlight's harsh glare. "To help in any way I can."

Mattie straightened up, looked toward the mall, then

back at Jake. "I'll keep that in mind." Her voice was cold, constricted. "Drive carefully," she said, shutting the car door and walking away without a backward glance.

Half an hour later Mattie walked into a small travel agency called Gulliver's Travel, located at the far west end of the Old Orchard Shopping Center, and dropped the two large shopping bags she was carrying in front of the first available desk. "I'd like to book a ticket to Paris," she said, sitting down before she was invited and smiling at the plump, middle-aged woman, whose name-plate identified her as Vicki Reynolds. Mattie quickly surmised that Vicki Reynolds was one of those people who made a habit of looking busier than she actually was, her hands constantly aflutter, her face pinched in mock concentration. Right now she was making a great show of entering information into her computer.

"If you'll just give me a second," Vicki Reynolds said, not looking up.

"I don't have a lot of time," Mattie told her, then laughed.

The travel agent glanced toward the two desks behind her, but both agents were busy with customers. "I'll be right with you."

Mattie sat back in her seat, grateful for the opportunity to sit down. She'd been running around like a lunatic since leaving Jake's car, racing from store to store, looking at this, trying on that, ultimately emerging with three new sweaters, including one in pink angora, two pairs of black pants, because you could never have too many pairs of black pants, a pair of Robert Clergerie shoes in forest green suede that the salesman assured her would go with anything, and a stunning new Calvin Klein jacket in bloodred leather. The jacket cost a small fortune, but the saleswoman claimed it was a classic and would never go out of style. She'd have it forever, the woman told her. "Forever," Mattie repeated, admiring herself in the full-length mirror. She'd worry about paying for it later.

She should also start thinking of buying a new car, she decided. She couldn't drive around in a rented Oldsmobile indefinitely. Sooner or later she'd have to buy a car of her own, so it might as well be sooner, although she'd never shopped for a car by herself. This would be a whole new experience for her, which was good, Mattie decided. It was time to experience new things. Maybe she'd buy herself a sports car, one of those spiffy little foreign jobs in bright tomato red. Or maybe something homemade, like a Corvette. She'd always wanted a Corvette. It was Jake who'd discouraged her, pointing out how impractical it was for her to have a two-seater car, especially if she had to chauffeur Kim and her friends around the suburbs. But Jake was no longer part of her decision-making process, and most of Kim's friends drove cars of their own. So, if ever there was a time for a shiny red sports car, this was it, finances be damned. Tomorrow morning she'd put on her pink angora sweater, her black pants, her green suede shoes, her Calvin Klein leather jacket, and go out shopping for a shiny new Corvette. Maybe she'd ask Roy Crawford to tag along.

"Now, what is it I can do for you?" Vicki Reynolds asked, finally looking up from her computer and greeting Mattie with an alarmingly line-free face, her skin so taut and stretched she looked as if she'd confronted a hurricane head-on.

"I'd like a first-class ticket to Paris," Mattie said, trying not to stare.

"Sounds good," the agent told her, hands fluttering, lips pulling back stiffly into something approximating a smile. "When would you like to go?"

Mattie ran through a number of options in her head. It was already October, and she didn't want her first time in Paris to be in winter, when the predominant color of the landscape would be gray. Summer was too crowded, full of students and tourists, and besides, what would she do with Kim? Much as she loved her daughter, Paris was a city she associated with romance, not teenage girls. She wanted her first time there to be carefree and romantic. Maybe she'd even talk Roy Crawford into joining her. "April," Mattie announced decisively. "April in Paris. What could be more perfect?"

"April in Paris it is," Vicki Reynolds agreed, her smile a straight line that twitched only slightly at the corners of her mouth, as Mattie leaned back in her chair and grinned from ear to ear.

"So, why do women do such terrible things to their faces?" Roy Crawford asked over his second glass of expensive red Burgundy.

They were sitting in an intimate corner of the small restaurant, its decor typical of most steakhouses, wood-paneled, masculine, dark even in the middle of the day, and they were eating fat, juicy steaks and baked potatoes heaped with sour cream, an indulgence Mattie hadn't permitted herself in years.

"Why do women do such things?!" Mattie's voice was incredulous. "How can you, of all people, ask a question like that?"

"What do you mean, Me, *of all people?*" Roy Crawford patted his full head of gray hair, smoothed a nonexistent wrinkle out of his pale blue silk tie.

"Because you keep trading in your wives for younger and younger models. You're living with a teenybopper, for God's sake."

"That has less to do with the way she looks and more with her general attitude toward life. You look very beautiful, I might add," he continued in the same breath.

"Thank you, but—"

"If you hadn't told me about the accident, I'd never have guessed."

"Thank you," Mattie said again, not sure why she was thanking Roy Crawford for being so unobservant. "But you can't seriously be trying to tell me that looks have nothing to do with why men go for younger women."

"I didn't say looks had nothing to do with it. I said looks were less important than attitude."

"So, if a middle-aged woman with great attitude walked in here beside a sullen young blonde with great tits, you'd choose age over beauty?"

"I'd choose neither, since I'm already lunching with one of the most attractive women in Chicago."

Mattie smiled, despite herself. "I suggest that the reason women, like the travel agent I was telling you about, feel the need to go under the knife is that they think they have no choice. They have to compete with women half their age for an ever-decreasing market of available men."

"Maybe they're not competing with other women," Roy Crawford said. "Maybe it's not men they're doing it for."

"What do you mean?"

"Maybe they're competing with themselves, with the image of who they used to be. Maybe they just don't want to get old."

"There are worse things than growing old," Mattie said.

"Name one." Roy laughed, took a huge bite out of his steak.

"Dying young," Mattie said, laying down her fork, her appetite rapidly evaporating. She shook her head, tucked her hair behind her ear.

"Live hard, die young, leave a beautiful corpse," Roy Crawford recited. "Isn't that how the saying goes?"

"Is that how you want to die?"

"Me? Die? No way. I'm going to live forever."

"Is that why you keep going after younger and younger women? As a way of staving off death?"

Roy Crawford stared across the small table, his fingers brushing invisible crumbs from the surface of the white linen tablecloth. "You're starting to sound a little like my ex-wives," he whispered.

"Why do men cheat on their wives?" Mattie asked, suddenly shifting gears.

Roy Crawford sat back in his chair, took a deep breath. "Is this some sort of test?" he asked.

"Test?"

"Do I get a prize if I come up with the right answer?"

"Do you *know* the right answer?"

"I have an answer for everything."

"That's why I asked you."

Roy Crawford took another sip of his wine, hunched his upper torso over the table. "Do you have a tape recorder hidden under that pretty silk blouse?"

"You want to search me?" Mattie asked, deliberately provocative.

"Now that's an interesting thought."

"First you have to answer the question."

"I forgot it," Roy said sheepishly, and they both laughed.

"Why do men cheat on their wives?"

Roy Crawford shrugged, laughed, looked the other way. "You know the old joke, Why does a dog lick its privates?"

"No," Mattie said, wondering at the connection.

"Because he can," Roy answered, and laughed again.

"You're saying that men cheat on their wives because they can? That's it?"

"Men are basically simple creatures," Roy said.

"Is that why you're here with me now?" Mattie asked.

"I'm here because you invited me to lunch to discuss buying some new art for my apartment," he reminded her.

"The one you share with Miss Teenage America."

"She's very mature," Roy said, with a sly twinkle.

Mattie smiled. "I'm sure she gives great attitude."

Roy Crawford threw his head back and laughed out loud, revealing a mouthful of perfect teeth. "That she does."

"Then, I repeat, what are you doing here with me?"

"Maybe the question would be better phrased, What are *you* doing here with *me?*"

"My husband's having an affair with another woman," Mattie said simply.

Roy Crawford nodded, the pieces of the puzzle falling into place behind his eyes. "And you're looking to return the favor?"

"That's part of it."

"And the other part?"

Mattie looked aimlessly around the darkened room, trying not to see her friend Lisa lurking behind the faces of the other women diners, struggling not to hear her ominous message in the hushed tones of the women's voices. "Maybe there is no other part," she said.

Again Roy Crawford laughed. "Well, thank you for your honesty, at least."

"You're angry," Mattie said.

"On the contrary. I'm flattered. I mean, I guess I would have been more flattered had you spoken of how handsome I am, how irresistible you find me, but revenge is good. I'll settle for revenge. When did you have in mind?"

Mattie searched his eyes for signs he might be mocking her, found none. "My afternoon is looking pretty free," she said.

"Then what say we get this show on the road." Roy grabbed his napkin from his lap, dropped it over what remained of his steak, and signaled the waiter for the check. "Where should we go?"

Mattie was slightly taken aback by the speed at

which things were progressing. This is what you wanted, she reminded herself, recalling the new satin underwear she'd purchased on her way out of the mall. "We might as well go to my place," she offered, knowing that Kim was planning to attend an after-school football game and wouldn't be home till dinner.

"Not a great idea," Roy said. "Outraged husbands have a way of turning up when you least expect them."

"There's no chance of that," Mattie said.

"He's out of town?"

"He's out, period," Mattie explained. "He moved out a couple of weeks ago."

"You're separated?" Roy Crawford looked stunned, as if he'd just crashed into a brick wall.

"Is that a problem?"

"It's a complication," Roy acknowledged, straining for a smile.

"A complication? I would have thought it was just the opposite."

"How can I put this?" Roy Crawford shook his massive head. "I quit school at sixteen, never even graduated. But I've done very well in life—why? Two reasons. One, I follow the opportunities, and two, I keep things as simple as possible. Now, if you were still living with your husband, then our getting together would be one of those great opportunities, a simple matter of two grown-ups getting together for a little fun. The only thing you'd expect from me is a good time. Opportunity without obligation." He paused, waved away the waiter, who'd approached with the bill. "The fact that you're no longer with your husband complicates things. It means your expectation level has changed."

"I don't expect anything from you," Mattie protested.

"You don't right now. But you will. Trust me, I speak from experience." He paused, looked around the room, then leaned in closer, as if about to impart some deep, dark secret. "At the very least, you'll expect a relationship. You *deserve* a relationship. But I don't want any more relationships. I don't want to have to remember your birthday or go with you to pick out a new car."

Mattie gasped.

"I've insulted you. I'm sorry. I didn't mean to do that."

"No," Mattie said, her head spinning from the combined speed of his rejection and the accuracy of his prediction. "You haven't insulted me. You're absolutely right."

"I am?" Roy laughed. "I think you're the first woman who ever said that to me."

"I give pretty good attitude myself," Mattie said. A woman with short, wavy hair passed by their table, and for an instant, Mattie thought maybe Lisa had followed her here, was about to shout her diagnosis for all to hear and assess. "I guess it wouldn't make any difference if I told you I might not be around that much longer."

"You're moving?"

Mattie shrugged, smiled sadly. "Thinking about it."

"Well, don't move too far away." Once again, Roy signaled the waiter for the bill. "My walls would be lost without you."

Live hard, die young, Mattie was thinking as Roy Crawford handed his credit card to the waiter. Leave a beautiful corpse.

TWELVE

Vou never tell me I look beautiful."

Jake groaned, flipped onto his back, then onto his left side, pulling the scratchy pink wool blanket up over his ears, trying to block out the sound of his mother's voice.

"How come you never tell me I look beautiful?"

"I tell you all the time. You don't listen," Jake's father said, his voice gruff, disinterested.

Jake heard the distant rustling of the newspaper in his father's hands. He groaned louder, in a vain effort not to hear what he knew was coming. He'd heard it before, had no desire to hear it again.

"Why don't we go out somewhere? Let's go dancing," his mother pressed, dancing into the forefront of Jake's dream, filling it with her blond hair and dark eyes, her wide floral skirt sweeping all other images aside. He saw her swaying suggestively in front of his father, who sat resolutely reading his newspaper and refusing to acknowledge her presence. "Did you hear me? I said, let's go dancing."

"You've been drinking."

"I haven't been drinking."

"I can smell the liquor on your breath from here."

His mother's pout filled the giant screen of Jake's unconscious mind. "You don't want to go dancing, fine. How about a movie? We haven't been to a movie in months."

"I don't want to go to a movie. Call up one of your girlfriends, if you want to go to a movie."

"I don't have any girlfriends," Eva Hart snapped. "You're the one with the girlfriends."

Jake flipped back onto his back, unconsciously humming his displeasure. *Time to wake up*, a voice inside his head was whispering. Whimpering. *You don't want to hear this.*

"Lower your voice," his father warned. "You'll wake the boys."

"I bet you don't tell your girlfriends to lower their voices. When they're screaming for more, you don't tell them to lower their voices."

"For God's sake, Eva—"

"For God's sake, Warren," she mocked. Jake saw his mother's face contort with rage.

Warren Hart said nothing, returned his attention to the newspaper in his hands, bringing it up in front of his face, effectively banishing his wife from his sight. No, Jake thought. That's the worst thing you can do. You can't ignore her. She won't just go away. His mother was like a tropical storm, her fury gradually building and gaining strength, sweeping away everything in her path, unmindful of whom she hurt, totally consumed by her need to wreak havoc, to destroy. She was a force of nature, and she could not be ignored. Didn't his father know that? Hadn't he learned it by now?

"You think I don't know about your little friends?" Eva Hart demanded. "You think I don't know where you go at night when you say you're going back to the office? You think I don't know everything about you, you miserable son of a bitch?"

Don't do it, don't do it, don't do it.

Eva Hart punched her hand through the middle of her husband's newspaper.

The memory lifted Jake's left hand into the air, brought it crashing to the bed with a thud.

His father jumped from his chair by the living room fireplace, tossing what remained of the newspaper to the beige broadloom at his feet. The small room seemed to shrink with his expanding rage. "You're crazy," he screamed, pacing back and forth behind the brown velvet sofa. "You're a crazy woman."

"You're the one who's crazy." His mother lunged forward, lost her balance, almost knocked over a lamp.

"I'm crazy for staying with a crazy woman."

"Then why don't you leave, you miserable bastard?"

"Maybe I will. Maybe that's just what I'll do." Jake watched his father grab his jacket from the hall closet and head for the front door.

You can't leave. You can't leave us alone with her. Please, come back. You can't leave.

"Don't think I don't know where you're going!

Don't think I don't know you're just using this as an excuse! Where the hell do you think you're going? You can't walk out. Goddamn you. You can't leave me here alone!"

Don't go. Don't go. Don't go.

"No!" Jake heard his mother scream, her fists pounding on the back of the door that slammed shut in her face, her anguished cries racing from the living room and down the hall of the tidy bungalow, pushing open the closed door to Jake's bedroom, the room into which his brothers had run at the first sound of trouble, the three of them piling up a mountain of books and toys against the door, the makeshift barricade useless against the force of their mother's growing hysteria.

Jake watched from behind closed lids as the three young brothers, ages three, five, and seven, huddled together in the safe space he had created at the back of his closet, his older brother Luke staring vacantly ahead, his younger brother Nicholas shivering with fear in his arms. "It'll be all right," Jake whispered. "We have water and a first-aid kit." He indicated the items he'd stashed away in the event of just such an emergency. "We'll be fine as long as we stay quiet."

"Where the hell are you, you miserable kids?" Eva Hart shouted. "Have you deserted me too?"

"No," Jake moaned, tossing back and forth in the queen-size bed. The child Jake put his fingers to his lips. "Ssh," he cautioned.

"How can you all desert me?" his mother cried out in the darkness of the tiny room. "Is there nobody in this miserable house who loves me?"

Jake's lungs felt the pressure of three children holding their breath. He groaned in pain, flipped onto his right side.

"I can't live this way anymore," Eva Hart cried. "Do you hear me? I can't live like this anymore. Nobody loves me. Nobody cares what happens to me. You don't care whether I live or die."

Nicholas started to cry. Jake lay a gentle hand across his mouth, kissed the top of his Buster Brown haircut.

"So, that's where you are," their mother said, her feet heavy on the brown carpet as she approached the closet door. Luke jumped up, grabbed the handle of the already locked closet door, held it tight as the knob twisted in his hands. "Damn you," their mother yelled, kicking the door before giving up. "It doesn't matter. Nothing matters." They heard a crash. My model plane, Jake thought, the one he'd spent hours painstakingly putting together. He bit his lip, refusing to cry. "You know where I'm going now? You know what I'm going to do?" Their mother waited. "You don't have to answer me. I know you're listening. So, I'm going to tell you what I'm going to do, because nobody loves me, and nobody cares if I live or die. I'm going into the kitchen, and I'm going to turn on the gas, and in the morning, when your father comes home from sleeping with his girlfriend, he'll find us all dead in our beds."

"No," Nicholas sobbed into Jake's arms.

"No," Jake said, pushing the blanket off his shoulders, kicking it away from his toes.

"I'm doing you a favor," their mother said, tripping over the books and toys she'd knocked over, falling down, picking herself back up, hurling a shoe at the locked closet door. "You won't even know what's happening. You'll die peacefully in your sleep," she muttered, stumbling from the room, a maniacal laugh trailing after her.

"No!" the child Jake cried, clinging tightly to his brothers.

"No!" Jake shouted now, his arms flailing out in all directions, slamming against his pillow, smacking into the space beside him. He heard a gasp, felt flesh and bone beneath his open palm, opened his eyes to the sound of Honey's terror-filled cries.

"My God, Jason, what's happening?"

It took several seconds for the child to grow back into the man, for the man's eyes to focus, for his brain to register where he was. "I'm sorry," he whispered, his forehead wet with perspiration, the sweat dripping into his eyes, mingling with his tears. "God, Honey, I'm so sorry. Did I hurt you?"

Honey wiggled her nose with her fingers. "I don't think it's broken," she said, reaching out to caress his bare arm. "What was it—that dream again?"

Jake lowered his head into his hands, his whole body clammy and cold. "I don't know what's the matter with me."

"You have a lot on your mind." Honey reached over and turned on the light by the side of the bed. Immediately, the distant browns of his childhood were replaced by the warm peach of his present surroundings. Honey tossed the red curls away from her face, smiled helplessly as they bounced right back. "Do you want to tell me about it?"

He shook his head, his hair wet against his forehead. "I don't remember half of it." A lie. He remembered every shrug, every shiver, every word. Even now, with his eyes wide open, he could see himself, a child of five, crawling out of his secret hiding place to open the window next to his bed, managing to pry it open only a few inches, but enough, he assured his brothers repeatedly, as they sat huddled together throughout the balance of the night, to make sure they were safe. The gas couldn't harm them now. "I guess I'm still not used to sleeping with the window closed," Jake offered sheepishly.

"You think the window has something to do with your nightmares?" Honey looked understandably confused.

Jake shrugged, shook his head, waved away her concern with a toss of his hand. He was a grown man, for God's sake. His mother had been dead for years. Surely he could learn to sleep with the window closed.

"I'm really sorry, Jason. It's the cats. Once somebody opened the window just a few inches and Kanga got out. It was days before I got him back."

As if on cue, both cats jumped on the bed. Kanga was an eight-year-old orange tabby; Roo was four years old and jet-black. Both were male, and neither had taken to the idea of sharing their space with a Johnny-come-lately, two-legged rival for their mistress's affection. Jake returned their dislike. He'd never been much of a cat person, preferring dogs, although Mattie had always refused to have a dog. Mattie, he thought, pushing Kanga off his leg and climbing out of bed, slipping a navy bathrobe over his naked body. Why was he thinking of her now?

He watched Honey disappear into the bathroom, her bare buttocks jiggling provocatively atop skinny legs, her hair a chaotic red mop. Seconds later, she emerged from the bathroom wearing a white terry-cloth robe, her hair gathered into an elastic band and piled atop her head in a conscious effort to impose order, although already several tendrils had come loose and were running down the back of her neck. "Why don't I make us some coffee?" Honey suggested, glancing at the clock on the end table beside the bed. "It's almost time to get up anyway."

"Sounds good."

"How about some bacon and eggs?" she offered.

"Coffee'll be just fine."

"Coffee it is."

You see, Jake thought. There was the big difference between Honey and Mattie right there. Mattie would have insisted on the bacon and eggs. "Are you sure?" she would have asked. "You should eat something, Jake. You know that breakfast is the most important meal of the day." And eventually, he would have given in, eaten the bacon and eggs he didn't really want, and felt stuffed and logy the rest of the morning. Honey took him at his word. No second-guessing for her. No trying to figure out what he really meant. He said coffee was all he wanted, then coffee was all he was going to get.

Honey wrapped her arms around him, kissed him full on the mouth. He tasted the toothpaste on her breath, smelled the scent of lilacs on her skin. "Maybe bacon and eggs would be nice," he said.

She smiled. "Nervous about today?"

"Maybe a little." He had an important meeting with a potential new client, a businessman of considerable wealth and influence who was charged with raping several women more than twenty years ago, something he adamantly denied. It promised to be the sort of high-profile, juicy case Jake loved. But he wasn't nervous about meeting the client. He was nervous about his meeting with Mattie, scheduled for later in the day.

Almost two weeks had passed since Lisa's devastating diagnosis. During that time, Mattie had sought a second, and then a third opinion. The doctors—one the chief neurologist at Northwest General, the other a neurologist at a private clinic in Lake Forest—were in complete agreement. Amyotrophic lateral sclerosis. ALS. Lou Gehrig's disease. A rapidly progressing neuro-muscular disease that attacked the motor neurons that carry messages to the muscles, resulting in weakness and wasting in arms, legs, mouth, throat, and elsewhere, eventually culminating in complete paralysis, while the mind remained alert and lucid.

And how had Mattie reacted to each fresh opinion? She'd gone out and bought a new Corvette, for God's sake, when it was dangerous for her to be driving at all. She'd rung up almost twenty thousand dollars worth of merchandise on her credit card. She'd booked a trip to Paris in the spring. What's more, she was still refusing to take her medication, despite the fact Jake had filled the prescription for her himself. What was the point in taking medication, she insisted, when she felt perfectly fine? The numbness in her feet had disappeared; her hands were operating splendidly, and she was having no trouble swallowing, talking, or breathing, thank you very much. The doctors were mistaken. If she had ALS, she was obviously in remission.

She was obviously in denial, Jake understood, wondering how he would have reacted to similar news. Mattie was a young, beautiful woman on the verge of a whole new life, and suddenly, boom! Weakness, paralysis, death. No wonder she refused to believe it. And maybe, just maybe, she was right, and everyone else was wrong. It wouldn't be the first time. Mattie was strong; she was stubborn; she was indestructible. She'd outlive them all.

"What are you thinking about?" Honey asked, although Jake could tell by her eyes that she already knew. "She'll be all right, Jason."

"She won't be all right," he said quietly.

"I'm sorry," Honey qualified. "I didn't mean to sound glib. I just meant she'll come to terms with what's happening. She'll start taking her medication. You'll see. You don't have to worry so much. Mattie knows you'll make sure she gets the best medical help available, that you'll be there for Kim. There's nothing else you can do." She kissed the side of his lips, entwined her fingers with his. "Come on. Let's get you something to eat. This is an important day for you."

"I'll be right there," Jake said. "I just want to shower, brush my teeth—"

"Okay. Holler when you're ready."

His eyes followed Honey out of the bedroom. Even beneath the bulk of her terrycloth robe, he could make out the dips and curves of her wonderful ass. He should have made love to her last night, Jake thought, instead of pleading exhaustion, allowing his worries about Mattie to drain him of energy. He'd make it up to Honey tonight. Or maybe even this morning.

He glanced at the mess he'd made of the bed, the blanket on the floor, the twisted pink-flowered sheets, the down-filled pillows pounded into near oblivion. Actually, the bed matched the rest of the impossibly cluttered room. Honey was one of those people who had trouble throwing anything away. She was a collector—of old magazines, of vintage costume jewelry, of unusual pens, of anything and everything that caught her curious eye. As a result, every square inch of apartment space was occupied by something. Loose coins and delicate chiffon scarves littered the top of her antique pine dresser; newspapers sat stacked on a small wooden chair, peeking out from underneath the array of silk blouses she rarely bothered to hang in her closet, a closet already overflowing with the more formal dresses and suits she never wore. Antique dolls, in dainty white lace, huddled together beneath the window, next to the colorful stuffed animal collection of her childhood. Baskets were everywhere. Small wonder there was barely room for any of his belongings. Already, they'd discussed finding a bigger place.

This couldn't be easy for Honey, Jake knew, entering the bathroom and tossing his robe over the two cats scratching at his toes. They protested loudly and darted from the tiny room as he stepped into the shower and turned on the tap full blast. Instantly a violent spray of hot water hit him in the face, stinging his flesh, like hundreds of malevolent insects. Bad boy, Jason, the water hissed.

Badboyjason. Badboyjason. Badboyjason.

Honey hadn't asked for any of this, Jake thought, positioning his head directly under the shower's wide nozzle, the steaming torrent of water washing away the sound of his mother's voice as the water tumbled off the top of his head and cascaded down his forehead into his eyes. Honey had fallen in love with an unhappily married man. She might have hoped he'd leave his wife. She might have hoped they'd eventually set up house together. He doubted she'd envisioned his moving in with her quite this quickly. He doubted she was prepared to deal with the fallout of his wife's lingering illness and premature death, that she was ready to be a mother to an angry and bewildered teenage girl.

The last several weeks had been a wild roller-coaster ride for all of them. They were still reeling, off balance, afraid for their lives. Except that he and Honey would escape with their lives. Mattie wouldn't be so lucky.

He'd been doing a lot of research in the weeks since Lisa Katzman had summoned them to her office. Not all patients succumbed as quickly as Lisa first suggested. Some lived as long as five years, and a full 20 percent of people with ALS reached a stage of the disease where, for no discernible reason, their condition plateaued. People like Stephen Hawking, the famous British physicist, who'd lived more than twenty-five years with the disease and functioned well enough to dump the wife who'd stood by him through most of those years, abandoning her for another woman.

Men, Jake thought, turning off the water with a sharp snap of his wrist. We really are cads.

He stepped out of the shower, dried himself with

one of Honey's rose-colored towels, wondered whether he'd ever get used to so much pink. Was it possible Mattie would live for another twenty-five years, slowly wasting away, a prisoner of her own body? Would she want to?

"Jason?" Honey called from the other room. He pictured her standing in the middle of the small galley kitchen amid her collection of antique pitchers and pink Depression glassware. "You almost ready?"

"Two minutes," he called back, using the edge of his towel to wipe the steam from the mirror over the sink, seeing his image in the glass blurred and distorted, appearing only to disappear again in the fine mist. How could he just abandon her? he thought, as Mattie's face superimposed itself across his own. She'd shared his life for almost sixteen years. How could he leave her when she only had a year or two left?

Or three. Or five.

How could he leave her to waste away into nothing?

You've already wasted over fifteen years of your own life.

How could he leave her to die alone?

We all die alone. Think of your brother. Think of Luke.

How could he leave her helpless, to choke on her own fear?

I've been slowly strangling to death all my life.

So, what's another year, maybe two?

Or three. Or five.

How could he go back when he didn't love her, when he'd finally worked up the courage to leave her?

You don't have to love her. You just have to be there for her.

What kind of man would walk out on her now? What kind of man would that make him?

Bad boy, Jason. Bad boy, Jason. Bad boy, Jason. Badboyjason, badboyjason, badboyjason.

Mattie had trapped him sixteen years ago, and she was trapping him again today. It didn't matter that she was dying, that she had no control over the situation, that she didn't want this any more than he did. The end result was the same. He was trapped. He was being buried alive along with her.

"Shit, goddamn, son of a bitch, shit!" he shouted, pounding his hand against the mirror, leaving a clear impression of his fist in the dull glaze.

"Jason, are you okay?" Honey stood in the doorway to the steam-filled room.

She seemed very far away, Jake thought, afraid that if he looked away, she would disappear altogether. How long would she wait? he wondered. "Honey—"

"Uh-oh. I don't think I like the sound of that."

Jake reached over, took her hands, walked her back into the bedroom, sat with her on the side of the bed. "We have to talk," he said.

THIRTEEN

I don't want to talk," Mattie protested loudly, storm-ing from the kitchen in an angry huff. "I already told you that. I thought I made myself very clear."

"We don't have a choice here, Mattie," Jake said, following her into the living room. "We can't just ignore what's happening."

"Nothing's happening." Mattie began circling the large room like a dog chasing its tail, extending her long arms, keeping her husband a comfortable distance away. She was wearing jeans, an old red sweater, a pair of ratty plaid slippers. He was in his lawyer's uni-form—conservative gray flannel suit, pale blue shirt, darker blue tie. Not an even match, Mattie decided, thinking she should have at least worn proper shoes. Except that she'd been having trouble with her shoes the last several days. She kept catching the toes against the floor, tripping over her feet. Slippers were easier.

She looked toward the windows that took up most of the living room's south wall, thinking of the recently drained pool lying outside beneath its protective winter cover, an ugly plastic thing that resembled a giant green garbage bag. Mattie always suffered from a kind of swimmer's withdrawal in those first few weeks after the pool was closed. This year was worse than most. Maybe next year she'd have the pool enclosed. It would be expensive, she knew, but worth every penny. That way she could swim every day all year long. Jake might balk, but what the hell. Let him balk.

Mattie was also considering reupholstering the two chairs in front of the window, replacing the gold-and-rose cotton stripes with something softer, maybe velvet, although she'd keep the beige-and-gold patterned wing chair and the floral needlepoint rug. Jake could have the baby grand piano that stood in the southwest corner of the room, unused and ignored since Kim gave up her lessons several years earlier. But she'd fight him tooth and nail for the small bronze Trova statuette that sat beside the piano, the two Diane Arbus photographs on the wall behind it, the Ken Davis painting at right angles to it, and the Rothenberg lithograph that occupied most of the opposite wall above the sofa.

Wasn't that why Jake was here? To divvy up the spoils?

That was what she'd assumed when he called yesterday, said he'd be over at around two this afternoon, that there were some issues they needed to discuss. But then he'd arrived on her doorstep, *her* doorstep, with a sad smile on his face, the kind of smile that made her want to kick his perfect teeth in, and a hangdog expression on his face that announced the seriousness of his intentions even before he opened his mouth, and she knew this discussion wasn't going to be about moving forward with their divorce, or deciding who got what. It was going to be a rehash of the last several weeks, more of the same subtle bullying that might work well with juries but didn't impress her one bit, the trying-to-get-her-to-see-it-his-way gentle pleading, the attempts to force her to face a truth she refused to acknowledge or accept.

In the last two weeks Jake had called at least once a day; he'd insisted on accompanying her to her doctor's appointments at Northwest General and the clinic in Lake Forest; he'd run to the drugstore to fill a prescription she told him she had no intention of taking; he'd made himself constantly available to her. In short, he'd suddenly turned into something he hadn't been during the almost sixteen years of their marriage—a husband. "Go back to the office," Mattie told him now. "You're a busy man."

"I'm finished for the day."

Mattie made no effort to hide her surprise. "God, I really must be sick," she said.

"Mattie—"

"Just a joke, Jake. What they call gallows humor. Anyway," she continued, before he could interrupt, "if you're finished for the day, why don't you spend it with your little friend? I'm sure she'd be thrilled to see you home so early."

"I'm not going back there," Jake said, his voice so low Mattie wasn't sure she'd heard him correctly.

"What?" she asked, in spite of herself.

"I can't go back there," he said, subtly altering his words, volunteering nothing further.

"She kicked you out?" Mattie was incredulous. He'd walked out on her after almost sixteen years for a woman who'd thrown him out after less than three weeks?! And now he expected her to just forget all about his betrayal, to bury her anger and hurt feelings and welcome him back with open arms? My house is your house? Fat chance, buddy. That's not the way it works.

"It was a mutual decision," Jake explained.

"You decided what, exactly?"

"That I should come home," he said.

"Home," Mattie repeated. "You're saying you expect to move back here?"

"I'm saying I *want* to move back here."

"And why is that?" The sinking feeling in the pit of Mattie's stomach told her she already knew the answer. He wanted to come back home, not because he loved her, not because he realized he'd made a terrible mistake, not because he wanted to be her husband, not even because his girlfriend had kicked him out, but because he believed she was dying. "This marriage doesn't need a second opinion, Jake," Mattie told him angrily. "It's over, finished, dead and buried. Nothing's changed since you left."

"Everything's changed."

"Oh, really? Do you love me?"

"Mattie—"

"Do you know that in over fifteen years of marriage, you never once told me you loved me? Are you trying to tell me that's changed?"

Jake said nothing. What could he say?

"I'll make this easy for you, Jake. You don't love me."

"You don't love *me*," he countered.

"So, what are we arguing about? We're in agreement. There's no reason for you to come back."

"It's the right thing to do," Jake said simply.

"According to whom?"

"We both know it's the right decision."

"And you made this decision when, exactly?"

"I've been thinking about it for several days now. It finally crystallized for me this morning."

"I see. And your girlfriend? When did it crystallize for her?"

Jake ran his fingers through his dark hair, sank down into the soft cushions of the sofa behind him. "Mattie, none of this is relevant."

"You're not in court now, counselor. I'm the judge here, and I find it very relevant. I direct you to answer the question."

Jake looked away, pretended to stare at Ken Davis's impressionistic rendering of a quiet street corner, the sun glowing pink through leafy summer trees. "We talked it over this morning. She agrees with me."

"Agrees with you about what?"

"That I should be here, with you and Kim."

"Your girlfriend thinks you should be home with your wife and daughter. How enlightened of her. And what is she going to be doing while you're here with your wife and child?"

Jake shook his head, lifted his hands into the air, as if to say he didn't know, as if to suggest it was no longer any of his concern.

"What did you tell her, Jake? I think I have the right to know," Mattie continued when he didn't answer.

"She knows the situation," Jake said finally.

"She thinks I'm dying." Mattie resumed her pacing back and forth in front of her husband, like a caged tiger, angry and ready to strike. "So, what, she's planning to wait me out, is that it? She figures she can hold on for a year or two, providing I don't drag it out too long?"

"She understands that I need to be here."

"Yes, she's very understanding. I can see that. And what? You'll keep seeing her on the side? Is that the plan? That way she gets to be noble and enlightened and understanding and a slut all at the same time."

"For God's sake, Mattie—"

"What's her name, by the way?"

Mattie saw a slight flicker in Jake's eyes, recognized it as a sign of indecision. Should he tell her or shouldn't he? Would it do any good? Would it advance his cause? What would she do with this information? Could she use it against him?

"Honey," he answered softly.

For an instant, Mattie thought he was talking to her. She felt her body sway toward him, her heart quicken, her defenses dissolve.

"Honey Novak."

"What?"

"Her name is Honey Novak," he repeated, as Mattie's body swayed to a stop.

"Honey," she said. "Isn't that sweet. Pardon the pun," she added, then laughed, a short, manic burst of energy. She was such a fool. One moment of imagined tenderness and she was ready to concede, give in, give up, agree to anything. "Is that her real name?"

"Apparently it was a childhood nickname that stuck," Jake said.

"How appropriate. Honey stuck because Honey's sticky." Once again, Mattie heard herself laugh, the sound sharper, more brittle, than the time before. "Honey's sticky," she said again, trying to stop the laugh from growing, metastasizing, spreading its poison. But it was as if the laugh existed quite apart from her, as if some alien life form had seized control of her body, and was using her lungs and her mouth to push forth its evil message. She couldn't stop it. She was its captive audience. "Oh God," she cried. "Oh God, oh God, oh God." And then she was gasping, gasping for air, gasping for breath, except that there was no air, she couldn't breathe. An alien force was laughing and gasping and coughing and choking the life right out of her body.

Instantly Jake was on his feet, surrounding her with his arms, holding her, until Mattie felt the awful sounds start to die in her throat, the coughing shudder to a halt, and her breathing gradually return to normal. Immediately she pulled out of her husband's arms, took a deep breath, then another, wiped the tears away from her eyes, swiped at her nose with the back of her hand. How long before her hands stopped working? she wondered, panic building inside the pit of her stomach. How long before she was no longer able to wipe away her own tears? Mattie walked over to the piano in the far corner of the room, slammed her hand down hard against the keys. A discordant fistful of sharps and flats shot into the air, howling their protest, like a wolf in the night. "Damn it," Mattie cried. "Goddamn it to hell."

For a moment nobody moved; nobody spoke. Then, "Can I get you anything?" Jake asked, his voice steady, although the color had drained from his face.

Mattie shook her head, afraid to speak. If she spoke, she'd have to acknowledge what they both already knew: that the test results were conclusive, that she was dying, that Jake was right—everything had changed. "I'm going to Paris in April," she said finally.

"That's good." The calmness of Jake's voice was betrayed by the bewilderment in his eyes. "I'll come with you."

"You'll come with me?"

"I've never been to Paris."

"You never wanted to go. You never had the time," Mattie reminded him.

"I'll make time."

"Because I'm dying," Mattie said quietly, a statement, not a question.

"Please let me help you, Mattie."

"How can you help me?" Mattie looked at her husband of almost sixteen years. "How can anybody help me?"

"Let me come home," he said.

Mattie sat alone on her living room sofa, slumped down in the same space Jake had occupied earlier, trying to make sense of the afternoon, of the last several weeks, of the last sixteen years, hell, she might as well make that the last thirty-six years while she was at it. She pushed her hair away from her face, wiped away what appeared to be a never-ending supply of tears.

Her eyes drifted toward the sun-dappled street of Ken Davis's large oil painting, on the wall to the right of the piano. It was a street much like the one she grew up on, Mattie realized, although this was the first time she'd made the conscious connection. Immediately, she saw a towheaded child of eight come skipping along that sun-filled street, on her way home from Lisa's house, eager to get home in time for lunch. Her father was taking her to the Art Institute. There was a major exhibition of impressionist paintings he wanted to show her. He'd talked of little else for weeks. Today was the big day.

Except where was his car? His car wasn't in the driveway, and it had been there when she went out this morning, just down the street, less than half a block away, to visit Lisa. And now her father's car wasn't there, although maybe he had to go out for a few minutes, to pick up something for lunch, and he'd be right back. There was no need to worry. Her father would be back in plenty of time.

Except that, of course, he didn't come back. He never came back. Her mother explained that her father had run off with some whore from his office, and although Mattie didn't understand what her mother meant by "whore," she knew it meant her father wasn't going to be back in time to take her to the Art Institute.

In the weeks immediately following her father's desertion, Mattie sat by her mother's side as her mother systematically erased any trace of Richard Gill from the house, disposing of his clothes in boxes she sent to the Salvation Army, burning whatever papers and documents he'd left behind, cutting his face out of each and every family photograph, so that after a while it was as if he'd never existed at all. Pretty soon, Mattie noticed her mother stopped looking at her as well. "Whenever I look at you, I see your father," her mother explained testily, shooing Mattie away, busying herself with her new puppy. And so, every day when Mattie came home from school, she raced to the photo albums to make sure she hadn't been decapitated, that she was still there, her child's smile assuring her that eventually everything would work out for the best.

It didn't. No matter how hard she tried or how desperately she prayed, nothing brought her father back or made her mother love her. Not the grades she received, not the scholarships she won. Nothing she accomplished accomplished anything.

And what exactly had she accomplished? Mattie thought now, extricating herself from the painting on the far wall, pushing herself off the sofa, shuffling toward the kitchen in her tatty plaid slippers. She'd exchanged one loveless home for another, devoted sixteen years to a man who'd left her for a whore of his own.

In the end, her life came down to three little words—she was dying. She chuckled, suddenly afraid. Afraid of the sound of my own laughter, Mattie realized sadly. An increasing occurrence.

Of course, there was still an outside chance the doctors were wrong. Perhaps if she saw another specialist, agreed to undergo more tests, went off to Mexico in search of a cure, she'd find someone who could give her a different prognosis, she'd find the happy ending she'd been searching for all her life. Except that there were no happy endings. There was no cure. There was only a drug called Riluzole. And all it offered was a few extra months. Mattie shuffled across the kitchen and lifted the bottle of pills from the counter.

"If I take them," Mattie said out loud, returning the bottle of pills to the white tile countertop, unopened.

How would her mother react to the news? Mattie wondered, tempted to pick up the phone right now and call her. Would her mother immediately start cutting her face out of the family photographs, or would she begin slowly with Mattie's feet, moving on to her arms and torso later, mimicking the course of the disease, so that eventually, only Mattie's head remained?

A father without a face. A daughter without a body. A mother without a clue. Some family.

And now Jake wanted to come home, to be a part of her life for however much of her life remained. He said it was because he wanted to do the right thing. But was it the right thing? And for whom?

"You'll need someone to drive you places," he'd argued, appealing to Mattie's practical side when all other approaches failed.

"I can drive."

"You can't drive. What if you have another accident? What if you kill someone, for God's sake?"

"Kim will have her license in a few months. She can drive me."

"Don't you think Kim will have enough to deal with?"

It was that question, startling in its simplicity, that

forced Mattie's capitulation. How could she ask Kim to be her sole means of emotional support, to pick her up when she fell down, to pick up after her when she was no longer able to pick up after herself, to pick up the pieces of their broken lives without breaking herself? Her beautiful little girl, Mattie thought, sweet little Miss Grundy. How would her daughter survive without her? "How can I tell you I'm leaving you?" she asked out loud, hearing the key turn in the lock.

"Mom?" Kim called from the front hall, the door opening and closing in one continuous arc. "What's the matter?" she asked, as Mattie appeared in the kitchen doorway. "You look like you've been crying."

Mattie opened her mouth to speak, but was distracted by the sound of a car pulling into the driveway.

Kim swiveled around, looked out the small window near the top of the front door. "It's Daddy," Kim said, clearly confused as she turned back to face her mother. "What's he doing here?"

FOURTEEN

"Do you swear to tell the truth, the whole truth, and nothing but the truth, so help you God?"

"I do."

"Please state your name and address."

"Leo Butler. One-forty-seven State Street, Chicago."

"You may be seated."

Jake watched from his seat at the defense table as Leo Butler, a balding and well-dressed man of sixty-two, withdrew his hand from the Bible and lowered himself carefully into his chair. Even sitting, he remained an imposing figure, his six-and-a-half-foot frame squeezed uncomfortably inside the small witness box, his shoulders broad beneath his brown cashmere jacket, his neck thick, his hands big and rough despite well-manicured nails. You can take the man off the football team, Jake thought to himself, but it wasn't so easy to take the football away from the man. Not when the man in question was Leo Butler, former college running back, who'd inherited his father's massive clothing empire at age twenty-five, only to run it almost into the ground ten years later. He'd been rescued by his wife Nora, who'd saved her husband's ass shortly after their wedding thirty-one years ago, only to shoot him in the back on the eve of their divorce.

Jake smiled at the small, fine-boned, white-haired woman beside him at the defense table, her hands neatly folded in the lap of her gray silk dress, the pronounced blue veins on the backs of her hands competing with the blinding array of diamonds on her fingers. "I paid for the damn things," she'd told Jake at their first interview. "Why shouldn't I wear them?" Clearly not as delicate as she looked, Jake understood then, as now. Tough on the inside, delicate on the out—the perfect combination for a defendant in an attempted murder trial, where stamina was as important as appearance, and appearance often as important as evidence. Jake knew that a jury often ignored what it heard in favor of what it saw. And wasn't one of the first things they taught you in law school that the *appearance* of justice being served was at least as important as justice itself?

In this case, the jury would hear about a bitter and unhappy woman, furious at having been abandoned by her husband for a woman younger than her daughter, embarrassed by the escalating openness of their affair, and desperate to retain her social standing in the community. The prosecution would show how she'd lured her estranged husband back to their home on New

Year's Eve just over one year ago, and pleaded with him to come back to her. They quarreled. He tried to leave. She shot him six times in the back. His girlfriend, waiting outside in the car, heard the shots and called the police. Nora Butler gave herself up to the arresting officer without a struggle.

Open and shut, the police proclaimed. Guilty as charged, the newspapers opined. Not so fast, said Jake Hart, signing on for the defense.

The assistant state's attorney, Eileen Rogers, an aggressive and attractive brunette in a tailored navy pinstriped suit, was on her feet in front of the jury, asking the witness to describe his business holdings and current social status, guiding him quickly and expertly through the years of his marriage, detailing the couple's bitter fights, the heavy drinking, the outright despair, right up until the day he asked for a divorce. Eileen Rogers then paused, took a deep breath, and lowered her voice to a dramatic whisper. "Mr. Butler, can you tell us what happened the night of December 31, 1997?"

Jake swiveled around in his chair, quickly searching through the rows of spectators until he found the one he was looking for. Unlike the rest of the spectators, Kim sat slumped in her seat in the middle of the fourth row, looking tired and uninterested. Even those who didn't know her could tell by her posture that she didn't want to be there. Her dark blond hair was twisted into a tight little bun on top of her head, and her bow-shaped mouth was twisted into an equally tight little pout that all but screamed her displeasure. Although her bored blue eyes stared straight ahead, Jake knew she was aware of his gaze. Pay attention, Kim, he wanted to shout. You might actually find what I do interesting. You might actually learn something about your father.

Not that she was remotely interested in anything concerning him, Jake understood. She'd made that very clear in the three months since he moved back home, speaking to him only when he addressed her directly, looking at him only when he got in her way, acknowledging his existence with eyes that wished he were dead. She was as protective of her mother as she was dismissive of him, as if one posture dictated the other. Clearly, if Jake wished to have a relationship with his daughter, he'd have his work cut out for him. So when he found out that today was a professional development day at school, he'd seized the opportunity to ask Kim to accompany him to court. "I think you'd enjoy it," he said. "It's a high-profile case, lots of drama. I'll take you out to lunch. We'll make a day of it."

"Not interested," came the immediate response.

"Be ready by eight o'clock," he insisted, still hearing the echo of Kim's loud groan in his ears. Something about his tone must have told her not to give him a hard time on this one, or maybe it was Mattie who'd been able to persuade her. Whatever the reason, Kim was dressed, albeit in sloppy jeans and a sweatshirt, and ready to go at the appointed time. She'd feigned sleep in the car on the drive to the courthouse, which was fine with Jake, who used the time to mentally fine-tune his strategy for the day's upcoming cross-examination. "Here we are," he said, pulling the car into the parking garage adjoining the courthouse, gently tapping Kim's arm. She pulled it away abruptly, and he felt as if his own arm were being torn from his side. Give me a chance, Kimmy, he wanted to say, running after her as she strode purposefully toward the elevators. "Kim—" he began, once inside the courthouse.

"I need to go to the bathroom." She immediately disappeared behind the doors of the women's washroom, not reappearing for a full fifteen minutes, until Jake wondered if she had any intention of ever coming out.

And now here she was, fourth row, fifth seat from the aisle, looking as if she'd been run over by a steamroller and was about to slide off the bench and disappear under the feet of the two middle-aged men sitting, ramrod-straight, to either side of her. I shouldn't have insisted she come, Jake thought, wondering what he'd been hoping to accomplish.

"Nora called my apartment at about seven o'clock that night," Leo Butler began, the deep baritone of his voice even and strong. "She said she had to see me right away, that there was a problem with Sheena, our daughter. She refused to elaborate."

"So you drove out to Lake Forest?"

"Yes."

"And what happened when you got there?"

"Nora was waiting for me at the front door. I told Kelly to wait in the car—"

"Kelly?"

"Kelly Myerson, my fiancée."

"Go on."

Leo Butler forced a cough into his open palm. "I went inside with Nora, who was crying and carrying on, not making any sense at all. I could tell she'd been drinking."

"Objection," Jake said.

"Your Honor," the prosecutor said quickly, "Leo and Nora Butler were married for over thirty years. I think he's qualified to know when she'd been drinking."

"I'm going to allow it," Judge Pearlman said.

"Go on, Mr. Butler," Eileen Rogers instructed.

"Nora admitted that our daughter was fine, that she'd just used her as a way of getting me to come out to the house, that she was upset because she'd received the divorce papers from my attorneys, that she was unhappy with my offer, that she didn't want a divorce, that she wanted me to come back home, that she didn't want me to go to the party with Kelly, on and on. She was becoming increasingly hysterical. I tried to reason with her. I reminded her that our marriage hadn't been good for a long time, that we were only making each other miserable."

That it was nobody's fault, that she'd be better off without him, Jake continued silently, squirming uncomfortably in his chair.

"Suddenly, Nora stopped crying," Leo Butler continued, his eyes reflecting his puzzlement, even now. "She got very calm, and this strange look came over her face. She said that as long as I'd come all the way out there, would I mind having a look at the fluorescent light over the kitchen counter because it had been making a funny noise. I said the light probably just needed to be changed, and she asked me if I'd do it for her. I thought, What the hell, change the damn thing and get out of there. I walked into the kitchen, and suddenly I heard this loud popping sound and felt a sharp tug on my shoulder, almost as if someone had pushed me. And then there was another pop, and another. Next thing I knew I was lying on the floor, and Nora was standing over me, with a gun in her hand and that eerie look on her face. It was then I realized I'd been shot. I said something like, 'My God, Nora, what have you done?' but she didn't say anything. She just sat down on the floor beside me. It was weird. I asked her to call nine-one-one, and she did. I found out later that Kelly had already called nine-one-one. I passed out in the ambulance on the way to the hospital."

"Exactly how many times had you been shot, Mr. Butler?"

"A total of six times, although, amazingly, all six shots missed my spine and vital organs. I'm only alive because my ex-wife was such a lousy shot."

The courtroom chuckled. Jake listened for traces of his daughter's laugh, was grateful not to hear any.

"Thank you," the prosecutor stated. "No more questions."

Jake was instantly on his feet. He walked toward the jury, which consisted of four men, eight women, and two alternates, also women. "Mr. Butler, you said your wife called you at approximately seven o'clock in the evening."

"My ex-wife, yes," Leo Butler corrected.

"Ex-wife, yes," Jake repeated. "The one you walked out on after thirty-one years of marriage."

"Objection."

"Counselor," the judge warned.

"Sorry," Jake apologized quickly. "So, your ex-wife called you at seven, said there was an emergency regarding your daughter, and you rushed right over. Is that correct?"

"Well, no. Kelly and I were getting dressed for a New Year's Eve party, and we decided to finish getting ready and stop at Nora's on our way to the party."

"So what time did you arrive at two-sixty-five Sunset Drive in Lake Forest? Seven-thirty? Eight o'clock?"

"I believe it was just after nine o'clock."

"Nine o'clock? A full *two hours* after your wife called and said there was an emergency involving your daughter?" Jake shook his head in feigned wonderment.

"Nora had pulled this sort of stunt before," Leo Butler replied, unable to keep the testiness out of his voice. "I wasn't convinced there was any real emergency."

"Obviously." Jake smiled at one of the older women jurors. Has your husband ever treated you so cavalierly? the smile asked.

"And I was right." Once again, Leo Butler coughed into his hand.

"I believe you said you were going to a New Year's party in the area," Jake said, suddenly shifting gears.

"The party was in Lake Forest, yes."

"A party at a friend's house?"

"Objection, Your Honor. Relevance?" Impatience played with the prosecutor's thin eyebrows, lifting them up and down.

"I believe the relevance will be clear shortly," Jake said.

"Go ahead," the judge instructed.

"A party at a friend's house?" Jake repeated.

"Yes," Leo Butler said. "Rod and Anne Turnberry."

"I see. Were the Turnberrys recent acquaintances?"

"No. I've known them for many years."

"How many?"

"What?"

"How many years have you known the Turnberrys? Five? Ten? Twenty?"

"At least twenty." Leo Butler's neck flushed red above the collar of his pale yellow shirt.

"Am I correct in assuming that the Turnberrys were also friends of your wife's?"

"They were friends of Nora's, yes."

"But Nora wasn't invited to the Turnberrys' New Year's Eve party, correct?"

"Rod thought it might be awkward to invite both of us, under the circumstances."

"The circumstances being that you were bringing your new girlfriend?"

"The circumstances being that Nora and I were getting a divorce, that I was starting a new life."

"A new life that didn't include Nora, but did include virtually all her old friends," Jake stated.

"Objection, Your Honor." The assistant state's attorney was on her feet. "Still waiting for relevance."

"Goes to the defendant's state of mind, Your Honor," Jake qualified. "It was New Year's Eve, the defendant was spending it alone while her husband was going to a party with all her old friends. She felt alone, abandoned, deserted."

"Objection," Eileen Rogers said again. "Really, Your Honor. Mr. Hart is making speeches."

"Save it for your closing statement," the judge admonished, instructing the jury to disregard Jake's later comments while overruling the prosecutor's objection.

"So, Mr. Butler," Jake continued, once again glancing toward the rows of spectators, trying to will his daughter's eyes to his, "you stated when you finally arrived at your former home, you found your wife in a highly agitated state."

"It had nothing to do with our daughter." Leo Butler tried clearing the defensiveness out of his voice.

"No," Jake agreed. "Your wife was upset about having received the divorce papers, you said. She wasn't happy with the offer of settlement. Isn't that right?"

"That's correct."

"What was the offer?"

"Excuse me?"

"What were you offering your sixty-year-old wife after more than thirty years of marriage?"

"It was a very generous offer." Leo Butler's eyes appealed to the prosecutor for help, but Eileen Rogers let the question stand. (He's doing my job for me, Jake could almost hear her thinking. Establishing a motive for the shooting. Damned if I'll object.) "She got to keep the house, her car, jewelry, fur coats, plus very generous alimony," Leo Butler said.

"And the business?"

"I inherited my business from my father," Leo Butler explained. "I didn't think Nora was entitled to any of it."

"Even though your business was falling apart when you married her? Even though she literally bailed you out of bankruptcy?"

"I think that's overstating—"

"Do you deny she used virtually all of her own inheritance to pay off your creditors?"

"I don't know the exact figures."

"I'm sure we could find out."

"Nora was very supportive," Leo Butler reluctantly agreed.

"But what had she done for you lately?"

"Objection."

"Withdrawn."

"You said your wife had been drinking before you arrived."

"That's right."

"You also stated she was a heavy drinker throughout your marriage. When exactly did she start drinking?"

"I couldn't answer that."

"Could she have started around the time you started beating her?"

The assistant state's attorney all but fell out of her chair in her rush to object. "Really, Your Honor. *When did you stop beating your wife?!*"

"I believe the question was, When did you *start* beating your wife," Jake said, as laughter filled the courtroom, "but I'm happy to rephrase that." He took a deep breath. "Mr. Butler, how often would you say you beat your wife during the course of your marriage?"

"Objection, Your Honor."

"Do you deny beating your wife?" Jake persisted.

"Objection."

"Overruled," the judge declared, as Eileen Rogers plopped back into her chair with an audible thud. "The witness will answer the question."

"I didn't beat my wife," Leo Butler announced, lowering his massive hands into his lap as if to hide them from the jurors.

"You're saying you never slapped her around from time to time?"

"I may have slapped her once or twice during the course of an argument."

"Once or twice a month, a week, a day?" Jake demanded, glancing over at Nora Butler, whose proud attempt to straighten her bony shoulders made her appear all the more vulnerable.

"Objection."

"Sustained."

"Isn't it true, Mr. Butler, that you once hit your wife so hard you burst her eardrum?"

"That was an accident."

"I'm sure it was." Jake spun around in a small circle, drawing the jurors effortlessly into his orbit. His eyes fell across the rows of spectators until they connected with the matching blue eyes of his daughter, her body now leaning forward in her seat. She pulled back as soon as she became aware of his gaze, resumed her earlier slouch. Jake almost smiled. "Isn't it true that virtually all your arguments ended with your slapping your wife around?"

"Objection, Your Honor. Mr. Butler is not the one on trial here."

"Sustained. Move on, Counselor."

"You fought with your former wife on the night in question, isn't that correct?" Jake asked.

"I didn't hit her," came the immediate response.

"But she had reasonable expectation to think you

might," Jake stated, waiting for the inevitable objection, which followed immediately. "You stated that your wife then became very calm and asked you to change a lightbulb in the kitchen."

"Yes." Leo Butler took a deep breath, visibly relieved at the change in topic.

"How did she look?"

"What?"

"Your wife. Ex-wife," Jake corrected, once again smiling at several of the middle-aged women on the jury. "How would you describe her demeanor?"

Leo Butler shrugged, as if he'd never given much thought to how he would describe the woman to whom he'd been married for more than thirty years. "She just became very still," he said finally. "Her eyes kind of glazed over."

"Glazed over? You mean, as if she were in some sort of trance?"

"Objection," Eileen Rogers said. "Mr. Hart is putting words in the witness's mouth."

"On the contrary, I'm just seeking clarification."

"Overruled."

"Did Nora Butler appear to be in a sort of trance?" Jake repeated.

Leo Butler went through his growing repertoire of assorted grunts, coughs, and squirms. "Yes," he admitted finally.

"And after she shot you, how did she appear?"

"The same."

"As if she were in some sort of trance," Jake repeated a third time.

"Yes."

"When you asked her to call nine-one-one, how did she respond?"

"She called them."

"No argument? No resistance?"

"No."

"How would you describe her movements? Sprightly? Sluggish? Did she run to the phone?"

"She moved slowly."

"As if she were in some sort of trance?"

"Yes," Leo Butler agreed.

"No further questions, Mr. Butler," Jake told him. "You may step down."

Jake watched the witness as he extricated himself from the witness stand and walked quickly, hunched slightly forward as if to disguise his great bulk, to his seat beside the assistant state's attorney. Score one for the good guys, Jake thought, sneaking another look at the spectator gallery, hoping to catch a congratulatory smile on his daughter's face. But when his eyes reached the fourth row, he saw only an empty space where Kim had been sitting. He heard movement behind him, and turned around in time to see his daughter as she slipped through the heavy wooden doors at the back of the courtroom and disappeared.

FIFTEEN

S o, what did you think?"

Kim shrugged, looked around the dark, decidedly dingy greasy spoon at the corner of California Avenue and Twenty-eighth Street. Her father had already apologized several times for the lack of fine restaurants in the area, although he assured her that Fredo's made one mean hamburger. Mean, Kim thought, thinking it an interesting choice of words. "I don't eat meat," she told him.

"Since when?"

"Since it's disgusting and cruel and fattening," she answered.

"You eat chicken."

"I don't eat *red* meat," she qualified. "Am I on the witness stand?"

"Of course not. I was just curious. I hadn't realized you didn't eat red meat."

Kim made a face meant to signal her supreme disinterest in the topic at hand. There were plenty of things her father didn't realize, she thought, wondering if there was any way she could get out of going back to court after lunch. That's when he'd asked what she'd thought of the morning's proceedings, although Kim knew what her father was really asking was what she'd thought of his performance.

"It was okay." She shrugged again, the gesture smaller, less defined than the previous shrug.

"Just okay?"

"What do you want me to say?" she asked.

"I'm just interested in what you thought."

"I thought it was okay." This time Kim didn't even bother to shrug. "Can we order now?"

Jake signaled for the waiter, who approached their small booth to the right of the rapidly crowding bar, pen poised to take their order.

"Do you have a Thai chicken salad?" Kim asked, ignoring the menu.

The waiter, whose wavy dark hair was almost the same shade as his skin, looked confused. "We have chicken salad sandwich," he replied with a heavy Spanish accent.

"I don't want a chicken salad sandwich," Kim said stubbornly. "They're loaded with mayonnaise. You might as well be eating a pound of butter."

"Chicken salad sandwich sounds good to me," Jake said, closing the menu and smiling at the waiter. Kim wondered if her father was deliberately trying to antagonize her.

"Two chicken salad sandwiches?" the waiter asked.

"No!" Kim all but shouted. "Oh, all right. But can you make mine with low-fat mayonnaise?"

"French fries or salad?" the waiter asked Jake, ignoring Kim altogether.

"French fries," Jake answered.

"Salad," Kim said, though the fries someone was eating at the next booth smelled delicious. "And could you put the dressing on the side?"

"Something to drink?" the waiter asked Jake.

"Coffee," he said.

"Diet Coke," Kim volunteered loudly.

"I read somewhere that diet pop isn't very good for you," Jake said as the waiter departed, shaking his head.

"Didn't I read the same thing about coffee?" Kim asked.

Jake smiled, which Kim found more than slightly irritating. Why was he smiling? She hadn't said anything funny or charming or even vaguely positive. Was he deliberately trying to provoke her? First he drags her into court to watch him browbeat some poor sucker on the witness stand until the jerk has to slink away with his tail between his legs, even though he was the one who got shot, for heaven's sake. Six times, no less. In the back! And then he gives her the choice of the courthouse cafeteria or this weird little diner for lunch. Who ever heard of a greasy spoon with a full bar, for Pete's sake, where visiting lawyers compete with local drunks for the bartender's attention, their clothes the only way to tell them apart?

"Where did you go this morning when you disappeared for so long?" Jake was asking.

"It wasn't long."

"Half an hour," Jake said.

Kim sighed, looked toward the door. "I needed some fresh air."

"Fresh air or a fresh cigarette?"

Kim's eyes shot to his. "Who said I had a cigarette?"

"Nobody had to say anything. I can smell it on your hair from here."

Kim thought about protesting, decided against it. "So?" she asked defiantly, as if daring her father to do something about it.

"So, you're not even sixteen. You know how dangerous smoking is."

"It'll kill me, right?"

"Good chance," Jake agreed.

"Mom never smoked."

"That's right."

"She's dying," Kim stated matter-of-factly, although she had to push the words out of her mouth.

"Kim—"

"I don't want to talk about this."

"I think we *should* talk about it."

"Not now," Kim stated.

"When?"

Kim shrugged, released a deep breath of air, heard her father do the same. "Did I miss something interesting while I was gone?" she asked. "You make mincemeat out of some other unsuspecting fool?"

Her father seemed genuinely surprised. "Is that what you think I do?"

"Isn't it?"

"I like to think I'm getting at the truth."

"The truth is, your client shot her husband six times in the back."

"The truth is, my client was in a hysterical dissociative state at the time."

"The truth is, your client planned the whole damn thing."

"It was temporary insanity."

"It was an act of cold-blooded premeditation."

Amazingly, Jake smiled. "You'd make a pretty good lawyer," he said.

Kim heard the unsolicited pride in his voice. "Not interested," she snapped, watching him wince. "I mean, really. How can you defend these people? You know they're guilty."

"You think all people charged with a crime are guilty?"

"Most of them." Did she? Kim wondered. Is that what she thought?

"Even if that were true," Jake argued, "our justice system is based on the premise that everyone is entitled to the best possible defense. If lawyers started acting as judges and juries, refusing to defend anyone they thought was guilty, the whole system would fall apart."

"Seems to me it's falling apart already. Look at you—you get guilty people off all the time. You call that justice?"

"To paraphrase Oliver Wendell Holmes, my job is not to do justice. My job is to play the game according to the rules."

"So this is nothing but a game to you?"

"That's not what I said."

"Sorry. I thought it was."

"You're telling me there's no room in your world for mitigating circumstances?" Jake asked.

Kim made the visual equivalent of a growl. What was he talking about now? "What's that?"

"Mitigating circumstances," Jake repeated. "Circumstances that lessen the severity of an act, that provide a justification—"

"For shooting your husband six times in the back? Good thing Mom didn't own a gun."

Jake paled, his chest caving forward, almost as if he'd been shot himself. "I'm just saying that things aren't always that cut-and-dried. Sometimes there are valid reasons—"

"For taking a life? I don't think so. I find it disgusting you would think so."

Kim braced herself for her father's outrage. Instead, she saw a smile playing with the corners of his mouth. "How about cruel and fattening?" he asked.

"What?"

"Sorry. I was just trying to be funny."

"By making fun of me?"

"Sorry," Jake said again as Kim fought back the sudden threat of unwanted tears. It was her father's outrage she'd been expecting, not her own. "Honestly, Kimmy, I didn't mean to hurt your feelings."

"Who said my feelings were hurt? You think I care about what you think?"

"I care about what *you* think," Jake said.

Kim sneered, looked away, focused her attention on the young man working behind the bar. She watched him pour a glass of scotch for one of his customers, continued staring at him as he wiped the counter, poured someone else a shot of vodka. Seconds later, he became aware of Kim's gaze and smiled. Kim did something with her lips she hoped was sexy and provocative.

"Is something wrong?" her father asked. "You have something caught in your teeth?"

"What? What are you talking about?"

The waiter approached with their drinks. "Sandwiches be out in a minute," he said.

"Can hardly wait," Kim said, letting her eyes wander across the small gathering of men and women around the bar. "Who's that?" Kim asked, referring to an attractive woman at the far end who was waving in their direction. "One of your girlfriends?"

"Her name is Jess Koster," Jake said evenly, although Kim detected a slight twitching of the muscles at his temples. He waved back. "She's an assistant state's attorney."

"She's very pretty."

Jake nodded.

"Ever sleep with her?"

"What?"

Kim watched the coffee cup almost slip through her father's hands. "Ever sleep with her?" she repeated, picturing her father leap across the scratched and narrow laminated table that divided them, his hands quickly surrounding her throat, throttling the life right out of her. How would he plead to the charge of murdering his only child? she wondered. Temporary insanity? Justifiable homicide? Mitigating circumstances?

"Don't be ridiculous," her father said, the words more painful than any imagined hands around her throat.

Kim felt her eyes fill with tears. She lowered her head before her father could notice them and slid out of the booth, grabbing her large black leather purse and pushing herself to her feet, looking helplessly around the room, eyes refusing to focus.

"What are you doing? Where are you going?" her father asked.

"Where's the washroom?" Kim demanded of the waiter as he approached with their sandwiches.

The waiter pointed with his chin to the back of the room. "Down the stairs," he called after her.

Kim walked briskly toward the back of the restaurant, watching the room blur with her tears. Damn it, she thought. How dare her father be so dismissive. Her question might have been out of line, but that didn't give him the right to mock her and call her ridiculous. She wasn't ridiculous. He was the one who was ridiculous, with his neat blue suit and sleeked-back hair, with his superior smirk and know-it-all attitude, lecturing her about the justice system when everyone knew there was no such thing as justice. If there was, her beautiful mother, who'd never done anything to hurt anyone in her whole life, wouldn't be dying of a stupid disease no one could even pronounce, let alone understand, while her father, who'd lied and cheated and devoted most of his life to keeping killers and other assorted lowlifes out of jail, was alive and well. Where was the justice in that?

Kim found the steep row of stairs at the back of the dimly lit main room and walked slowly down the steps, her purse slapping against her side as her hand trailed against the wall for support. In the background, John Denver was singing about the glories of nature. Sure, Kim thought, pushing open the door to the tiny women's washroom at the bottom of the stairs. Poor guy spends his life singing about mountains and sunshine and the simple joys of everyday life, and what happens to him? The experimental plane he's piloting runs out of gas, and he crashes into the ocean and dies instantly. Talk about justice!

Kim pushed open the door to the stall of the single cubicle and lowered the toilet seat, sitting down. She didn't need to pee. What she needed was a cigarette. And not some dumb ordinary cigarette either, but one of the special kind that Teddy had rolled for her on the weekend. "Come out, come out, wherever you are," she coaxed, searching through her floppy leather purse, finding several loose joints at the bottom of her bag and lifting one to her mouth. "What are you doing? You have something caught in your teeth?" she asked, mimicking her father as she lit the sloppily rolled cigarette, giggling even before she inhaled. She sucked in a big deep breath, felt the acrid smoke immediately scorch her lungs, as she held it for a full five seconds, the way Teddy had shown her. "All my troubles up in smoke," she said, slowly releasing her breath, the sweet taste of marijuana lingering on her tongue. She took another drag, leaned back against the exposed plumbing of the hospital-green wall, willed her body to relax. Teddy was right. Only two drags, and already her father's words had lost a large part of their sting. Mr. Self-Righteous. Mr. Mitigating Circumstances. Another drag, and nothing he said would hurt her. A few more, and who knew, even justice might return. My job isn't to do justice, he'd said, quoting Sherlock Holmes or somebody like that. His job was to play the game according to the rules.

Except that he didn't, did he? The rules of marriage dictated fidelity, loyalty, love. Jake Hart didn't play the game according to the rules there.

Kim closed her eyes, savoring the tightness in her chest. Why had her mother allowed her father to come home anyway? They didn't need him. She could take care of her mother until she got better. And she *would* get better, no matter what Kim had said earlier. The pills she was taking seemed to be working. She wasn't in any pain. She looked terrific. Occasionally her foot would fall asleep and she'd lose her balance, or she'd drop something, but that could happen to anybody. No way her mother was going to lose the ability to walk, to move, to speak, to swallow, like the doctors all said. Besides, scientists were *this* close to finding a cure, her mother had assured her. Surely the two of them could have coped until then without Jake.

Kim heard footsteps on the stairs outside the tiny room, listened as they stopped in front of the bathroom door. In the next second she heard the door open and close, bent down to see a pair of black pumps and shapely calves filling the narrow space between the toilet and the sink. Kim jumped to her feet, raising the lid and dropping the little that remained of her cigarette into the toilet. She flushed it down, watching as it disappeared. Then she frantically swatted at the air, trying to rid the small cubicle of smoke. Only when she was satisfied the air was clear did Kim venture out of her stall.

Kim immediately recognized the woman waiting by the sink as the assistant state's attorney who'd waved to her father. Jess Cousins, or Costner. Something like that. Kim smiled at the woman, who stared back at her without returning her smile. Sourpuss, Kim thought, washing her hands even though there was no need, leaving the room without a backward glance.

"Are you all right?" her father asked as Kim slid back into the booth.

Kim nodded, trying to concentrate on the chicken salad sandwich on the plate in front of her. But it kept slipping in and out of focus, and she had trouble getting it to stay still.

"I saved you some French fries," Jake said.

Kim shook her head, then immediately wished she hadn't. The motion made her dizzy. She lifted the sandwich to her mouth, took a large bite. "It's good," she heard herself say, as if her voice belonged to someone else.

"Look, Kimmy," her father said. "I know how difficult a time this must be for you. I know you have a lot on your plate."

"I'm eating as fast as I can," Kim said, and giggled.

"You know what I mean. I'm here if you want to talk about it."

"I already told you I don't want to talk about it."

"I do," Jake said, and Kim laughed out loud.

"So, what you really mean is that *I'm* here if *you* want to talk about it." She laughed again, very pleased with her cleverness.

"Kim, are you all right?"

"Fine." Kim took a huge bite of her sandwich, felt some of the chicken salad dribble down her chin. "This is very good," she said. "Fredo makes a *mean* sandwich."

"I know you've been upset about my moving back home," Jake persevered.

"Why *did* you move back?" Kim demanded, surprising herself with the vehemence of the question she hadn't meant to ask. "And please don't insult my intelligence by saying you did it for me."

There was a long pause.

"Do you even *know* why you moved back?" Kim asked. Then, "Never mind. It doesn't matter anymore. You're back. It's a moot point. Isn't that the expression you lawyers use?" She finished the first half of her sandwich, started on the other.

"You're very angry, Kim. I understand that."

"You don't understand anything. You never have."

"Maybe if you gave me half a chance—"

"Listen," Kim interrupted, slapping the remains of her sandwich down on her plate, watching it fall apart. "If my mother agreed to let you move back in after everything you've done, well, that's her business. I told her what I thought of the idea, but obviously she didn't agree with me, so what choice did I have? None. Whatever Jake Hart wants, Jake Hart gets. He wants to play around, he plays around. He wants to leave, he leaves. He wants to come back, he comes back. I guess my only question is how long you plan to stick around once Mom starts getting better." Kim struggled to put her sandwich back together, trying to scoop the errant pieces of chicken back between the thin slices of bread.

"Kim, sweetheart, she's not going to get better."

"You don't know that." Kim refused to look at her father. If she looked at him, she might toss what remained of her sandwich into his face.

"She's going to get worse."

"So now you're a doctor too, are you?"

"And it's important that we work together on this—"

"I'm not listening to you."

"—that we do everything in our power to make your mother comfortable and happy."

"To ease your conscience?" Kim shot back. "To make you feel better?"

"Maybe," Jake agreed. "Maybe that's part of it."

"That's *all* of it, and you know it."

Jake rubbed his forehead, shook his head, ultimately rested his chin in the palm of his hand. "You really hate me, don't you?" he said, more statement of fact than question.

Kim shrugged. "Aren't children supposed to hate their parents?" she asked. "You hated yours."

"That I did," he agreed.

Kim waited for him to defend himself, to point out the obvious differences between their two situations, but he said nothing. Her father rarely spoke about his childhood. Kim knew her father and his brothers had been abused. There were many times she'd wanted to ask him about it, and now he was handing her the perfect opportunity, and she wouldn't give him the satisfaction of her curiosity. He looks exhausted, Kim thought, almost feeling sorry for him. "Shouldn't we be heading back to court?" she asked.

Jake checked his watch, immediately signaling the waiter for the bill. Seconds later, leaving the cash on the table, Jake ushered his daughter toward the front of the restaurant.

"Jake," a woman called from somewhere behind them.

Kim turned to see Jess Cousins, or Koster, or whatever her name was, approaching. Her father quickly made the appropriate introductions.

"How've you been?" Jake asked.

"Fine," Jess Koster said, looking from Jake to Kim, then back again to Jake. "I was wondering if I could talk to you for a minute."

"Certainly."

"I'll wait outside," Kim volunteered.

"Is something wrong?" Kim heard her father ask, as she opened the door and stepped out onto the street, the sound of his words immediately picked up by the outside wind. Something wrong? the wind echoed. Something wrong? Something wrong?

Somethingwrong?Somethingwrong?Somethingwrong?

Sixteen

Mattie stood in the doorway to the guest bedroom, studying Jake's unmade bed. In typical fashion, he'd thrown the white-and-yellow-striped comforter over the top of the queen-size bed so that it *appeared* to have been made, but Mattie could tell from the checkered sheets peeking out carelessly beneath it that underneath the comforter they were a crumpled mess. How can anyone get a good night's sleep in an unmade bed? she wondered, slowly approaching. She reached over to fluff out the pillows, watching a pillow fly out of her hand and land on the night table beside the bed, almost dislodging the delicate pleated lamp shade from its white porcelain base. "That was cute," Mattie said out loud, plopping down on the bed. "And now for my next trick." She retrieved the pillow, propped it up behind her neck against the headboard, and lifted her legs to the top of the bed, checking her watch. Almost five o'clock. Jake and Kim would be home from court soon. She should probably start getting dinner ready, although she was feeling quite listless. Maybe they'd just order in.

Mattie closed her eyes, inhaling Jake's smell on the pillow behind her head. The pillow tickled her neck, like a lover's kiss. She'd always loved the way Jake smelled, Mattie acknowledged, imagining Jake's lips at her earlobe, his tongue grazing her hairline as he buried his face deep in her hair. She heard herself sigh, opened her eyes. "Don't go there," she said, unable to prevent Jake's hands from reaching through her subconscious to slide across her breasts and belly. Mattie reclosed her eyes, allowing her body to slide down the bed so that she was lying stretched out on top of it. Suddenly Jake was everywhere—beside her, above her, below her, on top of her. She felt the weight of his body as it pressed into hers, felt his legs gently prodding her own legs apart. "No way," Mattie said, sitting up sharply, knocking Jake's image roughly to the floor. "I am not doing this."

That's for sure, Mattie thought. In the three months since Jake moved back home, they'd had next to no physical contact. He'd simply moved his things into the guest bedroom without any discussion, as if he assumed this was what Mattie would want, or more likely, because it was what *he* wanted. For all intents and purposes, they were still separated. Jake's home consisted of the den and guest bedroom, while Mattie shared the rest of the house with Kim. Occasionally Jake visited, but for the most part he remained the outsider he'd always been, trying to be of help while maintaining a safe distance between them.

Even his routine hadn't changed that much. He was still working an average of ten hours a day. Assuming he *was* working, and not with his little friend, his honey, his Honey, Mattie thought derisively, knowing that even when Jake was home, his mind was a million miles away. At the courthouse. At *her* house. That on the rare occasions when his body actually sat by her side throughout an entire evening, his spirit was decidedly elsewhere.

His body, Mattie thought again, seeing it stretched out and naked beside her on the bed, her hand playing with the soft dark hairs on his chest, caressing his enviably flat stomach, his strong thighs. She pushed several fingers inside her mouth, sucked restlessly on their tips, heard a groan escape her lips.

The phone rang somewhere beside her head. Mattie extricated her fingers from her mouth, eyes still closed, and threw her hand toward the phone on the night table. "Hello?"

"It's Stephanie. Did I wake you?"

Mattie forced her eyes open, her body upright, her feet to the floor. "No, of course not. How are you?" She pictured her friend, short frosted hair, brown eyes, pudgy cheeks that perfectly suited the rest of her plump frame.

"How are *you*? You sound tired."

"I'm fine, Steph," Mattie said, with only a hint of impatience. Ever since she'd told her friends about her condition, they'd been flooding her with their solicitations and goodwill, offering to drive her to this appointment or that, to do her grocery shopping, pick something up for her downtown, anything she needed, they were ready, willing and eager to be of help.

Except they didn't help, Mattie thought, transferring the phone from one ear to the other. They hovered. Like waiting helicopters, poised to take flight.

"What can I do for you?" Mattie asked.

"Enoch and I were wondering whether you and Jake would like to join us for dinner tomorrow night. We're going to Fellini's, over on East Hubbard Street. It got a great review in last weekend's paper." Stephanie giggled, sounding disconcertingly like one of her ten-year-old twins. Enoch Porter had come into Stephanie's life six months ago, almost three years to the day since her ex-husband had wiped out their joint bank account and taken off for Tahiti with the babysitter. Enoch was Stephanie's revenge—ten years her junior, tall, gorgeous, and so black he shone.

"Sounds great," Mattie told her. "We'll be at Pende Fine Arts in the late afternoon, if you'd like to join us."

"I don't think art galleries are Enoch's thing," Stephanie said, and giggled again. "You're not doing too much?"

"What time should we meet?" Mattie asked, ignoring her friend's concern.

"Seven o'clock okay for you guys?"

"Seven o'clock is perfect. We'll meet you there."

Probably she should check with Jake first, Mattie thought, hanging up the phone. Maybe he had other plans. "Screw his other plans," she said, thinking of Honey, trying to imagine what the other woman looked like. In the next second, the phone was back against her ear. Mattie pressed in 411, waited as the automated voice welcomed her to the system.

"For what city, please?" the recording asked.

"Chicago," Mattie said plainly. What was she doing?

"Do you want a residential number?" the recording continued.

Did she? "Yes," Mattie stammered.

"For what name please?"

"Novak," Mattie said, clearing her throat. Was she crazy? What on earth was she doing? "Honey Novak. I don't know the street." Why had she added that? Did the recording care? What did she want with Honey's phone number anyway? Was she planning on actually calling the woman? Why? What exactly was she planning to say?

"I show no listing for a Honey Novak," a human voice announced suddenly, catching Mattie off guard.

Mattie nodded gratefully, about to hang up. Obviously someone was looking out for her. What had she been thinking?

"I do show three listings for an H. Novak," the operator continued, as the phone almost slipped from Mattie's hand. "Do you know the address?"

"No, I don't," Mattie told the woman. "But if you wouldn't mind giving me the three numbers . . ."

"There'll be a separate charge for each one," the operator explained, as Mattie grabbed a ballpoint pen from the drawer of the nightstand and searched in vain for a scrap piece of paper, ultimately scribbling the numbers on the inside of her left hand.

Not allowing herself time to think, Mattie dialed the first of the three numbers. The phone rang three times before being picked up. Mattie found herself holding her breath. What was she doing? What was

her objective? as Jake might say. What was she trying
to prove?

"Hello." A man's voice. Mattie quickly hung up the
receiver, her breath coming in short, uneven spurts.

Immediately, her phone rang.

Mattie stared at the ivory phone with growing
apprehension, raising it gingerly to her ear. "Hello?"
she asked.

"Who's this?" the man's voice demanded.

"Who's *this?*" Mattie asked in return.

"Harry Novak," the man answered. "You just
called my house."

Call display! Mattie realized with growing horror.
Or *69. Or another one of the growing number of
electronic horrors invading modern life. She hadn't
thought of that. She hadn't thought at all, for God's
sake. What was she doing? "I called the wrong number," Mattie explained. "I'm very sorry to have incon-
venienced you." The man hung up before she could
embarrass herself further.

"That'll teach me," Mattie whispered, noting her
hand shaking as she returned the receiver to its carriage, although even as she was saying the words, she
was remembering the number to circumvent the system. Once again, she lifted the receiver to her ear, tapping in *67 before dialing the second number.

This time the phone was answered almost immediately, as if the person on the other end had been sitting
by the phone, waiting for it to ring. Typical of a
woman involved with a married man, Mattie thought.
"Hello," the woman said. A low, somewhat raspy
sound. A nice voice, Mattie thought. A little saucy.

Was it her? Mattie wondered. "Hello," the voice said again. "Hell-lo-o." No, Mattie decided. The voice was too playful, too confident. Not the voice of a woman who lived alone, who didn't know the identity of the person on the other end of the line. Mattie was about to hang up, move on to the third and final number.

"Jason?" the voice on the other end asked suddenly, as Mattie's breath froze in her lungs. "Jason, is that you?"

Mattie dropped the receiver toward its carriage, watched it miss, land with a thud on the white carpeted floor. She quickly retrieved it, trying to return it to its proper place, but the receiver wiggled in her hands as if it were alive, and she dropped it again. Only on her third try was Mattie successful. "Goddamn," she whispered, her breathing increasingly shallow, almost painful. "Goddamn."

She sat on the side of the bed for several more minutes, the echo of her husband's name on the other woman's tongue repeating in her ear. "Jason," Mattie repeated out loud. Hadn't he always hated that name? Mattie threw her head back against the top of her spine, trying to regain control of her breathing, folding one shaking hand inside the other. "That was a very stupid thing to do," she admonished herself, pushing herself off the bed, quickly exiting the room. Time to get a grip. Splash some cold water on her face, put on a little makeup, give her husband something pleasant to look at, a reason to stay home.

Seconds later Mattie faced her reflection in the mirror of her bathroom as she reached across the cherry wood counter for her blush. She wondered what Honey looked like, whether she was tall or short, blond or brunette, slightly overweight or reed-thin. "I'm thinking Julia Roberts," she said, expertly brushing the powdered pink blush across her cheekbones. "That's better. A little color was definitely called for." As well as a healthy application of mascara, Mattie decided, reaching for the long silver tube, raising the mascara brush to her lashes. But the brush ignored her lashes and jabbed directly into her eye. "Damn it," Mattie cried as the brush dropped from her shaking hand and fell into the sink. She blinked furiously, the mascara jumping from her eyes to her freshly pink cheeks, leaving behind a series of little black streaks, like tiny scratches. "Oh, that's just great." Mattie sighed. "I look wonderful. The anti-Honey," she said, fighting back tears as she reached for a tissue, tried wiping the black stains from her face. "Now I look like I've been in a fight. And I lost," she said. You lost, she silently admonished her mirror image, using a wet washcloth to rub her face clean, watching traces of those thin black marks resurface, like a ghostly series of commas.

"Nonsense, I have only begun to fight," Mattie said, once again applying the soft pink blush to her cheeks. But her hand refused to cooperate, her fingers unwilling to close around the handle of the brush. She dropped it to the counter, watching her fingers shake as if being buffeted by invisible winds. "Oh, God," she said. "This is not happening. It's not happening." You're just upset because you did a stupid thing. Nothing else. Take a deep breath. Now another. Stay calm. Everything's going to be all right. This is nothing to get upset about. You're taking your medication.

You are not going to die. You're going to Paris in April. With your husband. "You're not going to die."

Mattie used both hands to lift the tube of mascara out of the sink. Slowly, she applied the mascara to her lashes with the greatest of care. "That's better," she said, as the trembling gradually came to a halt. "You're just tired and upset—and very horny," Mattie admitted with a laugh. "Your hands always shake when you're horny."

Things are going to change around here, she decided. Starting tonight. Starting with a little mascara. Continuing with a little wine at dinner. Maybe a midnight visit to the guest room. She'd never had any trouble seducing Jake Hart before. Of course that was Jake, not Jason. She didn't know this guy Jason at all.

Mattie heard the rumble of the garage door. "They're home," she announced to her reflection, satisfied that she looked all right. Better than all right, she decided, holding her hands in front of her face, satisfied the trembling had ceased. She fluffed out her hair, straightened the shoulders of her red sweater, took one last deep breath, and headed for the stairs.

She was almost at the bottom when the front door opened with a sharp whoosh and her husband and daughter exploded into the hall.

"Enough," Kim was shouting. "I don't want to hear anymore."

"I'm not through with you, young lady," Jake bellowed.

"No? Well, I'm through with you."

"I don't think so."

"What's going on?" Mattie reached the bottom of

the stairs just as her husband and daughter bounded into view. They look awful, Mattie thought, their eyes flashing daggers at one another, their cheeks flushed with rage. "What's wrong? What happened?"

"Dad's gone off the deep end." Kim threw her hands into the air, headed for the kitchen.

"Where do you think you're going?" Jake demanded.

"I thought I'd get a glass of water, if that's all right with you." There was no disguising the contempt in Kim's voice. What the hell happened? Mattie wondered, eyes appealing to Jake for an answer.

"She brought marijuana into the courtroom! Can you believe that?" The pained expression on Jake's face echoed the outraged disbelief in his voice.

"What? No! That's impossible."

"Of all the stupid, lame-brained stunts to pull," Jake sputtered.

"So you've said at least a hundred times since we got in the car," Kim yelled from the kitchen.

"I don't understand," Mattie said. "There has to be some mistake."

"The mistake was treating our daughter like a responsible human being."

"Responsible?" Kim called out over the sound of running water. "You mean like you?"

"Please, Jake. Tell me what happened."

"Can you imagine what would have happened if she'd been caught?"

"Think of the shame," Kim said from the kitchen doorway, lifting her glass of water into the air in a mock toast.

"You could have been arrested. You could have been charged and sent to juvenile hall."

"Would somebody please tell me what happened." Mattie was almost in tears.

"Nothing happened," Kim said flatly. "Dad's getting all bent out of shape over nothing."

"You smoked marijuana in court?" Mattie asked, incredulously.

Kim laughed. "Hardly."

"No," Jake said. "She saved that little stunt for the restaurant." Jake began pacing back and forth in front of Mattie. "I take her over to Fredo's—"

"A major dump," Kim interjected.

"She acts like a total spoiled brat—"

"Hey, I didn't want to be there in the first place. The whole stupid day was your idea."

"The place is crawling with lawyers and cops, and she goes down to the bathroom and smokes dope. Lucky it was a friend of mine who discovered her."

"Yeah. Real lucky," Kim said. "She should have minded her own damn business."

"She's an assistant state's attorney, for God's sake. She could have had you arrested."

"But she didn't, did she? So what's the big deal? I made a mistake. I said I was sorry. I won't do it again. Case closed. You win. Another poor sucker bites the dust."

"Kim, I don't understand," Mattie said, trying to make sense of what she was hearing.

"What is it you don't understand, Mother?" Kim snapped.

Mattie felt the word *Mother* slap against her cheek,

as if she'd been struck. Tears filled her eyes, ran down her face.

"Watch how you talk to your mother," Jake said.

"My mother is perfectly capable of speaking for herself. She isn't dead yet!"

"Oh, God," Mattie sighed, the air rushing from her body as if she'd been punctured by a sharp object.

Jake's face grew beet red, as if someone had wiped a paintbrush across his skin, starting with his neck and stroking upward until it reached his scalp. He looked as if he were about to burst. "How could you say such a horrible thing?" he asked.

"I didn't mean it," Kim protested. "Mom, you know I didn't mean it the way it came out."

"You disgust me," Jake told his daughter.

"*You* disgust *me*," came the immediate reply.

"That's enough. Both of you," Mattie interjected, the bottoms of her feet tingling ominously. "If we could just go into the living room and sit down, discuss this calmly."

"I'm going up to my room." Kim took several long strides toward the stairs.

"You're not going anywhere," Mattie said, grabbing her daughter's arm.

"What? You're taking *his* side?"

"You're not giving me much of a choice."

Kim wrestled her arm away from her mother with such force that Mattie lost her balance. She teetered for several seconds on feet she could barely feel, then crumpled to the floor, trembling hands extended in front of her in a vain effort to block her fall.

Kim was instantly at her side, on her knees, trying to

help her up. "Mom, I'm so sorry," she cried repeatedly. "It was an accident. You know it was an accident."

"Leave her alone," Jake ordered, approaching the two women, gathering Mattie into his arms. "Get away from her."

"I'm sorry. I'm so sorry," Kim kept saying, refusing to let go of Mattie's arm as Mattie struggled to her feet.

"Haven't you done enough damage for one day?" Jake demanded, pushing Kim aside, so that it was her turn to lose her balance. Kim's hands shot reflexively into the air, the glass she was holding flying toward the ceiling, the water spurting into the air like a geyser before the glass came crashing to the floor, bouncing across the rug and shattering against the wall. "Now look what you've done," Jake was shouting.

"What *I've* done?" Kim yelled back even louder.

"Please, can we just stop this now?" Mattie pleaded.

"Clean the mess up," Jake instructed his daughter. "You made it. You clean it."

"Goddamn you," Jake shouted, his hand swooping into the air, ready to strike.

"You want to hit me?" Kim screamed. "Go on, Daddy. Hit me. Hit me!"

Mattie held her breath as Jake's arm swayed in the air, lingering above his head for what felt like an eternity before it eventually collapsed at his side. Behind her, she heard Kim's footsteps racing up the stairs, the door to her room slamming shut. Mattie watched as Jake fell back against the wall, hands over his closed eyes, his skin ashen. "Are you all right?" she asked.

"I almost hit her."

"But you didn't."

"I wanted to. I came so close."

"But you didn't," Mattie repeated. She reached out her hand, withdrew it when she saw it shaking. She knew how disappointed Jake must feel, how much he'd wanted his daughter to be proud of him. *I'm proud of you*, she wanted to say, but said nothing, standing still by his side until she could no longer feel the bottoms of her feet. "I think I need to sit down."

Jake led her into the living room, wiping tears away from his eyes and nose, settling her into the soft beige sofa, all without a spoken word.

"Why don't you sit down?" she offered.

He swayed from one foot to the other, as if physically weighing his alternatives. "Listen, do you think you'll be all right if I go out for a few minutes? I could really use some air."

Mattie swallowed her disappointment. Why won't you let me comfort you? she asked silently. "I'll be fine," she said out loud.

"I'll clean everything up when I get back."

"Do you want me to come with you?" Foolish question, Mattie understood as Jake shook his head. Of course he didn't want her to go with him. What kind of man takes his wife along to visit his girlfriend?

"You're sure you'll be okay?"

"I'm fine, Jake," Mattie repeated.

"I'll be back soon," he said.

Mattie's eyes followed him out of the room. "Drive carefully," she said.

SEVENTEEN

"Jake? Jake, are you ready?"

Mattie stole a final glance at her reflection in the bathroom mirror, noting gratefully that everything seemed to be in its proper place, no unwanted black squiggles under her eyes, no stray hairs escaping their jeweled clasp at the back of her neck. Pretty in pink, she thought, adjusting the satin collar of her cashmere sweater, making sure the vintage rhinestones at her ears were securely fastened. The only discordant fashion note were three phone numbers scribbled across the palm of Mattie's left hand, fading reminders of yesterday's folly. The numbers had refused to disappear despite repeated scrubbings, clinging to Mattie's skin with the stubbornness of a tattoo. Hopefully Jake wouldn't notice, Mattie thought, deciding not to worry. It was doubtful Jake would get close enough to notice. A slight tremor teased her fingers. Mattie thrust her hands into the pockets of her gray slacks and exited the room.

"Jake? Are you almost ready?"

Still no response.

"Jake?"

Mattie walked down the hall to the guest room, peeked inside the open door. "Jake?" But the room was empty, the white-and-yellow-striped comforter tossed carelessly across the bed, exactly as it had been the day before. Had the bed even been slept in? Mattie wondered, turning away.

The closed door to Kim's bedroom stood before her like a silent and implacable rebuke. Her daughter had barricaded herself in her room last night and hadn't stirred since. She'd refused dinner and hadn't appeared for either breakfast or lunch. She must be very hungry, Mattie thought, knowing how proud her daughter was, how stubborn. Just like her father, Mattie thought, knocking gently on the bedroom door, cautiously pushing it open when she received no reply.

The room was in darkness, the shutters closed, no lights on. It took a few seconds for Mattie's eyes to adjust, to differentiate between the bed against the far wall and the chest of drawers beside it, the desk to her right and the straight-backed chair in front of it. Abandoned articles of clothing covered every available surface. Mattie inched her way forward, the toe of her black shoe hitting a discarded cassette on the floor, sending it flying into the closet door. The figure in the bed stirred, sat up, pushed a matted tuft of hair away from her face, stared toward Mattie, said nothing.

"Kim? Are you all right?"

"What time is it?" Kim asked, her voice husky with sleep.

Mattie peered through the semidarkness toward the clock on the wall. The clock was the size and shape of a small watermelon, its bright rosy pink face surrounded by a dark green frame, its minutes represented by a series of black seeds. "Almost four o'clock," Mattie said. "Have you been asleep all day?"

Kim shrugged. "On and off. What's it like out?"

"Sunny. Cold. January," Mattie said. "Are you all right?" she asked again.

"I'm fine." Kim pushed her hair away from her forehead, a gesture she'd inherited from her father, one that said she was already impatient with the conversation, and looked toward the windows. "You going somewhere?"

"A photography exhibit, and then we're meeting Stephanie Slopen and a friend of hers for dinner. You want to join us?"

Even in the darkness, Mattie had no trouble making out the sneer on her daughter's face. "I'm grounded till my fortieth birthday, remember?"

"What you did was very wrong," Mattie reminded her.

"Is that what you came in here to tell me?"

"No."

"What then?"

"I'm worried about you."

"Don't you have enough to worry about without worrying about me?"

Mattie began mentally straightening up the room,

picking her daughter's clothes off the floor with her eyes, returning each item to its proper place. Kim had always been so neat, so precise. When had she turned into such a slob? "But I do worry about you. I know how confusing a time this must be for you."

"I'm fine, Mom," Kim said.

"I was thinking, maybe you should talk to someone. . . ."

"Someone? You mean like a psychiatrist?"

"Maybe."

"You think I'm crazy?"

"No, of course not," Mattie said quickly. "I just think it might help if you had someone to talk to."

"I have you." Kim's large eyes raced through the darkness toward her mother. "Don't I?"

"Of course you do. But I'm part of the problem, Kim," Mattie told her.

"You're not the problem. *He* is." There was no need to specify who *he* was.

"Your father loves you very much. You know that."

"Yeah, sure. Enjoy your dinner." Kim flopped back down in bed, covered her head with her blankets, a clear signal the conversation was over.

Mattie hesitated for several seconds, then carefully backed out of the room, closing the door behind her. There was a great deal that still needed to be said, but she didn't have the energy to say it. Or the time, she thought, checking her watch. Where was Jake? They needed to get going.

"Jake?" Mattie called again, heading down the stairs.

She knew he was on the phone even before she saw

his closed office door, knew he was speaking to Honey even before she lifted the extension in the kitchen to her ear, knew what she would hear even before she heard him say the words. "I'm sorry," he was saying.

"Stop apologizing," Honey told him, in her now-familiar rasp.

"She made these plans without my knowledge. I can't get out of it."

"I'm the one who should be sorry. I should have been here for you yesterday."

"You had no way of knowing."

"I don't know why I picked yesterday, of all days, to go to the gym so early."

"Tomorrow night," Jake interrupted forcefully. "Tomorrow night, no matter what."

"Sounds good. Where should we go?"

"I was hoping we'd stay in."

"Sounds even better. Seven o'clock?"

"I can't wait to see you," Jake said.

"I love you."

Mattie hung up the phone before she could hear her husband's reply.

"What do you think?" Mattie asked, the eavesdropped conversation still echoing in her ears as she stood beside Jake in the center of the small gallery on Erie Street, around the corner from the Magnificent Mile. The floors of the gallery were bleached wooden strips, the lighting high and recessed. A large front window took up half the north wall. The other walls were filled with a stunning array of large color photographs: a young Mexican woman in a bright floral dress, with flowers in her hair and a crucifix around her neck, posing in front of a painted backdrop of the Virgin Mary floating in a cloud-flecked sky, the painted flowers beneath the Virgin's feet blending into the flowers along the bottom of the girl's dress; a group of hand-painted angels, on a cracked turquoise wall, watching over a small black-and-white photo of a young man; a large TV sitting incongruously on a table in front of a painted backdrop of an old-fashioned landscape; a fat, sour-faced Latina in a gold-flecked blue dress staring accusingly into the camera, more fearsome than the array of uniformed generals sitting behind her.

"I like them," Jake said.

(*I love you*, Honey whispered.)

"Why?" Mattie asked. (Why are you here?)

Jake laughed self-consciously. "I'm a lawyer, Mattie," he said. "What do I know about art? Do *you* like them?"

"I love them," Mattie said, then bit down on her tongue.

(*I love you*, Honey whispered.)

"Why?"

Why am *I* here? Mattie wondered, trying to force the earlier conversation from her mind. "The use of color and composition," she explained, using the sound of her own voice to banish unwanted echoes. "The way the photographer combines reality and artifice, using one to compliment and accentuate the other, occasionally blurring the boundaries between the two. The way he uses inanimate objects to make a statement about the self-image of a culture. The way these pic-

tures combine visual language with personal understanding."

"You see all that?"

Mattie smiled, despite herself. "I read the brochure
before we got here."

Again Jake laughed. Mattie realized how much she
liked the sound of his laughter, how little she'd heard
of it over the years. Does he laugh with Honey? she
wondered. (*I can't wait to see you,* he'd said.) She
focused her attention on a photograph of a young man
posed provocatively in front of a wall filled with
painted images of war—soldiers, tanks, guns, explo-
sions. The boy stood with his back to the camera, his
red T-shirt pulled up and away from his faded denim
jeans to expose a large white bandage that ran, like a
jagged scar, across his back.

"Powerful stuff," Jake said. "Who's the photographer?"

"Rafael Goldchain. Born in Chile in 1956. His
Jewish grandparents emigrated from Germany to
Argentina in the 1930s. His parents eventually moved
to Chile, where Rafael was born, then settled in
Mexico in the early 1970s. Rafael moved to Israel,
where he studied at the Hebrew University of
Jerusalem, and then, in 1976, he emigrated to Toronto,
Canada, where he's lived ever since."

"Pretty mixed-up guy."

He's not the only one, Mattie thought, glancing
back at the brochure in her hands. "He says that when
he's photographing in Latin America, he feels he's
engaged in a purposeful and meaningful process of

self-discovery," she read out loud. "By creating within that culture, he enhances his sense of belonging."

"So he's using his profession as a way of working out his own issues," Jake said.

I guess we all do that to one degree or another, Mattie thought.

"So now that you've viewed this exhibit," Jake continued, "what do you do now?"

He's asking what I've been doing for the last sixteen years, Mattie thought with wonder, not sure whether to be angry or pleased. Maybe if you'd taken the time to get to know me, she thought, the same kind of time you've squandered over the years on women like Honey Novak, then you wouldn't have to ask.

(*Tomorrow night,* she heard Jake say. *Tomorrow night, no matter what.*)

"I decide whether I have a client who might appreciate one of these images," she told him, pointing to a photograph on the far wall. In the picture, an old-fashioned jukebox sat in the corner of a blue-green room, the jukebox all but overwhelmed by posters of half-naked women pinned to the walls, the emphasis on one poster in particular, a woman wearing a pink corset and black nylon stockings, her fingers hooked into the sides of her panties, about to pull them down over her rounded backside. "I was thinking this one might look particularly good above the sofa in your office."

Jake laughed, clearly not sure if she was serious. "I'm not sure my partners would appreciate it. They still haven't gotten over the baked potato."

Mattie understood he was referring to the Claes

Oldenburg lithograph she'd persuaded him to hang on the wall behind his desk. "I was thinking of your office at home."

Jake nodded, a guilty blush suddenly flashing across his face. "I'm sorry, Mattie," he stammered. "I've been meaning to spend more time at home."

It took Mattie a few seconds to connect one thought to the other. "Jake, I didn't mean—"

"It's just been so hectic—"

"I only meant—"

"—what with the trial—"

"Honestly, Jake, I wasn't implying—"

"As soon as this trial is over—"

"Stop apologizing," Mattie said.

(*Stop apologizing,* Honey echoed.)

Mattie gasped, brought her hand to her mouth. Did her husband spend his life apologizing to women? she wondered. Apologizing and seeking absolution?

"What's that?" Jake asked.

"What's what?" Mattie looked toward a young couple gesticulating broadly in front of the photograph of the surly-looking woman in the gold-flecked blue dress.

"On your hand." Jake caught Mattie's left hand in his, turning it palm-up before she was able to twist it away.

Mattie mumbled something about needing a phone number and not being able to find a piece of paper. Not quite a lie. Not nearly the truth. Jake seemed to accept it. Why not? Mattie wondered, hiding her hand in her pocket. She'd been accepting similar mumblings for years.

"You really think this would look good over the sofa in my office?" Jake asked, his focus returning to the photograph.

Now it was her turn to wonder if he was serious. "What do you think?" she asked.

"I think it's perfect," he said, and laughed.

"Sold to the gentleman with the great laugh." Mattie found herself laughing as well.

"Thanks for letting me tag along today," Jake said, after they'd completed arrangements to purchase the photograph. "I really enjoyed myself."

"Thank *you*," Mattie said in return. "I'm sure there were places you'd rather be."

(*She made these plans without my knowledge. I can't get out of it.*)

"Can't think of one," Jake said, managing to sound as if he meant it. He checked his watch. "Hey, it's getting late. You hungry?"

Mattie nodded, allowing him to take her arm. "Starved," she said.

The restaurant was already full to the rafters by the time Mattie and Jake pushed through the glass-paneled front door just after seven o'clock. A large number of patrons were stuffed, like well-dressed sausages, into a small waiting area, and stood jostling for position around the self-satisfied maître d'. Several delicate perfumes fought a losing battle with a conflicting variety of more oppressive scents, including a cigar being smoked by a ponytailed young woman at the bar. "Excuse me, but we have a reservation," Mattie heard someone say.

"Everyone here has a reservation," came the maître d's chilling response.

"Half of Chicago must be here," Jake said, shouting to be heard above the persistent roar of the impatient crowd.

"That's what happens when the papers give you a good review," Mattie said, as Jake made a motion to indicate he couldn't hear her. He lowered his ear close to her mouth so that she could repeat what she'd said. Mattie leaned forward, her nose brushing against the side of his neck. He smells so wonderful, she thought, losing her balance as a woman in a low-cut black dress pushed into her. She stumbled, her lips grazing Jake's ear.

"Are you all right?" he asked, catching her before she fell.

Mattie nodded, looking past the crowd into the main room, which struck Mattie as no different from most of the other upscale restaurants in the area—a large square room with too many tables crowded between too many mirrors, a line of banquettes running along one side, an overstocked bar along the other. "There's Stephanie!" Mattie pointed toward the last of the banquettes, where a middle-aged white woman with frosted hair was passionately embracing a young black man.

Mattie and Jake began zigzagging their way through the tables toward the booth at the far end of the room.

"Mattie?"

Mattie felt a hand on her arm.

Roy Crawford jumped up from his chair, leaned forward to give Mattie a kiss on the cheek. "I see I'm not the only one who reads the restaurant reviews. How are you? You look wonderful."

"Thank you. So do you." He did look wonderful, Mattie thought, noting the mischievous eyes twinkling beneath his full head of silver hair.

"I'd like you to meet Tracey." Roy Crawford indicated the seated blonde to his right.

"With an *e-y*," Tracey said.

Mattie digested this piece of unnecessary information, introducing Roy to her husband.

"A pleasure." The two men shook hands.

"Roy is a client."

"Well, then," Jake said easily, as if he'd never entertained any other possibility, "Mattie will have to tell you all about the fabulous exhibit we just saw."

"She'll have to indeed," Roy Crawford said with a wink.

"Seems like a nice man," Jake said as they continued on to their table. "His daughter's a very pretty girl."

Mattie smiled, didn't bother correcting him. Tracey with an *e-y*, she thought, as they reached the banquette where Stephanie and Enoch sat gazing into each other's eyes, oblivious to everything but each other. Mattie cleared her throat. "Excuse me. I hate to interrupt," she said, realizing this was true.

Immediately Stephanie was on her feet. "There you are. I was starting to worry about you."

"I noticed."

"Let me introduce you to my honey," Stephanie enthused, as both Mattie and Jake looked self-consciously toward their toes.

Everyone should have a Honey, Mattie thought.

Enoch Porter leaned forward, kissing Mattie's cheek in almost the same spot as Roy Crawford had mere moments ago.

"Is he not the most delicious thing you've ever seen?" Stephanie whispered.

"He's pretty delicious," Mattie agreed as Enoch and Jake made their own introductions.

"His skin is like velvet," Stephanie whispered.

"He seems very nice."

"Forget nice," Stephanie confided, covering her mouth with her hand. "He has a tongue that just won't quit."

Mattie's smile froze on her face. As far as necessary information went, this was right up there with Tracey with an *e-y*. "Listen, if you'll excuse me, I have to go to the washroom," she said, already out of her chair.

"Are you all right?" Stephanie's voice trailed after her. "You just sat down."

"Be right back."

"You want me to go with you?"

Mattie dismissed her friend's offer with a wave of her hand. But Stephanie had already returned her attention to Enoch, her arm sliding around the back of his neck, her large breasts flattening against his side. *Everybody's having sex but me,* Mattie thought, locating the washroom beside the busy bar.

What was the matter with Stephanie? How could she be so brazen, so shameless, so obvious? She had two young children, for heaven's sake. How would they feel if they knew their mother was making a complete fool of herself, that she was throwing herself at a man ten years her junior, hanging all over him, for God's sake, letting him paw her in front of everyone, shouting his sexual prowess for all the world to hear? Had she no pride? No self-respect? No sense of propriety? Didn't she know this ill-matched relationship would never work?

Who cares? Mattie thought. She and Jake were the same generation, the same color, the same everything. Had it worked? "You're just jealous," Mattie told her reflection, which promptly hung its head in shame. What she wouldn't give for the opportunity to hang all over a young lover, to feel his velvet skin lying, like a blanket, across her own, to have him paw her mercilessly in front of her envious friends.

Everyone should have a Honey, she thought again, applying fresh lipstick to her mouth, although there was no need. But her fingers lost their grasp on the slender tube, and the lipstick shot across her cheek, leaving a line like a pale trickle of blood. "Oh, God," Mattie whispered, reaching for a tissue from her purse, watching helplessly as the purse fell to the floor, its contents scattering across the white-and-black mosaic of the tiles. Mattie slowly lowered herself to her knees, her hands sweeping the floor to retrieve a smattering of felt-tip pens, a packet of Kleenex, her sunglasses, her wallet, her checkbook, her house keys. What else? she wondered, noticing a pair of stiletto heels beneath one of the stalls, realizing for the first time that she wasn't alone in the room. How can anyone walk in those things? Mattie wondered, pushing herself to her feet, teetering for an instant on legs that refused to stand. "Please," she whispered into the collar of her pink sweater, grabbing the countertop for support. Please, she repeated silently, not bothering to finish the unspoken prayer.

Mattie heard a toilet flush and smiled at the young woman who emerged from the stall, her black hair as high as her stiletto heels, heels that, Mattie noted, she had no trouble at all managing. The young woman studied herself in the mirror while she washed her hands, seeming pleased enough with what she saw. As well she should be, Mattie thought, eyes trailing after her as she left the room. She was young, beautiful. Everything was working properly. No doubt she was returning to a boyfriend who adored her.

My turn, Mattie thought, taking a deep breath, straightening her shoulders and walking out of the washroom.

Roy Crawford was standing just outside the door. "You were in there a long time," he said.

"I dropped my purse." A stupid thing to say, she thought. Had he been waiting for her?

"What's on your face?" Without waiting for an answer, Roy Crawford gently rubbed at the skin beside her mouth. "Looks like lipstick." He lifted his index finger to his mouth, licked its tip provocatively, then returned it to her cheek, his eyes never leaving hers. Mattie felt the coolness of his saliva as it soaked into her skin, leaving her breathless. "There. That's better."

"Thank you," Mattie whispered, fighting for air.

"So that's your husband," Roy said, as if this were the most normal thing to say under the circumstances.

Mattie nodded, not trusting her voice.

"I thought you were separated."

"He came back."

Roy Crawford smiled a long, slow smile. "Call me," he said.

EIGHTEEN

They were lying in her bed, wrapped in newly purchased pink-and-white gingham sheets. "Special for the occasion," Honey had quipped as they tore off each other's clothes and jumped into bed, only seconds after Jake's arrival. Half an hour later, they lay side by side, naked in one another's arms, sweaty and unsatisfied, confused and conciliatory, the cats playing with their exposed toes near the foot of the bed.

"I'm sorry, Honey," Jake was saying, impatiently trying to shake the cats from his feet. "I don't know what the problem is."

"It's all right, Jason. These things happen. No apologies necessary."

"God knows I want to." Jake brushed an impatient hand across his eyes.

"I know that."

"I've been thinking about this all day."

"Maybe that's the problem—too much thinking." Honey sat up in bed, the sheet falling to her waist, exposing large pendulous breasts. She shooed the cats away from Jake's feet. One hopped to the floor, mewing in protest; the other remained silently at the end of the bed, yellow eyes focused accusingly on Jake.

"I guess I'm just tired."

"It's been a tough few weeks."

Honey flopped back down on the pillow, snuggled into the hook of Jake's arm, gently caressed the hairs on his chest. "How's the trial going?"

"Great. I think we have a good shot at an acquittal." Jake laughed. He'd been waiting all day for seven o'clock to arrive. He'd thought of little else since he awoke that morning, already hard. He'd made small talk with Mattie over breakfast, all the while imagining Honey's body and elaborately plotting in his mind the various things he was planning to do to her as soon as he got to her apartment. Nowhere in his elaborate scenario of sexual acrobatics had they ever taken a time out to discuss business. Never had the sexual acrobatics failed to get off the ground. "Actually," Jake heard his voice continue, "it's the prosecution's own witnesses who are winning the case for me."

"How's that?" Was it his imagination, or did Honey sound as confused by his sudden loquaciousness as he felt?

"Both the victim himself and the arresting officer admitted that my client was in a zombielike state at the time of the shooting. Even the court-appointed psychiatrist was forced to admit the likelihood my client was temporarily insane."

"Forced by whom?"

Jake laughed. "Well, by me, I guess."

"So you were good, were you?"

"I was very good." He felt a slight stirring in his loins.

"I'll bet you were." Honey's hand slid between his legs, taking his penis in her hands, encouraging it gently with her fingers.

Jake moaned, as if the sound might further encourage his body toward the proper response. "That feels good." A little verbal incentive, he thought, glancing toward his stubbornly limp organ. What was the matter with the damn thing? Why was it just lying there? Damn it! This had never happened to him before. He glared toward his groin, as if he could intimidate his penis into action.

"Try to relax," Honey encouraged, planting a series of soft kisses up the center of his chest. He felt the warmth of her breath, the soft touch of her lips as they fastened onto his own, the gentle prodding of her tongue as it explored his open mouth. "That's better," Honey said, a noticeable smile in her voice as her hand continued massaging his cock.

Jake closed his eyes and buried his hands in Honey's red curls as her head disappeared between his legs, her lips surrounding his penis, drawing it slowly in and out of her mouth until it began to respond. She was a wonderful lover, Jake thought, so adventurous, so expressive, so willing to do anything to make him happy. And she was being so patient, so understanding about this whole thing with Mattie. How many women would have put their lives on hold for him the way she had? The way Mattie had, he realized with a shudder, for almost sixteen years.

"Jason, what's happening?"

"What?" Jake looked from Honey's confused eyes to his once again flaccid organ.

"I thought we had something going there for a few minutes."

"I'm sorry."

"What were you thinking about?"

"Nothing." He took a deep breath, released it, glanced at the cat staring at him from the foot of the bed. Again he thought of Mattie. She'd seemed awfully chipper all day. He'd heard her singing along with the radio, one of those stations that specialized in golden oldies, while he was working in the den, and he could still picture her Mona Lisa-like smile when he said he had to go out tonight, that he might not be back till late. She hadn't even asked where he was going, although he had an explanation all prepared. "I'll be out too," she told him simply.

"You're thinking about Mattie, aren't you?"

"Mattie? No." Was he that obvious?

"How's she doing?" Honey continued, clearly not convinced.

"About the same."

"I hope she realizes what a wonderful man you are."

Jake forced a smile onto his face. Mattie knows exactly what kind of man I am, he thought ruefully. And therein lay the difference between the two women: one knew him all too well; the other didn't know him at all. Was that why he was here?

"I love you, Jason Hart," Honey was whispering, her face stretching toward his.

"I'm sorry," Jake said. "What?"

"I said, I love you."

"Why?" Jake asked, surprising himself. "Why do you love me?" Why was he asking that? He hated when women asked questions like that, as if feelings had to have reasons. And now he was doing the same thing. Why? he wondered, and almost laughed.

"Why do I love you?" Honey repeated. "I don't know. Why does anybody love anybody?"

That answer, which was word for word the answer he would have given had she asked it of him, was strangely, almost irritatingly unsatisfying. There were times for the truth, he realized, and times when the truth just wasn't enough.

"Let me see," Honey backtracked, as if sensing his displeasure. "I love you because you're smart, sensitive, sexy—"

"Not very sexy tonight," he qualified.

"Ah, but the night is just beginning," Honey reminded him. She laughed, though the laugh was hollow, the way Mattie sometimes laughed when she was unhappy. Jake shook his head, trying to shake thoughts of Mattie from his brain. You weren't invited on this excursion, he told her. Go home.

Except she wasn't home. She was out. Where? Probably at the movies with Lisa or Stephanie or another of her friends. Mattie had a lot of friends, Jake thought, realizing that aside from the friendships he'd made through Mattie, he had no real friends of his own.

"How's your book coming along?" Jake asked as Honey's tongue circled his nipples.

"My book? You want to talk about my book?"

It seemed as good a topic as any, Jake thought. At least until he could get Mattie off his mind. It was Mattie standing between his brain and his dick. He had to dislodge her in order to get his blood flowing freely. "I just wondered how it was coming along."

Honey pushed herself into a sitting position, crossed her legs, yoga-style, arranging the pink-and-white gingham sheet modestly across her lap. She looked close to tears, Jake thought, trying not to notice. "My book is coming along great."

"That's good."

"I finished chapter three this afternoon."

"That's very good."

"I'm really pleased with it."

"Good."

"Good," she repeated.

"Great."

"Great."

There was a long pause. What was the matter with him? Jake thought. Was he really making small talk when he could be making love?

"What's it about?" he heard himself ask, knowing Honey had always refused to talk about it before.

"A woman involved with a married man." Honey smiled self-consciously, her voice quivering. "They say you should write about what you know." Suddenly she burst into tears.

"Honey . . ."

"It's okay. I'm fine. Damn it. I'm fine." She quickly

erased her tears with an angry hand. "I promised myself I wouldn't do this, and I won't. I won't," she repeated, as if trying to convince herself. "I hate silly, weepy women."

"You're anything but a silly, weepy woman." Jake reached for her, cradled her in his arms, kissing her forehead. You're just confused, he thought. Almost as confused as I am. "You have every right to be upset."

"I know this whole thing isn't your fault. And I understand, really I do. I know we agreed that going back to your wife was the right thing to do, and I'm not trying to put any pressure on you. I know a demanding mistress is the last thing you need in your life right now. It's just not easy for me, Jason. Damn it. I guess I was really looking forward to tonight." A new set of tears clouded her eyes, fell down her cheeks.

"Please, Honey, don't cry."

"It's just that sometimes I feel you slipping away."

"I'm not going anywhere."

"I don't want to lose you."

"You won't."

"I'm not a fighter, Jason. That's always been part of my problem. I've never really committed to anything. That was true of my marriage, and it's true of my so-called novel. It's like I'm always holding back. I don't take chances, and I give up way too easily. Well, not anymore," she announced, shoulders straightening in fresh resolve. "For the first time in my life, I'm putting myself on the line. I'm serving warning, Jason. I intend to fight for you. I'll do whatever it takes to keep you."

Jake kissed away the fresh tears falling from Honey's eyes. It was the first time he'd seen her cry, he realized, licking the tears from the side of her mouth, his tongue gently pushing her lips apart. Honey groaned, wrapping her arms around his neck, her legs around his thighs. Jake felt a welcome stirring in his groin and quickly pulled Honey into position, pushing his way roughly inside her. Honey gasped, her nails digging into his shoulders. "Everything's going to be all right." Jake whispered, then again, "Everything's going to be all right." He kept pounding his way inside her, the words pounding simultaneously against the sides of his brain, until he almost believed them himself.

"Champagne?" Roy Crawford was asking.

"Why did I know you'd have champagne?" Mattie smiled at him from her seat on the edge of the king-size bed.

"Because I'm hopelessly predictable?"

Mattie's smile widened. "Because you're hopelessly romantic."

"And you're not?"

"Me? No. I'm much too practical to be romantic."

It was Roy Crawford's turn to smile. "Maybe we can do something about that."

"That's why I'm here."

Here was a beautiful blue-and-ivory room on the twenty-eighth floor of the Ritz-Carlton in downtown Chicago, where Mattie had suggested they meet when she called him first thing that morning. *Here* was a king-size bed and a bottle of champagne and a man walking toward her with a twinkle in his eye and two tall glasses of vintage Dom Perignon in his hands. *Here* was what Mattie had been thinking about all day.

Roy Crawford sat down beside her on the edge of the turned-down blue satin bedspread, his knees grazing hers as he handed her a glass of champagne and clicked it against his own. "To tonight," he said.

"Tonight," Mattie agreed, lifting the glass to her lips, taking a long slow sip as the champagne bubbles tickled at her nose. "Very nice," she pronounced.

"It is indeed," Roy Crawford said, though he'd yet to take a drink.

Mattie felt her pulse begin to race. How long had it been since anyone had looked at her with such unbridled lust? "I take it you had no trouble getting away tonight," she heard herself say over the loud beating of her heart.

"No trouble. Tracey knows I have an erratic schedule."

"Tracey with an *e-y*?"

Roy smiled. "She's very precise." He took a sip of his champagne, nodded appreciatively. "What about you? Any problems?"

"My husband has an erratic schedule of his own." Mattie laughed, although the thought of what Jake might be doing at that exact moment caused one of the champagne bubbles to burst in her throat, and Mattie had a hard time catching her breath.

"You all right?"

"Fine," Mattie gasped.

"Look up," Roy instructed. "Put your hands in the air."

"What? Why?"

"I don't know." Roy Crawford looked appropriately sheepish. "My mother always said that when you're choking, you should look up and put your hands in the air."

"I'm not choking," Mattie insisted, looking up and raising her hands in the air nonetheless.

"Better?"

Mattie nodded, careful not to speak.

"So, things are going well between you and your husband?" A look of fresh concern flashed through Roy Crawford's gray eyes.

"Things are just fine," Mattie assured him, the constriction in her throat rendering her voice a sexy growl.

"And this is what—payback time?"

Mattie stood up, walked to the window, slowly sipped on the champagne in her glass. "No, I don't think so," she said honestly. "I don't think I'm doing this to get back at Jake. Not anymore." She paused, took a deep breath, feeling her throat clear. "I'm doing this for me."

Roy was right behind her, his lips on the back of her neck. "I think I'm flattered."

Mattie felt the hairs at the back of her neck jump to attention. They swayed precariously under the weight of his warm breath. "I think I could use another glass of champagne."

Roy immediately refilled her glass, watched as she gulped it down. "You're sure you want to do this?"

"Very sure." Mattie lowered the glass to the table, raised her hands to Roy's face, brought her lips to his. His lips were soft and wide, wider than Jake's, she thought, as he expertly returned her kiss, his mouth open, with only a hint of tongue. Just the right amount of pressure, Mattie decided. Clearly a man who enjoyed kissing and had perfected its art. "You do that very well," she told him, her legs tingling as he danced her slowly toward the bed.

"I have four sisters. We used to practice all the time when we were kids."

They stopped in front of the bed, and he kissed her again. This time the kiss was deeper, although his tongue remained a soft tease. Yes, indeed, he'd practiced well, Mattie thought. Not that Jake wasn't a good kisser. He was. It had just been a very long time since he'd kissed her like this. Had he ever? she wondered, the back of her calves hitting the baseboard of the bed. Go away, Jake, Mattie thought, opening her eyes, Roy Crawford's large head blurring around her.

Roy pulled back slightly, though his lips remained fastened to hers. His hands found the front of her green silk blouse, his fingers tracing increasingly small circles across her breasts. So far, so good, Mattie thought, as his hands began unbuttoning her white pearl buttons. She felt a familiar tingle in the bottom of her right foot. It was nothing to worry about, she assured herself. Her whole body was tingling. There was nothing to worry about.

"How're you doing?" Roy whispered.

"Great," she told him.

"Great," he repeated, sliding the blouse down over her shoulders, his fingers returning immediately to the front of her black lace bra. "You're so beautiful," he told her, his hands sliding down to her hips.

He took his time, removing each article of clothing with care, marveling at the softness of her skin, the delicate curves of her body, her smell, the way she responded to each new caress. "Look at you," he said, lying down beside her on fresh white sheets. "Do you have any idea how incredibly beautiful you are?"

"Tell me again," she said, tears welling up in her eyes.

And so he did. Again and again. His hands were on her breasts, in her hair, between her legs, his lips tracing the path of his hands, his tongue retracing the path of his lips. Mattie closed her eyes, opened them when she found Jake lurking behind her lashes. Go home, Jake, she told him. This bed isn't big enough for all of us.

"Ready?" Roy Crawford was asking.

"Not yet." Mattie sat up, pushed Roy Crawford playfully down. "My turn," she said, studying his naked body. The last time she'd cheated on her husband, she'd closed her eyes and looked the other way. She had no intention of doing that now. No, this time, she was going to savor every second. She was going into this affair with her eyes wide open.

Roy Crawford was in great shape for a man his age, Mattie thought, running her fingers across his smooth chest. Slim, taut, muscular. He obviously took very good care of himself. Probably works out a few days a week at the gym. Like Jake does, Mattie thought. The gym—where Jake met Honey. Honey with an e-y, she thought.

She felt Roy Crawford flinch beneath her fingers. "Sorry," Mattie apologized quickly. "Did I hurt you?"

"Easy does it," Roy Crawford said.

"I guess I'm out of practice."

"You're doing great," he said, as Mattie's mouth took over from her fingers.

In the next minute Mattie was on top of him, fitting her body over him. She cried out as he entered her, and he reached up, held her, as he moved inside her. Soon they changed positions, so that he was on top, then again, so that he was at her side, then again, so that she was back on top. "You're so beautiful," he kept saying, over and over again. "So beautiful. So beautiful." He flipped her over, lifted her legs over his shoulders, rose onto his knees, pounding his way farther and farther inside her. Mattie arched her back to accommodate him, her hands grabbing his buttocks, pushing him deeper into her, as if trying to take his entire being inside her. She felt dizzy and euphoric, her body buzzing, as if it were about to explode. It was magic, she thought, as her body shuddered to a climax.

How much she'd missed that magic, Mattie realized. How much she needed it in her life.

"Are you all right?" Roy was asking from somewhere beside her.

"Fine," Mattie said, smiling gratefully. "You?"

He leaned over, kissed her bare shoulder. "Fine," he said.

Silence.

The magic was over.

Like any good magic trick, it had vanished without a trace. Great while it lasted, worthy of all the hosannas it received, but in the end, over before you knew it, before you could examine it for clues, for subtle sleights of hand, for telltale strings attached. Ooh and aah all you liked—in the end, there was nothing there.

Was that what she really wanted? Was that how she wanted to spend the last year of her life?

That was one of the things she loved about art, Mattie realized. It was precise, permanent, meticulous, inside the lines. Even the most outrageous scrawl was usually well thought out in advance. Life, on the other hand, was transient, fleeting, messy. It didn't care if it strayed outside the lines. Hell, it bulldozed right over them.

She looked toward Roy, self-made millionaire and perpetual adolescent, sprawled out naked beside her, not a false pretension in sight. *I yam what I yam what I yam.* Popeye as Plato. Simplicity itself. Exactly as advertised. She closed her eyes. If there was more to him, she didn't want to know.

The magic was over.

After several minutes, Mattie glanced toward the clock at the side of the bed. Already twelve minutes after nine o'clock. "I should probably think about getting back home," she said, thinking ahead to the long cab ride home.

Roy Crawford ran his hand through his thick gray hair. "Yeah. I should really get a move on."

They were like two strangers waking up from a night of drunken revelry to find themselves naked and sweaty and vaguely afraid of the person beside them, Mattie thought as Roy headed for the bathroom.

Seconds later, Mattie heard the shower running. She reached for her clothes, dragging her pants over her hips, her arms through the sleeves of her blouse. There'd be plenty of time to shower when she got home, she decided. It was unlikely that Jake would be home before midnight. She was still fumbling with the buttons of her green silk shirt when Roy came out of the shower, a large white towel draped casually around his hips.

"Problems?" he asked.

"The buttons don't want to cooperate." Mattie hid her shaking fingers behind her back.

"Allow me." Roy Crawford's hands returned to the front of her blouse. He hesitated, his fingers hovering over her breasts. "Better not," he said finally, fastening each button in turn.

"Thank you," Mattie said sincerely.

"Any time." Roy kissed her gently on the side of her lips.

"Thank you," Mattie said again.

Roy Crawford looked surprised. "For what?"

"For making me feel like a sex object."

They laughed. "My pleasure," he said, reaching for his socks. "You know, I'd really like to see that exhibition your husband mentioned the other night." He slid into his black pants, pulled his blue sweater over his head.

"I think you should," Mattie agreed, straightening her hair in the mirror across from the bed. "There are several photographs I think you'd really like."

"I'll call you. We can set something up."

"Sounds good."

"Good," he echoed.

"Good," she said.

NINETEEN

"Come on in. Hurry up." Kim quickly ushered Teddy Cranston through her front door, casting a furtive glance down the quiet dark street, mindful of potential prying eyes peeking out from neighboring homes. Not that she was doing anything wrong, she thought. At least, not technically. She was grounded. That meant she couldn't go out. It didn't mean she couldn't invite somebody *in*. Besides, her parents were out for the evening, so what difference did it make? What they didn't know wouldn't hurt them. Undoubtedly her mother or her father, possibly even both, would be calling home at some point in the evening to make sure she hadn't left the house, and she'd be ready for them. Just like she was ready for Teddy. Tonight's the night, she'd told him over the phone. Get your ass over here in half an hour or miss your chance. Exactly twenty-nine minutes later, he was at her door.

"My room's upstairs," Kim said, leading the way. Why waste time on preliminaries? They'd spent months on preliminaries. Now they had only a couple of hours to get the job done.

"Nice house," Teddy remarked, taking off his heavy brown leather jacket, dropping it over the banister as he followed Kim up the stairs.

"It's okay."

They didn't speak again until they reached the door to her room. Kim took a quick peek inside to make sure it looked presentable. After calling Teddy, she'd hastily tossed everything that wasn't weighted down into the closet. She'd even made her bed. Her mother was always going on about how uncomfortable it was to sleep in a bed that hadn't been made. Not that they'd be doing any sleeping, Kim thought with a silent chuckle, banishing her mother from the room with a shake of her blond hair.

"Cool," Teddy said vaguely, stepping onto the wheat-colored carpet and looking around. "Great quilt," he said, eyes coming to rest on the queen-size bed.

Kim nodded. Actually, the comforter was a mock quilt, made up of a series of brightly colored patches, each patch individual and distinct, red-and-white stripes beside blue-and-white gingham up against yellow flowers and large green dots. Her mother had selected the comforter, just as she'd chosen everything else in the room, although ostensibly it was Kim making the decisions. "Whatever you want," her mother had told her when they first moved in. "You're a big girl now. We'll decorate your room exactly the way you want."

Except what did Kim know of what she wanted?

She was only eleven when they'd moved in. She hadn't had time to develop a sense of taste or a semblance of style. And so she'd gone along with all her mother's suggestions. Even her walls were a reflection of her mother's personality. While most girls her age plastered their walls with posters of the latest Hollywood heartthrob, supermodel, or singing group, the sand-colored walls of Kim's room were covered with framed posters from the Art Institute, signed and numbered lithographs by the likes of Joan Miro and Jim Dine, even a wonderful black-and-white photograph of a mother embracing her daughter by famed photographer Annie Liebowitz.

What was she supposed to do when her mother was gone, Kim wondered helplessly, when she had no one to tell her what she liked and disliked, when she had no one to rely on for her sense of self?

"This is so cool," Teddy remarked, moving in for a closer look at a brilliant yellow rendering of the number 4 floating on a background of red and black. "Did you do it?"

Kim searched Teddy's face for signs he must be joking. "Hardly. It's by Robert Indiana." Immediately she bit down on her bottom lip. Had she gone too far by correcting him? Had she embarrassed him? Would he mumble some dumb excuse about having to be somewhere else, leaving her and her irksome virginity intact?

"Oh." Teddy shrugged. "Cool."

"It's a print." How could he mistake a print for an actual painting? How could she give herself to someone who couldn't tell the difference?

"Cool," he said again, plopping down in the center of the bed.

Was that all he ever said? Kim wondered, standing in the middle of the room. True, he wasn't the smartest boy in the school, but he wasn't the dumbest either. Think positive, Kim admonished herself. Don't dwell on the negative. Think about all the things you like about Teddy—his chocolate brown eyes, the dimples in his cheeks when he smiles, his tight lean body, his long tapering fingers, the way he kisses, the way his hands feel on your breasts. Let someone else love him for his mind, Kim thought, as Teddy patted the space beside him on the bed, beckoning her over. Wasn't it enough that he was older, more experienced, that he'd selected her over any of the other girls he could have chosen? Wasn't it enough that she was the envy of all her friends?

Except they weren't her friends. Not really. Caroline Smith, Annie Turofsky, Jodi Bates—they only liked her because Teddy liked her. They'd dump her like a hot potato as soon as Teddy did. No, the truth was she didn't have any close friends. The truth was that her mother had always been her best friend. *You and me against the world*, her mother used to sing to her when she was a little girl. What would happen to her when her mother deserted her? Who would she be able to turn to then? Her father?

"Your father's such a hunk," Jodi had all but swooned after he'd picked her up at school one day.

"I wouldn't mind a shot at him," Caroline volunteered with a rude laugh.

Go for it, Kim had been tempted to say, but didn't. Caroline had a way of getting the things she went after, and the last thing Kim needed was Caroline Smith for a stepmother. Kim groaned. Was there no limit to the baseness of her thoughts? Her mother wasn't even dead yet, and already she was thinking of her replacement.

"Aren't you going to join me?" Teddy was asking, looking at Kim expectantly.

Pushing thoughts of her mother roughly aside, Kim approached the bed, pulling her white turtleneck over her head as she walked, letting it fall to the floor.

"Wow," Teddy said, as she unhooked her plain white bra and tossed it aside.

Kim felt her body flush red with embarrassment. What was she doing? Was she really going to let Teddy see her naked?

"Wait for me," Teddy said, jumping to his feet, shedding his shirt, jeans, shoes, and socks in one easy motion, as if each article of clothing were part of the same cloth, as if they were attached to him by Velcro. He discarded them with no more embarrassment than if he were peeling off unwanted remnants of an old sunburn. He stood naked before her, his erect penis all but dancing in front of him.

"Oh," Kim said.

"Aren't you going to take those off?" Teddy indicated Kim's jeans and heavy black boots.

Kim sat on the edge of the bed, trying to ignore Teddy's dancing organ as she pulled off her boots and squirmed out of her jeans. "Did you bring a condom?"

"They're in my pocket." He nodded vaguely toward the floor.

"Don't you think you ought to put one on?"

Teddy moved like an automaton toward his jeans, quickly locating the small packet he was looking for and tearing it open. Kim pulled back the comforter and climbed underneath the blanket, gathering the pale yellow sheets up under her chin as Teddy struggled to put on the condom. "Dressed for success," he said finally, a triumphant smile across his handsome face.

"Are you sure that thing's going to work?"

"I won't let anything happen," Teddy assured her, crawling into bed beside her. "I promise."

"What if it breaks?"

"It won't break. These things are like steel." His hand moved to her breast. Kim pushed it away.

"Could you turn off the light?"

Wordlessly Teddy jumped to his feet and shut off the light beside the bed. He was back beside Kim almost before her brain had time to register he'd been gone.

"Maybe we shouldn't be doing this," Kim stammered, refusing to relinquish her grip on the blanket at her chin.

"What? Come on, Kim. You've been teasing me for months."

"I haven't been teasing you."

"You've been driving me crazy. That's what you've been doing." His tongue began exploring the inside of her ear.

Is sex all you ever think about? Kim wanted to ask, but didn't because she already knew the answer. Of course sex was all he thought about. It was all *all* boys thought about, and not just occasionally, the way girls did, but all the time. Literally every minute of every waking day. No wonder they could barely string two sentences into one coherent thought. No wonder they couldn't tell the difference between a painting and a goddamn print.

Besides, tonight had been her idea, not his. She was the one who'd telephoned his house and practically ordered him over. She was the one who'd invited him upstairs to her bedroom. She was the one who'd started the ball rolling by taking off her sweater. She was lying naked in bed beside a naked man, for God's sake. How could she call the whole thing off now?

"You'll be careful?" she asked.

"I won't let anything happen," he said, as he'd said moments ago. "I promise."

And the next thing she knew, Teddy was shoving his way roughly inside her, or at least trying to. "You have to relax," he whispered between grunts. "Just relax and let it happen."

"You're in the wrong spot," she told him impatiently.

"What do you mean, I'm in the wrong spot?"

"I don't think that's the right spot," Kim said, trying to shift her position, to crawl out from under him, her actions causing Teddy to pump all the more strenuously.

By accident or design, he finally stumbled into the right orifice, and immediately began thrusting his way farther inside her. Kim gasped as a sharp pain shot through her body, and her insides stretched to accommodate him. The parting of the Red Sea, she thought, feeling a sticky substance on the insides of her thighs, wondering if there was blood on the sheets and how she'd explain it to her mother. I'll just tell her I got my period, Kim decided, grabbing Teddy's buttocks in an effort to slow him down. But he either misunderstood her intentions or chose to ignore them. In any event, he did the exact opposite, quickening his already frantic pace until he cried out, a small frightened sound, as if he'd been hurt, and she felt his body shudder to a halt on top of her. Seconds later, he slid off her to lie on his back, his left hand stretched out over his head in a posture of either triumph or utter exhaustion. That's it? Kim thought. That's what all the fuss is about? She reached over to draw the comforter up under her chin.

"You okay?" Teddy asked, as if suddenly remembering she was there.

"Fine. You?"

"Great. You were great." He turned on his side, kissing her wet cheek. "You crying?"

"No," Kim replied indignantly, wiping her cheek. What was *that* all about?

"It'll be better next time."

"It was great *this* time," she lied, glancing at his naked torso, seeing his once charging organ now lying flaccid and vulnerable amid his soft tangle of pubic hair. Where's the condom? she thought. "Where's the condom?" she said.

The condom, of course, was still inside her, she realized with a sick feeling in her gut.

"Oh God, what are we going to do?" she wailed.

"Take it out," Teddy told her.

"What do you mean, take it out?"

"Just reach in and get it."

"I can't do that."

"Why not?"

"Because I can't." What was the matter with him? "You promised me you'd be careful. You promised you wouldn't let anything happen."

"I *was* careful."

"Then what's the stupid thing still doing inside me?"

"It must have slipped off when I pulled out."

"Oh God, oh God, oh God."

"All you have to do is—"

"I'm not doing anything. *You* do it. Oh God, oh God, oh God," she repeated, covering her face with her hands as Teddy disappeared under the comforter and began poking at her with his fingers.

"I've got it," he announced after several seconds, triumphantly displaying the spent condom. "And look, see, it's okay. It didn't rip. Everything's still in there."

"Oh God, gross," Kim exclaimed, feeling sick to her stomach, as Teddy dropped the condom into the nearby wastepaper basket. "How do you know none of it spilled out?"

"None of it spilled out," he said, as if his word should be enough to quell Kim's growing panic.

"How do you know?"

"I just know."

"Oh God, oh God, oh God."

"It'll be all right."

"Oh God."

"You think you could stop saying that?" Teddy asked. "You're making me kind of nervous."

"What if I'm pregnant?" Kim asked.

"Oh God," came Teddy's immediate reply.

Don't panic, Kim told herself. There's nothing to worry about. He wore a condom. It didn't break. No pesky little sperm escaped. Besides, you just finished your period two days ago. No way you could be pregnant. No way. No way. No way.

Oh God, oh God, oh God.

Is this how her mother felt sixteen years ago? Kim wondered. And was that why she'd taken such a stupid risk—as a way of getting to know her mother better?

"Kim?" Teddy was asking. "Are you all right? You suddenly got so quiet."

"I'm fine," Kim told him, feeling strangely calm.

"Kim?"

"Yes?" She felt his body stirring beside her.

"You want to do it again?"

Mattie sat in the backseat of the taxi, trying to ignore the persistent tingle between her legs where Roy Crawford had been. She felt the now-distant echo of his body thrusting into hers, the way one feels an amputated arm or leg, the sensation still present despite the absence of the limb. The sensation of absence, Mattie thought. So much preferable to the absence of sensation.

What was it they said about sex? When it was good, it was great, and when it was bad, it was still good. Yes, that was it. "Turn here," Mattie directed the cab driver. "Fifth house from the end."

The driver, a middle-aged man with a white crew cut, whose nameplate identified him as Yuri Popovitch, pulled to a halt in front of Mattie's house. Mattie noted the lights on in the front hall, though the rest of the house was in darkness. She checked her watch. Almost ten o'clock. It was possible Kim was already asleep. Mattie hadn't bothered calling to check up on her. If Jake wanted to keep tabs on his daughter, that was fine. Mattie had decided to trust her.

"Thank you," Mattie told the driver, handing him his fare along with a handsome tip. She pushed open the car door and swung her feet around. But Mattie's feet refused to find the ground, and her knees buckled under her, sending her flying facedown into the layer of fine snow at the side of her driveway.

The driver was instantly at Mattie's side, picking her up, dusting her off. "Missus, you all right? What happened to you?"

"I'm sorry," Mattie apologized, unable to stand without his assistance. Dear God, what was happening to her? "I must have had too much to drink." Yes, that was it, she told herself. Too much champagne. Champagne and sex—a deadly combination. Especially when you weren't used to it.

"Good thing you not sick in my car." Yuri Popovitch helped Mattie up the steps to the front door, waited while she fished in her purse for her keys.

"Would you mind—" She handed the keys to the driver.

Yuri opened the door, returned Mattie's keys to her outstretched hand. "You okay, Missus? You can manage now?"

"I should be fine. Thank you very much." Mattie grabbed the door handle as he released her. She watched him run down the steps to his cab, then drive off without looking back. I should be fine, she repeated silently. "But I'm not," she acknowledged out loud, as her body collapsed to the floor. "Jake!" she called out. No answer. Who was she kidding? Her husband wasn't home. "Kim!" she called, receiving a similar response.

Kim must have gone to bed early, Mattie thought, forced to crawl on her belly across the needlepoint rug to the kitchen. "Goddamn it," she cried, sliding across the ceramic tiles to the breakfast table, pulling off her coat, leaving it in a discarded heap on the floor as she used the back of one of the chairs to pull herself up. Sobbing and cursing, exhausted by her efforts, she collapsed into the chair. "Goddamn it. What's happening to me?"

You know exactly what's happening to you, her tearful reflection in the sliding glass door told her.

"No," Mattie insisted. "Not now. Not yet."

You have something called amyotrophic lateral sclerosis, she heard Lisa say, her friend's image appearing in the glass next to Mattie's.

"Sounds serious."

It is.

"How long do I have?"

A year. Maybe two, even three.

Mattie closed her eyes, wiping Lisa's image from her mind. But the voices continued, like a TV set whose picture tube is on the fritz, the screen suddenly blank, the sound remaining strong and clear.

"And what happens to me during that year or two or three?" Mattie heard herself ask even as she covered her ears with her hands.

As the disease progresses, you'll lose the ability to walk. You'll be in a wheelchair. Your hands will be rendered useless. Your body will start contorting in on itself.

"I'll be a prisoner of my own body," Mattie acknowledged, withdrawing her hands from her ears and opening her eyes, staring into the darkness of her backyard, her heart pounding against her chest, as if trying to get out while there was still time. "I'm dying," she said, forcing herself to her feet, pushing her legs toward the glass door, unlocking it and sliding it open, stepping slowly, carefully, onto the balcony. The cold night air quickly wrapped itself across her shoulders like an old sweater as she stared toward the pool, hidden beneath its protective winter cover. Would she ever swim again? Unlikely, she thought. "I'm dying," she repeated, the words no easier to digest or understand, despite their repetition. "But not yet. Not until I've see Paris."

Mattie laughed, forcing her legs forward until she was leaning against the railing. Paris was three months away. She could probably function well enough till then. She'd had these episodes before. They came and went, although each episode lasted longer, left her weaker. But after Paris, then what? Almost half a year would have passed since Lisa delivered her devastating diagnosis. Six months of the little time she had left would already be gone. What of the next six months? Could she sit helplessly by and watch as her nerve cells collapsed around her, until she could no longer speak or eat or breathe without choking? Could she do that?

Did she have a choice?

We always have a choice, Mattie thought. She didn't have to wait around for the ravages of the disease to claim her. She could take matters into her own hands while her hands still worked. She didn't have a gun, so shooting herself was out of the question, and she doubted she'd have the strength and accuracy a knife would demand, even now. Hanging was too complicated, and throwing herself down a flight of stairs too uncertain of success.

"I could drown," she said simply, her mind floating beneath the ugly green cover. Open the pool a few weeks early. Wait till everyone was out of the house and go for a little swim, disappear under the water quickly, quietly, with a minimum of fuss.

Except that Kim might find her, Mattie realized in horror. She couldn't risk that. No matter what, Kim had to be protected.

She'd have to find another way.

Mattie pushed herself away from the railing, teetering precariously on legs that were only now beginning to regain their bearings. She stepped back into the kitchen and slowly made her way across the room. "I'm going to die," she repeated in wonder, crossing the front hall to the stairs. "I have a year. Maybe more." Her hand reached for the banister, came to rest on an unfamiliar brown leather jacket.

Mattie examined the jacket. It was a man's jacket, she determined quickly, although it didn't look like anything Jake would wear. Was it Kim's? Had she borrowed it from one of the boys at school?

The jacket became too heavy for Mattie's hands to hold, and it slipped from her fingers and fell to the floor. "Maybe less than a year," Mattie whispered, tears filling her eyes as she slowly mounted the stairs.

Less than a year.

Mattie reached the top of the stairs, resting on the landing for several seconds. The door to Jake's room was open, as was the door to Kim's bedroom. That was unusual, Mattie thought, knowing Kim liked to sleep with her door closed. Was it possible Kim had disobeyed them and gone out after all?

"Kim?" Mattie called gently, approaching the open door to Kim's room, peering inside.

The room was dark, but even in the darkness, Mattie could see that Kim had done some serious straightening up. Poor thing, Mattie thought. She must be exhausted. That's why she went to bed so early. That's why she didn't hear me call. That's why she forgot to close the door.

Mattie inched her way into the room. She wanted to give her daughter a kiss good night, the way she used to when Kim was a little girl. Her sweet, beautiful baby, Mattie thought, approaching the bundle hidden beneath the heavy comforter, pulling it aside, about to kiss her daughter's forehead, when the bundle beside Kim suddenly moved.

And then all hell broke loose.

Mattie was screaming. Kim was screaming. The boy, whoever he was, was tearing madly around the room, gathering up his clothes, shouting his apologies as he ran from the room and down the stairs.

"How could you do this?" Mattie was yelling, hearing the front door slam.

"You think **we** fell asleep on purpose?" Kim yelled in return. "How could you embarrass me like that?"

Mattie stared at her defiant daughter, still a month

shy of her sixteenth birthday. My baby, she thought, with a bewildered shake of her head. Mattie wanted to grab Kim and shake her, but could she really yell at her daughter for doing the same thing she'd been doing herself? Surely the fact Kim was only fifteen years old was offset by her mother's adultery. "I can't deal with this now," Mattie said, retreating to the safety of her own room, hearing the door to Kim's bedroom slam shut behind her.

Mattie lowered herself to the side of her bed, stared numbly into space. Quite a night, she thought, falling back against the headboard. "And it's not over yet." She reached for the phone, pressing in the numbers she'd committed to memory, listening as the phone rang, once, twice, three times before being picked up.

"Hello?" The voice was raspy, familiar.

"Is this Honey Novak?" Mattie asked, already knowing the answer.

"Yes. Who's this?"

"This is Mattie Hart," Mattie said calmly, trying to picture the woman's face, hearing her sharp intake of breath. "I'd like to speak to my husband."

TWENTY

Less than an hour later, Mattie heard the low rumble of the garage door as it opened and closed. She climbed slowly out of her chair in the living room, pushing one foot in front of the other with studied precision, her heart bouncing so erratically in her chest she was afraid it might burst clear through. Like that creature from *Alien*, she thought, deciding this was as good a term to describe her as any. Her body had been invaded by some mysterious force beyond her control or understanding. It was causing her to behave in ways totally foreign to her personality. What was she if not some strange creature, alien even to herself? "Stay calm," she cautioned herself, inching her way toward the front door, running a still-trembling hand through her just-washed hair before burying it deep inside the pocket of her powder blue housecoat. "This is not the time for unnecessary histrionics."

Oh, no? a little voice asked. *You're cheating on your husband; your husband is cheating on you; you discovered your fifteen-year-old daughter in bed with some boy you've never even met. Not to mention the fact you're dying. Can you think of a better time for histrionics?*

Mattie reached the front hall at the same moment Jake's key turned in the lock. She took a deep breath, then another as Jake pushed open the front door, the wind howling dramatically behind him, gusts of freshly falling snow swirling around his head. A suitably grand entrance, Mattie thought, watching him.

At first Jake didn't see her standing there. His head was down, as if he were still braving the elements, and he was preoccupied with ridding his boots of the snow he'd acquired between the car and the foyer. It was only after he'd removed his boots and shrugged off his coat that he realized she was standing there. "That's quite a storm picking up out there," he said, hanging his coat in the closet and shaking the snow from his hair. "Lucky I had some boots in the car." He paused, looked directly into Mattie's eyes for the first time since walking through the door. Enough small talk, his eyes said. "Are you all right? Has something happened?"

"I'm fine," Mattie said.

Confusion brought Jake's eyebrows together at the bridge of his nose. "I don't understand. On the phone, you said I had to get home right away. You made it sound pretty urgent. Is something wrong?"

"You mean besides the fact I'm dying and you're fucking other women?"

There was a second's silence.

She'd gone too far, Mattie thought, holding her breath.

"Besides that," Jake said.

And suddenly they were laughing. A few nervous giggles that grew into great big whoops of glee, propelled by shock, driven by tension, effortlessly bridging the distance between them. They laughed with utter and complete abandon, until their sides ached and their insides threatened to explode, until they could barely catch their breath. They laughed so hard they temporarily forgot that she was dying and he was fucking other women.

And then she remembered, and he remembered, and the laughing stopped.

"I'm sorry," Mattie said.

"What have you got to be sorry about?"

"About calling you at your girlfriend's house. About ruining your evening."

Jake had the good grace to look embarrassed. He shuffled from one foot to the other, looked uneasily from side to side. "How did you know where to find me?"

"It wasn't exactly the puzzle of the century." Mattie smiled. Were men really as simple as Roy Crawford claimed? "Did you really think I didn't know where you were going?"

"I guess I was trying not to think," Jake admitted after a pause. "Looks like I should be the one apologizing to you."

"What's the point of an apology if you're not really sorry?"

Jake nodded, a sudden hardness appearing in his eyes, as if he'd just realized he'd been summoned home from his mistress's apartment in the middle of a budding blizzard for no discernible reason. "What's this about, Mattie?" he asked, bringing them back to the topic at hand, impatience replacing the concern in his voice, obliterating whatever traces of laughter remained.

"Maybe we should sit down." Mattie motioned toward the living room.

"Can't you just spit it out? I'm really tired. If it's nothing urgent—"

"Kim's having sex," Mattie blurted out. Was that really what she wanted to talk to him about?

"What?" Jake's eyes shot to the stairs.

"Not right now," Mattie qualified, afraid he was about to bound up the steps and confront their daughter right then and there. "Before."

"Before? Before when?"

"When I got home." Why was she talking about this now? This wasn't what she'd brought him home to discuss. "I walked in on her."

"You walked in on her having sex?"

"No, thank God." Too late to turn back now, she thought. "They were already finished. They were asleep." She watched Jake trying to digest this latest piece of information, to make sense of what he was hearing.

"Who's they?"

"Kim and—whoever." Mattie pictured a tall, good-looking, and unquestionably naked young man hopping around on one foot, struggling to pull up his jeans. "I don't know his name. We weren't exactly formally introduced."

Jake began pacing back and forth in front of Mattie,

his frustration filling the small front hall. "I don't understand. What's gotten into her lately? She smokes dope in a public place. She has sex practically under our noses. What's she thinking, for God's sake?"

"I'm not sure she's thinking very clearly about anything at this point."

"Does she want to get AIDS? Does she want to get pregnant? Does she want to—" He stopped abruptly.

"End up like us?" Mattie asked, finishing his sentence for him.

"That's not what I was going to say."

"Why not? It's the truth."

"It's just that she's so young. There's so much time."

"Not always," Mattie reminded him, her voice soft, barely audible.

The color drained from Jake's face. "Oh God, Mattie, I'm sorry. Jeez, that was a thoughtless thing to say." He brought his hand to his head, massaged his forehead, closed his eyes. "You know I didn't mean—"

"I know. It's okay."

"It's not okay."

"It's okay, Jake," Mattie repeated. "You're right— she's young, she has time."

"What did you say to her?"

"What could I say? That it's all right for her mother and father to be having affairs, but not her?" Mattie held her breath. Dear God, what had she said? She hadn't meant to tell Jake about her own infidelity. Or had she? Was this the real reason she'd summoned Jake home from his mistress's apartment?

"It's hardly the same thing."

Slowly, Mattie released the air in her lungs. "No, I guess it isn't." Obviously what she'd said hadn't registered.

There was a moment's pause. Mattie watched Jake's eyes flicker with confusion, indecision, and disbelief.

"What do you mean, it's all right for her mother and father to be having affairs?" Jake asked, as if hearing Mattie's remark for the first time. "What are you saying?"

"Jake, I—"

"You're having an affair?"

Too late for denials. Besides, what was the point? "Well, I don't know that I'd call it an affair exactly."

"That's where you were tonight? With another man?"

"Does that upset you?"

"I don't know." Jake looked stunned, as if he'd been struck over the head with a blunt object and was just about to lose consciousness.

Mattie found herself growing impatient with Jake's reaction. "You think you're the only one entitled to a sex life?"

"Of course not."

"I don't think you have any right to be upset."

"I think I'm more surprised than anything else."

Now Mattie was angry. "Why are you so damned surprised? You don't think a man might find me attractive?"

"That's not what I meant."

"As your daughter so eloquently put it the other day, I'm not dead yet!"

Jake staggered back as if he'd been pushed. "Mattie,

hold on. You have to give me a minute here to catch my breath. I just found out that both my daughter and my wife are having sex."

"We're *all* having sex," Mattie interrupted, still bristling.

"We're all having sex," Jake repeated numbly. "You know, I think we should sit down after all."

Mattie turned and walked into the living room, flopping down on the beige Ultrasuede sofa. Fatigue rushed to embrace her, climbing all over her, pulling on her neck and shoulders like a restless toddler. Why had she told Jake about her affair? Had it been accidental, something blurted out in the heat of the moment? Or had more sinister forces been at work? Had she deliberately been trying to shock him? To hurt him? If so, why was she so angry at his reaction? What had she been hoping to achieve? Why had she summoned him home from Honey's apartment? What did she really want to say?

Mattie watched Jake fold his body into one of the rose-and-gold-striped chairs across from where she sat, his feet stretched out their full length in front of him. He raised his face to hers expectantly. "Do I know him?" he asked.

For an instant, Mattie didn't know what Jake was talking about. "What? Oh. No," she said, picturing her husband and Roy Crawford shaking hands. "It's no one you know."

"How did you meet?"

"Does it matter?"

Jake shook his head. "I guess not." He looked helplessly around the room. "Do you love him?"

Mattie almost laughed. "No." There was a long pause while Mattie tried to impose order on the random chaos of her thoughts. The inside of her head was such a jungle of dangling participles and disconnected phrases, she'd need a machete to hack her way through. Why had she summoned him home from Honey's apartment? What was it she wanted to say to him? "Why did you come back, Jake?" she asked finally.

"You called," he reminded her. "You said I needed to get home as soon as I could."

"I don't mean tonight."

Jake closed his eyes. "I'm not sure I understand."

"You were gone. You were starting a new life. And then Lisa called us into her office and announced I was—" Mattie stumbled, quickly regrouped. "Dying," she said, forcing the word out of her mouth. "I'm dying," she repeated, still waiting for the word to make sense.

Jake reopened his eyes, waited for her to continue.

"That's not easy for me to say," Mattie said. "It's even harder for me to believe. I mean, I keep telling myself that it's not possible. How can I be dying when I'm only thirty-six years old? I still look pretty good. I still *feel* pretty good. Just because I fall over occasionally, and my hands shake almost all the time now—"

"They shake all the time?" Jake sat up straight in his chair. "Have you told Lisa?"

"I'm telling you," Mattie said quietly.

"But there may be something Lisa can prescribe."

"It's nothing I can't handle, Jake. Besides, that's not the point."

"The point is, you're experiencing difficulty—"

"The point is, I'm dying," Mattie reiterated, the words no easier to understand, despite the repetition. "And I can't keep denying it, much as I've tried. My body just won't cooperate. Every day when I wake up, I can feel a subtle difference. I tell myself it's my imagination, but I know it's not. I never had that great an imagination." She tried to laugh, but the sound threatened tears instead. "I can't keep pretending I'm going to get better, that this is all just going to go away," she said. "It's too much work. I don't have the strength."

"No one's asking you to pretend."

"You ask me to pretend every time you walk out the door," Mattie told him, her thoughts suddenly focusing, becoming clear. "Every time you call to say you're working late at the office, or that you have to meet a client for dinner, or go in to work for a few hours on a Saturday afternoon. You asked me to pretend tonight, for God's sake," Mattie said, her voice rising. "I can't do it anymore, Jake. I can't pretend any longer. That's why I called you at Honey's apartment. That's why I asked you to come home."

Jake said nothing for several long seconds. "Tell me what you want me to do," he said finally. "I don't know what you want me to do."

"Why did you come back, Jake?" Mattie asked again. "What did you think would happen? What was your objective?" A lawyer's phrase, Mattie thought. Jake's phrase.

"I felt I should be here," he said, as he had said before. "For you, and for Kim. We discussed this. You agreed."

"I changed my mind."

"What?"

"It's not enough," Mattie said simply. "I need more." She thought of Roy Crawford, felt his fingers on her breasts, between her legs. "And I'm not just talking about sex." She pushed Roy's hands aside. "I need more," she repeated.

Jake opened his mouth to speak, closed it when no words were forthcoming. He shook his head, looked helplessly into his lap.

"Did you see how happy Stephanie looked last night?" Mattie asked.

"What's Stephanie got to do with this?"

"She looked radiant," Mattie said, ignoring his question, talking more to herself than to Jake. "I kept looking at her and thinking, I want to feel like that. Please God, just give me one more chance to feel like that. Do you know what I'm trying to say?"

Jake shook his head. "I'm not sure."

Mattie pulled her shoulders back, pushed her body to the edge of the sofa. "Let me make this simple for you, Jake. The doctor tells you you have a year to live. How are you going to spend it?"

"Mattie, this is irrelevant."

"It's very relevant. Answer the question, counselor. One year—how do you spend it?"

"I don't know."

"Would you spend it living with a woman you didn't love?"

"It's not as simple as that," he argued.

"On the contrary, it's very simple. You married me because I was pregnant, because you're basically a decent man who wanted to do the right thing, the same reason you came back when we learned I was dying. And that's good and that's admirable and I appreciate it, I really do. But you've served your time. You're paroled for good behavior. You don't have to be here anymore."

"You're going to need someone to take care of you, Mattie."

"I don't need a babysitter," Mattie insisted. "What I need is to be with someone who loves me. What I *don't* need is to be with someone who loves someone else."

"What do you want me to do? Tell me what you want me to do, and I'll do it."

"I want you to figure out why you came back," Mattie said again. "Was it for me, or was it for you? Because if it was for you, so that you could feel good about yourself, then I'm not interested. I won't let you feel good about yourself at my expense. I'm the one who's only got a limited amount of time left to feel good, and I don't want to spend it with someone who makes me feel bad."

"God, Mattie, it was never my intention to make you feel bad."

"I don't give a shit about your intentions!" Mattie cried. "What I want is your passion. What I want is your loyalty. What I want is your love. And if I can't have those things, if you can't at least *pretend* to love me," she said, that word again, "for a year or two or however long I have left, then I don't want you here."

And then they said nothing, each one staring straight ahead, Mattie at the windows behind Jake's head, Jake at the Rothenberg lithograph over Mattie's right shoulder. It was so ironic, Mattie thought. She, who could pretend no longer, was insisting her husband do just that. For a year or two or three or five. Was it really so much to ask? Was she really so difficult to love?

Her father obviously thought so. He'd walked out of her life without so much as a backward glance. Years later, she managed to track him down to some artists' colony in Santa Fe, and she called him long-distance and demanded to know why he'd never once tried to contact her, and all he could do was mumble something lame about it being better this way, that they should let sleeping dogs lie, an expression her mother would surely have appreciated had Mattie confided in her. But her mother had long ago deserted her as well, emotionally if not physically. And Jake had only married her because she was pregnant. Yes, they were lining up to love her.

What was she going to do if Jake got up from his chair right now and walked out the door? Call Lisa? Ask if she could borrow her husband? Or Stephanie? Ask her if Enoch had a friend? Or Roy Crawford? Just think how he'd react to anything as complicated as a wheelchair, Mattie thought, too tired to laugh. Too frightened.

It was just a matter of time before a wheelchair was exactly where she'd be. And then what? Professional caregivers were expensive. She'd only be able to afford one for so long. And the next step? A chronic care facility? A state hospital? A place where she could be abandoned and ultimately forgotten. No one wanted to be around a woman whose every gasp was a reminder of their own mortality. At least Jake had been willing to stick around. What difference did his motives make? Who was she to be so proud, so foolish?

"Could you do that, Jake?" Mattie asked, her voice small but surprisingly stubborn. "Could you pretend to love me?"

Jake stared at Mattie for what felt like an eternity, his normally expressive face impossible to decipher. He rose slowly to his feet and walked across the room, stopping just in front of her, extending his hand for her to take. "Let's go to bed," he said.

They didn't make love.

There'd been enough sex for one night, they both agreed.

Mattie took off her robe, letting it fall to the floor, and climbed into bed as Jake walked to the window.

"Please leave it closed," Mattie said. "It's so cold out there."

Jake hesitated, standing in front of the window for several seconds, as if paralyzed, his body swaying precariously.

"Is something wrong?"

Jake shook his head. Then he pushed himself away from the window and quickly stripped to his boxer shorts before climbing into bed beside her. Mattie felt the mattress sink beneath his unexpected weight. She watched him fall back against his pillow, his eyes open wide, staring blankly at the ceiling.

He's trying to figure out what he's doing here, Mattie thought, watching him. He's trying to understand how he ended up back in the middle of this mess, this mess he thought he was finally clear of, the mess he's right back in the thick of, and he doesn't understand what happened. Would it help you to know that I don't understand it any better than you do? Mattie wanted to ask, suddenly overwhelmed by fatigue. Can you really pretend, Jake? she wondered. Can you pretend to love me?

As if he heard her thoughts, Jake rolled over on his side to face her. He kissed her softly on the lips. "Turn over," he said gently. "I'll hold you."

At first Mattie thought the sounds were part of her dream. She was being chased through the streets of Evanston by a young black man, his long serpent's tongue stretching toward her, threatening to ensnare her. She struggled to outrun him, her breathing increasingly labored and painful, as loud as her footsteps on the hard pavement. "No!" she gasped, through lips that didn't move. "No!"

A crowd suddenly gathered, and Mattie realized she was naked. The black man chasing her was naked as well, his long muscular legs gaining on her, his hands reaching out to slap at her sides. She felt his fist connect with her back, knocking the wind right out of her. Mattie stumbled, fell forward. "Watch out for the gas main," a bystander warned. "Watch out for the gas."

"No!" an onlooker shouted, slapping at her arm. "No!"

Mattie forced her eyes open, suddenly aware of Jake moaning beside her. It took her a minute to realize what was happening, that Jake was beside her in bed, that their dreams were interlapping, that she'd incorporated parts of his nightmare into her own. "No gas," he was saying over and over again, his arms flailing about in growing panic, so that Mattie had to jump back to avoid another blow. "No. No gas. Don't. Don't."

"Jake," Mattie said gently, touching his shoulder, feeling him cold and clammy beneath her fingertips. "Jake, wake up. It's all right."

Jake opened his eyes, stared at Mattie with no sign of recognition.

"You were having a nightmare," she explained, watching his face absorb the reality of his surroundings. He actually looks glad to be here, Mattie thought, smiling at her husband through the darkness. "It sounded like you were trying to stop someone from turning on the gas. Do you remember?"

Jake nodded. "My mother," he said simply, sitting up in bed, pushing his dark hair away from his forehead.

"Your mother?"

He looked toward the window. Mattie waited for him to brush her concern aside as perfunctorily as he had his hair, the way he usually did, to tell her to go back to sleep, that it was nothing. "When I was little," he said instead, surprising her, "my mother would get drunk and threaten to turn on the gas oven so that we'd all die in our sleep."

"My God."

"It was a long time ago. You'd think I'd be over it by now." He tried to laugh, but the laugh died in his throat. "I'm sorry I woke you up."

Mattie reached over to wipe the sweat from Jake's

forehead with the palm of her hand. There was so much about her husband she didn't know, so much he'd never told her. "Is that why—" she began, then stopped, so many things suddenly clear. Slowly Mattie edged away from Jake's side, climbing out of bed and walking to the bedroom window. In one sweeping motion, she brushed aside the heavy ivory curtains, and pushed open the window. The cold night air leaped into the room, like a hungry cat. Wordlessly, Mattie returned to the bed and crawled in beside her husband. "Turn over," she whispered. "I'll hold you."

TWENTY-ONE

So, what did you think of the article in *Chicago* magazine?"

Jake glanced briefly at the magazine on his desk, then back to the beautiful young woman sitting across from him. Her name was Alana Isbister— *"Was*bister," she joked when they were introduced. "I'm divorced." Definitely a come-on, Jake recognized, smiling as he motioned for the reporter from *Now* magazine to sit down in one of two dark blue chairs in front of his desk. A year ago he would have come back with something equally witty and seductive, a casual throwaway line that would have literally charmed the pants right off her. Even six months ago, at the height of his relationship with Honey, he would have been tempted to respond. Today he didn't have the energy, the strength, or even the desire to pursue anything more complicated than the preliminary interview she'd requested, so he simply smiled and answered her question.

"I thought the article was highly complimentary," Jake said.

"The picture doesn't do you justice." Alana Isbister's full coffee-colored lips settled into a provocative pout.

Jake pushed the magazine out of his line of vision. He'd never been comfortable with photographs of himself. They were such a lie. Every time he looked at one, like this one of him all decked out in lawyerly gray flannel for the cover of *Chicago* magazine, every hair in place, including the few artfully arranged strays that spilled across his forehead, his engaging smile a careful study in modest confidence, the blue of his eyes highlighted by the blue of his tie, he felt a rush of utter and pure revulsion. "Jake Hart, the Great Defender," the bold headline proclaimed. "The Great Pretender" was more like it.

"Your editor said you had a different sort of piece in mind," Jake prompted, sneaking a peek at the small digital clock on his large oak desk. Two-fifteen already. In less than an hour he was supposed to pick up Kim at school and drive her to her appointment with her therapist. Then he had to pick up Mattie at home, the two of them returning to get Kim at the end of her session, and then all of them were heading over to see Mattie's mother, a visit Jake was dreading almost as much as Mattie. He knew the visit would upset her, and when Mattie was upset, her condition seemed to worsen. She'd need his support more than ever, and he needed some time alone to prepare for what would undoubtedly prove to be a very difficult afternoon. The last thing he needed to be doing was wasting precious time talking to a reporter from some silly avant-garde magazine, no matter how popular a magazine it might be or how beautiful the reporter in question unquestionably was.

Jake had only agreed to a preliminary meeting with the woman from *Now* because the powers-that-be at the firm, the same powers who were considering him for a full partnership, had strongly indicated their desire that he continue to cooperate with the press. Money couldn't buy this kind of publicity, they told him. It doesn't matter what they say about you as long as they get the name of the firm right.

"We think our readers would like to get to know you more *personally,*" Alana Isbister was saying, smoothing her long straight brown hair behind one ear, blinking mascara-kissed eyes. "So much has been written about Jake Hart, the attorney—congratulations, by the way, on winning the Butler case—but almost nothing has been written about Jake Hart, the man."

"Ms. Isbister—"

"*Was*bister." She laughed, held up her empty ring finger.

"*Was*bister," he repeated.

"Why don't we just make that Alana?"

Jake nodded. Had flirting always been this exhausting? Maybe he just needed a good night's sleep. In the six weeks since he'd moved back into Mattie's bed, he'd rarely slept through the night without interruption. Mattie was always twitching or coughing, jumping up in bed gasping for air, occasionally falling down on her way to the bathroom in the middle of the night. He'd wake up and hold her, assure her he was up anyway. They'd talk for a few minutes, try to get comfortable again. At first, it had been difficult, pretending to be alert, pretending to be interested, pretending not to resent lying awake in the middle of the night for hours on end. But soon he'd found himself telling her about his day, discussing his growing frustration with office politics, occasionally regaling her with tales of former courtroom exploits. Occasionally some problem at work would disturb his sleep, and he'd find himself lying there, hoping Mattie would wake up so they could discuss it. Sometimes, when neither one of them could fall back to sleep, they'd end up making love. Afterward, he'd wonder about the other man she'd been involved with, whether she thought about him at all, whether she'd be with him if things were different. Was that the kind of personal information *Now* magazine had in mind? "I'm really not that interesting outside the courtroom," Jake demurred. "It's my caseload that's fascinating, not me."

Alana Isbister cast a skeptical eye around the room. "Somehow I tend to doubt that. Any man who would hang a painting of a baked potato on the wall behind his desk is a man to be reckoned with."

"My wife chose all the art in this room." Jake was surprised to note the trace of pride in his voice.

"You've been married for how long?"

"Sixteen years."

You married me because I was pregnant, he heard Mattie interrupt. *You've served your time. You're paroled for good behavior. You don't have to be here anymore.*

"Amazing," Alana Isbister said, fiddling with the

small tape recorder in her lap. "You don't mind if I put this on, do you?"

Jake shrugged, tapped the top of the charcoal gray phone on his desk. He'd promised to call Honey before three o'clock.

I don't need a babysitter, Mattie continued, unprompted. *What I need is to be with someone who loves me. What I don't need is to be with someone who loves someone else.*

He knew Honey was trying to be understanding about his decision not to see her for the next couple of months, but she was finding their enforced separation difficult. As was he, he assured her, although he certainly didn't miss those damn cats.

If you can't at least pretend to love me, then I don't want you here, Mattie insisted. *Could you do that, Jake? Could you pretend to love me?*

He hadn't answered her. Instead he'd pushed his fears and doubts aside and silently accompanied Mattie up the stairs to their bedroom, allowing instinct to prevail over reason, refusing to think on it further. "I'm sorry. Did you say something?" Jake asked, watching Alana Isbister cross and uncross long shapely legs beneath her short black skirt.

"I was asking if there were any more at home like you."

It took Jake a few seconds to understand the question. "My older brother is dead," he replied flatly. What did his family history have to do with anything? This was even more intrusive than questions about his marriage. If this was what she'd meant by getting to know him more personally, he wanted no part of it. "I haven't seen my younger brother in almost twenty years."

Alana Isbister hunched forward in her chair, displaying a formidable cleavage. "Now, you see, that's very fascinating. Tell me more."

"Nothing to tell." Jake tried his best not to look as uncomfortable as he was beginning to feel. As long as they get the name of the firm right, he reminded himself. "My older brother died in a boating accident when he was eighteen. My younger brother and I simply lost touch after I left home."

"And how old were you when you left home?"

"Seventeen."

"Even more fascinating."

"Not really." Jake stood up, walked to the row of bookshelves beside his desk, pretended to be looking for something in particular.

"Where did you go after you left home?"

"I rented a basement apartment over on Carpenter Street for a couple of years. Horrible little room, but I loved it."

"How did you support yourself?"

"Worked three jobs," Jake explained, lifting a book on criminal law and procedure from the shelf. "Delivered newspapers in the morning, worked at a hardware store after school, did telemarketing on weekends."

"And your parents? How did they feel about all this?"

"You'd have to ask them," Jake said, bristling as he walked around to the front of his desk, the collar of his pale blue shirt digging into his Adam's apple, threatening slow strangulation. "Ms. Isbister—"

"Alana."

"Ms. Isbister," he repeated, coughing into his hand, "I don't think this interview is going to work out." He motioned vaguely toward the door.

Alana Isbister was instantly on her feet, trying to balance the tape recorder in her hand while simultaneously smoothing her short skirt across her slender thighs. "I don't understand. Did I say something to offend you?"

"It's not you. It's me. I'm just not very comfortable discussing my personal life."

"Jake . . . ," she said.

"Mr. Hart," he corrected, watching her green eyes blink with amazement. "Really, I have to insist." He walked to the door, opened it, stood waiting.

"You're kicking me out?"

"I'm sure there are any number of other lawyers in the firm you'd find equally fascinating."

He waited as Alana Isbister returned her tape recorder to her large black floppy purse and gathered her long green tweed coat under her arm. She walked to the door, stopped in front of him, held out her card.

"Why don't you think about this some more and call me if you reconsider."

Jake took the card from her outstretched hand. As soon as she was out of sight, he dropped it into his secretary's wastepaper basket.

"That interview was almost as short as her skirt," his secretary observed, eyes twinkling mischievously beneath a long fringe of strawberry blond bangs.

"No more reporters, no more interviews," Jake said flatly, walking back into his office, about to shut the door behind him when his hand was stopped by the instantly recognizable voice of Owen Harris, one of the firm's more senior partners.

"Jake. Good, you're here. Hard man to find these days. Need to talk to you a minute. Like you to meet Thomas Maclean, his son Eddy." Owen Harris was a compact little man in every respect. He was short, trim, as precise in his diction as he was in his made-to-measure navy blue suits, a man who used only as many words as were absolutely necessary. He routinely dropped vowels, discarded verbs, and seemed to disavow conjunctions altogether. Still, he was an expert at getting his point across.

Jake. Good, you're here. Hard man to find these days. Hard to miss the point of that little barb. Had he really been spending that much time away from the office?

Jake shook hands with the imposing father-and-son duo, noting the father was by far the handsomer of the two men, although his son was easily the taller. He ushered the three men into his office, motioned them toward the green-and-blue sofa at the end of the small room. Only Eddy Maclean sat down, one long leg carelessly crossing over the other, his head lolling back against the top of the sofa as if he were bored with the whole proceedings before they'd even begun.

"Interesting art," the elder Maclean said, remaining on his feet even after Jake pulled over one of the chairs from in front of his desk.

"Jake's the maverick in the firm," Owen Harris stated, equal measures of regard and dismay weaving through his clipped tone.

"Every firm needs one." Jake forced a smile onto his face, wondering what they'd make of the Raphael Goldchain photograph now hanging on the wall of his office at home. He cast a furtive glance at his watch. Almost two-thirty. He hoped this meeting wouldn't take long. At this rate, he doubted he'd have time to call Honey.

"You're familiar with Mr. Maclean's chain of discount drugstores," Owen Harris began.

"Shop there all the time," Jake said. "Is there some problem?"

"I'll let Tom fill you in," Owen Harris said, already in the doorway, nodding his nearly bald head up and down. "Don't need me." He closed the door after him.

Once again Jake stole a quick glance at his watch.

"Are we keeping you from something?" Thomas Maclean asked.

Clearly a man who didn't miss a thing, Jake realized, resolving to be more careful. "We have time," he said. "What can I do for you?"

The senior Mclean looked from Jake to his son, who was the picture of studied nonchalance. "Sit up straight, for God's sake," Thomas Maclean snarled, and the young man's well-toned body snapped to attention, although the look on his face remained bored, disinterested. "It seems my son was involved in a rather unfortunate incident last night."

"What kind of incident?"

"Involving a young woman."

"She's a slut. Everybody knows it," Eddy Maclean sneered, rolling his light hazel eyes, running a lazy hand through his shoulder-length brown hair.

"What kind of incident?" Jake repeated.

"Apparently, there was a party at somebody's house. The parents were away on holiday. My son met this girl—"

"Why don't you let your son tell me what happened?" Jake interrupted.

Thomas Maclean pulled back his large, square shoulders, scratched the side of his long nose, and sat down in the blue straight-backed chair Jake had provided, waving his hand in the air to indicate his son had the floor.

"She came on to me, man," Eddy Maclean said immediately. "She's this real ugly chick, man. I never would have touched her if she hadn't come on to me."

"So you touched her," Jake said, already knowing the rest of the story.

"Not like she says I did. I didn't do anything she didn't want me to."

"What exactly did you do?"

Eddy Maclean shrugged. "You know."

"Apparently," the senior Maclean interrupted, "they had sex."

"How old are you, Eddy?" Jake asked.

"Nineteen."

"And the girl?"

"Fifteen."

"He didn't know how old she was till later," Thomas Maclean clarified. "Apparently, this girl looks much more mature than she is."

"Does this girl have a name?" Jake asked, trying not to picture his daughter naked in a bed with Eddy Maclean.

"Sarah something."

"Sarah something," Jake repeated, fighting the urge to wrestle the young man to the ground and pummel him into unconsciousness. Was that how his daughter's erstwhile lover referred to her? As Kim something?

"Ugly chick. We never would have touched her if she hadn't started it."

"We?"

"Apparently there were two other boys involved," Thomas Maclean volunteered.

Jake walked over to his desk, leaned against it. At least finding Kim with that boy had provided them with the leverage they needed to get Kim to a therapist. She was dealing with a lot of issues. She needed to talk to someone. "I think we have to start from the beginning."

"Apparently—" the senior Maclean began.

"In Eddy's own words," Jake interrupted. "If you don't mind."

Thomas Maclean nodded his permission. Eddy Maclean cleared his throat. Jake waited, aware of the small clock on his desk ticking behind him.

"We went to this party."

"Who went?"

"Me, Mike Hansen, Neil Pilcher."

"And what happened at the party?"

"Nothing. It was a real drag. A bunch of teenyboppers dancing to the Spice Girls. We were all set to leave. Then this chick comes up to us and says for us not to go, the party's just getting started."

"This girl was Sarah?"

"Yeah. She says she's seen me around and she thinks I'm real cute. You know, shit like that. What am I supposed to think?"

"What *did* you think?"

"Same thing any guy would think. You know—that she's interested."

"So what happened?"

"I say we'll stick around if she makes it worth our while. She says, sure thing. We go upstairs, into one of the bedrooms."

"And then what?"

He smiled. "We had sex."

"And your friends, Neil and Mike, where were they while this was going on?"

"At first they were outside the door. You know—standing guard."

"Standing guard against what?"

The boy shrugged. "We didn't want to be interrupted."

Jake rubbed his forehead, trying to keep a budding headache at bay. "You said 'at first.' I take it Neil and Mike got tired of standing guard and came inside."

"They wanted a piece of the action."

"The action being this fifteen-year-old girl."

"Just a minute," Thomas Maclean interjected.

"I thought she was older," his son reiterated.

"How did she feel about the others joining in?" Jake asked, trying to keep the disgust out of his voice, the image of his daughter out of his head.

"She didn't object."

"She didn't say no, or ask you to stop at any point?"

"She was saying a lot of things, man. It's not like we were listening to every word this chick was saying."

"So she could have said no," Jake stated.

"She wanted it, man. She's just crying rape because she found out who my old man is, and she wants a piece of the pie."

"She's claiming you raped her?"

"Surprise, surprise," the young man spat out in disgust.

"I have a friend in the state's attorney's office," Thomas Maclean clarified. "He called to tell me the girl and her family were at the police station, and it looked as if they'd be issuing a warrant for my son's arrest. We came here immediately."

Jake walked around his desk, sat down, stared openly at the clock. Two-forty-eight. "What else?" Jake asked.

"What do you mean, what else?" Thomas Maclean's voice stopped just short of indignant.

Jake pointed with his chin toward Eddy Maclean. "He knows what I mean." There was always something else, Jake knew, waiting.

"She claims she was a virgin."

"And you dispute this?"

"Hard to tell, man. I mean, you go in the back door, sometimes there's blood."

It took a minute for Jake to figure out exactly what the young man was talking about. "Are you saying you sodomized her?"

"*I* didn't, man. That's not my scene. But hey, Neil, he's an ass man from way back."

"Is this relevant?" Thomas Maclean demanded with

the skewered logic of those rich and powerful enough always to get their way. "If the girl consented, what difference does it make what she consented to?"

"I don't like surprises," Jake responded calmly. "If I'm going to represent your son, which, I assume, is why you're here, then I need to know all the facts."

"Of course," Thomas Maclean said, backing off. "So what happens now?"

"My advice would be to go down to the police station and have your son turn himself in. I'll call one of my associates and have him accompany you—"

"What do you mean, one of your associates? What about you?"

"I'm afraid I have a prior commitment—"

"Cancel it."

"I can't do that." Jake's voice was firm. He pressed the intercom. "Natasha, get a hold of Ronald Becker and ask him to come to my office immediately. Thank you," he said, clicking off before his secretary had a chance to reply. "Ronald Becker is a highly competent young attorney, and this is a very basic procedure."

"Owen Harris assured me that you would handle everything."

"I am handling everything."

"Personally."

Personally, Jake repeated silently. That word again.

Could he really do this? Could he really palm a very important client off on an associate, no matter how basic the procedure, so that he could drive his daughter to her therapist? So that he could chauffeur his wife to her mother's?

There was a knock on the door, and Ronald Becker, a young man with curly salt-and-pepper hair and a slight gut pushing on the buttons of his brown pin-striped jacket, walked into the room, his head bobbing up and down, rather like a pigeon, Jake thought, making the appropriate introductions.

"I need you to accompany the Macleans to the police station," he said. "Eddy will be turning himself in, but offering nothing further. You'll accompany him to the courthouse, where he'll enter a plea of not guilty to whatever charge is pending, and post whatever bond is necessary." He turned toward the father and son, now both on their feet and staring at him in open-mouthed amazement. "Mr. Becker will take care of whatever questions you have on the drive to the station. Trust me, there's nothing complicated here. You'll be home in time for dinner. In the meantime, I'll have my secretary schedule another appointment with you for early next week."

"Next week?"

"Let me give the matter some thought over the weekend and decide what I think would be the best way for us to proceed. Now, I really have to go," Jake said, one foot already out the door. "Mr. Becker will take good care of you."

It was only when Jake was alone in the elevator that he realized the full import of what he'd just done. He threw his head back and laughed out loud. When the elevator reached the lobby, he was still laughing.

TWENTY-TWO

"So, how did it go with Rosemary?" Mattie was asking, twisting around in her seat, staring at Kim expectantly.

Kim shrugged, pressed her nose against the car window, feeling it cold against her skin as her warm breath caused the window to fog up around her. She drew a stick figure of a woman with frizzy hair in the glass with her index finger. "Fine," Kim said, immediately rubbing the image away with the bottom of her coat sleeve.

"She seems like a very nice woman."

"I guess." Kim closed her eyes, waited until she heard her mother turn around before opening them again. She fell back against the plush leather interior of her father's car, stared out the side windows at the mounds of stubborn snow. Was winter never going to be over? Here it was the beginning of March, and there was still almost a foot of snow on the ground. Of course, the faster time passed, the less time there was. At least as far as her mother was concerned. Kim sat forward in her seat, reached out her hand to touch her mother's shoulder. But her mother and father were whispering conspiratorially, and Kim quickly withdrew her hand.

"Yes, sweetie?" her mother asked, as if she had eyes in the back of her head. "Did you want to say something?"

Kim grunted, watching a red sports car pass them on the inside lane. Her father had somehow managed to convince the car dealership to take back the red Corvette her mother had purchased at the time she first learned of her illness. Why should that surprise her? Kim wondered, absently counting the number of red cars on the road, the way she used to do when she was a child. If her father could convince seemingly sensible people to let murderers walk free, then surely it took no effort on his part to convince car dealers to take back their red Corvettes. He was Jake Hart, after all, the Great Defender, lionized, and all but canonized, in the most recent issue of *Chicago* magazine. He could convince anyone of anything.

"Did anyone at school say anything about the article on your father?" Mattie was asking, as if she were privy to every thought in her daughter's head.

"No," Kim said, although several of her teachers had in fact remarked on it.

"What did you think of it, Kimmy?" her father asked.

"Didn't read it," Kim lied. The truth was she'd read it so many times, she could have recited it by heart.

"I thought it was very complimentary," Mattie said, and Kim heard her father laugh. "What's so funny?" her mother asked.

"Same words I used this afternoon," Jake said, as Kim squirmed in her seat.

Suddenly they were so damned compatible, she thought. They never fought anymore. They never yelled. Never even raised their voices. Ever since her father had moved back into her mother's bedroom, they'd turned into Mr. and Mrs. Congeniality. Sometimes she'd wake up in the middle of the night and lie there in bed waiting for the once-comforting sound of their strained whispers, like the ones she grew up with, her signal to jump out of bed and rush to her mother's defense. But the only whispers Kim heard lately were usually followed by a muffled barrage of giggles, and one time, when she'd tiptoed over to her parent's bedroom to make sure everything was all right, she'd seen her father's body twisting inside the blankets as he positioned himself over her mother, and she realized, with no small degree of revulsion, that her parents were making love.

That was the way it went these days in the Hart household: her parents always agreeing with one another, laughing at each other's feeble jokes, conferring with each other over the best way to handle difficult situations. Like their insistence she see a therapist after discovering her with Teddy, she thought, stifling a groan in her throat. Not that experimenting with sex was synonymous with mental illness, they were quick to explain. It was natural for teenagers to experiment with sex, they stressed, not wanting to appear too hyp-

ocritical. Just that coupled with her recent behavior
and their own recent separation and reconciliation, not
to mention Mattie's condition, well, Kim obviously
had a lot on her plate. She needed someone to talk to,
to help her sort out some of her feelings during this
very difficult time.

What was there to talk about? Kim wondered,
remaining stubbornly silent throughout most of her
initial session with the therapist. Teddy hadn't even
called since his rather hasty exit from her bedroom
that night. He ran the other way whenever he encoun-
tered her in the school corridors. And of course the
whole student body had heard what happened, how
the condom had come off, how she'd screamed for him
to get it out, how her mother had burst in on them
while they slept, how he'd had to grab his clothes and
run for his life. Deflowered and deserted, Kim
thought, permitting herself a slight chuckle. A first
time to remember.

"How did you feel when you saw your mother
standing there?" Rosemary Colicos asked at Kim's
first session with the almost aggressively unattractive
social worker.

"Embarrassed," Kim answered reluctantly. "Angry."

"Relieved?" Rosemary asked.

Stupid question, Kim thought at the time. Why
would she be relieved at her mother discovering her in
bed with Teddy Cranston? And yet, the more sessions
Kim had with the middle-aged woman whose streaked
blond hair looked as if it had been plugged directly
into an electrical socket, the less stupid the question
seemed.

It was the same with most of the questions Rosemary asked: "What do you think motivated you to have sex with Teddy under your parents' roof?" "Are you angry at your mother for being sick?" "What would you be giving up if you forgave your father?"

"Lust." "Of course not." "Nothing," came Kim's immediate replies. But over the course of the last six weeks, Rosemary had subtly forced Kim to rethink her answers. Maybe she *was* relieved at having been discovered. Maybe being discovered was exactly what she'd had in mind when she invited Teddy over. And if she wasn't angry at her mother, then why did everything her mother said and did these days annoy her so much? As to what she would be giving up if she could somehow manage to forgive her father, well, Kim could sum that up in one word—power.

"So, how come we're going to Grandma Viv's?" Kim asked, a deliberate challenge in her voice. "I thought you didn't like to go there."

"It's been a long time," Mattie admitted.

"So why now? What's the special occasion?" Kim saw her mother's shoulders stiffen, noted the pinched look that filled her father's eyes in the rearview mirror. They were going to tell her grandmother about Mattie's condition, she realized in that instant. They were going to tell her grandmother that her daughter was dying. "I don't feel well," Kim cried suddenly. "Stop the car. I think I'm going to be sick."

Immediately, her father pulled the car to the side of the road. Kim pushed the door open, jumped out of the car, crouched in the middle of the sidewalk, a series of dry heaves racking her thin frame. She felt her mother squat beside her, her arms draping protectively across her shoulders. "Take deep breaths, sweetie," her mother was coaxing, smoothing Kim's hair away from her face. "Take deep breaths." Was this how her mother was going to feel? Kim wondered, fighting for air. Was this what it felt like to choke to death?

It wasn't the first time something like this had happened. It happened the other day at school as she was walking toward the cafeteria. This awful shortness of breath, the air literally freezing in her mouth, as if a large chunk of ice had wedged itself at the back of her throat. She'd run into the nearest washroom and locked herself inside one of the empty cubicles, circling the tiny space in front of the toilet like a caged tiger at the zoo, flapping her hands in front of her face, fighting to get air into her lungs. She was dying, she understood in that moment. She'd inherited her mother's awful disease.

Amyotrophic lateral sclerosis.

Standard run-of-the-mill anxiety.

At least according to Rosemary Colicos. "Which doesn't mean these attacks aren't scary and awful," the therapist told her. "Just not fatal."

"What about the fact my foot keeps falling asleep?" Kim demanded during today's session.

"It might be a good idea to get out of those heavy boots from time to time," Rosemary suggested, motioning toward Kim's tight knee-high black leather boots. "You sit all day in boots like those, your feet are bound to fall asleep occasionally. You're not dying, Kim," she assured her. "You're going to be all right."

Was she? If so, what was she doing on her hands and knees heaving bile into the middle of an icy sidewalk in the middle of Chicago in the middle of a wintry Friday afternoon?

After what seemed like an eternity, the gagging reflex stopped, and Kim felt her chest expand with air. She wiped the tears away from her eyes, lay her head on her mother's shoulder, felt the cold sun surprisingly warm against her cheek.

And then her father's shadow was looming over them, blocking out the sun. "Are you okay?" he was asking.

Kim nodded, slowly climbing to her feet, then turning to help her mother. But Jake was already beside Mattie, one hand under her arm, the other around her waist, and Mattie was leaning her full weight against him. She didn't need Kim's help.

"Are you all right, sweetie?" Mattie asked as they climbed back into the car.

"Fine," Kim said. "It must have been that hot dog I wolfed down at lunch."

"I thought you didn't eat red meat," her father said.

And then no one said another thing until the car pulled to a stop in front of her grandmother's house.

"Go ahead, pick one." Her mother was motioning excitedly toward the litter of eight new puppies crawling all over each other inside the large cardboard box on Grandma Viv's kitchen floor. Mattie had this huge loopy grin across her face, and there were tears in her eyes, the kind of tears you got when you were doing something you knew was going to make someone really happy. Even her father's face had that dumb smile plastered across it. And Kim could feel the same stupid expression tugging at her own lips. Her grandmother, smiling discreetly beside the old avocado-colored stove at the far end of the small green-and-white kitchen, with at least six other dogs circling her thick ankles, was the only person in the room who still looked like a human being, and not like some goofy sort of alien.

"Is this a joke?" Kim asked warily, afraid to approach the wriggling cardboard box.

"Which one do you want?" her mother asked.

"I can't believe this. You're letting me have a puppy?"

"Happy birthday, Kimmy," her father said.

"Happy birthday," her mother echoed.

"It's not my birthday till next week." Kim backed away from the box. Was there some reason they were celebrating her birthday a week early? Was there some new problem with her mother?

"It's all right, Kim," her mother told her, once again invading the deepest recesses of her daughter's mind without her permission. "We just wanted it to be a surprise. We were afraid if we waited until next week—"

"I don't know which one to choose," Kim squealed, throwing herself toward the box before her mother had a chance to finish her explanation and lifting one small white bundle after another into her hands. "They're all so cute. Aren't they the cutest things you ever saw in your life?" She held one puppy out at arm's length, watched his little legs dangle between her fingers, small button eyes the color of rich dark chocolate. Teddy's eyes, Kim thought, returning the puppy to the box, selecting another whose eyes were still half closed.

"What kind of dogs are they?" Mattie asked. Kim noticed that Mattie carefully avoided direct eye contact with her mother.

"Peekapoos," Grandma Viv announced, straightening already proud shoulders and patting her short, graying brown hair. "Half poodle, half Pekingese. Smarter than both those breeds combined."

"I want this one," Kim said, kissing the top of the puppy's white coat over and over again. The puppy lifted its tiny head and licked the underside of Kim's mouth.

"Don't let him lick your lips," Mattie cautioned.

Kim ignored her mother, continued to let the tiny puppy lick her mouth, felt his tongue, eager and wet, ferret its way between her lips.

"Kim . . . ," her father said.

"For heaven's sake, you two, it's all right. Their mouths are cleaner than ours." Grandma Viv dismissed their concerns with an impatient wave of her hand. "What are you going to call him, Kimmy?"

"I don't know. What's a good name?" Kim's eyes darted back and forth between her grandmother, her father, and her mother, afraid to stop too long on anyone. So they were finally letting her have a dog. Why? Her mother had always hated dogs. She'd even gone so far as pretending she was allergic to them the summer Kim brought home a stray from the pound, insisting they give the dog to Grandma Viv. Kim had gone every week to visit him, but it wasn't the same as having a dog in your own home, one who followed you around from room to room and curled up against your feet in bed. Why the sudden change of heart? Why now, when the last thing her mother needed was a small untrained puppy underfoot?

It was official, Kim understood in that moment, fighting back a sudden shortness of breath. Her mother was dying.

"What do you think would be a good name, Mom?" Kim pushed the words around the blockage at the back of her throat.

"He's your baby," Mattie said. "You choose."

"It's a big decision."

"Yes, it is," her mother agreed.

"How about George?"

"George?" Mattie and Jake asked in unison.

"I love it," said Grandma Viv. "George is the perfect name for him."

"George and Martha," Kim said, smiling at her mother. "They go together."

"I never understood why your mother hated the name Martha so much," Grandma Viv grumbled. "I always thought it was such a lovely name. You don't see Martha Stewart calling herself Mattie, do you? Who wants some tea?" she asked in the same breath.

"Tea sounds great," Jake said.

"Tea would be nice," Mattie agreed.

Kim watched her mother watching *her* mother out of the corner of her eye, trying to see Grandma Viv the way her mother did. They didn't look a lot alike. Her grandmother was shorter and stockier than her mother, and her short dark brown hair was curly and increasingly riddled with gray. Her features were coarser than her only child's, her nose broader and flatter, her jaw squarer, her eyes green as opposed to blue. Mattie had always insisted she looked exactly like her father, although there were no pictures of him anywhere to verify her claim. Unlike her mother, her grandmother never wore makeup, although her cheeks glowed bright red whenever she was angry or upset, blotches that rarely stained Mattie's perfect complexion. Still, Kim could see traces of her grandmother in the proud pull of her mother's shoulders, in the way both women held their heads, in the way each relied on her hands to express thoughts too difficult to stand on their own.

"What happened between you and Grandma Viv?" Kim used to ask.

"Nothing happened," her mother would reply.

"Then how come you never visit her? Why doesn't she ever come to our house for dinner?"

"It's a long story, Kim. There are no easy answers. Why don't you ask your grandmother?"

"I did."

"And?"

"She said to ask you."

Her mother had a strange look in her eyes, Kim thought now, as if she'd stumbled into the wrong house and wasn't sure how to extricate herself politely, which was probably exactly the way she was feeling. How long had it been since she'd been inside Grandma Viv's house anyway? How old had she been when she walked out the front door for the last time? Probably not much older than her father had been when he left home, Kim decided. It was strange, she thought, kissing the top of her new puppy's soft head. Her parents were more alike than she'd realized.

"Did you see the article about Jake in *Chicago* magazine?" Mattie asked her mother, in an obvious attempt to rekindle the conversation.

"No, I didn't." Grandma Viv walked to the sink, began pouring cold water into a kettle. "Did you bring a copy with you?"

"As a matter of fact, I have one in my purse." Mattie reached for her brown leather bag on the kitchen table.

"Tell me you didn't," Jake demurred.

Was he actually blushing? Kim rolled her eyes toward the ceiling.

"I did." Mattie giggled proudly, opening her handbag, pulling out the magazine, about to hand it to her mother when it shot out of her hands and flew across the room, sending the dogs around her mother's feet running for cover, loudly barking their consternation.

"Well, you don't have to throw it at me," Grandma Viv said testily. "That's okay, babies," she said to the assorted canines slowly creeping back into the room.

Kim saw that her mother's face had turned ashen, and that her eyes were frozen wide with horror.

"I'm so sorry. I don't know what happened."

"Are you all right?" Jake asked.

"Of course she's all right." Grandma Viv reached down to pick the magazine off the floor. "She was always a bit clumsy. Nice picture of you, Jake. The cover, no less."

"Apparently the article's very complimentary," Kim

said, watching the color return to her mother's face, purposely using her mother's word, the same word her father claimed to have used earlier. All in the family, she thought, fighting the urge to gag, taking several deep breaths.

"Are you all right, sweetie?" her mother asked.

She doesn't miss a thing, Kim thought, watching as her grandmother lowered the kettle to the stove and extricated a large white birthday cake from a box on the kitchen counter, all in one fluid motion.

"Why does everyone keep asking if everyone is all right?" Grandma Viv asked, depositing the cake in the middle of the kitchen table. "I noticed no one has asked me how I'm feeling."

"Aren't you feeling okay, Grandma Viv?"

"I'm fine, dear. Thanks for asking. So, who wants a rose?"

"I do," Kim and her mother said in unison.

They all sat down at the round Formica table, the tiny puppy sleeping in Kim's lap, Grandma Viv lifting a restless black terrier to hers, trying to get him to settle down.

"Do you think you could get the dog away from the cake?" Mattie asked her mother, although it was clearly more demand than request.

"He's nowhere near the cake." Small red blotches appeared magically on Grandma Viv's cheeks as she lowered the dog to the floor and jumped to her feet. "I seem to have forgotten the candles." Her grandmother began noisily opening and closing the kitchen drawers. "I know I have some around here somewhere."

"It's all right, Grandma Viv. I don't need candles."

"What are you talking about? Of course you need candles. What's a birthday cake without candles?"

"Kimmy," her father said, "can you put George down while we eat?"

"George is staying on my lap," Kim snapped. "And don't call me Kimmy."

"Found them," her grandmother proclaimed triumphantly, returning to the table and arranging the candles on the cake in four neat little rows. "Sixteen candles," she said, smiling at her only grandchild as she deposited an extra candle in the middle of a soft pink rose. "And one for good luck."

TWENTY-THREE

"Mom, can I talk to you a minute?"

"Of course, Martha."

Mattie inhaled a deep breath of air, letting it out slowly, trying to force a smile onto her lips. She's called you Martha all her life, Mattie reminded herself. It's too late to expect her to change now.

Her mother stared at Mattie expectantly from her seat at the kitchen table, two small dogs currently in her lap, five larger ones at her feet. Beside her, Jake sat reading the *Chicago Sun-Times*, occasionally glancing over at Mattie, smiling his support. Kim sat cross-legged on the floor beside the cardboard box of tiny puppies, cradling George in her arms, rocking him back and forth like a newborn baby. The only grandchild I'll ever see, Mattie thought wistfully, stepping into the doorway between the kitchen and the Lshaped living-dining area. "In the living room, if you don't mind." Mattie watched the puzzled look that settled on her mother's face as she lowered the dogs in her lap to the floor and rose to her feet.

"Do you want me to come with you?" Jake asked, as he'd asked several times earlier.

The last thing Mattie saw before she left the kitchen were Kim's eyes following her from the room. Be careful, the eyes warned. Mattie nodded silently, although she wasn't sure for whom the warning was intended, and backed out of the door.

The living room looked essentially the same as it always had: pale green walls and matching wall-to-wall carpeting, an unimaginative cluster of furniture that was decidedly more utilitarian than decorative, a series of muted Audubon prints on the walls. Mattie selected a relatively clean spot in the middle of the straight-backed mint green sofa by the front window, pretending not to notice the fine layer of dog hair that covered the velvet surface like a blanket. Mattie sat with her hands folded in her lap, her legs crossed at the ankles, her back arched and stiff, trying to connect with as little of the sofa as possible.

"I vacuumed right after you called," her mother said pointedly, plopping down into the green-and-white-striped corduroy chair to Mattie's left, tilting her head to one side like one of her dogs, waiting for Mattie to speak.

"The place looks nice," Mattie said, as a small brown dog with incongruously large and scraggly ears jumped onto the sofa beside her. Mattie had no idea what breed of dog it was. Probably her mother didn't either, she thought, quickly lowering the mutt to the floor, shooing him away with the toe of her shoe. Ever since she could remember, she'd been fighting with dogs for her mother's attention. The dogs always won.

"Come here, Dumpling," her mother instructed the dog, scooping him into her arms and laying him across her lap like a napkin. "Martha doesn't like dogs," she apologized, kissing the top of his head and deftly removing a gob of mucus from his eye. Immediately several more dogs flocked to her side, arranging themselves around her feet, like so many slippers. They all stared at Mattie accusingly.

"It's not that I don't like them," Mattie began, then stopped, lifting her eyes from her canine accusers to stare blankly at the wall ahead. I don't have to defend myself to a bunch of dogs, she thought. "At any rate, what I like isn't important. What's important today is what Kim likes, and Kim is certainly thrilled with George, even if he's too young to take home just yet. And for that, I thank you."

Her mother shrugged, squirmed in her seat, her cheeks acquiring a sudden faint blush. "You should thank Daisy for giving birth so close to Kim's birthday."

"I'll send her a thank-you note," Mattie said, then wished she hadn't. What was the point in being sarcastic? Especially now. Besides, her mother was much too literal for sarcasm. "Have you found homes for the other puppies yet?" she asked quickly, remembering how surprised her mother had been when she'd called several weeks earlier to ask if she might have any puppies available.

"Not yet. I wanted Kim to have first pick of the litter. But it's never a problem finding people to take them. I might even keep one or two myself."

"Isn't there some sort of city ordinance about having so many dogs?"

"Is that what you brought me in here to talk about?" her mother asked, not bothering to disguise her irritation. Again she tilted her head to one side, waiting.

"No, of course not," Mattie said, then stopped, unable to proceed. How do you tell your mother you're dying? she wondered—even a mother who's barely acknowledged your existence while you were alive? "There's something I have to tell you."

"Well, go ahead. Spit it out. It's not like you to be shy."

How would you know? Mattie wondered, but didn't ask. "You remember that actor from one of those soap operas you watch, *The Guiding Light*, I think it was—"

"I never watch *Guiding Light*," her mother corrected. "Only *General Hospital* and *Days of Our Lives*. Oh, and sometimes *The Young and the Restless*, although I can't stand the way they drag their story lines on forever."

"There was an actor on one of the soaps—he died a little while ago of something called amyotrophic lateral sclerosis," Mattie said, barely waiting for the end of her mother's sentence. "Lou Gehrig's disease," she qualified.

Her mother's eyes remained infuriatingly unresponsive, so that Mattie wasn't sure if her mother had any idea where she was going with this.

"Oh yes, I remember him. Roger Zaslow, no, Michael Zaslow, I think his name was. And you're right—he was on *Guiding Light*. It used to be *The* Guiding Light, but they changed it. Never understood why, exactly. They said they wanted to make the show more modern, bring it up-to-date. I don't see how dropping an article—"

"Mom—"

"I read about him in *People* magazine," her mother continued, one word running into the next. "They fired him. Said what good was an actor who couldn't say his lines, or something like that, according to *People* magazine anyway. He was very bitter about it, I read. Can't say I blame him. Terrible disease," she muttered, looking away, biting down on her lower lip, refusing to acknowledge the obvious, to ask why they were talking about this.

"I'm sick, Mom," Mattie said, answering the unasked, unwanted question. She watched as her mother stiffened in her chair, her eyes beginning to glaze over, the way they always did when she was confronted with unpleasant news. She'd barely begun, and already her mother was retreating, Mattie realized, leaning forward on the sofa, forcing her mother's eyes to hers. "You remember when I was in the hospital after my car accident?"

Her mother reacted with an almost imperceptible nod of her head.

"Well, the hospital ran some tests, and they discovered I have the same condition as that actor from *Guiding Light*."

Mattie heard a slight gasp catch in her mother's

throat, although her face remained immobile. "The doctors say they're very close to finding a cure, and hopefully—" Mattie stopped, cleared her throat, started again. "Realistically," she said, "I have maybe a couple of years. Confidentially," she added, lowering her voice to a whisper, "I don't think it'll be that long. New things are happening every day. It's like the disease is starting to pick up the pace."

"I don't understand," her mother said, staring past Mattie to the window overlooking the street, her long fingers purposefully stroking the dog on her lap. "You seem perfectly fine."

"Right now, I'm still functional. My arms and legs are working okay, for the most part, but that will change. The magazine that flew out of my hand before—things like that have been happening more and more often. Pretty soon I'll lose the ability to walk, and I won't be able to do anything with my hands. I won't be able to speak. Well, you know the rest." Mattie tried to read the look on her mother's face, but her expression had altered very little since she first sat down. "Are you all right?"

"Of course I'm not all right," her mother said, her voice low. "My daughter has just informed me she's dying. Did you really think I'd be all right?"

"I didn't mean—"

"I knew it was something," her mother said, eyes staring resolutely into space. "I mean, why the sudden change of heart about letting Kim have a dog? And when was the last time you called and said you wanted to come over? Never. So I knew something was up. I thought maybe you were going to tell me that you were moving to New York or California, now that Jake is such a big shot, or that he was leaving you for another woman. The usual. You know. Something. Something else. Not this. Not this."

"Mom, look at me."

"It's never what you think it's going to be," her mother continued, as if Mattie hadn't spoken. "Somebody says they have something to tell you, and you try and guess what it is, you consider all the possibilities, and they still pick the one thing you didn't imagine, the one thing you forgot to consider. That's always the way it is, don't you find?"

"Mom," Mattie repeated, "I need you to look at me."

"It's not fair of you to do this to me."

"This isn't about you, Mom," Mattie said simply, leaning over to take her mother's square chin in the palm of her hand, forcing her eyes back to hers. The dog in her mother's lap began a low growl. "I need you to listen to me. For once in my life, I need your complete, undivided attention. Do I have it?"

Wordlessly, her mother lowered the still-growling dog to the floor.

"Right now, I'm in the early stages of the disease. I'm coping pretty well. I can still work and do most of the things I did before. I've given up driving, of course, so I take a lot of cabs, and Jake and I have started going grocery shopping together. Kim helps out as much as she can—"

"Kim knows?"

Mattie nodded. "It's been very hard for her. She puts on a tough front, but I know she's having a difficult time."

"So you bought her a dog."

"We hoped it would ease her pain, give her something to focus on."

"She's a good girl."

"I know she is," Mattie said, fighting back tears. It was important to get through the rest of her agenda without tears.

"What do you want me to do? I'd be happy to take her for a few weeks. Kim tells me that you and Jake are planning a trip to Paris in April. I'd be happy to take her then," her mother said, deliberately ignoring the larger picture, her traditional method of coping. Focus on an irrelevancy, enlarge it until it blots out everything else.

"We can talk about that later," Mattie said. "*I* need you right now, Mom. Not Kim."

"I don't understand." Again, her mother's eyes returned to the window. "Do you need me to run some errands?"

Mattie shook her head. How could she make her mother understand what she was about to ask? A medium-size black dog leaped onto the sofa, making itself comfortable on the cushion beside Mattie, regarding her suspiciously through heavy-lidded eyes. "Do you remember when I was about five years old, we had a dog?" Mattie asked. "Her name was Queenie. Do you remember Queenie?"

"Of course I remember Queenie. You used to throw her over your shoulder and hold her upside down, and she never complained. She'd let you do anything."

"And then she got sick, and you said we had to put her to sleep, and I cried and begged you not to."

"That was a very long time ago, Martha. Surely, you still can't be angry at me for that after all these years. She was very sick. She was in pain."

"And she looked at you with 'those eyes,' you said, those eyes that told you it was time to put her out of her misery, that it would be cruel to keep her alive."

Her mother fidgeted restlessly in her chair. "I wonder how Kim's making out with George."

"Listen to me, Mom," Mattie said. "There's going to come a time when *I'm* going to look at you with those eyes."

"We should get back to the others. It's not right—"

"I'm going to be virtually immobile," Mattie persisted, refusing to let her mother rise from her chair, "and I'm not going to be able to move, not my legs, not my hands. I'm not going to be able to do anything to put an end to my suffering. I'm going to be helpless. I won't be able to take matters into my own hands." Mattie almost laughed at her choice of words. "The way this disease works," Mattie backpedaled, "is that the muscles in my chest are going to get weaker and weaker, resulting in breathing that's shallower and shallower, leading to shortness of breath."

"I don't want to hear this."

"You have to hear this. Please, Mom. Lisa has prescribed morphine for when that starts to happen."

"Morphine?" The word shook in her mother's mouth, wobbled into the space between them.

"Apparently morphine relieves the distress of being breathless. It acts on the respiratory center to slow the breathing down. Lisa says it's remarkable in its ability to remove anxiety, control panic, and restore calm. But there'll come a time when the morphine will be on the table beside my bed, and I won't be able to reach it. I won't be able to measure out the right amount to end my suffering. I won't be able to do what has to be done. Do you understand, Mom? Do you understand what I'm saying?"

"I don't want to talk about this anymore."

"Twenty pills, Mom. That's all it would take. You grind them up, mix them with water, pour it down my throat. In a few minutes I drift off to sleep. Ten or fifteen minutes later, I slip into a coma, and I don't wake up. Within a few hours, I'm gone. Easily. Painlessly. My suffering is over."

"Don't ask me to do this."

"Who else can I ask?"

"Ask Lisa. Ask Jake."

"I can't ask Jake to break the law. The law is his whole life. And I can't ask Lisa to risk her whole career. And I certainly can't ask Kim."

"But you can ask your mother."

"This isn't easy for me, Mom. When was the last time I asked you for anything?"

"I know you think I've been a lousy mother. I know you think—"

"None of that matters now. Mom, please, you're the only one I can ask to do this. I've been thinking about this for weeks. And I'm asking you now because, chances are, I won't be able to ask you when the time comes. All I'm going to be able to do is look at you with 'those eyes.'"

"This isn't fair. It isn't fair."

"No, it's not. None of it is fair," Mattie agreed, her

hands still gripping the sides of her mother's chair, blocking her escape, although her mother had grown still. "It's just the way it is. So I need you to promise you'll do this for me, Mom," Mattie told her. "You'll know when it's time for me to go. You'll know when it would be cruel to keep me alive, and you'll help me, Mom."

"I can't."

"Please," Mattie insisted, her voice rising. "If you ever loved me at all, promise you'll help me." Mattie held her mother's eyes with her own, refusing to let her turn aside, to look away, to hide from the choice that had been made for her. Around them, the dogs panted in unison, as if they too were awaiting her decision.

"I don't know if I can."

"You have to."

Mattie watched her mother's shoulders collapse, her eyes fall to her lap in silent acquiescence.

"Promise," Mattie pressed. "You have to promise."

Her mother's head nodded up and down. "I promise," she said.

"And you can't say anything about this to Jake. You can't say anything—"

"What's going on?" Kim asked from the doorway.

Mattie spun around in her seat, almost losing her balance and falling off the sofa. She steadied herself with her hand before scrambling to her feet. "How long have you been standing there?"

"I heard you yelling at Grandma Viv."

"I wasn't yelling."

"It sounded like yelling to me." Kim inched her way into the room, the tiny white puppy still cradled in her arms, fast asleep.

"You know how your mother just gets excited about things," Grandma Viv said.

"What's she excited about?"

"Your new puppy, of course," Mattie answered, walking to Kim's side. "May I hold him?"

"You have to be very careful," Kim cautioned, eyes shifting warily between her mother and grandmother as she deposited the puppy in Mattie's trembling hands.

The puppy was so soft, so warm, Mattie realized with surprise, lifting him to her cheek, rubbing him gently against her skin, her hands shaking visibly.

"You're not going to drop him, are you?" Kim asked.

"Maybe you better take him." Mattie returned the puppy to her daughter's eager hands. She glanced at her mother, red cheeks staining her otherwise pale face, as if she'd been struck. "We should probably get a move on," Mattie said.

"I'm not going," Kim announced.

"What?"

"Who's not going where?" Jake asked, coming into the room, looking from Mattie to her mother, then back to Mattie, his eyes asking if everything was all right.

Mattie nodded, tried to smile.

"I'm going to stay here tonight," Kim announced. "I don't want to leave George. That's all right with you, isn't it, Grandma Viv?"

"If it's all right with your parents," Mattie heard her mother say, her voice an unfamiliar monotone.

"Of course it's all right," Mattie said, full of sudden admiration for her only child. "You're a very sweet

girl," she told Kim on her way out the front door minutes later, planting a kiss on her daughter's wary cheek.
She understood Kim's decision to stay was as much
about not wanting her grandmother to be alone as it
was about not wanting to leave her new puppy.

"Sweet sixteen," Kim said with a self-conscious
curtsy.

"Watch your step," Mattie's mother cautioned as
Jake took Mattie's elbow and guided her to the car.
"It's still a bit icy in places."

"I'll be in touch, Mom," Mattie said.

Her mother nodded, a coterie of dogs barking at her
feet, and closed the front door.

"So, how'd it go?"

"It was harder than I thought it would be," Mattie
told Jake.

"She's your mother, Mattie. She loves you."

Mattie reached over and touched Jake's hand,
knowing how hard that was for him to say. Mothers
didn't always love their children, they both knew. "I
think in her own peculiar way, she does," Mattie
acknowledged, leaning back in her seat and closing her
eyes as Jake backed the car out of the driveway onto
Hudson Avenue. She pictured her mother's stony
expression when she was confiding the news of her
condition. Would her mother come through for her?
Was it reasonable to expect her to be there for her in
death as she'd never been in life? Had it been reasonable to ask? Mattie shook her head, determined not to
persevere in something that was out of her control.

"Feel like going to a movie?" Jake asked.

"I'm kind of tired. Would you mind if we just went home?"

"No, that's fine. Whatever you want."

Mattie smiled, her eyes still closed. Whatever you want. How many times had she heard her husband say that over the course of the last six weeks? He's trying so hard, she thought. Home for dinner every night, working out of the den whenever possible, running errands with her on weekends, watching television beside her in bed, even letting her control the remote. When he wasn't working, he was at her side. When he was at her side, he was holding her hand, or touching her thigh, and when they made love, which they did several times a week, it was as good as it had always been. Was he picturing Honey when he caressed the nape of her neck? Mattie wondered now. Was it Honey's breasts he suckled, Honey's legs he parted when he entered her? Mattie quickly dismissed the unwelcome image. As far as she knew, Jake hadn't seen Honey at all. There were only so many hours in the day, after all. There was only so much energy to go around. Still, where there's a will, there's a way. Wasn't that how the old saying went?

Where there's a will, there's a way, Mattie repeated silently, wondering why people knocked clichés. There was something enormously comforting about clichés. They spoke of predictability, of familiarity, of permanence. The more tenuous her health, the more Mattie appreciated their easy truths and sweeping generalities: Love makes the world go round; Love conquers all; Love is better the second time around.

Except there'd never been a first time.

"How about we stop at the supermarket and pick up a couple of steaks?" Jake was asking. "I make a terrific steak, if you recall."

"Sounds wonderful." Mattie marveled at the enthusiasm in her husband's voice. He'd have made a great actor, she thought, then decided that emoting in the courtroom was probably not all that different from emoting on the stage. Or emoting in the bedroom.

The car pulled to a sudden halt, and Mattie opened her eyes to find them parked in front of a medium-size supermarket on North Avenue. "I'll just be a minute," Jake said, already half out of the car.

"I'll come with you."

Immediately he was at her side, opening her door, helping her out of the car, escorting her inside the brightly lit store. "This way," Jake directed, guiding Mattie through the produce section, past the aisles full of canned goods and cereal boxes and fruit drinks and paper towels, toward the surprisingly large meat section at the far end of the store. The effortless way he moved, the sureness of his steps, told Mattie he'd been here before. With Honey? she wondered, trying to mask her sudden sadness with a smile.

"You seem to know your way around," she commented, despite her best efforts to remain silent.

"All supermarkets are pretty much the same, aren't they?" he said easily, reaching for several steaks, examining them closely beneath their tight plastic wrap, then returning them to the shelf, selecting several more.

"How about these?" Mattie grabbed a couple of

steaks. "These look pretty good." She was about to offer the steaks for Jake's inspection when a sudden tremor, like a small earthquake, caught hold of her arm, tossing it into the air as if it were weightless, as if it were no longer connected to the rest of her body. The steaks shot out of her hand and across the aisle, narrowly missing another shopper and knocking over a display of exotic cheeses in a nearby bin.

"What the—?" the woman shopper exclaimed, glaring at Mattie.

"Oh, God," Mattie cried, burying her hands beneath opposite arms, feeling queasy and faint, panic growing in her gut, threatening to erupt. It was happening again. Just like in her mother's kitchen. Except she was no longer in her mother's kitchen. She was in a public place. How could she do this to Jake? How could she embarrass him again by creating a scene in public? She couldn't bare to look at him. She couldn't stomach the look of horror and disgust she knew she'd find on his face.

And then another steak went flying across the aisle. And then another.

Mattie's eyes raced toward her husband, who was leaning over the meat section, gathering more packages into his hands, grinning impishly from ear to ear.

"My God, what are you doing?" Mattie asked, not sure whether to laugh or cry as he sent two more steaks flying across the aisle.

"This is fun," Jake said, unleashing two more. "Come on. It's your turn." The woman shopper ran for cover as Jake dropped another steak into Mattie's hand.

Before she could give herself time to think, Mattie hurled the packaged steak over her shoulder, hearing it land with a thud somewhere behind her as Jake followed suit with a barrage of lamb chops. By the time the manager arrived with the security guard, the entire meat section lay in scattered bundles across the floor, and Mattie and Jake were too limp with laughter to offer either explanations or apologies.

TWENTY-FOUR

I think I could use another drink." Jake looked around the old-fashioned Italian eatery known as the Great Impasta, silently signaling the busy waiter for another glass of red wine. The popular restaurant was located on East Chestnut Street, just north of Water Tower Place, only blocks away from his office, and was a favorite spot with many of the lawyers in his firm, two of whom Jake noticed dining together with their wives in a dimly lit corner of the room. So far they hadn't spotted him, for which Jake was inordinately grateful. They were two of his least favorite people—privately, he referred to them as Tweedle-Dum and Tweedle-Dumber—and besides, he'd had enough excitement for one day. He pondered again what strange force had overtaken him in the supermarket, deciding not to overanalyze what was clearly a simple act of spontaneity. Except that Jake Hart was anything but a spontaneous kind of guy. Honey claimed that even his ad-libs were carefully researched and rehearsed in advance. Honey, he thought, closing his eyes in consternation, remembering he hadn't called her all day, knowing how disappointed she'd be—with the situation, with the way things were going, with him. ("It just takes a minute to pick up a phone," he could hear her say. "Really, Jason, I don't think I'm asking for all that much.")

Bad boy Jason, bad boy Jason, bad boy Jason!

Badboyjason, badboyjason, badboyjason.

"Something wrong?" Mattie asked.

Jake opened his eyes, stared across the red-and-white checkered tablecloth at his wife of sixteen years. She didn't look that much older than the day he married her, he thought, watching as the candle from the middle of the table cast a warm glow on her otherwise pale complexion. Her hair was a little longer than when they'd first met, and she'd lost a bit of weight in the last few months, thinning out the natural oval of her face, but she was still a very beautiful woman, probably one of the most beautiful women he'd ever seen. "I just remembered that I forgot our anniversary," he said, realizing this was true. "January twelfth, wasn't it?"

Mattie smiled. "Close enough."

He laughed. "I'm sorry."

"That's all right. You made it up to me earlier." Her smile widened. "First time I've ever been thrown out of a grocery store."

"I have to admit I rather enjoyed that myself."

They laughed together, one laugh echoing the other, the two sounds overlapping, intertwining, harmonizing.

"This is a nice restaurant," Mattie said, looking around. "I love the plastic grapes and the old wine bottles. It's a nice change from the high-tech look you see everywhere these days."

"This place has been around forever," Jake said. "The food is wonderful."

"Well, I'm looking forward to it. Suddenly I'm starving."

Jake checked his watch. Almost seven-thirty. Service was very slow tonight. They'd placed their order—angel-hair pasta with red clam sauce for Mattie, beet-filled ravioli and a Caprese salad for Jake—almost forty minutes ago. Jake had already polished off two glasses of wine. He should have ordered a bottle, he thought, although there was something unseemly about ordering a whole bottle of wine when you were the only one drinking. Mattie was sticking to mineral water, which was probably a good idea. It had been quite a day for her. He reached over, took her hand in his, felt the familiar tremble.

"I'm okay, Jake," she assured him.

He smiled. Wasn't he the one who was supposed to be reassuring her?

"So you never told me about your interview with *Now*," Mattie said.

"Oh, God, that." Jake shook his head. "It was a disaster."

"A disaster? How so?"

Jake waved his hands in front of his face, as if trying to shoo away an unpleasant memory. "Ms. Isbister—"

"Who?"

"*Was*bister."

"What?"

Suddenly they were laughing, although Jake could tell by the puzzled look on Mattie's face she wasn't sure why. "The writer in question," Jake qualified, chuckling over the image of the startled reporter struggling with her tape recorder as he was kicking her out of his office, "was interested in a more personal angle than I was willing to provide."

Mattie cocked her head to one side. "How personal?"

"She asked about my parents, my brothers," Jake said, as the image of Alana Isbister was replaced by the sad faces of his brothers, Luke and Nicholas. He tried to blink them away, failed.

The waiter approached with Jake's glass of wine. "This one's on the house," he said as Jake reached out to claim his glass, "with our sincere apologies for the delay. There were some difficulties in the kitchen, but they've been resolved, and your food should be out momentarily."

"No problem," Jake said, raising his glass in a mock toast, seeing his brothers' reflection in the dark red liquid. "Thank you."

"Pas de problème," Mattie repeated quietly in French. "Merci."

"No fair. You've been studying."

"Every chance I get. I can't believe we're really going."

"Believe it, lady. Everything has been confirmed. Everything has been paid for in advance. Five more weeks, we are on our way to Paris, France."

"You sound excited."

"I *am* excited," Jake said, realizing this was true. He'd been pretending to be looking forward to this trip for so long, it had become a reality. And no one was more surprised by this unexpected development than he was. "My brother Luke always talked about going to Europe," he heard himself say. Why had he mentioned that?

"Anywhere in particular?" Mattie asked.

"Not that I can remember. He used to talk about hitchhiking from one end of the continent to the other." What was the matter with him? Hadn't he managed a successful detour away from his past? What was he doing circling around back? Clearly, the events of the afternoon had unsettled him, and the incident in the grocery store coupled with several glasses of expensive red wine had upset his normal equilibrium, loosening his tongue. Jake raised his glass to his lips, took a long sip. Might as well loosen it some more, he thought, as Luke winked at him from the bottom of the glass.

"Talk to me, Jake," Mattie encouraged softly. "Tell me about Luke."

Jake felt an immediate tug on his heart, as if the muscle had been caught by a fishhook and was about to be yanked, flopping about in useless protest, clean out of his chest. He looked to the corner of the restaurant, where Tweedles Dum and Dumber sat laughing easily with their wives. One of the Tweedle wives caught him staring and poked her husband, who turned, recognized Jake, and quickly poked his partner in turn. Soon all four Tweedles were smiling and waving at him from across the room. Jake dutifully returned their smiles, mimicked the exaggerated jauntiness of their waves. "My earliest memory is of my brother Luke screaming," he said between tightly clenched teeth, returning his full attention to Mattie. Hell, he was the one who'd started down this road. He might as well go all the way.

"Why was he screaming?"

"My mother was beating him." Jake shrugged. Standard procedure, the shrug said.

Mattie's face clouded over with pain. "How old was he?"

"Four . . . five . . . six . . . seven . . . seventeen," Jake recited. "The screams kind of blended together after a while. She beat him every day of his life."

"That's so awful." Tears filled Mattie's eyes. "He never struck back?"

"He never struck back," Jake repeated. "Not even when he was bigger than she was. Not even when one good snap of his wrist would have sent the wicked witch flying into kingdom come."

"And your father?"

Jake pictured his father in his brown easy chair in front of the living room fireplace, his face hidden behind the omnipresent newspaper in his hands, the thin paper as protective, as repellent, as a shield of heavy armor. "He never did anything. He just sat there reading his damn newspaper. When things got really bad, he'd put down the paper and walk out the door."

"He never tried to stop her?"

"He had more important things to do than be a

father to his children." Jake paused, looked directly into Mattie's eyes. "Just like me."

"You're not like him, Jake."

"No? Where was I when Kim was growing up?"

"You were there."

Jake scoffed. "I was gone in the morning before she got up, and I usually didn't get home until after she was asleep for the night. When was I actually there for her?"

"You're there now."

"It's too late now."

"It's not too late."

"She hates me."

"She loves you." Mattie reached across the table, grabbed Jake's hand. "Don't give up on her, Jake. She's going to need you very much over the next while. She's going to need her father. A girl always needs her father," Mattie whispered, recalling the afternoon she'd phoned Santa Fe to tell her father of his new grandchild, only to be informed that Richard Gill had died of a sudden heart attack three months earlier. "You're a good father, Jake," Mattie said now. "I've watched you with her. You're a wonderful father."

Jake tried to smile, his lips twisting from side to side, eventually collapsing with the effort, disappearing one inside the other as tears gathered force behind his eyes. He felt a shaking in his arm, could no longer be certain if the trembling hand was Mattie's or his own. "I'm a fraud, Mattie. I've been a fraud my whole life. My mother knew that. She recognized that about me from day one. If she were here now, I'm sure she'd give you an earful."

"Why would I listen to anything that horrible woman had to say?" Mattie asked vehemently. "Why would you?"

"You don't know the whole story."

"I know you loved your brother very much."

Jake took another long sip of wine, emptying his glass. A quiet buzz settled in at the top of his spine, separating his neck, just slightly, from his shoulders, so that his head felt as if it were suspended, floating on air. He pictured Luke floating beside him, a tall, gangly kid, never really comfortable in his own skin. Always very quiet. Very sensitive. "In many ways, it was like I was the firstborn, not Luke," Jake said, his thoughts translating themselves into words, sliding with surprising ease off his tongue. "I was the instigator, the organizer, the know-it-all, the one who took care of business. He was the dreamer, the one who talked about hitchhiking across Europe, joining a rock 'n' roll band . . ."

Mattie nodded encouragement, staring past Jake's deliberately opaque blue eyes directly into his soul. He tried to look away, couldn't. He didn't want anyone looking into his soul. It was a dark, evil place he shared with no one. So he was amazed at the sound of his own voice continuing on, as if possessed of a will of its own.

"When I was Kim's age," Jake heard himself say over the soothing buzz that had settled around his ears, "my parents rented a cottage on Lake Michigan for a couple of weeks. It was a pretty isolated spot, just a few other cottages in the area. Luke had just turned eighteen. Nicholas was fourteen. Nick was pretty much of a loner, even then, and he'd disappear first thing every morning. We wouldn't see him again until it got dark. So, it was pretty much Luke and me together every day.

"At first it was okay. As long as the weather was good, we'd swim, go for canoe rides, toss a baseball around. My father would sit on the dock and read his newspaper. My mother would lie out in the sun. But then it started raining, and it must have rained for three days straight. It didn't bother the rest of us, but it drove my mother crazy. I can still hear her railing. 'We didn't put out all this money to sit inside some goddamn ugly cottage all day!' Then she'd slap at whoever was closest. Usually Luke. 'Put that goddamn book away. What are you, some kind of faggot?' " Jake shook his head, trying to rid his mind of the unpleasant memory.

"Anyway, one of those rainy days, Luke and I were sitting in the kitchen playing Monopoly, and my mother was bored and irritable, and she started in on Luke, ragging him because he couldn't beat his younger brother at a simple board game, the usual garbage that had been coming out of her mouth for as long as any of us could remember. And Luke just sat there and took it, the way he always did, waiting for the storm to blow over. Usually she'd run out of steam after a while, but she was angry because my father had gone into town, and she'd been drinking. When Luke didn't respond, she grabbed Luke's neat little stacks of Monopoly money from the table and tossed them into the air. Luke didn't move, just sat there and gave me this little look we gave each other when things got really bad—it was kind of our little signal that we had things under control. Which, of course, we didn't."

"What happened?"

"She started calling Luke a fag and a disgusting queer, whatever filth she could think to throw at him. I told her to shut up, which normally would have shifted the focus of her anger to me, at least for a few minutes, but this time she just ignored me. I mean, she was cooking, she was on a roll. She was tossing cards and dice and fake money all over the damn place. Finally she picked up the board and whacked Luke over the head with it.

"No reaction. He didn't even lift his hand to block the blow. Just gave me that little look again. And my mother saw it, and of course it enraged her all the more. So she picked up a ketchup bottle that was sitting on the counter, and she threw it at the back of his head."

"My God."

Jake followed the scene in his mind as if he were watching a movie on TV, narrating it as it went along. "The bottle bounced off him and crashed to the floor. There was ketchup everywhere. My mother was screaming at Luke to clean it up. And Luke got up from the table really slowly, slower than I'd ever seen him move, and I thought, this is it, he's going to kill her. He's going to kill her.

"But instead he just grabbed some paper towels from the counter and started cleaning up the mess. And he didn't stop until he'd picked up every bit of broken glass, and wiped away every speck of ketchup from the floor, the table, even the walls. And my mother stood there laughing at him the whole time, calling him a dumb faggot over and over again. And he was down on his knees and he shot me that little look, and I knew he was waiting for me to give it back, but I couldn't do it. I was so disgusted with him, so ashamed of him, so *angry* at him for *not* killing her, that I thought I was going to burst. You want to know what I did?"

Mattie said nothing, staring at Jake with those wonderful blue eyes, those eyes that told him that it was all right, that *she* understood. Even if he didn't.

"I called him a dumb faggot, and I ran from the room."

Mattie's eyes never wavered, even as tears began falling the length of her cheek.

"And my mother threw her head back and laughed," Jake continued, still hearing the horrible sound of his betrayal echoing through his mother's victory laugh. "I ran out the door in the middle of that awful rain, and I kept running until my legs gave out. Then I hid in the woods until it stopped raining and got dark.

"By the time I got home, everyone was asleep. I went into Luke's room to apologize, to tell him that the person I was really angry at, ashamed of, disgusted with, wasn't him. It was me. For not killing her myself.

"But he wasn't there.

"I sat up waiting for him, but he didn't come back." Jake held his breath, released it in one painful whoosh. "We found out the next morning that he'd hitchhiked into town, got himself good and drunk, stole a boat, crashed it into somebody's pier. He died instantly. We never knew if it was an accident or not."

"My God, Jake, I'm so sorry."

"Nice guy you married, huh?"

"You were sixteen years old, Jake."

"Old enough to know better."

"You couldn't know."

"He's dead," Jake said simply. "I know that."

Mattie wiped the tears from her eyes. "And Nicholas?"

Jake pictured the sad-eyed, vaguely scruffy adolescent he hadn't seen in over fifteen years. "Nick coped by drinking, doing drugs, dropping out of school. He had a few brushes with the law, spent some time in jail, moved out of town, dropped off the face of the earth about ten years ago. I have no idea where he is now."

"Have you tried to find out?"

Jake shook his head. "What's the point?"

"Peace of mind," she said simply.

"You think I deserve peace of mind?"

"I think you do," she said.

Jake felt a fresh gathering of tears behind his eyes. Had Mattie always been so damned understanding? he wondered, looking around for the waiter. Hadn't he said their food would be out momentarily? What the hell was going on? How much difficulty could there be in preparing two orders of pasta?

"My father moved in with one of his girlfriends shortly after Luke's death," Jake continued, unprompted. "He died of cancer a few years later. My mother claimed she put a curse on him, which I don't doubt for a minute, but he must have put one on her too, because she died of the same cancer during my first year in law school." Jake paused, laughed out loud. Better than crying, he thought. "So there you have it," he said, in his best lawyer's voice. "The whole sordid tale."

"And you've been carrying around all that guilt for all these years."

"It's guilt I've earned, don't you think?"

Mattie shook her head. "I think guilt is a waste of precious time."

Jake felt a vague stirring of anger, although he wasn't sure why. "What do you suggest I do about it?"

"Let it go," Mattie said.

"Just like that?"

"Unless you enjoy torturing yourself."

Jake felt the anger ferret its way into the center of his brain, disturbing the pleasant buzz around it, sending it scattering in all directions. "You think I enjoy feeling guilty?"

Mattie hesitated, lowered her eyes. "Is it possible you've been using your guilt as a way of hanging on to Luke?" she offered softly.

"That's a load of crap," Jake shot back, startling not only Mattie but himself with the unexpected ferocity of his words. What was Mattie talking about? What kind of simplistic New Age garbage was she spouting? How dare she! Dying or not, what gave her the right? Who did she think she was, Joyce-fucking-Brothers, for God's sake? Damn her anyway. Who the hell did she think she was?

"I'm sorry," Mattie apologized quickly. "I didn't mean to upset you. I was just trying to he—hel—huln."

Jake watched Mattie's mouth contort around the strange sequence of sounds. Instantly his anger was forgotten. "Mattie, what's happening? Are you all right?"

"F—foi—fo—"

Jake could see the growing panic in his wife's eyes. What the hell was going on? He should never have snapped at her. Damn it. This was all his fault. "Do you want some water?"

Mattie nodded, took the water from Jake's out-stretched hand, her own hand shaking so hard Jake couldn't let go of the glass. She sipped at it gently, swallowed carefully. "I'm okay," she said slowly, after what felt like an eternity. But she didn't look okay, Jake thought. She looked flushed and scared, her eyes those of a terrified woman confronting a would-be assailant.

"Do you want to leave?"

She nodded without speaking.

The waiter approached with their dinners. "I'm afraid we can't stay." Jake dropped a hundred-dollar bill into the middle of the plate of steaming ravioli, then helped Mattie from her seat and quickly led her toward the front entrance, the waiter watching after them in stunned silence.

"Jake . . . Jake!" Jake recognized the voices of his partners calling after him in unison, heard their foot-steps close behind as he handed his coat check to the maître d'. "Surely you weren't leaving without coming over to say hello."

Jake turned to face the Tweedles, better known as Dave Corber and Alan Peters. "Sorry. My wife isn't feeling very well."

The two men eyed Mattie suspiciously. No doubt they were remembering her infamous outburst in court last fall, Jake surmised, and wondering about the rumors that had been circulating throughout the firm ever since about the state of Jake's marriage.

"I don't believe we've ever had the pleasure." Dave Corber grabbed at Mattie's hand even as she struggled to get her arm through the sleeve of her coat.

Mattie offered a weak smile. "Ma—Mor—Mana—"

"I'm sorry. I didn't catch that."

"We really have to go," Jake said, gathering Mattie under his arm, feeling her shaking through the thickness of her heavy wool coat as he hustled her toward the door.

"So, the little woman has a big problem holding her liquor," Jake heard Alan Peters whisper, just loud enough to be heard.

Before he could stop himself, before he even realized what he was doing, Jake spun around and grabbed his startled partner by the throat, lifting him off his short little legs and into the air, watching the man's pale eyes bulge with terror, his round face flush red with the sudden lack of oxygen. "What did you say?" Jake demanded, as all around him, patrons gasped and jumped from their seats. "Do you have any idea what kind of moron you are? I'll kill you, you stupid son of a bitch!"

"Help me! Help me!" Alan Peters cried, his voice a frightened croak.

"Jake, what are you doing? For God's sake, put him down," Dave Corber yelled.

"Somebody call the police."

Jake felt hands on his back, his sides, his arms, all of them trying to get him to loosen his grip on Alan Peter's short, squat neck.

"Jake, he can't breathe. Put him down. What are you trying to do?" Dave Corber demanded, his face almost as red as his partner's.

And then he heard her, her voice soft, unsteady, then clearer, stronger, floating above the chaos. "Jake," Mattie was pleading. "Jake, put him down. Please put him down."

Instantly Jake released his grip on the man's throat, watching him collapse in a crumpled heap on the wood floor. Ignoring the continuing screams of the Tweedle wives and the astonished exclamations of assorted onlookers, Jake turned and swept Mattie into his arms, rushing her out the door of the restaurant and into the night.

TWENTY-FIVE

Jake, do you have a few minutes?"

It was more command than request, and Jake knew it. "Certainly."

"In my office," Frank Richardson said, hanging up the phone before Jake had time to ask what the meeting was about.

Not that he didn't know. Everyone in the office knew. Everyone in the building knew. Hell, by now the entire legal profession was undoubtedly aware of the incident that had taken place at the Great Impasta last Friday night. One lawyer attacking another in the middle of a popular Italian restaurant—it was right up there with the gunfight at the OK Corral. Especially when one of the lawyers was the Great Defender himself, Jake Hart.

Rumor had it his wife was somehow involved. So

drunk she was slurring her words, the story went. Yes sir, completely unintelligible, couldn't even say her name. Not surprising. Wasn't she the one responsible for that outburst in court just last fall? And hadn't she gotten drunk and smashed up her car, ending up in the hospital? Something like that. Hadn't Jake left her soon after? Moved in with a girlfriend? Hadn't he always had a little action on the side? Maybe that's what they were arguing about in the Great Impasta. Maybe that's why she'd been drinking so heavily. Poor Alan Peters. All he did was try to say hello. Did you hear? You could actually see the indentations of Jake's fingers on his throat. Poor man was positively covered with bruises. He hadn't been able to speak all week.

Jake dropped the brochure he'd been perusing on the Hotel Danielle, located in the heart of Paris's Latin Quarter, onto the small pile of other travel brochures he'd been accumulating over the weeks and pushed his chair away from his desk. He stood up, buttoned the jacket of his olive green suit, smoothed out the nonexistent creases in his yellow-and-green print tie, and took a deep breath before throwing open his office door and stepping out into the hall. "I'll be in Frank Richardson's office if you need to reach me," he informed his secretary.

"You have an appointment in twenty minutes. Cynthia Broome," she reminded him, answering the question mark on his face.

"Have I seen her before?" Why couldn't he remember anything? Surely they'd already had this conversation at least once today.

"First time."

Jake nodded, relief mixed with agitation, and started down the long hall, dismissing the gentle landscapes and floral still lifes that hung along the walls with a shake of his head. Since he'd started accompanying Mattie on scouting missions to various galleries, he'd learned to distinguish between art that was real and art that was merely decorative. Jake had never given much thought to art of any kind before. Truth be known, he'd always considered its study something of a waste of time, a distraction from the things that were truly important. What real difference was there between impressionism and expressionism, classicism and cubism, between Monet and Mondrian, Dali and Degas?

Jake laughed. A big difference, he'd discovered, aware his movements were being monitored by at least a dozen pairs of eyes. What are you looking at? he was tempted to bellow at the secretaries as he passed each cluttered desk. Give them their money's worth. But he said nothing, ignoring their impish smiles and not-so-quiet whispers as he disappeared around the corner, heading toward the far end of the cream-colored corridor. "Cynthia Broome," he repeated out loud several times, trying to get himself back on the legal track, wondering who she was, why she wanted to see him. She better not be some damn reporter, he thought, hoping her case was a simple one, something that wouldn't demand too much of his concentration. He'd been having trouble concentrating all week. Probably because he'd been half expecting the police to burst through his door at any minute, read him his rights, arrest him for assaulting a fellow member of his esteemed profession.

"You should really call him and apologize," Mattie had been urging all week, her speech pretty much back to normal.

"Not a chance," Jake insisted stubbornly. No way he was going to apologize to some egg-shaped jerk who'd insulted his wife. The asshole had been very wise to stay clear of him all week. If he were to run into him in the hallway, Jake wasn't sure what he might do. His thick neck had felt awfully good in Jake's angry hands.

Not that Jake hadn't done his share of apologizing these last few days. "I'm sorry I was such a jerk," he told Mattie repeatedly.

"I'm the one who was out of line," she was quick to reply. "I had no business playing amateur psychologist."

"You said I was using my guilt as a way of hanging on to Luke. Is that what you really think?"

"I don't know," she admitted.

What did she mean, she didn't know? Jake stopped dead in his tracks. How could Mattie do that? Open up a huge can of worms and then just drop it, leaving the worms to crawl out of their comfortable darkness and confront the dangerous light of day.

Jake made a quick detour, ducking into the nearby men's room, grateful to find it empty. Women were always looking for deeper meanings where none existed, he thought, glaring at his image in the large mirror over the green marble sink, surprised to see how composed, how in control he appeared. Ask a guy why he likes sports, and he'll tell you it's because he likes sports. Dig deeper and you'll find a guy who *really* likes sports. But women couldn't accept that. That was why, according to Mattie, it wasn't enough for him to feel guilty because he'd deserted his brother and that desertion had contributed to his death. No, the real reason he'd held onto his guilt all these years was because it was his way of not letting go, his way of keeping all other emotions at bay. As long as he felt guilty, he didn't have to feel much of anything else. There was only so much room after all. And guilt had a way of taking up a lot of space.

Jake splashed some cold water on his face. Mattie hadn't said anything about his using guilt as a way of avoiding other emotions. Now who was playing amateur psychologist? he wondered angrily, pushing open the bathroom door with more force than he intended. It slammed against the outside wall, narrowly missing an approaching tax specialist. "Sorry," Jake apologized to the shaken attorney, who backed quickly out of Jake's way. Getting very good at apologizing, Jake thought.

Frank Richardson's office occupied the southeast corner of the thirty-second floor, and was by far the largest and most desirable office in the firm, which was fitting, considering the older man's stature as one of the firm's original founding fathers. His secretary, Myra King, who at age sixty-seven was almost as old as her boss, was already standing in front of his door, waiting to show Jake in.

"Myra," Jake acknowledged, stepping past her into Frank Richardson's office.

"Mr. Hart," she replied, closing the door after him, retreating to the safety of her desk.

Frank Richardson was standing by the window, feigning interest in the street below. He was a man of medium height and weight, with a smattering of flyaway gray hair clinging precariously to his temples. His was not an impressive profile, the brow too pronounced, the chin too weak, the nose too flat. However, all that changed when he turned his face toward you. It was then you felt the full force of the almost oppressive intelligence behind his dark hazel eyes, eyes that rendered the rest of his features an unnecessary afterthought. "Jake," Frank Richardson said warmly, motioning Jake toward one of three deep red tub chairs that were grouped around a small glass coffee table at one end of the room. A large desk, in the shape of a quarter moon, curved into a corner at the other end, its top littered with pictures of Frank's children and grandchildren. The wall behind his desk was dotted with framed diplomas and citations. A large painting would have worked better in that space, something bold and dramatic by an artist like Tony Sherman, Jake found himself thinking, recalling the exhibit Mattie had taken him to the previous week. Or maybe one of Rafael Goldchain's exotic photographs, something that would bring a splash of color and daring to an otherwise dull wall. Jake lowered himself into one of the chairs, not surprised to find it wasn't very comfortable. Sit down, but don't stay too long, the chairs said, as Frank Richardson took the seat beside him.

"I understand you turned down the Maclean case," Frank said, not wasting any time on preliminaries.

Clearly a man who didn't believe in foreplay, Jake thought, his mind drifting back to last night in bed,

Mattie's tongue licking at the sides of his cock. She wanted to try everything, she'd told him. "I won't break," she said. "Don't treat me like a china doll."

"Jake," Frank said, eyes searing into Jake's brain. "The Maclean case," he repeated. "Mind telling me why you turned it down."

Jake forced Mattie's tongue into the far recesses of his mind, away from Frank's penetrating gaze. "The kid's guilty."

Frank Richardson looked stunned. "Your point?"

"I didn't think I could provide him with the best possible defense he's entitled to under the law," Jake said dryly.

"May I take a moment to remind you that the kid's father is Thomas Maclean, founder and chief executive officer of Maclean's Discount Drugstores, one of the fastest-growing franchises in the state. He's worth millions to this firm, not to mention this case is right up your alley. It'll be front-page news for months."

"Eddy Maclean and two of his Neanderthal friends raped a fifteen-year-old girl."

"According to the boy's father, the girl looks closer to twenty, and she was more than a willing participant."

"You're telling me she consented to being gang-banged and sodomized? Frank, I have a daughter who's fifteen years old."

"Your daughter didn't invite some boy she'd just met at a party into the nearest bedroom." Frank Richardson folded his long, elegant hands in his lap. "Something funny?" he demanded, as Jake tried to suppress a smile.

"No, sir." Jake almost laughed. When was the last

time he'd addressed anyone as "sir"? And why was he smiling, for God's sake? He tried not to think about Mattie's description of a skinny young man hopping naked around his daughter's bedroom.

"Look, Jake, I can appreciate your sensitivity in this area, but this case is tailor-made for you, and you know it. You could win it in your sleep."

"I've already given it to Taupin."

"Maclean wants you."

"Not interested."

Frank Richardson rose to his feet, returned to the window, again pretending to focus on the street below. "How are things at home, Jake?"

So the Maclean preamble was foreplay after all, Jake marveled. "Fine, sir," Jake said again, feeling as if he'd been drafted into the army.

"Your wife—"

Jake felt the muscles in his throat constrict. "Fine," he said again, the word squeezed between reluctant vocal chords.

"Naturally I've been informed of the unfortunate episode last Friday night."

"I'm sure Alan Peters couldn't wait to provide you with all the grisly details."

"Actually, no," Frank Richardson said, catching Jake by surprise. "It was Dave Corber who told me what happened. Alan has said nothing. I understand he's decided to let the matter drop."

Jake sighed with relief, in spite of himself.

"Apparently he feels you've been under considerable stress, that there are problems at home of which we are obviously unaware."

Jake rose to his feet. "I prefer to keep my personal life private, if you don't mind, sir. It's really none of anybody's business—"

"Everything is my business when it affects this firm." Frank Richardson motioned toward the chairs. "Please sit down. I'm not finished yet."

"With all due respect—" Jake began.

"Save your due respect," Frank interrupted. "It's been my experience that whenever someone says 'with all due respect,' they show you none at all."

"Look, Frank," Jake said, lowering his voice, softening his position. "I screwed up last Friday, lost my temper, reacted inappropriately. I assure you it won't happen again." Should he tell Frank the truth about his wife's condition? he wondered, wavering. Mattie had told all her friends, most of her business associates, some of her clients. So far, he'd said nothing to anyone. He'd been carrying around a very heavy load for months, and he was starting to stumble under the strain. It was affecting his judgment, his work, possibly even his career. Maybe it would help if he unburdened himself to Frank.

"Jan Stephens tells me you turned down her offer to serve on the Associate Development Committee," Frank Richardson continued, unaware of Jake's interior monologue.

"I really don't have the time right now, Frank."

"Really? I was given to understand that you have quite a bit of time on your hands, that in the last six months your billable hours have declined considerably, that you are rarely here before nine in the morning, and that you're often gone by four o'clock, not to mention it's been months since anyone's seen you around the office on weekends. Am I mistaken?"

"I've been working out of my office at home."

"I understand you're also planning a holiday this April," Frank Richardson continued, dismissing Jake's explanation with a slight arching of his eyebrows. "I'd like you to postpone it."

"Postpone it? Why?"

"As you're no doubt aware, there's an international convention of lawyers coming to town this April, and Richardson, Buckley and Lang has agreed to serve as one of the hosts. All the partners will be expected to take on a very active role."

"But I've never been involved—"

"Time to start, wouldn't you say?"

"With all due resp—" Jake started, stopped, started again. "I'm afraid I can't change my plans, Frank."

"Care to tell me why?"

"I haven't taken a holiday since I joined this firm," Jake said, hoping this would be enough to satisfy the firm's most senior partner, knowing it wouldn't. "I've made a promise, Frank. Don't ask me to break it."

"I'm afraid that's exactly what I'm asking you to do."

"You're putting me in an impossible position."

"You're very good in impossible positions," Frank reminded him, walking to his office door, about to open it. "You're on the verge of being made a full partner, Jake. I'm sure you wouldn't want to jeopardize that. Talk to Tom Maclean again. I know he's most anxious to have you in his son's corner."

"Frank—" Jake began, as Frank opened the door. "There's something I need to talk to you about."

Frank Richardson immediately reclosed the door, signaled that he was listening with a wary tilt of his head.

"It's my wife." Jake paused, released a deep breath. "She's very sick."

"I've heard the rumors," Frank conceded, a flush of embarrassment sweeping across his face, settling into the deep creases below his piercing hazel eyes. "Alcoholism is a very insidious disease. Your wife deserves your sympathy and support. But you mustn't allow her to drag you down. There are many fine clinics where she can go."

"She's dying, Frank." Jake pushed the words angrily from his throat.

"I don't understand."

"She doesn't have a drinking problem. She has something called amyotrophic lateral sclerosis. Lou Gehrig's disease."

"Dear God."

"We don't know how long she's got—" Jake felt the catch in his voice, like a trigger being cocked, heard the words explode, flying from his mouth like so much shrapnel, as a barrage of tears, like drops of blood, streamed down his cheeks. What was happening to him, for God's sake? "I'm sorry," Jake cried, catching the look of horror in Frank Richardson's eyes as he tried to stanch the flow of unseemly tears. But the tears kept coming, refusing to abate, no matter how violently he pushed them aside. "I don't know what's the matter with me. . . ." Was he really breaking down in front of the firm's most senior partner?

What was the matter with him? Where was his self-control? Why was he so goddamn upset?

True, he and Mattie had grown closer in these last few months since he'd agreed to play her lover. But that's all it was—playacting. He was just trying to make a dying woman's last months as pleasant as possible. He didn't really love her, for God's sake. What was the matter with him? What was he doing breaking down in public? What was he doing jeopardizing his entire career?

"Look, about the conference in April—" Jake began.

"I'm sure we can work something out, Jake, even if it means putting off the partnership deal for another year."

"I'm sure I can rearrange my schedule." Jake cleared his throat, coughed into his hand. "There's no reason Mattie and I couldn't take our trip in May or June."

"Of course, that would be wonderful," Frank agreed, the muscles in his face relaxing, although his eyes remained on the alert for a renewed outburst.

"And I'll get in touch with Tom Maclean. I'm sure there's a way we can work something out."

"He's waiting to hear from you," Frank said, as if there'd never been any doubt.

Jake took a deep breath, forced a smile onto his lips. "Thank you," he said, although he wasn't sure what he was thanking the older man for. Probably for putting things back into their proper perspective, he thought, stepping into the corridor.

"Thank you for stopping by," Frank said. "Please convey our heartfelt good wishes to your wife."

"Shit, goddamn, son of a bitch, shit!" Jake was muttering as he strode past his secretary. What the hell was he supposed to do now? How was he supposed to tell Mattie their trip was off, even temporarily? Was there anything he could say to soften the blow, to ease her disappointment? What could he tell her? That it was beyond his control? That there were mitigating circumstances? That there was nothing to prevent them from going in May? Surely one month wouldn't make that much difference. Surely Mattie would understand the impossible predicament she'd put him in. Not that it had been her intention to derail his career. But that's precisely what was happening. And just because he'd agreed to participate in this continuing pretense of a marriage didn't mean he'd agreed to forfeit everything he'd worked so hard for all these years. It was time to regain his perspective, time to put his life back on track. Make-believe could only take you so far. Eventually you had to return to the real world. Mattie would simply have to understand.

"Cynthia Broome is waiting—" his secretary said, following after Jake. "In your office," she continued, as the woman smiled up at Jake from her chair in front of his desk.

Jake felt his breath catch in his lungs.

"Can I get you another cup of coffee, Ms. Broome?" the secretary asked.

"No, thank you."

"I'm right outside if you change your mind." Jake's secretary made a quick exit, pulling the door shut after her.

Jake stared at the small woman in front of his large desk as she rose from her chair, her red curls all but swamping her round face, the collar of her white silk shirt half in, half out of her navy blazer. What was she doing here?

"Planning a trip?" Honey asked, motioning toward the brochures on Jake's desk. "I've heard of the Hotel Danielle. It's supposed to be quite wonderful."

"Honey, what the hell is going on? What are you doing here?"

Honey's face flashed embarrassment, shame, defiance, hope, in quick equal measures. "I wanted to see you. I couldn't think of any other way."

"Who the hell is Cynthia Broome?"

"She's the heroine of my novel."

Jake smiled, took a step toward her, stopped short, his body swaying into the space between them. "I'm sorry I haven't called all week."

"That's all right."

"It's been frantic around here."

"I understand. I know how busy you are."

"How've you been?" Jake asked.

"Fine. You?"

"Fine."

Honey laughed awkwardly. "Listen to us. Next thing you know, we'll be talking about the weather."

"Honey—"

"Jason," she said, smiling self-consciously.

Jake flinched at the sound of his given name. "You look great."

"I've been going to the gym every day, hoping I'd run into you."

"I haven't been to the gym in ages. I'm sorry."

"Don't be. I think I've lost a few pounds." Honey

tried to laugh, but the weak sound slid into more of a cry. "I've missed you so much, Jason."

"I've missed you too."

"Have you?"

Had he? Jake wondered. The truth was, he'd pushed her so far into the recesses of his mind that he'd barely thought of her all week.

Honey brushed her unruly mop of red hair away from her face. "I've been thinking of cutting it all off," she said.

"Don't do it."

"I don't know. I think it's time for a change."

"I love your hair."

"I love *you*," she told him, tears filling her eyes. "Damn it, I promised myself I wasn't going to do this." She pushed the tears aside, took a deep breath, smiled her crooked smile, and stuck a defiant finger up her nose. "How's that?" she asked.

"Much better."

They laughed softly. "I could really use a hug," she said.

"Honey—"

"Just a little one. Just enough to let me know you're not some figment of my imagination, like Cynthia Broome."

What would be the harm? Jake wondered, taking her in his arms.

"God, I've missed this," she whispered, lifting her face toward him, her lips begging to be kissed.

She felt so awkward in his arms, Jake realized. Short while Mattie was tall. Round where Mattie was firm. Plump where Mattie was flat. He wasn't used to holding her anymore. He wasn't used to having to contort his body to accommodate hers. Mattie was a much more natural fit, he thought, pulling Honey closer to him, as if trying to squeeze Mattie out of his mind.

"I love you," Honey said again.

Jake knew she was waiting for him to say the same thing, that her declaration of love was really a request to hear it from him. Why couldn't he say it? He loved Honey, didn't he? Hadn't he left his wife and daughter for her? He'd only returned home because Mattie was gravely ill. He'd only agreed not to see Honey as a way of keeping Mattie happy, because not seeing one allowed him to concentrate on the other. He had every intention of returning to Honey as soon as this whole awful mess was over. Didn't he?

Didn't he?

What was the matter with him? Not only had he almost deep-sixed his career, but if he wasn't careful, he'd lose Honey as well, and all because he'd almost let a little game of let's-pretend get perilously out of hand. Just as his visit with Frank had been a wake-up call, Honey's unexpected appearance as Cynthia Broome was a reminder to him of everything he could lose if he allowed the extended charade he'd been playing to get the better of him.

He looked down at Honey, staring at him expectantly through gold-flecked brown eyes, still moist with tears. She'd been so patient, so understanding. And she felt so good, he thought, kissing her firmly on the lips, his hands grasping her buttocks, as he imagined the pliant flesh beneath the harsh denim of her jeans.

"Oh, Jason. Jason," she was moaning, her hands reaching under his jacket, tugging at his shirt. "Lock the door," she said, pulling her own blouse free of her blue jeans, planting his hands on her breasts, kissing him again and again, her hungry mouth threatening to swallow him whole. "Lock the door, Jason," she urged, guiding him toward the sofa at the end of the room.

It would be so easy, Jake thought. Lock the door, tell his secretary he wasn't to be disturbed for anyone. Not his partners, not his clients, not his wife.

His wife, Jake thought as Honey's tongue slid between his open lips. Could he really do this to Mattie? Wasn't it enough he was about to break his promise regarding their trip to Paris? Did he have to break her heart as well?

God, Mattie, it was never my intention to make you feel bad.

I don't give a shit about your intentions. What I want is your passion. What I want is your loyalty. What I want is your love.

How would she ever know? Jake wondered, kissing the tears from Honey's eyes, then pulling back, seeing Mattie's eyes staring back at him from Honey's face.

Mattie would know, he understood. She would know the way she always did.

"I can't," he said, his hands falling helplessly to his sides.

"Jason, please—"

"I can't. I'm sorry."

Honey said nothing, her lower lip quivering as her eyes restlessly circled the room.

Jake leaned forward, buried his face in Honey's soft red curls, the texture of her thick hair so different from Mattie's, whose hair was finer, silkier. The unmistakable odor of stale cigarettes filled his nostrils. "I thought you'd given up smoking," he said quietly.

"I can only give up so many things at once," Honey told him, her voice an uneasy mix of resignation and tears. "Besides, I read this report. They took two hundred people, a hundred of whom smoked and a hundred who didn't. And guess what? They all died."

Jake smiled. It *was* good to see her. He really *had* missed her.

"Speaking of the dead, how's Mattie doing?" Honey gasped, closed her eyes, shook her head, jabbed her hands into the air in frustration. "I can't believe I said that. Please forgive me, Jason. I didn't mean to say that. I don't know what came over me. I'm so sorry. God, that was awful. How could I say such a horrible thing?"

"It's okay," Jake tried to reassure her, although his head was spinning. How *could* she have said anything so insensitive? "I know you didn't mean it the way it sounded."

"Do you?"

"Of course."

"Good. Because to be perfectly honest," Honey admitted, tears once again filling her large brown eyes, "I'm not so sure."

"What?"

"I'm scared, Jason. Something awful is happening to me."

"I don't understand."

"Neither do I. That's what scares me."

"Are you feeling all right?"

"This has nothing to do with my health," Honey snapped. "Not everyone is suffering from a fatal disease, Jason. God, there I go again. Listen to me. I'm turning into some sort of monster."

"You're not a monster."

"No? What am I? I'm spending all my time waiting for someone to die, *praying* for someone to die."

Jake said nothing. What could he say?

"Do you have any idea what it's like to go to bed every night hoping you'll call me in the morning to tell me Mattie is dead? God, sometimes I really hate myself."

"I'm so sorry."

"I'm so afraid of losing you."

"You're not going to lose me," Jake said, surprised by how unconvincing he sounded, even to himself.

"I'm losing you already." Honey walked back to Jake's desk, lifted the Paris brochures into her hands. "April in Paris. What a lovely romantic idea. When were you planning to tell me about it? Or were you just going to drop me a postcard?"

"It was just an idea. It doesn't look like we'll be going after all."

Honey dropped the brochures back onto his desk. "I'm jealous, Jason. I'm actually jealous of a dying woman."

"There's no reason to be jealous. You know why I went home. You agreed."

"I agreed to stay in the background. I never agreed to disappear." She shook her head, red curls flying about her face. "I don't think I can do this anymore."

"Please, Honey. If you could just bear with me a little while longer."

"Are you sleeping with her?"

"What?"

"Are you sleeping with your wife?"

Jake looked helplessly around the room, a sudden headache gathering force behind his temples. This was worse than the altercation in the restaurant, worse than his meeting with Frank. "I can't abandon her, Honey. You know that."

"That's not what I'm asking you, Jason."

"I know."

Jake waited for Honey to ask the question again, but she didn't. Instead she smiled her crooked smile, wiped the tears away from her eyes, and tucked her blouse back into the waist of her jeans. Then she straightened her shoulders, took a deep breath, and walked to the door.

"Honey—" he called after her. But she was already gone.

TWENTY-SIX

Mattie sat at her kitchen table, a French textbook open in front of her, staring out the sliding glass door into the backyard. She'd been sitting this way for over half an hour, she realized, glancing over at the two clocks on the other side of the room. It was amazing how much time could be spent doing absolutely nothing—not moving, not speaking, barely breathing. It wasn't so bad, she decided, trying to project ahead to a time when such stillness would no longer be voluntary, when she would be forced to spend hours, days, weeks, months, possibly even years, unable to move, unable to speak, barely able to breathe. "Oh, God," she sighed, panic building in her chest. She would never let that happen.

But the inescapable fact was that every day she felt weaker, as if her muscles had developed a slow leak, like tires infested with tiny nails, and each day she lost more energy along the side of the road. When she walked, she pulled her legs along as if she were dragging heavy steel girders. As for her hands, there were days Mattie felt she lacked the strength to make a simple fist. Sometimes Mattie found it hard to swallow, harder to catch her breath. Increasingly, pens dropped from uncooperative fingers, buttons remained open, sentences unfinished, food untouched.

She tried to keep optimistic by reminding herself of recent medical miracles. Using genetic manipulation, a scientist in Montreal had reported being able to slow the progression of Lou Gehrig's disease by 65 percent in laboratory mice. Now that they had the target gene, scientists were screening for drugs that would activate this gene in order to get it to produce more of the protein needed to slow the disease. But Mattie knew that no matter how fast the scientists worked, they would be too late. At least for her. "Just give me Paris," she said quietly, returning her attention to the French textbook on the table.

How would she manage in Paris? she wondered, as the pages slipped through her fingers, and she found herself back on page one. Would she be able to navigate the charming cobblestone streets of the Latin Quarter? How would she manage the mountain of stairs at Montmartre? How much energy would she have for the magnificent treasures of the Louvre, the Grand Palais, the Quay d'Orsay? Would the time difference affect her? Would she be plagued by jet lag? What about the long plane ride over? Lisa had already warned her that the shifting of oxygen levels in the plane might cause her some increased discomfort. Would she be able to cope?

She'd be fine, Mattie assured herself. Jake had bought her a cane, and she'd agreed to a wheelchair at the airports in both Chicago and France. She had sleeping pills and Riluzole and her trusty bottle of morphine. She'd rest when she got tired. She wouldn't be too proud to say she'd had enough. Maybe she'd even get herself one of those motorized tricycles Lisa had told her about, race through the streets of Paris on one of those.

The phone rang.

Mattie debated letting voice mail pick it up, decided she'd better answer in case it was Kim or Jake. Mattie barely saw her daughter these days—when Kim wasn't at school, she was at her grandmother's, tending to her new puppy until he was old enough to be separated from his mother. As for Jake—something had been troubling him the last few weeks, Mattie knew, wondering if and when he'd tell her what it was. "Better answer it," Mattie said out loud, struggling to her feet and slowly dragging herself across the room to the phone. "Hello?"

"Mrs. Hart?"

"Speaking." The woman's voice on the other end of the line was unfamiliar.

"This is Ruth Kertzer, from Tony Graham's office at Richardson, Buckley and Lang."

Mattie fought to keep the barrage of names in line. Why would someone from her husband's firm be calling her? Had something happened to Jake?

"Mr. Graham is in charge of coordinating the dinners that some of the partners will be hosting during the international lawyers' convention in Chicago next month, and he wanted me to clear a couple of possible dates with you."

"I'm sorry?" What on earth was this woman talking about? "I'm afraid I'm not following you."

"Mr. Graham thought it would be a nice gesture if we had a number of small dinner parties in people's homes, say twelve or fourteen people, instead of a larger, more formal affair at a restaurant or hotel. We have your husband's name down as a host for one of the dinners. The firm is covering all expenses, of course. Did your husband forget to mention any of this to you?"

Apparently, Mattie thought, wondering if this was what had been troubling Jake. How was she going to cope with twelve to fourteen strangers in her house? Oh, well, as long as she didn't have to cook, she'd manage somehow. Truth be told, she was a little flattered. In the past Jake had always shied away from bringing her into firm functions. That Jake thought her capable of handling such an event at this particular time made her feel happy, even optimistic. "When exactly is all this scheduled to take place?"

"The convention is from April fourteenth through April twentieth. The nights in question are—"

"That's impossible. We'll be away from April tenth till the twenty-first."

"You'll be away? But Mr. Hart is leading one of the seminars."

"What?" Mattie bit down on her lower lip. "No, that's impossible."

"I spoke to him myself just the other day," Ruth Kertzer said.

"Um, listen, there's obviously some sort of mixup here. Can I get back to you on this?"

"Certainly."

Mattie hung up the phone without saying good-bye. What was going on? Jake hadn't mentioned anything about a convention in April, and they'd been actively planning their trip to Paris for months. There had to be some mistake. Don't get upset, she urged herself, feeling her heartbeat quicken. The stupid woman obviously had her dates mixed up. The convention was probably not till May, or quite possibly not till April of next year. Didn't they usually plan these things years in advance? No way Jake was going to renege on his promise to accompany her to Paris, especially now that the trip was mere weeks away. No, Jake would never do that to her.

The old Jake, maybe. The Jake who was cold and distant and withholding, who valued work above family, work above everything. That Jake would have thought nothing of canceling their plans at the last minute. The old Jake wouldn't have given a second thought to hurting her feelings or spoiling her holiday. But that Jake had checked out months ago. The Jake who'd taken his place was thoughtful and kind and sensitive, a man who listened to her and confided in her, who talked to her and laughed with her. Jake Hart had become a man Mattie could trust with her feelings, a man she could depend on to be there when she needed him. A man she could love.

A man she thought might be capable of loving her in return.

"This can't be," Mattie said, picking up the phone, using both hands to press in the numbers for Jake's private line.

"Mattie, what's up?" Jake answered, without saying hello. She heard a trace of the old impatience in his voice, wondered whether she was imagining it. Probably she'd interrupted him in the middle of something important.

"I had a disturbing phone call," she said, deciding to plunge right in.

"What kind of phone call? From Lisa?"

"No, nothing like that."

"Something about Kim? A crank? What?"

"It was from Ruth Kertzer."

There was silence.

"Ruth Kertzer from Tony Graham's office," Mattie clarified, although his continuing silence made it clear he knew exactly who she was. The silence was so heavy Mattie felt she could hold it in her hands.

"What did she want?" he asked finally.

"She wanted to clear a few dates with me."

"Dates? For what?"

He sounded genuinely confused. Was it possible he didn't know after all? That the whole thing was indeed a misunderstanding? That Ruth Kertzer had gotten her dates, or her lawyers, confused?

"Apparently, there's some big convention coming to town in April," Mattie began, preparing to laugh with her husband over the secretary's incompetence. But even as she spoke the words, Mattie could feel the color draining from her husband's face, and she knew Ruth Kertzer had confused neither her lawyers nor her dates. "I understand we're hosting one of the dinners," she said softly, holding her breath.

"None of that has been decided," came the unsatisfactory response.

"Ruth Kertzer seems to think it has. Do you want to tell me what's going on, Jake?"

"Look, Mattie, it's a little complicated. Can we talk about it when I get home?"

"She said you're speaking at one of the seminars."

Silence. Then, "I've been approached."

"And you've accepted?"

Jake cleared his throat. "It wouldn't mean canceling our trip, only putting it on hold for a couple of weeks. Mattie, please, I'm already late for a meeting. Can we talk about this when I get home? I promise I'll straighten everything out."

Mattie bit down hard on her bottom lip. "Sure," she said. "We'll talk when you get home." She waited until the line went dead in her hands before slamming the phone against its carriage, then watched in horror as the plastic shattered and the receiver came apart, falling to the floor in jagged chunks. "Goddamn you, you miserable son of a bitch! I'm not postponing our trip. Not for a few weeks. Not even for a few days. I'm going to Paris, as scheduled, with you or without you. Do you understand?" Mattie burst into a flood of bitter, angry tears. "How can you do this?" she wailed, her breathing growing tight, emerging from her chest in a series of short, painful spasms. She gripped the counter, tried to steady herself. It's not that you can't breathe, she reminded herself. It's just that your chest muscles are getting weaker, resulting in breathing that's shallower, which leads to a shortness of breath, which results in panic. But you're fine. You're fine. "Stay calm," she gasped, her eyes darting about the kitchen, bouncing frantically off the various surfaces like balls in a pinball machine.

Mattie thought of the small bottle of morphine in the upstairs bathroom. One little five-milligram tablet was all that was necessary to remove the anxiety, control the panic, restore calm.

Twenty tablets would be enough to stop her breathing altogether.

What was she waiting for? Paris? That was a joke. "Who am I kidding?" she asked out loud, her breathing returning to normal, her face moist with sweat. How could she go anywhere by herself? It had all been a stupid fantasy, a game of let's-pretend that had gone too far. Jake had no doubt gone along with the pretense because he'd assumed she'd be too weak or incapacitated by now to even think of following through. How could she have fooled herself into thinking he ever had any intention of keeping his promise? He had his own life to worry about, his girlfriend, his career, his fucking dinner parties and seminars to look forward to.

And what did Mattie have to look forward to? A life of wheelchairs and feeding tubes and slow strangulation.

What was she waiting for? Could she really rely on her mother to end her suffering when the time was right? Maybe the right time was right now. She'd leave a note for Kim, in case she got home before Jake, telling her she was taking a nap and instructing her not to disturb her. She wouldn't leave a note for Jake. What was the point? *The time for hesitating's through,* Mattie hummed, slowly propelling herself toward the stairs. *Come on, baby, light my fire.*

Light my fire. Light my fire. Light my fire.

Mattie was still humming when she reached her bathroom and opened the medicine cabinet, still humming when she lifted the small bottle of morphine into her trembling hands. She poured herself a glass of water, emptied the contents of the bottle into her open palm, counted out twenty pills, then pushed all twenty into her mouth at once.

"Good day, gentlemen, Ms. Fontana," Jake said, acknowledging the three young men, their fathers, and their attorneys, gathered around the impressive oblong conference table that filled most of the large boardroom. On either side of the table sat twelve high-backed armchairs in rust-colored leather. Jake scanned the occupants of the seats on one side of the table: rapist, father, lawyer, he enumerated silently. Then again, on the other side: lawyer, father, rapist. There was a certain symmetry to that, Jake thought, noting that only the Macleans distanced themselves from the others present, the younger Maclean sitting off by himself at the far end of the long table, his father standing in front of the impressive expanse of windows overlooking Michigan Avenue. It was a beautiful day—sunny and clear. Too nice a day to waste indoors, Jake thought restlessly, wondering what the weather was like in Paris. He assumed his seat at the head of the table, motioning for Thomas Maclean to join them.

"You're late," the senior Maclean stated, declining the invitation.

"Sorry. I had a last-minute phone call. It couldn't be helped." Jake faked a smile. Why was he apologizing? He didn't owe this man any explanations. He was here, wasn't he? Wasn't that enough? "Did I miss anything?"

"Party doesn't really start until you show up, Jake," Angela Fontana said. She was an impeccably groomed woman with dark hair that was pulled into a French roll at the back of her head, and a wide mouth that seemed to stretch from one side of her narrow face to the other, even in repose. Jake estimated her as in her late forties, as was Keith Peacock, the other attorney present. Despite his surname, Keith Peacock was as bland in appearance as he was humorless in temperament, although he always seemed to be smiling. Both attorneys came from large firms and had stellar reputations. Normally Jake would have considered it interesting, even fun, to be working with them, but today he found himself more than mildly irritated by their presence. How could three of the best legal minds in the city be the mouthpieces for such callow and despicable young men?

Jake shifted his attention from the attorneys to their clients. Mike Hansen was a good-looking boy, as tall and thin as his lawyer, although his face, unlike Keith Peacock's, seemed frozen in a perpetual scowl. His dark brown hair was neatly trimmed, and he wore a shirt and tie underneath his red-and-white leather jacket. The jacket clashed with the chairs, Jake thought, eyes wandering to Neil Pilcher, who was shorter and heavier set, although he too would probably have been considered handsome under more pleasant circumstances. He sat nervously biting his nails, every so often glancing toward Eddy Maclean, who stared lazily off into space, an unlit cigarette dangling between bored fingers.

"Put that damn thing away," Thomas Maclean told his son, and Jake watched as the boy casually crushed the cigarette inside the palm of his hand, the tobacco filtering through his fingers and falling to the oak tabletop like dried flecks of manure.

"This is Neil Pilcher," Angela Fontana said, introducing Jake to her client. "And this is his father, Larry Pilcher."

Jake nodded at the pale man, whose eyes seemed to sag with the weight of the heavy bags pulling at them. Were the bags there before his son raped and sodomized a fifteen-year-old girl? Jake wondered, trying not to think of Kim, of how he would feel if she were ever the victim of scum like these, of how scornful she would be at his taking this case.

"My job isn't to do justice," he'd told her the day she'd come to watch him in court. "My job is to play the game according to the rules." Except there were times lately when Jake was no longer sure what the rules were.

"Jake—" Keith Peacock was saying.

"Sorry, what?"

"I was introducing you to Mike's father, Lyle Hansen."

"Sorry," Jake said, nodding toward the balding bulldog of a man leaning forward in his seat, muscular arms crossed one over the other. "I guess we should get started." All eyes turned to him. Show us how brilliant you are, their eyes shouted collectively. Show us how to get three guilty, unrepentant rapists off the hook. Give us a strategy and show us the way. It doesn't matter that the girl they raped is the same age as your daughter, or that your daughter will hate you for defending them. She'll hate you anyway after you disappoint her mother. After you break your promise and Mattie's heart. Hell, what difference will it make? Jake thought with a small chuckle. She hates you now.

"Something you find amusing, counselor?" Tom Maclean demanded.

Jake cleared his throat. "Sorry. I was just thinking about something."

"Care to share your thoughts?"

"Not really, no." Jake turned to Angela Fontana. "Angela, how do you see this case progressing?"

"I think it's pretty straightforward—the word of a girl with a questionable past against the word of three upstanding young men whose roots go as far back as the *Mayflower*. I thought you could give the opening and closing statements to the jury, I could handle the testimony of the police detectives and the doctors, Keith could cross-examine the forensic expert, and we could all take turns with the girl."

"Sort of like the boys did," Jake said.

"What did you say?" Thomas Maclean demanded.

"Just a little jailhouse humor." Jake watched Angela's eyes widen with astonishment and the smile disappear abruptly from Keith Peacock's face.

"I'm afraid I see nothing humorous in either the remark or the situation."

What a pompous, self-righteous son of a bitch, Jake thought. Thomas Maclean didn't give a shit about that poor girl. He didn't even give a shit about his son, except insofar as how the boy's behavior impacted on his precious reputation. No, the only person Thomas Maclean really cared about was himself. Sound like anyone you know, Jake?

"I wondered if we could set aside a few dates," Keith Peacock said.

Ruth Kertzer called, Jake heard Mattie say. *She wanted to clear a few dates with me.*

Dates for what?

"I have next Monday and Wednesday afternoon free," Angela Fontana said, checking her appointment calendar.

"I'm not available Monday," Lyle Hansen said.

Do you want to tell me what's going on, Jake? Mattie asked.

It's a little complicated. Can we talk about it when I get home?

Except what was there to talk about? He'd made his decision. He couldn't go to Paris. Not now. Not when Frank Richardson had made it perfectly clear that by going on this trip he'd be putting his partnership on the line, not to mention his entire career. He couldn't do it. Mattie had no right to ask it of him.

Except she hadn't asked him. He'd volunteered, practically begged to come along. She'd agreed against her better judgment, and he'd had to work hard to win her trust. He knew how much Mattie was looking forward to the trip, how the mere mention of it kept her spirits up and her hopes high. He also knew how much she'd come to rely on him these last few months, and he understood that any postponement, however brief, would be too long. He knew if they didn't go in April, they wouldn't go at all, that even if Mattie agreed to a postponement, she'd never trust him to keep his word again, that he would never trust himself. Something had come up this time; something would come up again. Something always did for men who put their own interests ahead of everyone else's. For men like Thomas Maclean. For men like Jason Hart.

Bad boy, Jason. Bad boy, Jason. Bad boy, Jason. *Badboyjason, badboyjason, badboyjason.*

Except things were different now. He was no longer the man his mother had programmed him to be. His priorities had changed. By pretending to be a good husband and father, he'd actually become one, and Jake was surprised to discover he liked the man he'd been pretending to be. He felt comfortable in his skin, secure in his decency. In the end, Jake realized, the face we show the outside world is often truer than the one we see in the mirror every day.

We are who we pretend to be.

And damn it, he'd been looking forward to accompanying Mattie to Paris. Sometime over the last few months, in the middle of all the planning and guide books, false pretense had given way to genuine enthusiasm. So was he really preparing to abandon his plans, abandon all he'd become, for the dubious pleasure of being made partner in some stuffy downtown law firm? Was he really planning on skipping Paris so he could attend some mind-numbing legal convention in Chicago? Was he willing to lose the respect of his wife and daughter so that he could win an undeserved acquittal in court? Was he willing to risk losing everything, including himself?

"Jake—?" Angela Fontana was regarding him expectantly. Obviously, she'd asked for his opinion. Clearly, she was waiting for a response.

"I'm sorry," Jake said again. How many times had he said that since walking in the room?

"Are we boring you?" Eddy Maclean asked.

Jake looked from Eddy Maclean to his father, to the other boys, to their fathers, to their respective lawyers, then back to Eddy Maclean. "As a matter of fact, you are," Jake said, rising from his chair and heading for the door.

"What?" he heard Keith Peacock gasp above the shocked laughter of Angela Fontana.

"What the devil is going on here?" Thomas Maclean demanded, racing around the desk to confront Jake at the door. "Where do you think you're going?"

"I'm going to Paris," Jake said, opening the door and stepping out into the corridor. "And you, sir," he said with a smile, "can take that miserable kid of yours and go to hell."

"Mattie?" Jake called from the front hall. "Mattie? Mattie, where are you? Mattie!"

Mattie heard the voice as if it were part of a dream. She tried to block it out, to will the voice away. She'd been sleeping so peacefully. She didn't want to be disturbed by dreams, by reminders, by ghosts and false images. Go away, she muttered to herself, a slight murmur the only sound escaping her lips.

"Mattie," she heard again, as the bedroom door opened. "Mattie?"

Mattie pictured herself standing over her bathroom sink, sprinkling twenty deadly tablets into the palm of her hand, like so much salt. She peeked through half-closed eyes, saw Jake's handsome face looming above her. "Jake? What are you doing home so early?"

"I'm through for the day." He laughed. "Actually, there's a good chance I'm through for good." He laughed again, a short manic burst of sound.

She tasted the bitter pills that had crowded against the sides of her mouth, spilling across her tongue, ferreting beneath it, as she'd raised the glass of water to her lips. "Jake, are you all right?" Mattie forced herself into a sitting position.

"Never better," came the immediate response. He leaned over, kissed her gently on the forehead.

"I don't understand."

"Well, let me see. About an hour ago I told a client to stuff it, told Jan Stephens I wouldn't be able to serve on the Associate Development Committee after all, and informed Ruth Kertzer I wouldn't be speaking at any seminars or hosting any dinner parties because I was going to Paris with my wife."

Mattie was momentarily speechless. She saw herself standing in the bathroom with her mouth full of pills. Jake wouldn't let her down, she'd told the frightened face in the mirror. He wouldn't disappoint her. And even if he did, she'd realized in that moment, her shoulders stiffening in quiet resolve, she wasn't going to lie down and die. At least not yet. Mattie watched her image spit the pills into the sink, following their path as they snaked their way across the porcelain basin and disappeared down the drain. "What will they do about the seminar, the dinner party?" she asked. "Can they get someone else?"

"There's always someone else, Mattie."

"No one like you," Mattie whispered, touching his cheek.

He took her in his arms, leaned back against the headboard, closed his eyes. "Tell me about Paris," he said.

Mattie snuggled in against her husband's side. "Well, did you know that most Parisians are great animal lovers?" she asked, as Jake began kissing away the happy tears that were falling freely down her cheeks. "That they allow dogs and cats into their restaurants, sometimes even giving them seats at the table? Can you imagine sitting next to a cat in a fancy restaurant?" She laughed and cried simultaneously, the words colliding with her tears. "But much as they love animals, they aren't so crazy about tourists, especially ones who can't speak French. Which isn't going to stop us from doing all the touristy things," she stressed. "I want to go to the top of the Eiffel Tower and the Arc de Triomphe. I want to walk the streets of Pigalle, take a boat ride on the Seine, all that stuff, Jake. And the Louvre and the Quai d'Orsay. And the Luxembourg Gardens. And Notre Dame and Napoleon's Tomb. I want to see it all." Mattie pulled away, enough so that she could look directly into her husband's eyes. "And I was so scared before, when you said you couldn't go, because I realized that, as much as I wanted to see Paris, I didn't want to see it without you." She paused, wondering if she'd said too much, unable to stop herself from saying more. "I couldn't imagine seeing it without you."

Tears filled Jake's eyes. "I wouldn't let you see it without me," he said simply.

"I love you," Mattie heard herself say, snuggling back into his arms.

I love you, the walls echoed. *I love you, I love you. I love you.*

Iloveyou, Iloveyou, Iloveyou.

TWENTY-SEVEN

It was just after nine o'clock on the morning of April 11 when their taxi pulled up in front of the Hotel Danielle on rue Jacob in the heart of Paris's Left Bank. "Is this not the most beautiful city you've ever seen in your entire life?" Mattie exclaimed. How many times had she asked that since they'd left the airport?

"It's by far the most beautiful city I've ever seen in my entire life," Jake agreed.

Mattie laughed, not quite believing they were really here. Months of planning and dreaming, and suddenly it was a reality. And it didn't matter that she was exhausted from the flight and hungry because she'd had difficulty swallowing the overcooked piece of meat that claimed to be steak Diane. "No one can swallow airplane food," Jake assured her, returning his tray to the stewardess untouched.

"Shall we?" Jake asked now, helping Mattie out of the cramped backseat of the small French car as the taxi driver carried their bags into the stylized Art Deco lobby of the charming old hotel.

"Oh, Jake. It's beautiful. C'est magnifique," Mattie said to the exotic-looking woman behind the front desk. The woman, whose name tag identified her as Chloe Dorleac, had dark violet eyes, thick black hair, and impeccable posture. She looked at Mattie the way one regards a child getting ready to misbehave, cautiously, skeptically, as if she were afraid Mattie might start doing somersaults around the room. No danger of that, Mattie thought, leaning on her cane.

"Bonjour, madame, monsieur. Can I help you?"

"How did you know we speak English?" Mattie asked.

Chloe Dorleac smiled indulgently, said nothing. Her mouth, Mattie noted, was a thin red slash that made only minimal adjustments when she altered her expression.

"We have a reservation." Jake fished in his pocket for the appropriate piece of paper, sliding it across the high ebony desk. "Hart, Jake and Mattie." He handed the woman their passports.

"Hart," Chloe Dorleac repeated, scrutinizing their passports with even more care than the customs officer at the airport, scribbling their passport numbers into her book. "Jason and Martha."

Who are *they?* Mattie wondered, scanning the small lobby for a place to sit down, seeing her image reflected repeatedly in the huge gilt-flecked mirrors lining the walls. She hadn't realized how tired she looked. "We're from Chicago."

"I believe we have another guest from Chicago staying with us," the woman said.

"Chicago is a big city."

"Everything in America is big, no?" Chloe Dorleac gave them another of her indulgent French smiles, though clearly she was bored with the conversation, and pushed a blank form across the desk. "Could you fill this out, please?"

Mattie took several measured steps toward a dark green velvet love seat that sat in a small alcove in front of the window overlooking rue Jacob. I'm in Paris, she thought, feeling the cushions balloon around her as she sank into the small sofa. "I'm really here," she whispered under her breath, glancing over her shoulder at the narrow, busy street that was everything she'd imagined, and more. "I did it. *We* did it."

Would she be able to navigate that street, with its constant parade of pedestrians, cars, and motorcycles, without the need for her cane? Probably not. But at least the cane was better than a wheelchair. She'd used wheelchairs at both airports, and discovered she hated them. Wheelchairs create barriers, however helpful they are designed to be. Your whole perspective changes. You are always looking up at people; they are always looking down. If they acknowledge you at all. Even the customs official at Charles de Gaulle airport had virtually ignored her, directing all his questions at Jake, even the ones concerning Mattie, as if she were a child incapable of intelligent response, as if she had no voice of her own.

She was going to lose her voice soon enough as it was. She had no intention of surrendering it prematurely.

Mattie felt movement, looked up, saw Jake approaching, a worried look on his tired face. "Something wrong?"

"Apparently our room won't be ready for at least another hour."

"Oh." Mattie tried to keep the worry out of her voice. She tried smiling without moving her mouth, like Chloe Dorleac, but the result was an expression more pained than indulgent. The truth was that, as much as she was thrilled to be here, as anxious as she was to see every inch of the city, Mattie desperately needed to lie down, at least for a few hours. Her legs felt as if she'd swum across the Atlantic, her arms as if she'd flown over by herself. She'd barely slept all night, unable to find a comfortable position despite the first-class seats. She'd nod off occasionally, only to jolt awake a few minutes later. What she needed now was a chance to recharge her batteries. What she needed was a few hours' sleep. "I guess we could go somewhere for a cup of coffee."

"I think we should stay here," Jake said. "Apparently, there's a lovely outdoor courtyard right in the middle of the hotel, and it has some comfortable lounge chairs where we can curl up and maybe sleep for a bit until the room is ready."

"Sounds good."

Jake helped Mattie to her feet, guided her through the lobby toward the tiny courtyard, a postage-size enclosure containing several uncomfortable-looking wooden chairs and one rather weatherbeaten chaise longue. "Well, it's not exactly the Ritz," Jake said.

No, it's certainly not, Mattie thought, but didn't say. The Ritz-Carlton was a lifetime ago. For both of them. "It's charming. Very French. C'est très bon," she said, as Jake helped her into the flimsy lounge chair. "Very comfortable." She was surprised to discover this was true. "But what about you?"

Jake sat on the edge of one of the nearby wooden chairs. "Perfect," he said, though the pinched look on his face told Mattie otherwise.

She smiled, sleep already tugging at her eyelids. He's as exhausted as I am, she thought. The last few weeks couldn't have been easy for him, regardless of what he claimed. To take a leave of absence from the firm, to put his career in jeopardy, his life on hold, how many men would do that? Especially for a woman they didn't love. Jake was already talking about where they'd go on their next trip. Hawaii, he'd suggested. Or maybe a Mediterranean cruise. She was a very lucky woman, Mattie thought, allowing her eyes to drift to a close, smiling at the irony of her thoughts. She was dying, her husband didn't love her, and she was the luckiest woman she knew.

She awoke with a start, almost tumbling from the chair. It took Mattie a moment to remember where she was, that she was actually in Paris, in the courtyard of a charming little French hotel, waiting while her room was readied. How long had she been asleep? She looked around the small enclosure, the sun falling across her eyes like a lazy chiffon scarf. Mattie squinted toward Jake, but there was a woman in a floppy beige hat occupying his chair. Mattie smiled, but the woman was engrossed in the guidebook on her lap and didn't notice. Mattie heard voices, noticed a man and woman leaning against one wall, conversing easily in French. She tried to recognize a familiar word or turn of phrase, but the couple was speaking much too fast, and Mattie quickly abandoned the attempt. Where was Jake? "Excusez-moi," Mattie said to no one in particular. "Mon mari—" No, that was no good. "Qui a vu—?" What exactly was she trying to say? "Damn! This isn't going to work."

The woman in the floppy beige hat looked up from her book. "It's okay. You can speak English." There was a laugh in her voice, a voice that was strangely familiar, maybe because it was so reassuringly American.

"I was wondering if anyone had seen my husband. He seems to have disappeared."

"Yes, they have a way of doing that. But no, sorry, I can't help you. You were alone when I got here. About five minutes ago," she added before returning her attention to the book in her lap.

Mattie tried to push herself into a more upright position, but her hands refused to cooperate and she was forced to lie back, pretend to be comfortable. An audible sigh escaped her lips.

"Are you okay?" the American woman asked.

"Fine. A little tired." Mattie struggled to make out the details of the woman's face, but the combination of the sun in her eyes and the woman's floppy hat made it difficult.

"Just arrived?"

Mattie glanced at her watch. "About an hour ago. What about you?"

"I've been here a few days."

"Anything to recommend?"

"I've just been walking the streets mainly, trying to get reacquainted." She waved the guidebook in her lap. "I haven't been here since college."

"This is my first time in Paris."

"Well, the first time is always special."

Mattie smiled agreement. "It's even more beautiful than I imagined."

"We're very lucky with the weather. It isn't always this nice in April."

"Are you here with your husband?" Mattie asked, eyes straining toward the lobby. Where could Jake have gone?

"No, I'm traveling alone."

"Really? You're very brave."

The woman laughed. "Desperate's probably a better word."

"Desperate?"

"Sometimes you want something so badly, you just have to take matters into your own hands," she said.

"I know that feeling." Mattie smiled. "I'm Mattie Hart, by the way."

There was a moment's hesitation. The sun flashed across the woman's face, turning it a ghostly white.

"Cynthia," the woman said, removing her hat, unleashing a barrage of wild red curls. "Cynthia Broome."

· · · ·

"Where were you?" Mattie struggled to her feet as Jake entered the small enclave and walked toward her, a large brown paper bag in his arms.

"I decided to do a little grocery shopping." He indicated the contents of the bag with a nod of his head. "Some bottled water, some biscuits, some fresh fruit." He kissed Mattie's forehead. "You were sleeping so soundly, I didn't want to disturb you. When did you wake up?"

Mattie checked her watch. "About twenty minutes ago. I met a nice woman. Turns out she's the one from Chicago the dragon lady mentioned."

"The dragon lady?"

"That's what Cynthia calls her. Cynthia . . . God, I can't remember her last name. Something useful." Mattie shrugged. "Oh, well. It'll come to me eventually. She's here by herself."

"Very brave."

Mattie smiled. "That's what I said. I was thinking maybe we could ask her to join us one day."

"Sure, if that's what you'd like."

"Well, maybe if we run into her again." Mattie looked toward the lobby. "You think our room is ready yet?"

"We're on the third floor," Jake said, escorting her toward the tiny elevator beside the winding staircase at the end of the lobby. "The bags are already in the room."

"It's like a bird cage," Mattie marveled as they squeezed inside the minuscule space, Jake pulling the wrought-iron door closed after him. Several seconds later the elevator bounced to a jerky halt on the third floor, where half a dozen rooms were grouped around a small landing, its dark blue carpet fading and frayed.

Jake used the large old-fashioned key to unlock the door to their room, pushing open the heavy door to reveal a small but beautifully appointed room overlooking the street.

"It's lovely," Mattie said, eyes falling on the thick, downy cotton pique comforter all but enveloping the wrought-iron double bed in the middle of the room. Impressionist prints lined the walls. A small armoire sat beside the window. The en suite bathroom featured a mosaic reproduction on the floor of Renoir's *Girl on a Swing*. "I love it."

"I see the French aren't big on wide-open spaces," Jake remarked, walking to the window, trying to pry it open.

"What's the matter?"

"It seems to be stuck."

"Is that a problem?" Mattie bit down hard on her tongue. Of course it was a problem. How could she be so insensitive? "I'm sorry, Jake. We'll change rooms."

"No, don't be silly. This is fine."

"It's not fine. I'm sure they have other rooms."

They didn't. Jake called Chloe Dorleac, who informed him the hotel was all filled up, and no other rooms would be available for several days. "The dragon lady says that Americans are always complaining it's too noisy with the window open, so they haven't bothered to have it fixed," Jake told Mattie, lying down beside her in the middle of the voluminous white comforter, which bounced around them like a parachute. "It's okay, Mattie. I'll be fine."

"You're sure?"

"Positive." He stared at the ceiling. "My mother doesn't even know I'm here."

"The Eiffel Tower was built in a record two years for the 1889 World Exhibition," Mattie said, reading from the guidebook, as she and Jake sat on a nearby bench looking up at the magnificent cast-iron structure. The temperature was a pleasant 72 degrees, and they'd changed out of their traveling clothes into inadvertently matching uniforms of khaki slacks, white shirts, and lightweight jackets. "The tower was never intended to be a permanent feature of the city, and only its potential use as a radio antenna kept it from being torn down," Mattie continued in amazement. "However, in 1910, it was finally saved for posterity, and each year it attracts over four million visitors."

"All of whom decided to visit this afternoon," Jake said.

Mattie smiled. "The tower weighs over 7,700 tons and is 1,050 feet high. It's made up of 15,000 iron sections, and 55 tons of paint were needed to repaint it. Its nickname is the 'staircase to infinity,' and it sways no more than five inches in high winds. Three hundred and seventy people have committed suicide here by jumping off the top platform, which is 906 feet from the ground."

"Ouch."

"It's beautiful, isn't it? I mean, it should be a cliché, but it isn't."

"It's beautiful," he agreed.

Mattie stared with growing envy at the seemingly endless number of people waiting in line for the slow-moving elevators. She and Jake had calculated it would take at least an hour to get to the front of the line. There was no way she could stand for that long, and climbing the hundreds of stairs to the top was obviously out of the question, so she and Jake had retreated to an empty bench to wait for the crowds to thin out. So far, they showed no sign of doing so, but Mattie was happy just to sit beside Jake and wait.

There was nothing like people-watching, no matter where you were, she thought, her attention captured by a pair of teenagers kissing with great abandon under a magnificent cherry tree. Another couple was locked in a passionate embrace beside a small kiosk, yet another as they walked along the busy pathway in front of the tower, seemingly oblivious to all but each other, just like the famous photograph by Robert Doisneau. The city of love, Mattie thought, eyes focusing on Jake.

"It says here we can avoid the long lines for the elevator by visiting the tower at night," Jake said, reading from a pamphlet he'd picked up.

"Really?"

"Apparently it's even more romantic at night," Jake said, "because it's all lit up."

"Could we do that—come back later?"

"How about we come back after our boat ride on the Seine?"

Mattie burst into tears.

"What it is, Mattie? If you're too tired, we can just wait here. I didn't mean to push you. We can do the boat ride another night."

"I'm not too tired," she assured him through her tears. "I'm just so happy. God, talk about clichés."

Jake wiped her tears away with a soft stroke of his fingers.

"What about you? You must be exhausted. At least I slept for a few hours at the hotel." Mattie knew Jake hadn't even closed his eyes.

"I slept on the plane," he reminded her. "What's the matter? Think I can't keep up?" Jake jumped to his feet, then helped Mattie to hers. "Just a minute," he said, corraling a passing Japanese tourist, dropping his camera into the man's startled hands. "Could you take a picture? *Un photo?* You just press down here," he added, quickly positioning himself beside Mattie in front of the magnificent tower, draping a protective arm across her shoulder. "One more," he directed, his hands instructing the young man to turn the camera into a vertical position. "Great. Thank you. That's going to be a great picture," he said after retrieving the camera and returning to Mattie's side. "Ready?"

Mattie slipped her arm through his as Jake slowly led her through the crowd. She caught sight of a woman in the floppy beige hat and was about to call out, but on closer inspection, she saw that the woman looked nothing at all like Cynthia Broome. Broome. Yes, that was her name. Cynthia Broome. From Chicago. "Ready or not," Mattie said.

TWENTY-EIGHT

The nightmare started the same way it always did.

Jake's mother was dancing around the predominantly beige-and-brown living room of his childhood, tossing her blond hair from side to side, raising her wide floral skirt to reveal provocative flashes of thigh, trying to lure her husband out from behind his newspaper. "You never tell me I'm beautiful," she was saying. "How come you never tell me I'm beautiful?"

"I tell you all the time," came the time-honored reply. "You don't listen."

"Why don't we go somewhere? Let's go dancing. Did you hear me? I said, let's go dancing."

"You've been drinking."

"I haven't been drinking."

"I can smell the liquor on your breath from here."

Jake moaned in his sleep, tried to block out the

sound of their voices the way he always did, despite knowing such efforts were futile.

"How about a movie? We haven't been to a movie in ages."

"Call up one of your girlfriends if you want to go to a movie."

"You're the one with the girlfriends," Jake heard his mother snap.

"Lower your voice. You'll wake the boys."

Yes, wake up, a little voice whispered inside Jake's head. *Wake up. You're not a child anymore. You don't have to listen to this. Wake up. You're not in your parents' house. You're on the other side of the world. And you're all grown up. She can't hurt you here. Wake up. Wake up.*

But even as Jake was admonishing himself to ignore the voices in his head, his attention was diverted by the sight of three small boys in their pajamas joining forces, constructing a futile barrier of books and toys at the base of his bedroom door.

"You think I don't know about your little friends? You think I don't know where you go at night? You think I don't know everything about you, you miserable son of a bitch?" Eva Hart was yelling, raising the ante along with her voice, a voice strong enough to pierce through solid walls, span decades, cross oceans.

Jake watched his mother drive her fist through the middle of his father's newspaper, feeling the full impact of that fist in the middle of his gut. He grabbed his stomach, doubled over in bed, as if he'd been sucker-punched.

His father leaped from his chair, threw his newspaper to the floor. "You're crazy," he was screaming as he headed to the door. "You're a crazy woman. You should be committed to an institution."

The three small boys raced for the closet, locking the door after them, huddling together at the back of the small dark space, Luke shaking in Jake's arms, Nicholas off by himself, staring blankly ahead.

Jake watched his mother lunge toward his father as if she were about to pounce on his back, ride him like a bucking bronco. Instead she lost her balance, fell against the skinny standing lamp next to the front door. It teetered back and forth like a metronome, counting off the seconds till his father's furious farewell. "I'm crazy for staying with a crazy woman."

"Yeah? Then why don't you leave, you miserable excuse for a man."

Don't leave, Jake cried silently. Please, Daddy. Don't leave. You can't leave us alone with her. You don't know what she'll do. "It'll be all right," he whispered to his brothers, reminding them of the water and first-aid kit he'd safely stashed away. "We'll be fine as long as we don't make a sound."

You don't have to watch this, the little voice whispered in Jake's ear. *This may have been your reality once upon a time, but it isn't anymore. Now it's nothing but a bad dream. Wake up. You don't have to be here anymore.*

But it was too late. His mother was already pounding her fists on Jake's closet door, demanding access, demanding loyalty, demanding his very soul. He watched her stumble around his room in a drunken rage, kicking at his shoes, emptying drawers of his clothes onto the floor, swooping up his model airplane, the one he'd spent weeks putting together, the one he'd been planning to present to his teacher and classmates during next week's show-and-tell.

Wake up before she can send it smashing to smithereens, the little voice admonished, invisible hands on Jake's sleeping shoulders, trying to shake him awake, as if he were standing outside himself. *Wake up. Wake up.*

For several seconds Jake straddled the peripheries of his dream, one foot inside, the other out. "Wake up," he repeated out loud, the sound of his voice pushing him over the periphery, across the invisible border that divided his present from his past.

Jake opened his eyes, hearing his ragged breathing ricochet off the walls of the small hotel room. It took him a minute to focus, to figure out where he was, to realize *who* he was. You're Jake Hart, he told himself. Adult. Lawyer. Husband. Father. You're not some frightened little boy anymore. You're all grown up. And still frightened, still running scared, Jake acknowledged, wiping the perspiration from his brow, releasing a deep breath of air from his lungs. How long had he been holding his breath? he wondered.

All your life, the little voice said.

Jake looked over at Mattie, asleep beside him in the old-fashioned, less-than-standard-size double bed. When the French described something as charming and old-world, Mattie had said earlier, he could translate that to mean small and just plain old. Jake smiled, feeling the warmth of Mattie's legs against his own. There was something to be said for the forced intimacy of old-fashioned, less-than-standard-size double beds.

"What a day," Jake said out loud, careful not to disturb Mattie as he climbed out of bed and walked to the window overlooking the street. Paris was truly an amazing city. Mattie had been right about that, as she was right about so many things. He should have listened to her years ago, when she first suggested coming here, when her steps had been as unfettered as her enthusiasm. She wouldn't have had to wait for any crowded, slow-moving elevator to take her to the top of the Eiffel Tower. She would have challenged him to a race to the top. And won.

"Don't start feeling guilty," she'd told him, reading his thoughts, as they stood on the top observation deck of the tower, overlooking the breathtaking panorama that was Paris at night. "I'm having the best time. There's nothing better than this."

"Better than the boat ride?" he'd asked playfully, and they'd laughed, as they did often these days. ("Why do they call it Bateaux Mouches?" he'd asked, checking his pocket dictionary as they boarded the large boat earlier in the evening for a one-hour tour of the Seine. "Doesn't that mean Boat Bugs?" Ten minutes later, as he and Mattie sat swatting pesky hordes of flying insects away from their faces, they understood.)

She never seemed to tire, although she was having obvious difficulty walking. At times she dragged one foot behind the other. Still, she refused to call it a night. They had dinner at a crowded bistro on rue Jacob called Le Petit Zinc, where a young couple sat making out at a nearby table. Ultimately Jake was the one to plead exhaustion. Mattie immediately put her arm through his, and they crossed the busy street to their hotel.

Even at four in the morning the street still wasn't empty, Jake marveled now, as a young man on a motor scooter stalled under Jake's window. The young man, who wore a black leather jacket and a deep purple helmet, looked up, as if he knew he were being watched, and waved when he saw Jake. Jake smiled, waved back, his attention quickly diverted by a small band of teenagers skipping down the middle of the road, their arms around one another's waists, their mouths open in easy laughter. At the corner, he noticed a middle-aged couple cuddling under the awning of a closed café. Did Parisians never sleep?

Maybe, like him, they were afraid to.

Jake returned to the bed, sat for several minutes watching the steady rise and fall of Mattie's breathing. Probably a result of the morphine he'd insisted she take. She'd resisted. "You have to sleep, Mattie," he told her. "You have us on one hell of a schedule. You're going to need all your strength."

"You're all I need," she said, drawing him into her arms, guiding him gently inside her.

And yet, at the moment of climax, she'd had trouble catching her breath, her body growing rigid in his arms as she fought for air, her arms flailing about in helpless abandon, as if she were choking on a piece of steak, her face growing red, her eyes wide with terror as she tried to gather the air around her into her open palms, to literally push oxygen into her lungs. Ultimately she collapsed beside him, coughing and crying, her body soaked in sweat. Jake wiped her forehead with a soft white towel, then held her tightly against his chest, trying to regulate her breathing with his own, if necessary to breathe for both of them.

It was then that Mattie agreed to take the morphine. Soon after, curled inside Jake's arms, she drifted off to asleep.

She'd lost so much weight, Jake realized with a shudder, staring at the delicate arm resting atop the billowy white comforter, like a small wiggly line. At least ten pounds, maybe more. She tried to hide it, wearing loose bulky clothing in the daytime, shapeless nightgowns at night. But lying here now, with the Parisian moonlight streaming in from the nearby window, the extent of her weight loss was impossible to dismiss or ignore. She seemed more bone than flesh. Even her hair seemed thinner. Jake brushed several fine strands away from Mattie's pronounced cheekbones, his fingers lingering on her pale skin, as if reluctant to leave her. *Disappearing before my very eyes*, he thought, bending toward her, his lips caressing Mattie's forehead with the softness of a feather. "You're so beautiful," he whispered, suddenly overwhelmed by a sadness so strong, it hurt to breathe. Was that how Mattie felt, he wondered, when she struggled for air?

"I love you," she'd told him the day he'd come home early to tell her they were going to Paris on schedule after all. She'd offered the words without prompting, without waiting for, or even expecting, him to say the words back. And he hadn't said them. Not then. Not since. How could he? he wondered, not trusting his voice. Not trusting himself. And so the words lingered provocatively on the tip of his tongue when they were together, playing with his lips, taking refuge behind his closed mouth. How ironic, he thought now, climbing back under the comforter and arranging his body around hers, that just as Mattie's life was ending, he couldn't imagine life without her.

Mattie stirred in her sleep, fitting the convex curve of her backside into the concave curve of his stomach, as if they were two pieces of the same puzzle, which was as good a way to describe them as any, Jake thought. He kissed her shoulder, inhaling the gentle remnants of her lilac perfume, purposefully holding her scent in his lungs for as long as he could, as if by doing so he could somehow keep her safe. Then he released it, slowly, reluctantly, his head falling against his pillow, sleep tugging at his eyelids.

He felt his nightmare lurking, waiting to sputter into action, like a video he'd stopped in midreel, jumping forward and back, trying to find the right spot, his father's face, his mother's fist, the pathetic stockpile of books and toys on the bedroom floor, his mother ransacking his room, hurling her vile threats against his closet door. "I can't live this way any longer," she was shouting. "Do you hear me? I can't live this way anymore. Nobody loves me. Nobody cares whether I live or die."

Still awake, Jake heard Nicholas whimper, watched Luke tightly clutch the handle of the closet door, his stomach twisting with each twist of the knob. Trembling, Jake withdrew his arm from Mattie's side, covered his ears to the sickening thud of his model plane crashing to the ground.

"Damn you," his mother yelled, kicking at the door. "Damn all of you spoiled little brats. You know what

I'm going to do? You know what I'm going to do now? I'm going into the kitchen, and I'm going to turn on the gas, and in the morning, when your father comes home from sleeping with his girlfriend, he'll find us all dead in our beds."

"No!" Nicholas cried, burying his head beneath his hands.

"I'm doing you a favor," Eva Hart shouted, tripping over the books and toys now strewn across the floor, aiming a shoe at the closet door. "You'll die in your sleep. You won't suffer the way I have. You won't even know what's happening."

"No!" Jake said now, opening his eyes, drawing strength from Mattie's steady breathing, refusing to be cowed any longer. There was no gas. There was nothing to be afraid of. He had a wife who loved him, who knew him better than any living soul, and still she loved him. Because he deserved to be loved. Because he was worthy of love, Jake understood for the first time.

If Mattie could face such a cruel, unfair future with such courage, then surely he could come to terms with a past he'd allowed to control him for way too long, a past that was slowly suffocating him to death.

He looked over at Mattie. No point in both of us suffocating to death, he heard her say, a wink in her voice.

And suddenly Jake was on his feet in the middle of the tiny room, an adult amid the chaos and debris of his childhood, and he was laughing. His mother was at the door, her back to him. His laughter filled every available space, assuming a life of its own, blocking his mother's exit. It was the force of his laughter that grabbed his mother by her shoulders and spun her around.

If she was startled to see him, she didn't let on. She stared at her grown son in drunken defiance. "What are you laughing about?" she growled. "Who do you think you are, laughing at me?"

"I'm your son," Jake said simply.

Eva Hart snorted, distinctly unimpressed. "Leave me alone," she said, twisting toward the door.

"You're not going anywhere," Jake told her.

"I'll do whatever I damn well please."

"You're not going anywhere," Jake repeated, standing his ground. "No one's leaving this room. No one's going to turn on the gas."

Now it was his mother's turn to laugh. "You can't tell me you took that silly threat seriously. You know I'd never do such a thing."

"I'm five years old, Mother," the adult Jake responded. "Of course I take your stupid threats seriously."

"Well, you shouldn't." His mother smiled, almost coquettishly. "You know I'd never do anything to hurt you. You've always been my favorite."

"Have you any idea how much I hate you?" Jake asked. "How much I've always hated you?"

"Really, Jason. What kind of way is that to talk to your mother? You're a very bad boy, Jason."

Bad boy, Jason. Bad boy, Jason. Bad boy, Jason. *Badboyjason, badboyjason, badboyjason.*

"I'm not a bad boy," Jake heard himself say.

"You take things far too seriously. You always did. Come on, Jason. Don't be a whiner. You're starting to sound like your brothers."

"The only thing wrong with my brothers was their mother."

"Well now, that's not very nice, is it? I mean, I wasn't such a bad mother. Look at you. You turned out okay." She winked. "I must have done something right."

"The only thing you did right was die."

"Oh my. Well, aren't we the melodramatic one. Maybe I should go turn on the gas after all."

"You're through terrorizing us. Do you understand?" Jake squeezed his mother's arm so tightly, he felt his own fingers meet through her skin.

"Let me go," his mother protested. "I'm your mother, damn it. How dare you talk to me this way."

"You're nothing but a drunken bully. You can't hurt me anymore."

"Let go of my arm. Get out of my way," Eva Hart said, but her voice was weakening, and her image was blurring, smudging at the edges, like a chalk drawing, growing fainter with each word.

"You have no more power over me," Jake said, his own voice clear and strong.

A puzzled look crossed his mother's flirtatious hazel eyes. And then she was gone.

Jake stood absolutely still for several seconds, relishing the silence, then returned to the bed, dropping down beside Mattie, his hand absently caressing the gentle curve of her hip as his mind began picking up the books and toys that lay scattered on the floor, returning each to its proper place. With great care he retrieved the pieces of his broken model airplane and deposited them on the small table where the plane normally sat. Then he watched himself walk to the closet door and open it, staring at the three small boys huddled together on the other side. "You can come out now," he said silently. "She's gone."

Immediately, Nicholas bolted out the closet door and ran from the room.

"Nick," Jake called out after him, watching him vanish into thin air. "Catch you later," he said softly, returning his attention to the two boys still cowering in the closet. Luke sat closest to the door, his eyes open wide, staring blankly into space. "I'm so sorry, Luke," Jake said, squeezing his ample frame inside the cramped space, kneeling beside the young boy who was his older brother. "Please, can you forgive me?"

Luke said nothing. Instead he leaned his child's body into Jake's side, allowing Jake to take him in his arms and rock him gently back and forth until he disappeared.

And then only the child Jake remained. "You're a good boy," Jake told him simply, without words, watching the boy's smile reflected in his eyes. "A very good boy, Jason. A very good boy."

"Jake," Mattie was saying, sitting up beside him, her voice lifting him out of his past into the dawn of a new day. "Are you okay?"

"Fine," he answered. "Just a little trouble sleeping."

"I had a dream you were laughing."

"Sounds like a good dream."

"What about you?" Mattie asked, concern returning to her voice. "Any more nightmares?"

Jake shook his head. "No," he said, folding her inside his arms, lying down beside her, and closing his eyes. "No more nightmares."

TWENTY-NINE

Kim was daydreaming again.

She sat at the back of the classroom, her math text open to the appropriate page, her eyes focused on the pear-shaped teacher in the sloppy brown suit standing in front of the chalkboard, as if she were actually paying attention to what old Mr. Wilkes was saying—something about letting X represent the problem, as if anything could actually be solved by letting one thing pretend to be something else—when in fact her mind was thousands of miles away, across the ocean, in Paris, France, strolling arm in arm with her mother down the famed Champs Elysées.

Her mother had called last night to find out how Kim was managing at school, with Grandma Viv, with her new puppy, with her therapist.

Fine, fine, fine, fine, Kim responded to each fresh inquiry. How about you?

Everything was great, came the enthusiastic response. They'd already seen the Eiffel Tower, the Louvre, Montmartre, Notre Dame, the Quai d'Orsay. Today they were heading off to the Champs Elysées and the Arc de Triomphe. The weather was wonderful; Jake was wonderful; she was wonderful.

Except then she'd started coughing and gasping for air, and Jake had to take over, finish the conversation for her. How was she doing? her father asked. How was school? Mattie's mother? The new puppy? Her sessions with Rosemary Colicos?

Fine, fine, fine, fine, Kim said. Put Mom back on the line.

It was hard for her mother to talk for long stretches, her father explained, although generally speaking she was managing very well, he was quick to assure her. They'd call again in a few days. Paris was great, he said. Next year, they'd take her with them.

Sure thing, Kim thought now, tugging at the tight little bun at the back of her head, loosening several of the bobby pins and feeling them drop from her hair, hearing the soft *ping* as they bounced off her shoulder and fell to the floor. She reached down to pick them up, eyeing the strange combination of open-toed summer sandals and heavy winter boots that adorned her classmates' feet. All it took was one nice day, when the sun came out and the temperature rose a few degrees above freezing, and half the student body was already in bare feet and sleeveless T-shirts. Couldn't wait for summer, Kim thought, straightening up, stabbing at her head with the errant bobby pins. Couldn't wait for time to bring them one season closer to death.

"Kim?"

The sound of her name crashed against her ears, like cymbals colliding. It filled the inside of her brain, echoing and reverberating, bouncing around her skull as if desperately searching for a way out.

"Sorry?" Kim heard herself ask Mr. Wilkes, who was staring at her as if he'd been expecting a more pertinent response.

"I believe I asked you a question."

"I believe I didn't hear you," Kim replied before she had time for a more considered response.

Displeasure flickered across Mr. Wilkes's watery green eyes. "And why is that, Kim? Were you not paying attention?"

"I would think that was fairly obvious, sir," Kim replied, stunned by her rudeness but enjoying the assorted gasps and giggles of her fellow classmates. It had been the most response she'd drawn from any of them in weeks.

The bell rang. The twenty-seven somnambulant teenagers slumped in their seats immediately sprung to life, rose up as one, and headed noisily for the door. "Kim?" the teacher asked as Kim was about to leave.

Kim turned reluctantly back toward Mr. Wilkes.

"I know about your situation at home," he began. "Your father informed the school about your mother's condition," he continued when she said nothing. "I just wanted you to know that I'm here for you, in case you ever wanted to talk to someone."

"I'm fine, sir," Kim told him, gripping her books tightly to her chest.

Fine. Fine. Fine. Fine.

How dare her father call the school? How dare he inform her teachers of her mother's illness? What right did he have to do something like that? "Can I go now?" she asked.

"Of course."

Kim fled down the halls to her locker. What else had her father blabbed to the school about? Jake Hart, the Great Defender, she thought derisively. The Great Blabbermouth was more like it, she decided, fiddling with her combination lock, mixing up the numbers, having to do it again. On the third try the locker opened, and Kim threw her books inside, retrieved her lunchbag, carried it to the cafeteria.

She found an empty table in the far corner, sat facing the wall, her back to the rest of the student population. She opened her lunchbag, frowning at the peanut butter and jam sandwich her grandmother had made. "I don't want your mother saying I didn't feed you," Grandma Viv explained. "If you're nothing but skin and bones when they get back from France, whose fault do you think it'll be?"

It would serve them right, Kim thought then and now, throwing the sandwich toward the yawning garbage bin in the corner, the sandwich hitting the top of the large container and coming apart, falling to the floor, sticky sides down. "Damn," Kim said, retrieving the sandwich and tossing the two halves directly into the bin, leaving the remnants of peanut butter and jelly on the linoleum floor. Yes, sir, it would serve her parents right if she were nothing but a bag of bones by the time they returned from their trip to Gay Paree. That would teach them to abandon her. Not that she didn't understand their desire to get away, but just because she understood it didn't make it any easier, didn't make her less alone.

Kim's stomach growled, part hunger, part protest. She checked the rest of her lunchbag. A box of 2 percent milk and a Snickers bar. Kim felt her mouth begin to salivate. Immediately she retrieved the chocolate bar from the bag and hurled it toward the garbage bin, watching it score a direct hit, disappear inside. She'd given up chocolate bars. They weren't good for you. Too much fat. Too much sugar. It was important she watch her diet, exercise some control over the things she put in her mouth. Probably if her mother had been more careful about what she'd eaten, if she'd avoided all those sweet desserts and those ridiculous marshmallow strawberries she so loved, she'd be all right now. No, you couldn't be too careful. So many chemicals, so many additives and dyes in everything we ate. You practically took your life into your hands every time you opened your mouth.

Even milk, Kim thought, tearing open the wrong corner of the small cardboard box and watching the warm milk bubble up and ooze across her fingers. Who knew what the dairy industry was adding to the milk to disguise the poisons the cows ingested daily. Look at the number of people who were lactose-intolerant these days. There had to be a reason people were becoming more prone to all sorts of dreadful diseases.

Kim lifted the small container to her lips, smelled the tepid liquid, felt it curdle on the tip of her tongue. Next thing she knew, the milk had joined the rest of her lunch in the garbage bin, and she was on her feet and heading toward the gym. If she wasn't going to eat, she might as well get an early start on her exercise program.

She'd started working out regularly after the debacle with Teddy. At first she did only ten minutes a day, a few crunches, a few lunges, some easy stretches, a few laps around the track. But every day a few more exercises got added to the mix, so that now she was exercising almost two hours daily. First came a series of simple stretches, then half an hour of low-impact aerobics, then more stretches, then more aerobics, this time high-impact, for at least thirty minutes, followed by two hundred stomach crunches and one hundred pushups, then more stretches, in addition to running and skipping and jumping and a few more stretches for good luck. Even when she was holding George, her stomach was busy crunching in and out, in and out, because you could never be too fit. You could never be too healthy.

Kim laced up her running shoes, checked her watch. She had over forty minutes before her next class. Enough time to get a good run in, she decided, beginning her first circle around the gym. In another month she could add swimming to her list. Kim pictured her mother in their backyard pool. Back and forth, back and forth, one hundred lengths, every day from May till mid-October. And what good had it done her? Kim wondered, stopping abruptly. All that chlorine in the water. So hard on your hair. Think what it must do to your insides. And you were bound to swallow some of it. It was unavoidable. Kim resumed her running, deciding swimming might not be such a good idea after all.

"Hey, Kimbo," someone shouted. "What's the hurry?"

Kim looked toward the wide double door to the gym, saw Caroline Smith flanked by her two clones, Annie Turofsky and Jodi Bates, resplendent in matching red sweaters.

"Where you going?" Jodi asked.

"Someone chasing you?" asked Annie.

Kim tried to ignore them. They'd barely spoken to her in months. They were only interested in her again because she'd been rude to old Mr. Wilkes in class, which meant she was potentially interesting, potentially dangerous. Why should she cater to their cruel whims? Why should she feel obliged to answer them? Except she didn't feel obliged, she realized, slowing down and jogging toward them. She felt grateful. "What's up?" she asked, as if the last several months had never happened.

"What did old man Wilkes say to you after class?" Caroline asked. "We took bets he was going to suspend you."

"No such luck."

"Who's the old bag who's been driving you to school all week?" Annie asked.

"My grandmother," Kim answered. "And she's not an old bag."

Caroline shrugged, her two companions immediately following suit. Nothing interesting here, the shrugs said.

"I've been staying at her house while my parents are away in France," Kim volunteered.

"Your parents are away?" Caroline asked.

"Why didn't you tell us?" Annie Turofsky said, her high-pitched voice an accusation.

"When did they leave?" asked Jodi Bates.

"More important," Caroline said, "how long will they be gone?"

"They left last week," Kim answered, basking in their renewed attention. "They'll be back Wednesday."

"So, let me get this straight," Caroline was saying. "You've been staying at your grandmother's while that nice big house of yours sits empty?"

"Seems a shame, doesn't it?" Kim said.

"A real waste," Caroline agreed.

"Are you thinking what we're thinking?" Jodi Bates asked.

"That it's a shame for a nice big house like that to be all by itself for the weekend?" Kim asked in return.

"Especially when there's a party looking for a place to happen."

"You supply the accommodations," Caroline offered. "We'll supply the guests. Everybody'll bring their own refreshments. How does that sound to you?"

"Sounds great."

"I can get the word out before the next class," Annie said.

Kim took a deep breath. What would be the harm? Her grandmother wouldn't question her going out for a few hours on Saturday night. Her parents were halfway around the world. No way they'd ever find out. She'd be careful. Insist everyone behaved. No drugs. No hard liquor. "No crashers," she said out loud.

"No problem," Jodi said.

"The A list only," Caroline concurred.

"I don't know." Kim wavered. "Maybe it isn't such a good idea."

But Annie was already halfway down the hall, shouting to everyone who passed by, "Party at Kim Hart's house. Tomorrow night. Nine o'clock."

Party at Kim's house, the halls echoed. *Tomorrow night. Nine o'clock.*

Party at Kim's. Party at Kim's. Party at Kim's.

"What do you think are the chances I could persuade our waitress to exchange one of these rolls for another croissant?" Jake was asking, smiling at Mattie as he knocked the rock-hard roll against the side of the small table. They were sitting in the small window-lined, flower-filled breakfast area located behind the elevator shaft at the rear of their hotel. It was nine o'clock in the morning. Outside the rain was coming down with such ferocity, it all but obliterated the by-now-familiar row of small boutiques and cafés.

It had been raining for at least four hours, Mattie calculated, stifling a yawn. It was raining when she woke up at five o'clock this morning to go to the bathroom, raining as she tried maneuvering her way across the room without waking Jake, who was snoring with such obvious contentment she hadn't had the heart to wake him, raining even harder when she collapsed onto the toilet seat some five minutes later, now fully awake. The rain pounded against the bathroom window behind her head, as if trying to get inside, as she wrestled with the toilet paper, trying to tear off the necessary strip, to bring it to her body. How soon before this most private of functions was no longer within her control, when something as basic as wiping herself would be, quite literally, taken out of her hands? The rain accompanied her back to bed. She crawled in beside her husband, spent the hours until Jake woke up listening to the rain as it slammed angrily against their hotel room window. It was easier not to think when it was raining, Mattie thought, strangely lulled by the storm's growing fury.

"You know the laws of the land," Mattie said now. "One soft croissant, one jaw-breaking roll." She raised her cup of black coffee to her lips, hoping a jolt of caffeine would provide her with enough energy to kick-start her day. In truth, all she wanted to do was go back upstairs and climb into bed. Hadn't she promised Jake that she wouldn't overdo, that she'd tell him when she was tired? A few hours more sleep—that was all she needed. Maybe in a few more hours, the rain would have stopped.

"I'm really looking forward to this morning," Jake was saying, a guidebook miraculously appearing in his hands. "Listen to this: 'More than a mere landmark in the extensive facelift that Paris has undergone in the last twenty years,' " he read, " 'the high-tech Georges Pompidou Center is a hive of constantly changing cultural activity. Contemporary art, architecture, design, photography, theater, cinema, and dance are all represented, while the lofty structure itself offers exceptional views over central Paris.' "

Mattie's shoulders slumped in anticipated exhaustion. Art, architecture, design, photography, theater, cinema, dance—the words slapped against her skull with the careless precision of the outside rain on the windows.

"'Take the transparent escalator tubes for a bird's-eye view of the piazza below,'" Jake continued reading, "'where musicians, street artists, and portraitists ply their trades for the teeming crowds.'"

Escalator tubes, bird's-eye views, street artists, teeming crowds, Mattie repeated silently, growing dizzier with each fresh image.

"Since it's raining," Jake continued, "we might as well taxi over to the gallery, do the inside first. Maybe by the time we're finished, the rain will have let up, and we can go outside and have our portrait painted." He stopped, dark blue eyes widening in alarm. "Mattie, what's wrong?"

"Wrong?" Mattie felt the coffee cup about to slip through her fingers. She tried to hold on to its delicate porcelain handle, but her fingers refused to retain their grip. Mattie pictured the cup sliding through her fingers and crashing to the marble floor, waited helplessly for this image to become reality.

Suddenly Jake's hands were on top of hers, catching the cup before it could fall, returning it to its saucer before a drop of the murky brown liquid could stain the thick white tablecloth, his eyes never leaving hers. "You're pale as a ghost."

"I'm fine."

"You're not fine. What's happening, Mattie? What aren't you telling me?"

Mattie shook her head stubbornly. "Honestly, Jake, I'm fine. I'm just a little tired," she conceded reluctantly, realizing it was pointless to protest further.

"When you say you're a little tired, it means you're exhausted," Jake translated. "The French aren't the only ones who've mastered the art of euphemism."

Mattie signaled her surrender with a smile. "I didn't sleep very well last night. Maybe it wouldn't be such a bad idea for me to take the morning off."

"Great idea. We'll go back upstairs, lie down until this rain lets up. I didn't get a lot of sleep myself."

"You slept like a baby."

"So, I'll watch you sleep."

Mattie pushed her hands across the table, caressed her husband's cheek with increasingly useless fingers. How long before she could no longer touch him this way? How long before even the slightest acts of tenderness would be denied her? "I want you to go to the Pompidou Center," she told him.

"Not without you," came the immediate reply.

"Jake, it's silly for both of us to miss it."

"We'll go tomorrow."

"No. You'll go this morning," Mattie insisted. "If it's any good, we'll go together next year. With Kim," she added, recalling his phone conversation with their daughter.

Jake brought Mattie's fingers to his mouth, kissed each one in turn. "I think she'd really love it here," he said.

"Then you'll make sure to bring her." Mattie's voice was soft, pleading.

"I'll make sure to bring her," Jake agreed, his voice a whisper.

They sat for several minutes in silence. "You should get going," Mattie said finally.

"I'll take you upstairs first."

"That's not necessary."

"Mattie, I'm not going anywhere until I know you're safely tucked in bed."

"I'm not an invalid, Jake," Mattie snapped, the sudden harshness in her voice surprising both of them. "Please don't treat me like one," she said, her voice returning to normal.

"God, Mattie. I'm sorry. I didn't mean—"

"I know," she assured him quickly. "I'm the one who should be sorry. I had no right to snap at you like that."

"You had every right."

"It's just not a good day, I guess."

"What can I do?" he asked helplessly.

"You can go to the Georges Pompidou Center and have a good time, that's what you can do."

"Is that what you really want?"

"It's what I really want."

Jake nodded, rose to his feet. "I guess the faster I go, the faster I can get back."

Mattie smiled up at him. "Don't rush. I'm not going anywhere. Now go. Get out of here."

He leaned over, kissed her, the feel of his lips lingering on hers long after he'd left the room. Mattie sat alone for several minutes watching the other diners: a young couple arguing quietly in Spanish in a corner table; two elderly women chatting excitedly in German; an American couple trying unsuccessfully to keep their two young sons in their seats. What had happened, she wondered, to the woman she'd met in the courtyard? Cynthia something. Broome. Cynthia Broome. Yes, that was it. She hadn't seen her since that first day.

Mattie pushed herself to her feet, noting with a smile that while all the croissants had disappeared from the baskets in the center of the tables, most of the hard rolls remained. Who had the strength to chew those damn things anyway? she wondered, slowly making her way across the room. Certainly not her, she thought, as one of the American youngsters bolted out of his chair and crashed into her legs. Mattie felt her knees buckle. She stumbled, grabbed hold of a nearby chair, managed through sheer force of will to stay on her feet.

"Will you sit down!" the boy's mother hissed, forcibly returning the towheaded child to his chair, pushing it in as close to the table as possible. "I'm so sorry," the woman said as Mattie walked past her toward the lobby, the woman's New England accent bouncing off the echo of the outside rain.

Chloe Dorleac, resplendent in a deep purple silk blouse and dark burgundy lipstick, nodded coolly in Mattie's direction as Mattie headed for the tiny elevator. The dragon lady, Mattie thought with a chuckle. Abruptly, Mattie swiveled on her heel and approached the desk. "Can I help you?" Chloe Dorleac said without looking up.

"I wanted to inquire about one of the guests," Mattie said, continuing when no further questions were forthcoming. "Cynthia Broome. She's American."

"Cynthia Broome," the dragon lady repeated. "This name is not familiar."

"She was here when we arrived. She told me she was staying several weeks."

Chloe Dorleac made an elaborate show of looking

through her register. "No. No one by that name has ever been here."

"Well, that can't be," Mattie persisted, eager to prove the dragon lady wrong, though she wasn't sure why. She was exhausted, and her legs were beginning to ache. She needed to get upstairs and lie down before she collapsed. "Not too tall. Attractive. Red curly hair."

"Oh, yes." The dragon lady's violet eyes flashed recognition. "I know who you mean. But her name is not Cynthia Broome." The phone rang, and Chloe Dorleac excused herself to answer it. "One minute," she said, holding up her index finger. "Une minute."

Okay, Mattie thought, waiting as Mademoiselle Dorleac spoke animatedly in French to whomever was on the other end of the line. So she'd gotten the last name wrong. It wasn't Broome. It was something else useful, although she was too tired to think what it might be. What difference did it make? Cynthia Not-Broome was obviously very busy seeing the sights of Paris and happy to be doing it all by her lonesome. Why was Mattie even thinking about her?

"Never mind," Mattie said to Chloe Dorleac, with an ineffectual wave of her hand. The dragon lady ignored her, laughing into the receiver, although her mouth barely moved. The sound of her laughter followed Mattie into the tiny wrought-iron cage and up the open elevator shaft to the third floor. It pursued Mattie into her room and into her bed, competing with the rain, as Mattie closed her eyes and surrendered her weary body to sleep.

THIRTY

In her dream, Mattie was rushing to meet Jake at the top of the Arc de Triomphe. Jake had warned her not to be late. Checking her watch, Mattie climbed into the backseat of an idling cab in the middle of the traffic-choked place de la Concorde.

"Vite! Vite!" Mattie instructed the driver.

"Chop! Chop!" came the reply from the front seat. "Did you know that King Louis XVI and Marie Antoinette were guillotined in this square during the French Revolution? In fact, between 1793 and 1795, a total of 1,300 people lost their heads in this very spot."

"My father lost his head when I was eight years old," Mattie said. "My mother cut it off."

Suddenly Mattie was out of the cab and running along the crowded sidewalk of the Champs Elysées. She checked her watch again, noting she had only two minutes to make it to the top of the wide tree-lined avenue, whose name meant Elysian Fields, but which was now home to an unsightly number of fast-food outlets, car showrooms, and airline offices. "Excuse me," she said, bumping into a woman in a floppy beige hat.

"What's the big rush?" the woman asked as Mattie flew by.

"The Arc de Triomphe was commissioned by Napoleon in 1806, but not completed until thirty years later," Mattie heard a tour guide shouting in English over the jostling crowd as she began her arduous climb to the top of the imposing structure. "Has anybody seen my husband?" she asked a group of tourists racing down the spiral stone staircase.

"You just missed him," said a woman with curly red hair. "He went to the Georges Pompidou Center."

A group of boisterous schoolboys hoisted Mattie over their shoulders and carried her back to the foot of the stairs, where they promptly disappeared, leaving Mattie alone in a small windowless room. "Somebody help me," she shouted, banging her body futilely against a heavy metal door. But her voice grew weaker as her efforts increased, and soon all she heard was the echo of her body slapping against the cold stone walls.

Knock, knock.

Who's there?

Knock. Knock.

Qui est là?

Knock. Knock.

Mattie opened her eyes, her breathing labored, her forehead covered in tiny beads of sweat. God, she hated dreams like that. She sat up and stared toward the window. Still raining, she thought, noting she'd slept barely an hour. Probably she should lie back down, try for another hour, make sure she was well rested for when Jake returned.

Knock. Knock.

Not her dream, Mattie realized. Someone was actually at the door. "Yes? Oui? Who is it? Qui est là?" Probably the cleaning lady, she thought, wondering why the woman didn't just use her key. Or possibly Jake—maybe he'd forgotten his. Mattie swung her legs around the side of the bed.

"Mattie?" the voice asked, as Mattie's hand froze on the doorknob.

Mattie opened the door to a vision of wet red curls.

"Miserable morning," the woman said, dusting some rain from the shoulders of her navy jacket and staring at Mattie through gold-flecked brown eyes. "I tried going out, but I had to come back. It's unbelievable out there. It's Cynthia," she said, almost as if she were asking a question. "Cynthia Broome? The dragon lady said you were looking for me."

Mattie stood back, motioned the other woman inside the small room, nodded toward an unsteady wooden chair by the window. "I was asking about you, yes." Mattie lowered herself carefully to the edge of the bed as Cynthia plopped her ample backside into the narrow seat and slipped out of her wet jacket. "Madame Dorleac said there was no one here by the name of Cynthia Broome."

The other woman looked momentarily caught off guard. She gathered a fistful of red curls into the palm of her right hand and shook them, several drops of water staining the thighs of her denim jeans. "Oh, of course. My passport," she said. "It's still in my married name. I should change it, I guess. I've been divorced almost four years." Cynthia looked warily around the room. "Did you want to see me about anything in particular?"

Mattie shook her head. "No, not really. I was just curious what happened to you. I hadn't seen you since that morning in the courtyard."

"When you were looking for your husband."

"I found him."

Cynthia looked toward the washroom. "Where'd you put him?"

Mattie laughed. "He went to the Georges Pompidou Center. I was a little tired, so I came back upstairs to lie down."

"And I woke you up?" Concern fell across Cynthia's face like a heavy blanket.

"It's all right," Mattie assured her. "Really. I'm fine."

"You're sure?"

"I was having a bad dream anyway. You rescued me."

Cynthia smiled, although the concern never left her round face. "What was the dream about?"

"Just one of those stupid dreams where you're trying to get somewhere and you can't."

"Oh, I hate those," Cynthia concurred. "They're so frustrating."

"Can I offer you anything? Some biscuits, Evian water, chocolates?"

"No, nothing. What kind of chocolates?" she asked, almost in the same breath.

"Cream-filled, sticky, gooey things. Absolutely sinful." Mattie stretched toward the open box of truffles sitting on the tiny table beside her pillow. But the box felt like a lead weight, and it tumbled from her hand, spilling its contents to the floor. "Oh, no."

"It's okay. I'll get them," Cynthia offered quickly, on her knees and scooping up the chocolates with eager fingers. In seconds the truffles were safely ensconced in their brown paper wrappers. "There. No harm done."

"I'm so sorry."

Cynthia reached back into the box, selected the biggest of the truffles and popped it into her mouth. "Um, yummy. Champagne filling. My favorite."

"Even covered in dust?"

"Yes, but it's French dust, don't forget. Makes a big difference."

Again, Mattie laughed, deciding she liked Cynthia Broome, wondering what man had been fool enough to let her get away.

"Where'd you get these?"

"I don't know. Jake picked them up at some little shop on the Right Bank."

"How long have you two been married?" Cynthia asked, eyes scanning the remaining chocolates in the box.

"Sixteen years."

"Wow. You must have been a child bride."

"Actually, the bride was *with* child," Mattie qualified, surprised to hear herself volunteer such personal information to a virtual stranger.

"But you're still together sixteen years later,"

Cynthia said, a touch of muted envy in her voice. "You may have had to get married, but you didn't have to stay together."

Mattie nodded. "I guess that's true." She laughed. But the laugh stuck in her throat, attaching itself to her larynx like a gooey piece of chocolate, preventing the outside air from reaching her lungs. Mattie jumped from the bed, the box of candies dropping from her lap to the floor as she waved her arms frantically in front of her face.

"My God, what can I do?" Cynthia asked, immediately on her feet, her own arms flapping helplessly into the space between them.

Mattie shook her head. There was nothing anyone could do, she realized, trying to calm herself down. She wasn't actually suffocating, she told herself, beginning the familiar litany. It was just that her chest muscles were getting weaker, resulting in breathing that was shallower, which just made it feel as if she couldn't breathe, but she was breathing fine. Stay calm. Stay calm.

How could she stay calm when she was choking on what little air she could force into her lungs? She was going to die right here and now unless she got out of this room immediately. She had to get outside, get outside where there was fresh air. And raindrops the size of grapefruits to drown her fears. Better to drown than to suffocate, Mattie decided, propelling herself toward the door, tripping over her feet, losing her balance, tumbling toward the floor, her hands unable to break her fall, her cheek hitting the dark wood floor, her lip splitting open, blood sneaking into her open mouth as she lay there, staring at the wisps of dust beneath her bed and gasping for air. Like a fish flopping helplessly at the bottom of a fisherman's boat, Mattie thought, feeling Cynthia Broome's hands on her shoulders as the other woman gathered her into her arms and pressed her against the white silk of her blouse, rocking her gently, like a baby, until Mattie's breathing returned to normal.

"It's okay," Cynthia kept repeating. "It's okay. You're okay."

"Don't get blood on your nice blouse," Mattie warned the other woman a few minutes later, wiping the tears from her eyes, the blood from her lip.

"No big deal."

"You're very kind."

"Not really," Cynthia replied cryptically. "Are you all right?"

"No," Mattie said. Then, softly, "I'm dying."

Cynthia Broome said nothing, although Mattie felt her body stiffen, her breathing grow still beneath her large breasts.

"Something called amyotrophic lateral sclerosis. Lou Gehrig's disease," Mattie added, almost by rote.

"I'm so sorry," Cynthia said.

"There's some morphine in my purse." Mattie indicated the brown canvas bag on the floor beside the armoire. "If you wouldn't mind getting me one pill and a glass of Evian."

Cynthia was instantly on her feet, stepping gingerly around the scattered chocolates on the floor, rifling through Mattie's purse, locating the small bottle of pills. "Just one?"

Mattie smiled sadly. "For now," she said. In the next second, Mattie felt the pill on the tip of her tongue and the glass of water at her lips, the Evian transporting the pill smoothly down her throat. "Thank you." Cynthia resumed her seat beside Mattie on the floor, the two women leaning against the foot of the bed. "You don't have to stay," Mattie told her. "I'm okay now. My husband shouldn't be too much longer."

"Tell me about him." The other woman settled in, clearly not going anywhere.

Mattie pictured Jake's dark blue eyes and handsome face, his strong hands and gentle mouth. "He's a wonderful man," Mattie said. "Kind. Good. Loving."

"Good-looking too, I'll bet."

"Great-looking."

The two women laughed softly. "So, you got a good one," Cynthia said.

"Yes, I did," Mattie agreed.

"I had a good one once."

"What happened to him?"

"Circumstances," Cynthia said vaguely.

"Circumstances change."

Cynthia nodded, looked toward the floor. "Yes, they do."

"Are we talking about your ex-husband?" Mattie asked.

"God, no." Cynthia laughed. "Although, who knows? He didn't stick around long enough for me to find out."

"Doesn't sound like you missed anything."

"I don't know. I always felt maybe I could have tried harder, you know." Cynthia tapped the side of her head. "Never been too bright where men are concerned." She glanced at Mattie. "Is there some reason we're sitting on the floor?"

"It's not as far to fall," Mattie said simply, as Cynthia helped her back onto the bed, propping some pillows behind Mattie's head and stretching her legs across the top of the white comforter.

"We're not going to let you fall," Cynthia said, examining Mattie's face with a careful eye. "You know, I think maybe we should put some cold water on that cheek. It's starting to swell up a bit." She walked into the bathroom. "Oh, look," she called out over the sound of running water. "You've got Renoir on your floor. I got Toulouse-Lautrec on mine. Jane Avril doing the can-can at the Moulin Rouge. Pretty neat, huh?"

Between the rain hitting the window, the water running in the bathroom, and the sound of Cynthia's voice, Mattie didn't hear the key turning in the lock. She didn't see the doorknob twist, didn't realize Jake was back until he was closing the door behind him. "The damn gallery was closed for renovations," he was saying, almost in slow motion, as he shucked off his jacket and smiled toward the bed, the smile immediately disappearing. And then suddenly, everything was happening very quickly, as if the whole scene had been prerecorded and the action was being fast-forwarded. Even later, when Mattie tried to recall the precise order of events, she found it difficult to pin them down, to separate one development from the next, one sentence from another. "My God, what happened to you?"

"I'm fine, Jake," Mattie assured him. "I just had a little fall."

He was instantly on his knees beside her. "Damn it, I knew I shouldn't have left you alone."

"It's okay, Jake. I wasn't alone."

"What do you mean?" He looked toward the bathroom. "Is the water running?"

"Cynthia's here," Mattie said. "She's making me a cold compress."

"Cynthia?"

"The woman from Chicago that I met in the courtyard when we first got here. You remember. I told you about her. Cynthia Broome."

The color drained from Jake's face, like water rushing from a tap. First, his cheeks, then even his eyes, seemed to pale. "Cynthia Broome?"

"Did I hear my name?" Cynthia stepped out of the bathroom and approached the bed as Jake rose clumsily to his feet. "You must be Jake," she said, transferring the wet towel to her left hand and extending her right toward him.

"I don't understand," he said, his hands stiffly at his sides. "What are you doing here?"

"Jake!" Mattie said. "Isn't that a little rude?"

"I'm sorry," he stammered, trying to laugh. "You just caught me off guard, I guess." He cleared his throat, lifted his hands into the air. "I go away for an hour, and I come back to find my wife covered in bruises and a stranger in my bathroom."

Was it her imagination, Mattie wondered, or did Cynthia wince at the word *stranger*, almost as if she'd been struck? And what was the matter with Jake? It wasn't like him to be so nonplussed, regardless of the situation.

"It's been a frustrating morning for you," Mattie said, as Cynthia walked around the bed and sat down beside her, gently applying the compress to Mattie's cheek.

Jake stood frozen to the spot. "Is somebody going to tell me what's going on?"

"I had an attack," Mattie explained. "I couldn't breathe. I fell. Luckily, Cynthia was here. She helped me."

"What was she doing here in the first place?" Jake asked, speaking about Cynthia as if she weren't in the room.

"I was told your wife was looking for me." Cynthia's voice was suddenly as cool as the compress. "I dropped by as a courtesy."

"A courtesy?"

There was no mistaking the anger in Jake's voice. What was the matter with him? Mattie wondered. It wasn't like him to be so reactive. Although he'd always been impatient with people he didn't like. She thought of the incident in the Great Impasta, his outrage when his partners jumped to the wrong conclusions about her behavior. But what did he have against Cynthia Broome? Why would he be angry at her? Surely he didn't hold her responsible for Mattie's attack. "Jake, what's going on? Are you all right?" Mattie asked.

Jake ran a shaking hand through his dark hair, took a long deep breath. "I'm sorry," he said again. "I guess the morning kind of got to me. I trudge all the way over to the damn gallery in this goddamn rain, and then it's closed, and I can't get a cab for over half an hour, and I finally get back, and I find—"

"Your wife covered with bruises and a stranger in your bathroom," Cynthia said, completing the sentence for him.

"Thank you for helping my wife," Jake said.

Cynthia nodded. "It was my pleasure. I'm glad I could be of help. Anyway," she continued in almost the same breath, holding the compress out toward Jake, "time for you to take over. This room really isn't big enough for three people." She pushed herself off the bed, retrieving her jacket and dropping the compress into Jake's hand as she walked past him. "Watch out for the chocolates," she advised.

"Maybe we could all have lunch together later," Mattie said as Cynthia opened the door.

Cynthia checked her watch. "Actually, I'm booked on some mystery tour of the city this afternoon. The mystery is whether we'll be able to see anything in all this rain."

"How about tomorrow?" Mattie pressed, although she wasn't sure why. Clearly the woman was as eager to leave as Jake was eager to see her go. Sometimes there was just a natural negative chemistry between two people, Mattie was forced to admit. Her mother claimed that was true of dogs. There was no reason why it couldn't apply to human beings as well. Why was she pushing for something that nobody really wanted?

"I'm kind of booked up for the rest of my stay." Cynthia swayed from one foot to the other.

"I understand," Mattie said, though she didn't really. "Maybe back in Chicago. You'll have to give me your address and phone number."

"I'll leave it with the dragon lady." Cynthia checked

her watch a second time, although the glance was so brief, Mattie doubted the hour had time to register. "Take care," she said. "Nice meeting you, Jason."

"I'll walk you downstairs," Jake volunteered suddenly. "I'll be back in a minute," he told Mattie, who said nothing as he followed Cynthia into the hall and closed the door behind him.

"Oh, my God," Mattie whispered as soon as they were gone, the words falling from her lips as she pushed herself off the bed and began pacing back and forth, dragging her legs across the narrow space between the bed and the wall. "Oh, my God. Oh, my God."

It couldn't be true. It couldn't.

"Oh, my God. Oh, my God."

Nice meeting you, Jason.

Jason. Jason. Jason. Jason.

What did it mean? What *could* it mean?

No wonder Chloe Dorleac had never heard of Cynthia Broome. There *was* no Cynthia Broome.

"Oh God, oh God, oh God."

No wonder her voice had always felt so familiar. Mattie had heard that same voice on the telephone more than once. *I love you, Jason.*

Jason. Jason. Jason. Jason.

She'd been here all along, probably trysting with Jake whenever they could find the time. How French, Mattie thought. To go to Paris with both your wife *and* your mistress. "Oh God, oh God, oh God."

I had a good man once.

What happened to him?

Circumstances.

"I have to get out of here," Mattie muttered, rifling

through the drawer of the small table beside her bed, quickly locating her passport beside her return ticket to Chicago. She stumbled around the bed, squishing several chocolates beneath her feet as she grabbed her purse from the floor and stuffed her passport and airline ticket inside. "I have to get out of here."

She opened the door, peeked into the hall. No one was there, although voices wafted up the elevator shaft from the lobby. She wondered where Jake had gone with Cynthia.

No, not Cynthia.

Honey. Honey Novak.

Honey with an *e-y*, she thought bitterly, dragging herself toward the elevator, realizing she'd forgotten her cane, and pushing the button repeatedly with the back of her right hand. She didn't have time to go back. She had to get out of this damn hotel right now. Before Jake returned. She had to get to the airport. Get on an earlier flight. Hopefully, by the time Jake figured out where she'd gone, she'd be on a plane back to Chicago.

She could manage by herself, even without her cane. She didn't have any luggage. It shouldn't be too difficult to change her ticket. She'd take an extra morphine tablet, sleep all the way back home. First thing she'd do when she got to her house was change all the locks.

"Where's the damn elevator?" Mattie slammed her open palm against the button, sighed with relief when she heard the elevator begin its ascent. What if Jake were on it? she wondered, stepping back, flattening herself against the velvet-flocked blue wallpaper, holding her breath.

Seconds later the elevator bounced to a halt, empty

and anticipatory. Slowly, Mattie pushed open the wrought-iron gate and stepped inside. Her fingers fumbled with the buttons, and she accidentally pressed two at once, so that the elevator made an extra, unwanted stop before finally arriving at the lobby. When it got there, Mattie remained motionless, peering through the wrought-iron bars, as if imprisoned, not sure if she had the strength to proceed.

"Aren't you getting out?" a little voice asked.

Mattie nodded at the towheaded youngster standing beyond the bars, the same rambunctious child she'd seen in the breakfast room earlier in the day. Had it really been only a few hours ago? she wondered, stepping out of the elevator. It seemed so much longer ago than that. A lifetime ago, she thought.

"Stand back and give the lady some room," the boy's mother instructed.

"She walks funny," Mattie heard the boy squeal as she limped toward the hotel's double front door with as much speed as she could muster.

"Ssh!" his mother said.

"Why was she crying?" the boy asked as the hotel door shut behind her.

Mattie stepped outside, the rain immediately soaking through her clothes, plastering her hair against the sides of her face. Seconds later, a taxi pulled up and she crawled inside. "Charles de Gaulle Airport," she said, grinding the mixture of rain and tears into the bruise on her cheek. "Vite." And then again, remembering her dream, "Vite."

THIRTY-ONE

Y ou want to tell me what the hell is going on?" Jake
demanded angrily, his hand on Honey's elbow as he
pushed her toward the stairs. Although he was whispering, there was no mistaking the fury in his voice.

"Jason, calm down. It's not what you think."

"Really? And what am I thinking, exactly?"

"I never meant for this to happen."

They reached the top of the narrow spiral staircase.
Jason hesitated, not sure in which direction to proceed,
his fingers digging into the crook of Honey's arm. He
knew he was hurting her, but he didn't care. In truth,
he wanted to kill her. It was taking all his strength to
keep from hurling her down the three winding flights
of stairs to the lobby below. What the hell was she
doing in Paris? In this hotel? What had she been doing
with Mattie? What had she said to her?

As if reading his thoughts, Honey said, "My room's on the fifth floor. Come upstairs, Jason. We can talk. I'll explain everything."

Without allowing himself time to think, Jake pushed Honey up the two flights of stairs to the fifth floor. What had she been doing in his hotel room? What had she said to Mattie to precipitate her attack? If Honey had said anything at all to upset Mattie, he'd throttle her on the spot.

Except that Mattie hadn't seemed upset, he reminded himself. If anything, she'd seemed grateful for Honey's presence, disappointed she was leaving, astounded at Jake's rudeness. How was he going to explain his strange behavior to Mattie?

"My key's in my jacket pocket," Honey was saying. "I can't get at it if you don't let go of my arm."

Jake released his grip, watched while Honey unlocked the door, then, after taking a furtive glance around, pushed her inside a room that was virtually identical to his own. "What the hell is going on?" he demanded, slamming the door behind them.

Honey threw her jacket across the unmade bed, disturbing the tousled sheets, dislodging her lingering smell. It wafted toward Jake's nostrils, reminding him of their months together, of the days and nights he'd spent in the whimsical clutter of her bedroom back home. For an instant he felt his outrage abate, his body start to uncoil, and then he pictured Mattie, sitting bruised and vulnerable on that same bed two floors below, and he felt his anger return, his fist clench at his side. He forced his eyes away from the bed, noting parcels covering every available surface—the chair, the night tables, even the top of the suitcase that lay on the floor by the window.

"I've started collecting French dolls," Honey told him, following the path of Jake's eyes. "I'm not sure how I'll get them all on the plane—"

"I'm not interested in any goddamn dolls," Jake snapped. "I want to know what you're doing here."

"I've always wanted to see Paris," Honey answered, her shoulders stiffening in quiet, if unmistakable, defiance.

"Cut the crap, Honey. Why are you here?"

The sharpness of his rebuke hit her with almost visible force. Her shoulders collapsed instantly, as if she'd been stabbed. Her body caved forward. Tears welled in her eyes. "I would think that's pretty obvious," she said after a brief pause, turning away.

"Enlighten me."

Honey walked to the window, stared out at the rain-soaked street. "I was very confused after what happened in your office," she began, swallowing her tears, refusing to look at him. "Confused and angry. And scared."

"Scared?" What was she talking about?

"I knew I was losing you. That I'd lost you," she corrected immediately. "You denied it, and I tried to deny it, even when you didn't call for weeks. That afternoon in your office, the way we left things, the way I just walked out, I couldn't leave it like that. I couldn't let it end without one more try. So I called your office, found out when you'd be away, booked a nonrefundable ticket so I couldn't back down, paid for the hotel room in advance, got here a few days before you did. I didn't really have a plan. I certainly wasn't going to reveal myself to Mattie. I just wanted to be here for you, just in case."

"In case of what?"

"In case you needed me. In case you wanted me," she added with a whisper.

"It's not about what *I* want," Jake said. "I thought you understood that."

"I understand a great deal, Jason. More than you think I do. More than I think *you* do."

"What are you talking about?"

"I understand that the man I love is in love with someone else."

"This isn't about love," Jake protested. "It's about need."

"It's about love," Honey said firmly. "Why is that so difficult a concept for you to grasp? You love your wife, Jason. It's as simple as that."

Jake shook his head, as if trying to keep Honey's words from penetrating his brain.

You love your wife, Jason. It's as simple as that.

You love your wife, Jason.

Jason. Jason. Jason. Jason.

"Oh, God," he moaned out loud.

"What's the matter?"

"She knows."

"What? What are you talking about?"

"Mattie knows."

"I don't understand. How could she—?"

"You called me Jason."

"What?"

"Downstairs. When you were about to leave, you said, 'Goodbye, Jason.' "

"No, I . . . oh, God, yes I did. Do you think she realized—"

He didn't answer. In the next second, Jake was out the door and running down the two flights of stairs to the third floor, Honey fast on his heels. "Stay there," he ordered her as he reached the third-floor landing and began banging on the door to his room. "Mattie! Mattie, let me in. I left my key inside. Mattie," he called again, feeling her absence, knowing the room was empty, that she was already gone. "Mattie!" he shouted, as the door to the next room opened, and a large woman in a yellow chenille bathrobe stuck her head out the door.

"Americans," she muttered under her breath before retreating back inside her room and closing the door.

"Excuse me," Jake heard Honey call to someone above her head. "Can you open a door for us?"

Who was she talking to? Jake wondered, turning to see a cleaning lady following Honey down the remaining stairs. "I forgot my key," he said, although the cleaning lady was obviously uninterested in his explanations. She opened the door with one of the keys on her large key ring, then retreated back up the stairs without a word. "Mattie!" Jake called, stepping into the empty room, checking the bathroom before opening the armoire, ascertaining her clothes were still there. As was her suitcase, he thought with relief, even as he understood she'd have neither the time, the strength, nor the inclination to pack. "Where the hell is she? Where could she have gone?"

"Her cane is still here," Honey said hopefully. "She can't have gone very far."

But Jake was already out the door and leaping down the stairs two at a time, jumping down the last three, hurling himself toward the front desk, where Chloe Dorleac was going over a map of the city with two German tourists. "Have you seen my wife?" Jake demanded. "Ma femme?" he said when Chloe Dorleac refused to acknowledge his presence. "Goddamn it," he shouted, banging on the desk. "This is an emergency."

"I don't know where your wife is," the dragon lady said coolly, her eyes never leaving her map.

"Did you see her go out? It can't be more than ten minutes ago."

"I cannot help you, monsieur," came the reply.

"She's not in the breakfast room," Honey said, appearing at his side.

Jake frantically scanned the lobby. His behavior had attracted the attention of the handful of tourists standing around, waiting for the rain to let up. "Has anybody seen my wife?" he pleaded to several blank pairs of eyes. "Does anybody speak English?" He paused, looked toward the street. "Did anybody see her? Tall, thin, blond hair around her shoulders. She has trouble walking—"

"I saw her," came a little voice from behind a large potted plant in the far corner of the lobby.

Jake was instantly on his knees, coaxing a reluctant towheaded youngster out from behind the tall plant. "You saw her?"

"I'm playing hide-and-seek with my brother," the boy said.

"You saw my wife—"

"She walks funny," the boy said, and giggled.

"Where did she go?"

The boy shrugged. "I have to hide before my brother finds me."

"You didn't see where she went?"

"She got into a taxi," the boy explained. "I don't know where it went."

"A taxi?" Jake repeated. Where the hell would she go? Especially in this downpour. The little boy ran from his side, disappeared around the corner just as his mother appeared.

"Lance, where are you?" the concerned woman called out. "Damn it. I've had enough of this nonsense. The game is over."

"Should we call the police?" Jake heard Honey ask as he pushed by her, racing back up the stairs to the third floor, relieved to find the door to his room still open. He ran to the night table on Mattie's side of the bed, pulled open the drawer, quickly locating his passport and his airplane ticket, knowing Mattie's were missing even before he checked.

"Oh, God," he said, collapsing with fatigue, his breath coming in short ragged bursts, his whole body shaking. He sank onto the side of the bed, his head in his hands. "She's gone," he said as Honey stepped into the room. "She's taken her passport and her ticket, and she's probably halfway to the airport by now."

Honey's voice was soft and direct. "Then I suggest you get up off your ass and get moving," she said.

• • •

The Roissy–Charles de Gaulle Airport is an enormous complex located nineteen miles north of Paris. It has two main terminals, the second of which is located several miles away from the first, and is comprised of two linked buildings in four sections. There is also a separate terminal catering to charter flights. In all, the airport is served by at least forty scheduled airlines and sixteen charter companies. Jake had had enough difficulty trying to figure it all out when he and Mattie first arrived. How would Mattie manage on her own? he wondered now, urging the cab driver to hurry through the congested Parisian streets. Despite the airport's proximity to the city, travelers were advised to allow a full hour to get there, and Jake well understood why, especially in difficult driving conditions such as these. "Do you think you could go a little faster?" Jake urged. "Plus vite," he said, as the cab-driver shook his head in time to the overworked windshield wipers. "It's very important I get to the airport as fast as possible."

"More important to get there alive," the driver told him in heavily accented English.

Jake leaned back against the cracked green vinyl seat of the ancient taxi. At least the Charles de Gaulle Airport was well outfitted to deal with the handicapped. Special telephone facilities were available, as well as restrooms, elevators and air bridges, wheelchairs, and baggage assistance. Agents wearing specially designated uniforms were available for assistance. Would Mattie find them? Would she be able to make herself understood?

Jake almost smiled. No matter what her difficulty,

Mattie never had any trouble making herself understood.

Would he be able to find her? Would he get to her in time? It was entirely possible she wouldn't even bother trying to change her ticket. She might simply go to the first counter she saw and get on the first available flight. She had her credit cards. There was no law that said she had to fly directly to Chicago. She might choose New York or Los Angeles, worry about catching a connecting flight later. Jake sighed audibly, pressing down on the invisible gas pedal at his feet. Mattie was upset. She was angry. There was no telling what she might do. He had to find her.

The taxi pulled into the terminal, and Jake tossed several hundred francs into the front seat, not bothering to wait for change. He ran into the terminal, his eyes scanning the large monitors for departing flights. "Excuse me," he said to one of the agents. "Where are the flights to Chicago?" He was running even before the startled young woman completed her directions.

"Excuse me," he said to the elderly gentleman he bumped into. "Excusez-moi," he apologized to the young woman whose suitcase he sent flying halfway across the floor. "Excuse me. Excusez-moi. Excusez-moi," Jake kept repeating, when what he really wanted to say to everyone was, "Get the hell out of my way." He was running blind, not sure where he was going, not seeing anything but his final destination. "Excuse me. Excuse me. Excusez-moi."

And then he saw her. She was sitting in a wheelchair at the end of a row of attached orange plastic seats, staring into her lap. She'd done it. All by herself.

She'd commandeered a taxi in the pouring rain and navigated the twists and turns of this busy airport without any help from him. She'd found the correct counter, gotten herself a wheelchair, no doubt secured a seat for herself on an earlier flight. God, she was amazing, Jake thought, stopping to catch his breath.

She took his breath away.

Now what? he wondered, reviewing all the things he'd thought about saying to her on the seemingly endless drive from the city. He'd prepared a few carefully chosen words in his own defense, silently rehearsed a few key phrases. This was going to be the most important closing argument of his life, he realized, walking toward her. It was important he get it right.

Suddenly Jake felt his body being propelled violently forward. He fought to maintain his balance as a red-faced, middle-aged man hurtled by in the opposite direction. "Excusez-moi," the man muttered, not stopping, not even turning around to see if Jake was still standing.

"Tsk, tsk," Jake heard someone mutter.

"Ça va?" someone asked. Are you all right?

"Thank you, I'm fine," Jake said, straightening his shoulders, steadying his feet. "Merci. Merci." He looked toward Mattie.

She was staring right at him, and for an instant their eyes connected. And then, in the next instant, she was trying to get away, to maneuver the wheelchair out of the space in which she'd been confined, the wheels twisting this way and that, refusing to move, as Mattie's hands struggled to release the brake.

"Mattie! Mattie, please." Jake rushed toward her, his carefully rehearsed words disappearing with each step. Mattie's hands connected with the brake, releasing it, and the wheelchair shot forward, almost running over his toes.

"Get out of my way, Jake," Mattie cried.

"Please, Mattie. You have to listen to me."

"I don't want to listen to you."

"Is there a problem here?" someone asked.

Jake looked over to see a muscular young man with an American flag sewn across his backpack getting up from his chair.

"No problem," Jake said. "Mattie—"

"It looks like the lady doesn't want to talk to you," the young man said.

"Look, this isn't any of your business." Jake blocked Mattie's continuing efforts to get away.

"Isn't that Jake Hart, the lawyer?" someone asked. "I saw his picture on the cover of *Chicago* magazine a while back."

"Is it?" her companion asked.

"I'm sure it's him. That woman in the wheelchair called him Jake."

"That woman is my wife," Jake snapped, spinning around angrily, watching as the various travelers waiting for their flight to Chicago shrank back into their seats. "And it's very important I talk to her."

"Go back to the hotel, Jake," Mattie shouted. "Your girlfriend's waiting for you."

"Oh, my," someone said.

"Please, Mattie, it's not what you think."

"Don't try to tell me that wasn't Honey Novak,"

Mattie said. "Don't you dare try to insult my intelligence that way."

"I'm not going to deny it."

"Then what could you possibly have to say that would interest me?"

"I had no idea she was in Paris," Jake began, the truth sounding more lame than any excuse he might have dreamed up. Since when was the truth any defense? he recognized. Hadn't his years practicing law taught him anything at all? "Please believe me, Mattie. I'd broken it off with her. I hadn't seen her in months."

"Then how did she know about our trip? How did she know where we'd be staying?"

"She came by the office—"

"You just said you hadn't seen her in months."

Jake looked helplessly around the large waiting area, feeling like a reluctant witness on the stand. "It was just for a few minutes. She dropped by unannounced."

"She does that quite a lot."

"I had no idea she was in Paris until I saw her in our hotel room."

Mattie shook her head, dislodging bitter tears. "You couldn't wait, could you? You couldn't pass up a romantic trip to Paris. Couldn't let it go to waste on your sickly wife."

"That's not true, Mattie. You know it's not true."

"What's the matter, Jake?" Mattie cried out, her anguish palpable. "Am I taking too long to die?"

A gasp escaped the lips of several of the onlookers.

"Mattie—"

"You want to hear something funny?" Mattie continued. "I like her. I actually like her. Congratulations. Jake Hart has great taste in women."

"I told you it was him," someone whispered loudly.

"Go back to her, Jake," Mattie said, resignation replacing indignation. "She loves you."

"I don't love her," he said simply.

"Then you're a fool."

"God knows that's true," Jake agreed.

For an instant, it appeared as if Mattie might soften, as if she might choose to believe him after all. But then suddenly a curtain of fresh resolve fell across her eyes, and she was once again trying to back out of the small space, her hands sliding helplessly against the sides of the wheelchair. "Move, damn you." Instinctively, Jake's hands shot out to help her. "Go away, Jake," she shouted. "Go away. I don't need you."

"You may not need me, lady, but damn it, I need *you!*" Jake cried, surprising even himself. "I love you, Mattie," he heard himself say. "I love you."

"No," Mattie said. "Please don't say that."

"I love you," Jake said again, falling to his knees in front of her wheelchair.

"Get up, Jake. Please. You don't have to pretend anymore."

"I'm not pretending. Mattie, I love you. Please believe me. I love you. I love you."

There was a long silence. It seemed everyone around them was holding their breath. Jake felt his own breath still in his chest. He couldn't breathe without her, he realized. What would he do if she were to leave him now?

"I love you," he repeated, his eyes holding Mattie's

until tears blinded them. He made no move to wipe the tears away. "I love you," he said again. What else was there to say?

Another silence. Longer than the first. Interminable.

"I love *you*," Mattie whispered.

"Oh, God," Jake cried. "I love you so much."

"I love *you* so much," Mattie repeated, crying with him.

Love you, love you, love you, love you.

"We'll go back to the city, find another hotel," Jake began.

"No," Mattie interrupted, her hand brushing awkwardly against his cheek. He grabbed it, held it steady, kissed it. "It's time, Jake," Mattie said, as Jake nodded sadly, knowingly. "It's time to go home."

THIRTY-TWO

They arrived back in Chicago at four o'clock in the afternoon, two days ahead of schedule. "Something's wrong," Mattie said, as the limo pulled to a halt in front of their house. An unfamiliar white van sat in the driveway next to her mother's beat-up old green Plymouth. Why would her mother be here? Mattie wondered, reading the elaborate logo on the side of the van. "Capiletti's Housecleaning Service," it announced in swirling red letters.

"Don't jump to any conclusions," Jake cautioned, paying the driver and helping Mattie from the backseat of the limousine.

"Do you think there was a break-in? Or a fire?" Mattie scanned the front of the house for signs of smoke damage.

"Everything looks okay."

"Hello?" Mattie called as Jake pushed open the front door. "Hello? Mother?" Mattie stepped nervously into the foyer. A woman wearing jeans, a sloppy shirt, and a bandanna over her brown hair suddenly marched across the front hall toward the kitchen, carrying a large green garbage bag. She smiled. "Who are you?" Mattie asked. "What's going on?"

"Martha?" her mother called from upstairs as the strange woman disappeared into the kitchen. "Is that you?"

"Mother? What's going on here?"

"Try not to get upset," Jake urged.

"You're early," her mother said instead of hello, as she hurried down the stairs, stopping abruptly at the bottom. Like the woman in her kitchen, Mattie's mother was dressed in jeans and a sloppy sweatshirt. Her gray hair was pulled into an awkward bun at the back of her head, more hairs on the outside of the purple scrunchie than inside it. "We weren't expecting you home for another couple of days."

"What's all this about?" Mattie asked again, not bothering to explain.

"It's not as bad as it looks," her mother began. "Maybe we should sit down."

"What's going on?" Mattie repeated.

"There was a party. I'm afraid things got a little out of hand. I'd hoped to have everything cleaned up by the time you got back."

"You had a party?" Mattie asked in disbelief. When had her mother ever entertained anyone but her dogs?

"Let's sit down," her mother urged, as a burly young man in a white T-shirt and black jeans stepped out of Jake's office, carrying the Raphael Goldchain photograph Jake had recently purchased, its frame cracked, its glass shattered, the picture of the scantily clad pinup sliced into two neat halves above her buttocks.

"What do you want me to do with this?" the young man asked, waving the bottom half of the photograph, the pinup's half-naked backside rippling provocatively.

Jake was immediately at the young man's side, lifting the picture from his callused hands. "My God, what happened? Who did this?"

"The police are trying to find that out," Mattie's mother explained. "Please, let's go into the living room and sit down. You must be exhausted from your trip."

Mattie watched Jake drop the torn photograph to the floor, his face a mirror of her own disbelief. What was going on? What had happened here? Suddenly she felt dizzy and faint, collapsing into Jake's arms as he led her into the living room and sat her down on the edge of the Ultrasuede sofa whose once-smooth surface was stained with beer and ashes.

"Apparently, Ultrasuede is something of a miracle fabric," her mother was saying. "Mr. Capiletti says he's sure he can clean the sofa up as good as new."

"That was Mr. Capiletti?" Jake asked, nodding toward the hall.

"His son. It's a family business. You might have seen Mrs. Capiletti when you walked in."

"What are all these Capilettis doing in my house?" Mattie asked, wondering if she were in the middle of one of her more ridiculous dreams. That's it, she decided, her body relaxing with the thought. She was still somewhere over the Atlantic, her head nestled against Jake's chest, the sound of his *I love yous* echoing in her ear. She'd wake up any minute, she told herself, and he'd still be beside her, still whispering the words she'd waited all her life to hear.

Except even as Mattie was trying to convince herself this was just another silly, nonsensical product of her overactive imagination, she knew she was wide awake, that she was actually sitting in the middle of her ash-covered, beer-stained sofa in the middle of what looked like a war zone, but was in fact her living room. "There was a party?" she asked again, her eyes absorbing the two rose-and-gold chairs whose fabric had been slashed along its vertical stripes, the baby grand piano whose shapely black legs had been gouged and mutilated, the needlepoint rug whose surface was littered with crumbs and other less identifiable debris, the Ken Davis painting that was splattered with what looked to be raw eggs.

"I was afraid to touch that," her mother was saying, following the direction of Mattie's eyes. "I was afraid if I tried cleaning it, the paint might come off."

"When did this happen?"

"Saturday night."

And suddenly, what had happened was very clear. Mattie sighed, closed her eyes, leaned back against the sofa, the smell of stale cigarettes reaching inside her nostrils, the bitter taste of spilled beer settling on her tongue. "Kim," Mattie said, her voice void of expression.

"It wasn't her fault," Mattie's mother was quick to explain. "She tried to stop it. It was Kim who called the police."

"You gave Kim permission to have a party?" Jake held tightly onto Mattie's hand.

"No," Viv admitted after a pause. "She told me she was *going* to a party. She didn't say where."

"She neglected to mention she was the hostess of this little shindig," Jake said.

"It was just supposed to be a few kids from school, but apparently some people showed up who hadn't been invited. Kim asked them to leave, but they refused, and things very quickly went from bad to worse. Kim called the police, but whoever the trouble-makers were, they got away before the police arrived. Unfortunately, not before they made quite a mess. The Capilettis have been here since first thing this morning. Most of the damage was to the main floor. You'll have to check and see if anything is missing."

"The Falling Man," Mattie said, referring to the small bronze sculpture by Ernest Trova that used to sit by the piano. "It's gone."

"That funny-looking bald guy, looks sort of like an Oscar?" her mother asked, and Mattie nodded. "The police found it outside on the front lawn. I thought it was some kind of elaborate pepper mill, so I put it in the kitchen."

"You thought it was a pepper mill?" Mattie asked incredulously.

"I never claimed to be an authority on art," her mother said defensively.

"Where is Kim now?" Jake asked.

"She was going to see Rosemary Colicos after school," Viv said. "Please don't be too hard on her, Jake. I know what she did was very wrong, but she's a good girl. She really is. She was terribly upset about what happened, and I know she plans to make it up to you. She's going to get a summer job, pay for everything that isn't covered by insurance."

"It's not a question of money."

"I know that." Viv lowered herself carefully into one of the gold-and-rose-striped chairs. "*She* knows that."

Mattie watched a strip of fabric float across her mother's lap. She'd been meaning to get those chairs re-covered for some time now, Mattie thought absently.

"So, how was your trip?" her mother asked, as if this were a perfectly normal thing to be asking under the circumstances, as if there were nothing odd or unusual about the situation, as if everyone returned home prematurely from a trip abroad to find their house in ruins.

"The trip?" Mattie repeated numbly. "The trip was wonderful."

"How was the weather?"

"The weather was great."

"Except for yesterday," Mattie heard Jake say. "It rained pretty hard yesterday."

"Yes, it did," Mattie agreed.

"And you saw everything you wanted to see?"

"We didn't miss much," Jake answered.

"You had no trouble getting around?"

"No trouble at all," Jake said, staring at Mattie, who was staring straight ahead, at the empty space where the Trova used to sit. "Mattie, are you all right?"

"She thought it was a pepper mill," Mattie said, the

absurdity of her homecoming hitting her with such force she could barely breathe.

And suddenly Mattie was laughing, laughing with such abandon, she felt her sides would split wide open. And Jake was laughing with her. And even her mother, who seemed incomplete somehow without at least one of her beloved dogs at her feet, was laughing, although the guarded look on her face told Mattie she wasn't quite sure what was so damn funny.

"Maybe you should go upstairs and lie down," her mother was saying. "It wasn't too much of a mess up there, but I changed the sheets on your bed, just in case. Really, I think you need to rest," she continued over Mattie's and Jake's raucous laughter. "The Capilettis and I will take care of things down here. You can call your insurance guy in the morning. I'll keep Kim with me tonight."

"Thank you," Mattie managed to squeak out between hoots.

"Tell Kim I'll be picking her up after school tomorrow," Jake said, as their laughter faded away. "And tell her we love her," he added softly, helping Mattie to her feet.

Viv nodded, pushing herself off the chair.

"Mom?" Mattie's voice stopped her mother before she reached the hall.

"Yes, Martha?"

"Thank you," Mattie told her. "It means a great deal to me, knowing I can count on you."

Mattie watched her mother's shoulders stiffen. Viv nodded without speaking, and left the room.

Mattie was upstairs resting, stretched out on top of her bed, when she heard the front door open and close, heard footsteps on the stairs, saw Kim in the doorway. Kim was wearing a zippered yellow sweatshirt over faded blue jeans, and as usual, the mere sight of her unspoiled beauty made Mattie's heart sing. Sweet little Miss Grundy, Mattie thought. Does she have even the slightest idea how beautiful she is? "Hi," Mattie said simply.

She'd been rehearsing this moment ever since Jake left her side to pick Kim up at school, adjusting, then readjusting her position on the bed, trying to find a suitable compromise between stiff-backed and casual, her voice seeking a balance between stern and loving, as she tried out numerous approaches for confronting her daughter, hearing all her efforts evaporate with the single word, "Hi."

"How are you?" Kim's voice trembled into the space between them. She tucked some imaginary stray hairs behind her ears, looked toward the floor.

"I'm okay. Lisa's coming by tonight to check me over. What about you?"

Kim shrugged as Jake walked into the room. "I'm okay."

Mattie patted the space beside her on the bed. "Why don't you sit down?"

Kim looked from Mattie to her father, as if she weren't sure for whom the invitation was intended, then looked back at Mattie, shook her head, her bottom lip quivering dangerously.

"Tell me what's going on," Mattie said softly.

"I screwed up," Kim said defensively. "I invited a

bunch of kids over. I thought I could control them, but—"

"I know what happened at the party," Mattie interrupted. "I want to know what's going on with you."

"I don't understand." Kim looked imploringly toward her father.

"What are you feeling, Kimmy?" Jake asked.

Kim shrugged, laughed, a short brittle sound that threatened to break upon contact with the air. "You sound like my therapist."

"Talk to us, sweetheart."

"There's nothing to talk about. You went away. I threw a party. It was a mistake, and I'm sorry."

"Were you angry because we went away?" Mattie asked.

"Angry? Of course not. Why would I be angry?"

"Because we didn't take you with us."

"That's just silly. I'm not a baby." Kim shifted her weight restlessly from one foot to the other. "Besides, how could I go with you? I have school, and anyway, this was your holiday. I understand that."

"Understanding something doesn't always make it easier to deal with," Jake said.

"What are you saying? That you think I did this on purpose?"

"Nobody said you did anything on purpose," Mattie said.

"Because I was angry at you for going away? Is that what you're saying?"

"Were you?" Jake asked.

Kim's eyes shot frantically around the room, as if she were looking for a way out. "No. Of course not."

"You weren't the least little bit angry at me for taking your mother away from you?"

"You're her husband, aren't you?"

"Not a very good one, as you've pointed out on more than one occasion." Jake's voice was steady, even gentle. "If there was any kind of a marriage here," he conceded, "it was between you and your mother. God knows I was never around." He paused, his eyes appealing to both mother and daughter for forgiveness. "For almost sixteen years, you had your mother all to yourself, Kimmy. And then suddenly, everything changed. Your mother got sick. I came back home. You felt increasingly left out. And then I whisk your mother off to Paris, leaving you at home."

"So . . . what? I'm like the spurned wife? Is that what you're saying?"

"I guess that's exactly what I'm saying," Jake agreed. "And you felt abandoned and betrayed and scared because you thought you were losing your mother. I'm the other woman, Kimmy," he acknowledged with a sad smile. "And I don't blame you one bit for being angry."

Kim looked helplessly toward the window, her lips twisting frantically, as if she were literally trying to digest the things Jake was saying. "So, bottom line, what you're saying is, I was angry at you for leaving me, for taking my mother away, and I invited a bunch of kids over, knowing they'd trash the house? Is that it?"

"Is it?"

"No! Yes! Maybe!" Kim shouted in almost the same breath. "I don't know. I don't know." She started pacing, increasingly small circles between the bed and the window. "Maybe I *was* angry at you for going away and leaving me here alone. Maybe I *did* invite those kids over knowing something like this would probably happen. Maybe I really *wanted* it to happen. I don't know. I don't know anything anymore. I just know I'm so sorry," she cried. "I'm so sorry. I'm so sorry."

"It's okay, baby," Mattie said, aching to surround her daughter with comforting arms.

"I'll get a job. I'll pay for everything."

"We'll work something out later," Jake said.

Kim's shoulders began to shake, her face dissolving, like heated wax, around her open mouth. "I'll go live with Grandma Viv. I know she'd let me stay with her."

"Is that what you want?"

"Isn't it what *you* want?"

"We want you to stay here." Tears fell the length of Mattie's cheeks.

"But why? I'm a horrible person. Why would you want anything to do with me?"

"You're not a horrible person."

"Look what I did!" Kim cried. "I let them wreck the house. I let them destroy all the things you love."

"I love *you*," Mattie said, once again patting the empty space beside her on the bed. "Please sit down, Kim. Please let me hold you."

Slowly, Kim lowered herself to the bed, collapsed against her mother's chest.

"You're just a little girl who made a big mistake," Mattie said, kissing Kim's forehead, weak fingers pulling at the bobby pins in Kim's hair, until it fell free and loose around her shoulders. "You're my sweet baby. I love you so much."

"I love you too. I'm sorry, Mommy. I'm so sorry."

"I know, baby."

"All your things—"

"That's all they are. Things," Mattie told her, as an unexpected smile reached her lips. "Elaborate pepper mills."

"What?"

"Things can be replaced, Kimmy," Jake said, joining them on the bed.

"What if they can't?"

"They're still just things," he said.

"You don't hate me?"

"How could we hate you?" Mattie asked.

"We love you," Jake said, making a spot for himself on the bed. "Just because we're not happy with what you did, that doesn't mean we don't love you, that we'd ever stop loving you." Mattie watched him reach out, remove the several bobby pins still dangling from his daughter's head, then smooth back her silky hair with his gentle hand.

In the next instant, Kim was crying in his arms. Jake held her for several minutes, then wordlessly, without disturbing his daughter, he reached out and touched Mattie's fingers. The three of them sat this way, in their tight little circle, until it grew dark.

THIRTY-THREE

Mattie sat in her wheelchair on the balcony off the kitchen, watching her daughter swim. It was cool, cooler than normal for late September, and gusts of steam wafted up from the overheated pool. Mattie's eyes followed the graceful arc of her daughter's arms as they sliced through the water, her long, lithe body propelled by the steady kick of her feet, her dark blond hair streaming freely behind her head. Like a beautiful young mermaid, Mattie thought, imagining herself swimming by her daughter's side. She shivered.

"Are you cold, Mrs. Hart?" a voice asked from somewhere behind her.

"A little," Mattie managed to spit out with great effort. Immediately, Mattie felt a cashmere shawl wrap around her shoulders. "Thank you, Aurora," she whispered, not sure whether the petite Mexican housekeeper Jake had hired at the beginning of the summer had heard. Her voice was so low these days, so quiet. Every word was a struggle. On everyone's part. She struggled to speak, to keep from choking on her thoughts; those around her struggled to hear, to understand what she was trying to say.

"Come on in, George," Kim called toward the frisky puppy who was running back and forth along the side of the pool as she swam. "The water's really warm."

George barked his refusal and bounded up the balcony steps, jumping into Mattie's lap and licking her face. No trouble understanding what he had to say, Mattie thought, savoring the feel of his wet tongue on her lips, as Kim waved happily from the pool and returned to her swimming.

"No, no," Aurora said, lifting the puppy from Mattie's lap and depositing him on the cedar planks. "Mustn't lick Mrs. Hart on the lips."

"It's okay, Aurora," Mattie tried to say, but she coughed instead, the cough becoming a desperate gasp for air. In months gone by, Mattie's hands would have shot from her side as she fought to get oxygen into her lungs, but now her skinny arms hung lifeless at her sides, gnarled fingers folded neatly in the middle of her lap. Only her head moved, bouncing violently on top of her shoulders with each strangled breath.

"It's okay. You okay," Aurora told her steadily, no longer panicking at such episodes, eyes locking on Mattie's until the spasm was complete. "You okay," she repeated, wiping the tears from Mattie's eyes with a tissue, smoothing back Mattie's hair, patting Mattie's useless hands, hands that rested across equally useless legs. "You want something to drink? Some water or juice?"

"Water," Mattie said, hearing only the first syllable clearly, the second syllable disappearing, like steam from the pool, into the cool air.

As soon as Aurora retreated to the kitchen, George jumped back into Mattie's lap, licking her twice across the lips before his tongue disappeared eagerly inside her left nostril. Mattie laughed, and the puppy settled comfortably into her lap, warming her cold hands with his furry little body, so that she felt as if she were wearing fleece-lined mittens. What was the old saying? Happiness is a warm puppy? They certainly got that one right, Mattie marveled, watching the puppy as he closed his eyes in instant sleep. All she had to do was provide a comfortable spot for him to curl up in, and he loved her. Unconditionally.

And she loved him, she realized with no small degree of amazement. After all these years of refusing even to consider allowing a dog into the house, she was totally smitten, completely head-over-heels in love. Sweet baby, she thought, aching to pet him.

"Oh no, off you go," Aurora said, shooing George from Mattie's lap before Mattie could protest. Aurora lifted the glass of water to Mattie's lips. Mattie took a slight sip, felt it trickle uneasily down her throat. "Have some more," Aurora instructed.

Mattie shook her head, although she was still thirsty. But the more she drank, the more she peed, and Mattie had learned to dread the prospect of nature's call. Of the many things she hated about this disease, the thing Mattie hated most was the way it gradually robbed you of everything you once took for granted—your mobility, your freedom, your privacy, and ultimately, most cruelly, your dignity. She could no longer even go to the bathroom by herself. She needed someone to take her there, to lift her out of her wheelchair and adjust her clothing, to sit her down on the toilet, to wipe her when she was through. Aurora was a godsend. She did all these things without complaint. As did Kim, and Jake, after Aurora left for the day. But Mattie didn't want her daughter playing nurse or her husband wiping her backside. "You have to eat and drink," everyone kept telling her. "You have to keep up your strength." But Mattie was tired of being strong. What was the point in being strong when you still had to be fed and carried and have your bottom wiped? She was weary of this forced infantilization. It could drag on for years, and it was not the way she wanted to be remembered. She'd had enough. She wanted to die with at least a semblance of dignity.

It was time.

"Brrr," Kim squealed, stepping out of the pool and wrapping herself in several layers of large magenta towels. "It's so cold once you get out." George was instantly at her feet, eagerly licking the water from between Kim's toes. "So, what do you think?" Kim asked, running up the steps, George at her heels. "Fifty lengths. Pretty good, huh?"

"Don't overdo," Mattie said slowly, quietly.

"I won't. If I start getting obsessive again, I'll stop. I promise."

Mattie smiled. The days of punishing two hour

workouts and monitoring everything she ate were mercifully over. Kim was in a new school and off to a promising start. She continued to see Rosemary Colicos once a week, as did Jake. Sometimes they went together. Kim and her father were getting closer every day.

It was time.

"What time's the ball game?" Mattie asked as Kim strained forward to hear her.

"I think Dad said seven o'clock." She checked her watch. "I guess I should start getting ready. It's almost five o'clock now. I want to wash my hair before we leave."

Mattie nodded. "You go. Get ready."

Kim leaned over, kissed her mother's bony cheek. Mattie felt the softness of her daughter's cold cheek against her own.

"You know how much I love you, don't you?" Mattie asked.

"I love you too," Kim said, scooping up George and running inside before Mattie could say anything more.

"We go inside too," Aurora said, spinning Mattie's wheelchair around and pushing it into the kitchen.

What if I don't want to go inside? Mattie wondered, understanding it was useless to protest. Her decision-making powers had been usurped, the latest in a gradual eroding of her basic rights. What good were choices when one had no power to act on them? Mattie didn't blame Aurora. She didn't blame anyone. She was no longer surprised by the well-meaning insensitivity of others. She was no longer angry. What good did it do to be angry?

What was happening to her was nobody's fault, not her mother's, not her own, not God's. If there was a God, Mattie decided, He hadn't wished this condition on her. Nor could He do anything to alleviate it. After months of watching helplessly as her body steadily dropped pounds and collapsed in on itself, of feeling her flesh grow slack and her features stretch and distort as if she were trapped inside a funhouse mirror, she had finally surrendered to what Thomas Hardy once described as "the benign indifference of the universe." Was it Hardy or Camus? Mattie wondered now, too tired to remember.

She was so tired.

It was time.

It was the best of times. It was the worst of times, Mattie recited silently. Charles Dickens. No doubt about that.

The worst year of her life.

The best year of her life.

The last year of her life.

It was time.

"Hi, sweetheart, how're you doing?" Jake entered the kitchen from the hall as Aurora was locking the sliding glass door.

Mattie smiled, as she always did when she looked at her husband. He'd lost a few pounds these last months, and his hair had acquired a few streaks of gray, the byproducts of her insidious disease, but he still managed to look as handsome as ever, if possible even more distinguished. He claimed the weight loss and gray hairs were the price he paid for going back to work. Not that he'd returned to Richardson,

Buckley and Lang, but over the summer he'd been asked to consult on a number of difficult cases, and he'd been contacted by several other renegade young lawyers who were thinking of opening their own firm sometime after the first of the year. Not interested, Jake told them, claiming he was satisfied working out of his office at home. But Mattie couldn't help but notice the fire in his eyes whenever he spoke to them, and she knew he missed the excitement of daily hand-to-hand combat. How long could she continue to hold him back? What more could he do for her than he'd already done? She couldn't even touch him anymore, she thought, as Jake lowered his lips to hers.

It was time.

Everything was falling into place. The private detective Jake had hired to find his brother had turned up several promising leads. Apparently there were three Nicholas Harts who were the right age and fit Nick's general description—one in Florida, one in Wisconsin, one in Hawaii. It was possible one of these men could be Jake's brother, and even if they weren't, at least the first steps had been taken. It wasn't necessary for Mattie to stay and watch Jake cross the finish line. He'd already won, she thought, relishing the feel of his lips as they lingered gently on hers.

"There's a new photography exhibit starting at Pende Fine Arts next week," Jake told her, lowering himself into the kitchen chair so that he could be at Mattie's eye level. "I thought maybe we could go next Saturday, take Kim with us."

Mattie nodded. Jake had replaced the Raphael

Goldchain photograph that had been destroyed, and Kim was paying him back ten dollars a week out of her allowance. As a result, she'd begun to take an almost proprietary air toward the picture, and had started to develop a genuine interest in photography.

"I was thinking we might buy Kim a new camera," Jake was saying, as if reading Mattie's thoughts. "The one she's got now is pretty basic."

Again Mattie nodded.

"Oh, dear, we're almost out of milk," Aurora announced, removing the container from the refrigerator and shaking it.

"I'll pick some up later," Jake offered.

"And some apple juice," Aurora added.

"I'll pick them up after the ball game."

He did so much, Mattie thought. He'd given up so much. Honey. His career. The last year of his life. All for her. She couldn't ask him to give up any more.

It was time.

"Do you have any idea how much I love you?" Mattie asked. "Do you have any idea how much joy you've brought to my life?"

"Do you have any idea how much you've brought to mine?" he asked in return.

The doorbell rang.

"It's Lisa," Mattie said, as Aurora headed for the door, the dog bounding down the steps from upstairs and barking at her feet.

"How's Mattie doing today?" Mattie heard Lisa ask as Jake walked into the hall to greet her.

"Seems a little down," she heard Jake say. "Maybe I shouldn't be going out."

"Nonsense," Mattie spat out, the effort resulting in a terrible series of spasms that only abated after Jake promised not to alter his plans. "You look great," Mattie said to Lisa, admiring her friend's short new hairdo, wondering how she'd look with that kind of severe geometrical cut, trying to remember the last time she'd been to a hairdresser's salon.

"Thank you," Lisa said, reaching into her black doctor's bag and removing the apparatus for measuring Mattie's blood pressure, strapping it around Mattie's arm, as if this were as normal as shaking hands. "You're looking pretty good yourself."

"Thank you," Mattie said. No point in arguing. She weighed less than a hundred pounds, her skin was so fine it was almost transparent, and her body was twisted in on itself like a pretzel. Still, everyone insisted on telling her she was beautiful, as if her condition had robbed her of her ability to judge for herself, to discriminate between what was and what one wished it to be. "Thank you," Mattie said again. Why not believe she was still beautiful? What harm was there in pretending?

"I was talking to Stephanie and Pam, and we were thinking we'd like to have a little party next month. How's October twelfth sound to you?"

"Sounds great," Jake answered for her.

"Great," Lisa said, listening to the sound of Mattie's blood as it pulsed through her veins. "I'll tell the others. Let you know the time and place." She dropped the stethoscope into her lap, loosened the tight wrap from Mattie's arm. "Everything sounds okay here," she said, although her eyes said otherwise. "So, have you heard the latest about Stephanie's ex?" Mattie shook her head. "You know he started making custody noises when he found out about Enoch."

"I think I'll leave you two alone while I finish up a couple of things in my office," Jake said, kissing Mattie on the forehead before he left the room.

Lisa continued without blinking an eye. "Well, Stephanie had the shithead followed. Turned out the turd has been leading something of a double life."

Mattie listened for the next forty-five minutes as Lisa filled her in on all the salient and salacious details, catching her up on all the latest gossip involving both people Mattie knew and those she didn't. She learned who was dating whom in the celebrity world, which new movies lived up to their hype and which disappointed terribly, what actresses had implants, and who of Hollywood's aging elite had recently undergone cosmetic surgery.

"Trust me," Lisa intoned knowingly. "Any woman over forty who doesn't have wrinkles has had a facelift."

Mattie smiled, knowing she wouldn't live to have the luxury of such petty concerns. What she wouldn't give to have a few wrinkles! What she wouldn't give to turn into a wizened old prune.

"Apparently, there's a great new book out on tape. I forget the name," Lisa was saying, "but I wrote it down somewhere, and I'm going to bring it over on my next visit. Is there anything else you need?" she asked, checking her watch as Mattie glanced toward the clocks on the far wall. 6:05 or 6:07. Take your pick.

Either way, it was time, Mattie thought.

"I need you to call my mother," she said, the words emerging slowly but clearly. "I need you to ask her to come over. Tonight."

Lisa immediately located Mattie's address book in the drawer by the phone and called Mattie's mother. "She'll be here in an hour," Lisa said, hanging up the phone.

"Who'll be here in an hour?" Kim asked, coming into the kitchen, showered and changed, her long hair hanging loose under her Chicago Cubs cap.

"Off to Wrigley Field?" Lisa asked.

"This is definitely our year," Kim said with a laugh. "Who'll be here in an hour?" she repeated.

"Your grandmother."

"Grandma Viv? Why?" A look of concern flashed through Kim's blue eyes.

"Ready to go?" Jake asked, joining the women in the kitchen.

"Maybe we shouldn't go," Kim said.

"Something wrong?" Jake asked.

"Mattie's mother's coming over," Lisa said.

"That's great. What's the problem, Kimmy?"

"Mom?" Kim asked. "Is there a problem?"

Mattie lifted her face to her husband and child, her eyes a greedy camera lens, snapping picture after picture, her mind racing back through time, uncovering memory after memory—the first time she'd seen Jake, the first time they'd made love, the first time she'd held her beautiful baby girl in her arms. "I love you both so much," she said clearly. "Please always remember how much I love you."

"We love you too," Jake said softly, kissing Mattie gently on the lips. "We won't be late."

"You're a wonderful man, Jake Hart," Mattie whispered in his ear, savoring his taste, his smell, his touch.

Kim approached, bent forward, folding her mother in her arms, as if she were the mother, Mattie the child.

"Be patient with your father," Mattie said before her child had a chance to speak. "Please try to accept whatever makes him happy."

Kim stared directly into her mother's eyes. As if she understood. As if she knew. "You're the best mother anybody could ever have," she said so softly only Mattie could hear.

"My beautiful baby." Mattie pressed her face into her daughter's hair, memorizing its texture, its feel against her skin. "Go now, sweetie," she urged gently. "It's time."

"I love you," Kim said.

"I love you," Jake repeated.

I love you, Mattie called silently after them, watching them disappear, their images imprinted forever on her soul. Take care of each other.

"You say something, Mrs. Hart?" Aurora asked.

Mattie shook her head as Aurora approached with a bowl of freshly made soup.

"Chicken noodle. Very good for you." Aurora advanced a spoonful toward Mattie.

"I'll do that, Aurora," Lisa said, lifting the bowl from Aurora's hands. "Why don't you go home? I'll stay with Mattie until her mother gets here."

"You sure?" Aurora hesitated, looked toward Mattie.

"You go," Mattie told her. "And thanks, Aurora. Thanks for everything."

"I see you tomorrow."

"Good-bye," Mattie said, watching her leave. Another picture for her soul's scrapbook.

"Soup's on," Lisa said when they were alone, lifting the spoon to Mattie's lips. "Smells very good."

"Thank you," Mattie said, opening her mouth like a baby bird, feeling the warm tickle of the liquid as it slid down her throat. "Thank you for everything."

"Don't talk. Eat."

Mattie allowed Lisa to spoon her the remaining contents of the bowl, saying nothing until not a drop was left.

"Somebody was hungry," Lisa observed, her lips struggling valiantly with a smile.

"You're a good friend," Mattie said.

"I've had a lot of practice," Lisa reminded her. "We've been friends for a long time. It's got to be, what—over thirty years?"

"Thirty-three," Mattie qualified. Then, after a moment's careful thought, "Do you remember the first time we met?"

Lisa took a moment of her own. "No." She shook her head guiltily. "Do you?"

Mattie smiled. "No."

They both laughed.

"I just remember you were always there," Mattie said simply.

"I love you," Lisa said. "You know that, don't you?"

Mattie knew. "I love you too," she said.

· · ·

"Thanks for coming," Mattie told her mother. It was obvious her mother had taken considerable effort with her appearance. She was wearing a lavender-colored blouse tucked into neat gray trousers, and a hint of color was brushed across lips that were curled into an uneasy smile.

"How are you feeling?" her mother asked, looking restlessly around Mattie's bedroom before fixing on the small dog curled up against Mattie's feet on the bed. "You're looking well."

"Thank you. So do you."

Her mother patted her hair with a self-conscious hand. "George seems to have found a friend."

"I think he likes it here."

Her mother reached out and petted the puppy's back. Immediately, the dog rolled over, exposing his stomach, his front paws making small arcs in the air, beckoning her closer, asking for more. How easily he makes himself understood, Mattie thought, watching her mother gently rub the puppy's delicate underside. How effortlessly he makes his wishes clear. "It was nice seeing Lisa again," Viv was saying. "It's amazing. She has the exact same face she had when she was ten years old."

"She never changes," Mattie agreed, realizing how comforting this was.

"Hard to picture her as a successful doctor."

"It's all she ever wanted to be," Mattie said, remembering. "When Lisa played doctor, she really meant it."

Her mother laughed. "You're sounding so much better," she said with obvious relief. "Your voice is nice and strong."

"It comes and goes," Mattie told her.

"So it's important not to give up, not to lose hope."

"There is no hope, Mother," Mattie said, as gently as she could. Her mother stiffened, backing away from the bed, retreating to the window. She stared without focus at the growing darkness.

"The days are getting shorter."

"Yes, they are."

"Be closing the pool soon, I guess."

"Another few weeks."

"Kim says she's become quite the little swimmer."

"Kim will do well at whatever she sets her mind to."

"Yes, she will," Mattie's mother agreed.

"You'll look out for her, won't you? You'll make sure she's all right?"

Silence.

"Mother—"

"Of course I'll look out for her."

"She loves you very much."

Mattie's mother looked toward the ceiling, her chin quivering, her lower lip swallowing the one on top. "Did you see the picture she took of me with all my dogs?"

"It's a beautiful picture," Mattie said.

"I think she has a real talent. I think it's something she might consider pursuing."

Mattie smiled sadly. "I think you need to listen to me now."

"I think you need to sleep for a while," her mother insisted. "You're tired. A little rest will do you a world of good."

"Mother, please, listen to me. It's time."

"I don't understand."

"I think you do."

"No."

"Please, Mother. You promised."

Silence.

Then, "What is it you want me to do?"

Mattie closed her eyes. "Thank you," she whispered, releasing a deep breath of air. She opened her eyes, looked toward the bathroom. "The bottle of morphine is in the medicine cabinet. I need you to grind up twenty pills and mix them with water, feed them to me a little bit at a time, until I've swallowed them all."

Her mother gasped, held her breath, said nothing.

"Then maybe you could just sit with me until I fall asleep. Would you do that?"

Her mother nodded slowly, her teeth chattering, as if she were cold. "In the medicine cabinet?"

"There's a spoon by the sink. And a glass," Mattie called after her, although her voice was fading. She said a silent prayer, although no words formed, even in her head. She was doing the right thing.

The time for hesitating's through.

It was time.

And suddenly Mattie's mother was standing at the foot of the bed, the bottle of morphine in one hand, the glass of water in the other. "The spoon," Mattie reminded her.

"Oh, yes." Viv put the glass of water and the bottle of pills on the nightstand next to Mattie. Then she walked back to the bathroom, her movements slow yet jagged, like an automaton. She retrieved the spoon, returned even more slowly to the bed, as if she were a wind-up toy taking its last awkward steps.

"It's all right," Mattie told her. "You'll put every-thing back where it was in a few minutes. No one will ever know."

"What will I tell them? What will I tell Jake and Kim when they get home?"

"The truth—that I'm fine, that I'm asleep."

"I don't think I can do this." Viv's hands were trem-bling so badly, she had to lock the spoon between both palms to secure it.

She looks almost as if she's praying, Mattie thought. "You *can* do it," she insisted. "You have to."

"I don't know. I don't think I can."

"Damn it, Mom. You did it for your animals. You understood about not letting them suffer."

"This is different," her mother pleaded. "You're my flesh and blood. I can't do this."

"Yes, you can," Mattie insisted, her eyes forcing her mother to look at her, directing her to the night table beside her bed, instructing her hands to lay down the spoon and open the bottle of morphine tablets.

"I know I wasn't a very good mother, Martha," her mother said, tears accenting the deep red blotches staining her cheeks. "I know what a disappointment I've been for you."

"Don't disappoint me now."

"Please forgive me."

"It's okay, Mom. It's okay."

"Forgive me," her mother repeated, pulling away from Mattie, backing away from the bed. "But I can't do this. I can't. I can't."

"Mom?"

"I can't. I'm so sorry, Martha. I just can't."

"No!" Mattie cried as her mother fled the room. "No, you can't leave me. You can't do this. Please. Please, come back. Come back. You have to help me. You have to help me. Please, Mother, come back. Come back."

Mattie heard the front door open and close shut with a terrible finality.

Her mother was gone.

"No!" Mattie screamed. "No! You can't go. You can't leave. You have to help me. You have to help me."

And then she was coughing and gasping for air, flailing about on the bed like a fish flopping around on the bottom of a fisherman's boat, her body a series of useless twitches, as the dog barked with growing alarm at her side. "Somebody help me," Mattie shouted at the empty house. "Please, somebody, help me."

Mattie hurled herself toward the end table, knocking over the glass of water and the bottle of pills, watching them bounce to the floor, her own body tumbling after them, as she landed with a sickening thud on her left shoulder, the taste of the carpet filling her mouth and nose, the dog whimpering by her side.

Mattie lay that way for what felt like an eternity, as the air slowly returned to her lungs. The dog lay beside her throbbing shoulder, every so often licking the side of her face with his eager tongue. The morphine lay less than two feet from her nose, but she couldn't reach it. Even if she could, what good would it do her if she couldn't open the bottle?

Mattie looked toward the window at the darkness beyond, willing it inside the room, praying for it to wash over her, end her suffering once and for all. Then she heard the sound of footsteps on the stairs, approaching, drawing nearer.

She opened her eyes.

"Oh, God, Martha," her mother cried, gathering Mattie into her arms, rocking her back and forth like a baby. "I'm so sorry. I'm so sorry."

"You came back," Mattie whispered. "You didn't leave me."

"I wanted to."

"But you didn't."

"I opened the front door. I heard you crying. I wanted to leave, but I couldn't," her mother said, her breath trembling into the space between them. "Let's get you back in bed," she said, somehow managing to get Mattie off the floor, to lift her back into her bed.

She arranged the pillows at Mattie's head, gathered the blankets around her, then slowly, wordlessly, retrieved the empty glass from the floor and carried it into the bathroom. Mattie heard the water rushing from the tap, watched her mother's slow trek back across the room, the glass of water in her hand. She put the glass on the night table beside the bed, then bent to the floor, secured the bottle of pills, opened it, and quickly crushed twenty pills into the waiting spoon, dissolving them in the water. Then she cradled Mattie's head in her arms and brought the glass to Mattie's lips, gently guiding the solution into Mattie's mouth.

It tasted bitter, and Mattie had to fight to keep it

down. The taste of darkness, she thought, embracing it. Slowly, determinedly, she watched the liquid drain from the glass until there was nothing left. "Thank you," she whispered as her mother returned the glass to the night table, then fitted her body awkwardly around Mattie's, laying Mattie's head against the loud banging of her heart.

"I love you, Mattie," her mother said.

Mattie closed her eyes, secure in the knowledge that her mother would stay with her until she fell asleep. "That's the first time you've ever called me that," she said.

For a while Mattie lay still in her mother's arms, but gradually she felt the air around her start to swirl, felt the loosening of her arms and legs as they began to unfold and straighten. Her fingers and toes stretched and flexed, and soon her hands were swooping out in front of her, her legs kicking from behind. She was swimming, Mattie thought with a silent laugh, swimming out of darkness toward the light, her mother watching after her, ensuring her safe passage.

Mattie thought of Jake and of Kim, how beautiful they were, how much she loved them. She threw both of them silent kisses and then slipped quietly behind a cloud and disappeared.

THIRTY-FOUR

Mattie was smiling.

Jake stared lovingly at the photograph in his hands, his fingers tracing the line of Mattie's curved lips as she smiled at him from her chair in front of the Tuileries. "C'est magnifique, n'est-ce pas?" he heard her ask, as he moved to the next photograph, this one of Mattie leaning happily against a bronze nude statue by Maillol. "Magnifique," he agreed softly, glancing toward the window of his den, watching the still-green leaves of the outside trees dancing in the surprisingly warm October breeze. He looked back at the stack of photographs in his hands. Had it really been six months since their trip to Paris? Was that possible?

Was it possible that almost three weeks had passed since Mattie's death?

Jake closed his eyes, reliving the last night of Mattie's

life. He and Kim had left the baseball game at the bottom of the eighth inning, picked up some milk and apple juice from a nearby 7-Eleven, and returned home a little earlier than expected. Viv's car was still in the driveway, and he heard her shuffling around upstairs for several seconds before she made her delayed appearance. "How is she?" he asked. "Sleeping peacefully," Viv replied.

Sleeping peacefully, Jake repeated now, watching himself approach their bed, his hand reaching out to smooth some hairs away from Mattie's face, careful not to disturb her. She felt warm, her breathing slow and steady. He watched himself undress and climb into bed, his arm falling gingerly across Mattie's side. "I love you," he whispered now, as he'd whispered repeatedly as he lay beside her, his eyes struggling to stay open, to keep watch over her, to carry her safely into the light of day. At some point, he must have drifted off to sleep. And then, suddenly, it was three o'clock in the morning and he was wide awake, as if something, or someone, had tapped him on the shoulder, shaking him gently until he opened his eyes.

His first thought was that it was Mattie, that she'd somehow regained the use of her arms and was poking at him playfully, but then he saw her, still lying in the same position she'd settled in hours earlier, and he found himself holding his breath. It was only then he heard the profound and utter silence that filled the room, and realized it was this awful stillness that had shaken him awake. He sat up, bent forward, grazed Mattie's forehead with his lips. She felt unnaturally cool, and he automatically secured the blanket across her shoulders, stubbornly waiting for the steady rise and fall of her breathing. But there was none, and he understood, in that instant, she was dead.

Jake glanced back at the pictures of Mattie in Paris, tears blurring his vision, as he watched himself gather his dead wife in his arms and lie beside her till morning.

"What are you doing?" Kim asked from the doorway, her voice tentative, as if she were afraid of disturbing him.

"Looking at pictures of your mother," Jake replied, swiping at his tears while making no attempt to disguise them. He smiled at the small dog glued to Kim's left ankle. "Trying to decide which ones to frame."

Kim sank down beside him on the sofa, leaned against his arm, George immediately jumping up, curling into a little ball on her lap. "She looks beautiful in all of them."

"Yes, she does. I guess that's what makes it so hard to choose."

"Well, let's see." Kim lifted the photographs from his hands, sifting through them with care. "Not this one," she said, straining to sound objective, although Jake noted the slight quaver in her voice. "It's not focused. And you didn't frame this one properly. Too much sidewalk. But this one's nice," she said, stopping on a picture of Mattie in front of Notre Dame cathedral, her hair attractively tousled, her eyes bluer than the clear Parisian sky.

"Yeah," Jake agreed. "I like that one."

"And this one." Kim held up a picture of Jake and Mattie in front of the Eiffel Tower, taken by the Japanese tourist Jake had corralled.

"Even though it's not quite centered?"

"It's a beautiful picture," Kim told him. "You guys look really happy."

Jake smiled sadly, squeezed his daughter tightly against him, mindful of George's jealous eyes. "How're you doing today?" he asked.

"Okay, I guess. How about you?"

"Okay, I guess."

"I really miss her."

"Me too."

The outside sun poured in from the windows, ricocheting off their backs, scattering across the room, like dust. A sound, like a distant rumble, filtered through the air.

"Sounds like someone's car in the driveway," Kim said, gently lowering George to the floor and extricating herself from her father's side. She walked to the window, peered outside. "It's Grandma Viv."

Jake smiled. Mattie's mother had visited often since Mattie's death, dropping by for an impromptu cup of coffee or a surprisingly heartfelt hug.

"Looks like she brought something with her." Kim stretched to see what it was.

Jake joined his daughter at the window as Viv struggled to retrieve something from the backseat of her car.

"What is it?" Kim asked.

Whatever it was was large, rectangular, and completely covered in brown paper. "Looks like it might be a painting of some sort," Jake said.

Mattie's mother saw them watching her from the window, almost dropping her parcel as she reached up to wave.

"What've you got, Grandma?" Kim asked, opening

the door, George jumping excitedly around Viv's feet.

"Okay, George, make way. Make way." Viv propped the parcel against the wall, hugged Kim, nodded warmly toward Jake. "Let me get my coat off. That's a good dog."

Jake hung Viv's coat in the closet beside Mattie's, the arm of one falling across the arm of the other. He hadn't yet dealt with Mattie's clothes, although he knew he'd have to attend to it soon. It was time. Time for him to go back to work, for Kim to resume her classes, for all of them to resume their lives. *The time for hesitating's through*, he hummed absently to himself, wondering why that old chestnut had suddenly popped into his head.

"What is it, Grandma?" Kim repeated.

"Something I thought you might like to have." Viv carried the parcel into the living room, arranging herself on the sofa, waiting as Jake and Kim occupied the two chairs across from her. Then she tore off the protective brown paper to reveal a painting of a little girl with blond hair, blue eyes, and the slightest hint of a smile. The painting was amateurish, its technique limited, its execution crude, a series of bold, colorful strokes that never quite connected, a curious amalgam of styles that never coalesced. And yet the subject of the painting was unmistakable.

"It's Mattie," Jake said, getting out of his chair to examine the painting more closely, propping it against the coffee table in the middle of the room.

"That's Mom?"

"When she was about four or five." Viv cleared her throat. "Her father painted it."

Both Kim and Jake stared at Viv expectantly.

Viv cleared her throat again. "I must have put it in the attic after he left. Forgot all about it till this morning. For some reason, I woke up thinking about it. Must have had a dream." Her voice drifted to a halt. "Anyway, I went up there, which was no easy feat, let me tell you, and I rifled around, and there it was, still in pretty good condition, and much better than I remember it being. Anyway, I thought you might like to have it."

Jake brushed some invisible hairs from the child's painted forehead. Mattie had been such a beautiful little girl, he thought. She'd only grown more beautiful with age. "Thank you," he said.

"Thank you, Grandma." Kim rose from her seat, buried herself against her grandmother's side.

"I could never understand how he could just leave the way he did," Viv said to no one in particular. "How he could just walk away from his daughter like that. They'd always been so close." She shook her head. "I used to be so jealous of the bond they shared. I used to think, why is it always Mattie-this and Daddy-that? Why is it never me? Stupid," she continued before anyone could interrupt. "Stupid to resent your own flesh and blood, to turn your back on a child who needs you."

"You didn't turn your back on her," Kim said.

"I did. All those years when she was growing up—"

"You were here when she needed you the most. You kept your promise, Grandma," Kim whispered as Mattie's mother covered her mouth with her hand to stifle a cry. "You didn't turn your back."

Jake watched the exchange between Kim and her grandmother, a chill traveling the length of his spine, confirming what he'd suspected all along. He closed his eyes, took a long deep breath. Then he sank down on the sofa, drawing both women into his arms.

They rocked together for several minutes in silence, the dog moving restlessly from lap to lap, trying to find a comfortable spot in which to settle. "What will we ever do without her?" Mattie's mother asked.

Jake knew the question was rhetorical, answered it anyway. "I'm not sure," he told her. "Carry on, I guess. Take care of each other, the way Mattie wanted."

"Do you think we'll ever be happy again?" Kim asked.

"Some day we will," Jake told her, kissing Kim's forehead, looking at the painting propped against the coffee table, seeing Mattie's grown-up smile shining through the face of the shy little girl. "In the meantime," he said softly, "we'll just have to pretend."

DOUBLEDAY CANADA
PROUDLY PRESENTS

GRAND AVENUE

JOY FIELDING

Hardcover available October 2001
from
Doubleday Canada

Turn the page for a preview of
Grand Avenue. . . .

We called ourselves the Grand Dames: four women of varying height, weight, and age, with shockingly little in common, or so it seemed at the time of our initial meeting some twenty-three years ago, other than that we all lived on the same quiet, tree-lined street, were all married to ambitious and successful men, and each had a daughter around the age of two.

The street was named Grand Avenue, and despite the changes the years have brought to Mariemont, the upscale suburb of Cincinnati in which we lived, the street itself has remained remarkably the same: a series of neat wood-framed houses set well back from the road, the road itself winding lazily away from the busy main street it intersects toward the small park at its opposite end. It was in this park—the Grand Parkette, as the town council had christened the tiny triangle of land, unaware of the inherent irony—that we first met almost a quarter of a century ago, four grown women making a beeline for three children's swings, knowing the loser would be relegated to the sandbox, her disappointed youngster loudly wailing her displeasure for the rest of the world to hear. Not the first time a mother has failed to live up to her daughter's expectations. Certainly not the last.

I don't remember who lost that race, or who started talking to whom, or even what that initial conversation was about. I remember only how easily the words flowed amongst us, how seamlessly we moved from one topic to another, the familiar anecdotes, the understanding smiles, the welcome, if unexpected, intimacy of it all, all the more welcome precisely because it was so unexpected.

More than anything else, I remember the laughter. Even now, so many years later, so many tears later—and despite everything that has happened, the unforeseen, sometimes horrifying detours our lives took—I can still hear it, the undisciplined, yet curiously melodious collection of giggles and guffaws that shuffled between octaves with varying degrees of intensity, each laugh a signature, as different as we were ourselves. Yet, how well those diverse sounds blended together, how harmonious the end result. For years, I carried the sound of that early laughter with me wherever I went. I summoned it at will. It sustained me. Maybe because there was so little of it later on.

We stayed in the park that day until it started raining, a sudden summer shower no one was prepared for, and one of us suggested transferring the impromptu party to someone's house. It must have been me, because we ended up at my house. Or maybe it was just that my home was closest to the park. I don't remember. I do remember the four of us happily ensconced in the wood-paneled family room in my basement, shoes off, hair wet, clothes damp, drinking freshly brewed coffee and still laughing, as we watched our daughters parallel play at our feet, guiltily aware that we were having more fun than they were, that our children would just as soon be in their own homes, where they didn't have to share their toys, or compete with strangers for their mothers' attention.

"We should form a club," one of the women suggested. "Do this on a regular basis."

"Great idea," the rest of us quickly agreed.

To commemorate the occasion, I dug out my husband's badly neglected Kodak Super 8 movie camera, at which I was as hopeless as I am with its modern counterpart, and the end result was something less than satisfactory, lots of quick, jerky movements and blurred women missing the tops of their heads. A few years ago, I had the film transferred to VHS, and strangely enough, it looks much better. Maybe it's the improved technology, or my wide-screen TV, ten feet by twelve, that descends from the ceiling with the mere push of a button. Or maybe it's that my vision has blurred just enough to compensate for my failure as a technician, because the women now seem clear, very much in focus.

Looking at this film today, what strikes me most, what, in fact, never fails to take my breath away, no matter how many times I view it, is not just how ineffably, unbearably young we all were, but how everything we were—and everything we were to become—was already present in those miraculously unlined faces. And yet, if you were to ask me to look into those seemingly happy faces and predict their futures, even now, twenty-three years later, when I know only too well how everything turned out, I couldn't do it. Even knowing what I know, it is impossible for me to reconcile these women with their fate. Is that the reason I return so often to this tape? Am I looking for answers? Maybe it's justice I'm seeking. Maybe peace.

Or resolution.

Maybe it's as simple—and as difficult—as that.

I only know that when I look at these four young women, myself included, our youth captured, *imprisoned*, as it were, on videotape, I see four strangers. Not one feels more familiar to me than the rest. I am as foreign to myself as any of the others.

They say that the eyes are the mirror of the soul. Can anyone staring into the eyes of these four women really pretend to see so deep? And those sweet, innocent babies in their mothers' arms—is there even one among you who can see beyond those big, tender eyes, who can hear the heart of a monster beating below? I don't think so.

We see what we want to see.

So there we sit, in a kind of free-form semicircle, taking our turns smiling and waving for the camera, four beguilingly average women thrown together by random circumstance and a suddenly rainy afternoon. Our names are as ordinary as we were: Susan, Vicki, Barbara, and Chris. Common enough names for the women of our generation. Our daughters, of course, are a different story altogether. Children of the seventies, and products of our imaginative and privileged loins, our offspring were anything but ordinary, or so each of us was thoroughly convinced, and their names reflected that conviction: Ariel, Kirsten, Tracey, and Montana. Yes, Montana. That's her on the far right, the fair-haired, apple-cheeked cherub kicking angrily at her mother's ankles, huge navy-blue eyes filling with bitter tears, just before her chubby little legs carry her rigid little body out of the camera's range. No one is able to figure out the source of this sudden outburst, especially her mother, Chris, who does her best to placate the little girl, to coax her back into the safety of her outstretched arms. To no avail. Montana remains stubbornly outside the frame, unwilling to be cajoled or comforted. Chris holds this uneasy posture for some time, perched on the end of her high-backed chair, slim arms extended and empty. Her shoulder-length, blond hair is pulled back and away from her heart-shaped face into a high ponytail, so that she looks more like a well-scrubbed teenaged baby-sitter than a woman approaching thirty. The look on her face says she will wait forever for her daughter to forgive her these imagined transgressions and come back where she belongs.

It seems inconceivable to me now, and yet I know it to be true, that not one of us considered herself especially pretty, let alone beautiful. Even Barbara, who was a former Miss Cincinnati and a finalist for the title of Miss Ohio, and who never abandoned her fondness for big hair and stiletto heels, was constantly plagued by self-doubt, always worrying about her weight and agonizing over each tiny wrinkle that teased at the skin around her large brown eyes and full, almost obscenely lush, lips. That's her, beside Chris. Her tall helmet of dark hair has been somewhat flattened by the rain, and her stylish Ferragamo pumps lie abandoned by the front door amidst the other women's sandals and sneakers, but her posture is still beauty-pageant perfect. Barbara never wore flats, even to the park, and she didn't own a pair of blue jeans. She was never less than impeccably dressed, and from the time she was fifteen, no one had ever seen her without full makeup, and that included her husband, Ron. She confessed to the group that in the four years they'd been married, she'd been getting up at six o'clock every morning, a full half hour before her husband, to shower and do her hair and makeup. Ron had fallen in love with Miss Cincinnati, she proclaimed, as if addressing a panel of judges. Just because she was now a Mrs. didn't give her the right to fall down on the job. Even on weekends, she was out of bed early enough to make sure she was suitably presentable before her daughter, Tracey, woke up, demanding to be fed.

Not that Tracey was ever one to make demands. According to Barbara, her daughter was, in every respect, the perfect child. In fact, the only difficulty she'd ever had with Tracey had been in the hours before her birth, when the nine-pound-plus infant, securely settled in a breech position, and not particularly anxious to make an appearance, refused to drop or turn around and had to be taken by caesarean section, leaving a scar that ran from Barbara's belly button to her pubis. Today, of course, doctors generally opt for the less disfiguring, more cosmetically appealing crosscut, one that disturbs fewer muscles and lies hidden beneath the bikini line. Barbara's bikini days were behind her, she acknowledged ruefully. Something else to fret over. Something else that separated the Mrs.'s from the Miss Cincinnatis of this world.

Watch how regally Barbara slides off her chair and onto the floor, casually securing her skirt beneath her knees while showing her eighteen-month-old daughter the best way to stack the blocks she's been struggling with, patiently picking them up whenever they fall down, encouraging Tracey to try again, ultimately stacking them herself, then restacking them each time her daughter accidentally knocks them over. Any second now, Tracey will climb into her mother's protective arms, the dark curls she has inherited from Barbara surrounding her porcelain-doll face, and close her eyes in sleep.

"There was a little girl," I can still hear Barbara say, in that soothing, singsongy voice she always affected when talking to her daughter, as I watch her lips moving silently on the film, "who had a little curl, right in the middle of her forehead. And when she was good, she was very, very good. And when she was bad, she was—"

"A really bad girl!" Tracey shouted gleefully, chocolate brown eyes popping open. And we all laughed.

Barbara laughed the loudest, although her face moved the least. Terrified of those impending wrinkles, and, at 32, the oldest of the women present, she'd perfected the art of laughing without actually breaking into a smile. Her mouth would open and a loud, even raucous, sound would emerge, but her lips remained curiously static, refusing either to wiggle or curl. This was in marked contrast to Chris, whose every feature was engaged when she laughed, her mouth twisting this way and that in careless abandon, although the resulting sound was delicate, even tentative, as if she knew there was a price to pay for having too good a time.

Amazingly, Barbara and Chris had never even seen each other before that afternoon, despite that we'd all lived on Grand Avenue for at least a year, but they instantly became the best of friends, proof positive of the old adage that opposites attract. Aside from the obvious physical differences—blond versus brunette, short versus tall, fresh-faced glow versus Day-Glo sheen—their inner natures were as different as their outer surfaces. Yet they complemented each other perfectly, Chris soft where Barbara was hard, strong where Barbara was weak, demure where Barbara was anything but. They quickly became inseparable.

That's Vicki, pushing herself into the frame, making her presence felt, the way she did with just about everything in her life. At twenty-eight, Vicki was the youngest of the women and easily the most accomplished. She was a lawyer, and, at the time, the only one of us who worked outside the home, although Susan was enrolled at the university, working toward a degree in English literature. Vicki had short reddish-brown hair, cut on the diagonal, a style that emphasized the sharp planes of her long, thin face. Her eyes were hazel and small, although almost alarmingly intense, even intimidating, no doubt a plus for an ambitious litigator with a prestigious downtown law firm. Vicki was shorter than Barbara, taller than Chris, and at 105 pounds, the thinnest of the group. Her small-boned frame made her look deceptively fragile, but she had hidden strength and boundless energy. Even when sitting still, as she is here, she seemed to be moving, her body vibrating, like a tuning fork.

Her daughter, Kirsten, at only twenty-two months, was already her mother's clone. She had the same delicate bone structure and clear hazel eyes, the same way of looking just past you when you spoke, as if there might be something more interesting, more engaging, more *important*, going on just behind you that she couldn't chance missing. The toddler was forever up and down, down and up, back and forth, clamoring for her mother's attention and approval. Vicki gave her daughter an occasional, absentminded pat on the head, but their eyes rarely connected. Maybe the child was blinded, as we all were initially, by the enormous diamond sparkler on the third finger of Vicki's left hand. Watch how it temporarily obliterates all other images, turning the screen a ghostly white.

Vicki was married to a man some twenty-five years her senior, whom she'd known since childhood. In fact, she and his eldest son had been high school classmates and budding sweethearts. Until, of course, Vicki decided she preferred the father to the son, and the resulting scandal tore the family apart. "You can't break up a happy marriage," Vicki assured us that afternoon, stealing a quote from Elizabeth Taylor's résumé, and the rest of the women nodded in unison, although they couldn't quite hide their shock.

Vicki liked to shock, the women quickly learned, just as they learned to secretly enjoy being shocked. For whatever her faults, and they were many, Vicki was rarely less than totally entertaining. She was the spark that ignited the flame, the presence who signaled the party could officially begin, the mover, the shaker, the one whom everyone clucked over and fussed about. Even if she wasn't the one who got the ball rolling—surprisingly, it was usually the more unassuming Susan who did that—Vicki was invariably the one who ran with it, who made sure her team scored the winning touchdown. And Vicki always played to win.

Next to Vicki's coiled intensity, Susan seems almost stately, sitting there with her hands clasped easily in her lap, light brown hair folding neatly under at her chin, the quintessential Breck girl, except that she was still carrying around fifteen of the thirty-five pounds she'd gained when pregnant and hadn't been able to shed since Ariel's birth. The extra pounds made her noticeably self-conscious and camera-shy, although she'd always preferred the sidelines to center stage. The other women offered their encouragement and advice, shared their diet and exercise regimes, and Susan listened, not out of politeness, but because she'd always enjoyed listening more than speaking, her mind a sponge, absorbing each proffered tidbit. She'd make note of their suggestions later in the journal she'd been keeping since Ariel was born. She'd once had dreams of being a writer, she admitted when pressed, and Vicki told her that she should speak to her husband, who owned a string of trade magazines and was thinking of expanding his growing empire.

Susan smiled, her daughter tickling her feet as she played happily with Susan's bare toes, and changed the subject, preferring to talk about her courses at the university. They were more tangible than dreams, and Susan was nothing if not practical. She'd quit school when she got married to help put her husband through medical school. Only now that his practice was established and going strong had she decided to return to school to finish her degree. Her husband was very supportive of her decision, she told the women, and her mother was helping out by looking after Ariel during the day.

"You're lucky," Chris told her. "My mother lives in California."

"My mother died just after Tracey was born," Barbara said, eyes instantly filling with tears.

"I haven't seen my mother since I was four years old," Vicki announced. "She ran off with my father's business partner. Haven't heard from the bitch since."

And then the room fell silent, as was so often the case after one of Vicki's calculated pronouncements.

Susan glanced at her watch. The others followed suit. Someone mentioned the lateness of the hour, that they should probably be getting home. We decided on a group picture to commemorate the afternoon, and together we managed to prop the camera on top of a stack of books at the far end of the room and arrange ourselves and our daughters so that we all fit inside the camera's scope.

So there we are, ladies and gentlemen.

In one corner, Susan, wearing blue jeans and a sloppy, loose-fitting shirt, balancing daughter Ariel on her lap, the child's wiry little body in marked contrast to her mother's quiet bulk.

In the other corner, Vicki, wearing white shorts and a polka-dot halter top, trying to extricate daughter Kirsten's arms from around her neck, small eyes mischievously ablaze as she mouths a silent obscenity directly into the lens of the camera.

In between, Barbara and Chris, Chris wearing white pants and a red-and-white-striped T-shirt, straining to prevent her daughter, Montana, from abandoning her yet again, while Tracey sits obediently on her mother's skirted lap, Barbara manipulating Tracey's hand up and down, as both mother and daughter wave as one.

The Grand Dames.

Friends for life.

Of course, one of us turned out not to be a friend at all, but we didn't know it then.

Nor could any of us have predicted that twenty-three years later, two of the women would be dead, one murdered in the cruelest of fashions.

Which, of course, leaves me.

I press another button, listen as the tape rewinds, shift expectantly on my chair, waiting for the film to start afresh. Perhaps, I think, as the women suddenly reappear, their babies in their laps, their futures in their faces, this will be the time it all makes sense. I will find the justice I seek, the peace I desire, the resolution I need.

I hear the women's laughter. The story begins.

Look for

Grand Avenue

Wherever Books Are Sold

Hardcover available October 2001

from

Doubleday Canada